“My name is Kendi Weaver. I’m a Child of Irfan.”

“Who’s Irfan?” Sejal asked.

“We’re an order of monks.” Kendi met Sejal’s gaze square on, willing himself to look trustworthy and honest. “We find people who are Silent and we train them.”

A strange look passed over Sejal’s face. “I’m not Silent. I was tested for it at birth.”

“Sejal, only the Silent can possess other people like—well, not like you do, but similar to the way you do.”

“I’m not Silent,” Sejal repeated, though Kendi detected an odd note in his voice, as if Sejal were parroting something he had heard many, many times.

“Listen.” Kendi leaned forward. “Do you sometimes hear voices whispering at you? Voices you can’t quite hear?”

Sejal’s eyes went wide. “How did you know that?”

“When you dream at night, is it sometimes so real, you wake up and it feels like you’re still dreaming?”

“Yes,” Sejal almost whispered.

“You’re Silent then.”

Sejal bit his lip. The shifty arrogance had left his face and he looked like a frightened twelve-year-old instead of a streetwise teenager. “Mom said the Unity ran tests when I was born. If I was Silent, I’d be a slave right now. I *can’t* be Silent. . . .”

DREAMER

A NOVEL OF THE SILENT EMPIRE

STEVEN HARPER

A ROC BOOK

ROC
Published by New American Library, a division of
Penguin Putnam Inc., 375 Hudson Street,
New York, New York 10014, U.S.A.
Penguin Books Ltd, 27 Wrights Lane,
London W8 5TZ, England
Penguin Books Australia Ltd, Ringwood,
Victoria, Australia
Penguin Books Canada Ltd, 10 Alcorn Avenue,
Toronto, Ontario, Canada M4V 3B2
Penguin Books (N.Z.) Ltd, 182–190 Wairau Road,
Auckland 10, New Zealand

Penguin Books Ltd, Registered Offices:
Harmondsworth, Middlesex, England

First published by Roc, an imprint of New American Library,
a division of Penguin Putnam Inc.

First Printing, September 2001
10 9 8 7 6 5 4 3 2 1

Cover art by Paul Youll
Cover design by Ray Lundgren

ROC REGISTERED TRADEMARK—MARCA REGISTRADA

Printed in the United States of America

To my mother, Penny, with thanks.

ACKNOWLEDGMENTS

I would like to offer heartfelt gratitude to Sarah Zettel for her invaluable contributions to this novel. Without her creativity and insight (and ice cream supply), this book would not exist. Thanks, Comrade!

I would also like to thank the Untitled Writers Group of Ann Arbor (Erica, Jonathan, Karen, Lisa, Sarah, and Sean) for their patience in reading chapter after chapter and offering comment after comment.

PROLOGUE

Planet Rust

For one thing to begin, another must end.
—Rustic Proverb

In the end, they walked to Ijhan. Vidya Vajhur started with swift steps, but Prasad slowed her down.

"You'll tire quickly at that pace," he told her. "We have a long way to go."

Vidya nodded. She set her shoulders more firmly into the shoulder harness Prasad had made for the wheelbarrow and forced herself into a steady trudge. The wheelbarrow was piled with clothing, a tent, food, and other necessities. It was hard to think of it as everything she owned, so she didn't.

Gravel crunched as Vidya walked. Beside her, Prasad pushed a cart containing the rest of their food. Hidden at the bottom were a few trinkets he said he didn't want to leave behind. One was their wedding knot. Another was a set of red data chips, red for medical histories and gene scans. Prasad had tried to slip them into the cart without her seeing. Vidya had wordlessly compressed her lips. Prasad's cart was topped by a crate of a dozen quacking ducks, the only animals unaffected by the Unity blight.

"Imagine if the blight had left the kine," Prasad had said. "Too valuable to leave and too difficult to take on the road. We're lucky there."

Leave it to Prasad, Vidya thought wryly, *to find blessings in a pile of horse shit.*

The harness bit into Vidya's shoulders and she spared a glance at her husband of five years. He was a head taller than she was, with brown skin to match her own. His black hair had gotten shaggy of late. Dark whiskers dusted chin and cheeks, though he had shaved only yesterday, and curly hair coated his strong forearms as they strained against the hand cart. His beautiful black eyes were lined with stress and strain, though he was barely twenty-five.

Vidya's eyes were a lighter brown beneath thin brows and a high forehead. Her face was a pleasing oval, and her body was long and lean. Too lean.

The crated ducks on Prasad's cart quacked in annoyance. Vidya wished they would shut up. They were getting a free ride, weren't they? She'd trade places with them in a second. It would be nice to be a duck. You could root around in a quiet pool to find food, and if there wasn't any, you only had to fly somewhere else.

She found she was striding again and forced herself to slow down. Her legs wanted to carry her fast and far so she wouldn't be tempted to look back at their ruined farm. She kept her eyes firmly on the gravel road before her. Watching out for the blast craters that made wheeled transport impossible was a good excuse to avoid looking at the fields. She could not, however, block out the smell. Every breath brought her the damp, moldy stench of standing crops destroyed by the Unity blight. Sometimes she caught a whiff of rotting meat, and once she smelled burned feathers. This made her speed up, and Prasad lengthened his own pace. Without a word, they pushed on as fast as they dared until the smell faded. Chickens mutated the blight into a form that attacked humans, and burning feathers could only mean a poultry farm someone was trying to cleanse. Except in that one instance, the blight—actually a series of diseases—left humans alone. Only now was Vidya realizing how that was, in some ways, even more horrible.

They trudged on, Vidya's eyes on the ground, until Prasad gasped. Vidya looked up. They had reached the main road, and it was in worse condition than the one they had been traveling. Flyers from the Empire of Human Unity had bombed and strafed it thoroughly. Crates pocked some places, piles of shattered pavement blocked others. It was passable, but only with difficulty. Prasad, however, was looking straight ahead. Vidya set the wheelbarrow down with an angry thump.

"This is a treat!" she cried. "A gift!"

"Hush," Prasad murmured. "We shouldn't call attention to ourselves."

Vidya glared at him, then swallowed her sharp retort. Sarcasm wouldn't improve the situation, and it wasn't Prasad who deserved her anger.

"What do you think we should do?" Vidya asked at last. "I have no ideas."

Prasad shrugged. "What else can we do?"

He lifted the handles on the handcart and trudged forward. The ducks quacked again. Vidya hesitated, then set her shoulders, hefted the wheelbarrow, and joined him.

The streaming mass of people on the road made grudging space for them. Thousands, perhaps hundreds of thousands, crowded the broken pavement. Most carried bundles or pushed carts and barrows. Many were injured. All were heading toward Ijhan.

The crowd shuffled along in eerie silence. Those who spoke did so in subdued voices. Occasionally a baby whimpered or a small child cried, but the sounds were quickly hushed. It was as if the throng feared being noticed.

"They must have heard the rumors, too," Vidya murmured. Her eyes flicked left, right, forward, behind, constantly scanning the crowd.

"Relief in Ijhan," Prasad agreed softly. "I wish we could've checked with Uncle Raffid to see how true it is. I wish—"

"You make a hundred wishes before breakfast," Vidya said. "Wishing will not take the networks from the Unity's hands or make it possible to call—"

"Poultry!" shrieked a voice. "My god—*birds*!"

Vidya's head snapped around. A silver-haired man was staring at Prasad's duck crate in horror. Prasad blinked. The people around them began to draw away.

"The blight!" the man screeched. "They'll bring the blight!"

He lunged for the crate, intending to smash it, but Vidya was already moving. Her hand snatched a small bundle from the wheelbarrow and whipped the cloth away.

"Stop!" she barked. "Or die."

The man froze. So did the people around him. After a split-second, the crowd edged away, leaving the man in an ever-widening circle. Vidya held a short rod in rock-steady hands. It glowed blue, and a single spark crackled at the end.

"This is an energy whip for herding kine," she said, standing in the wheelbarrow harness. "At half power it stuns a full-grown bull. It is now set to full. Leave the ducks alone."

"The blight—" the man gasped.

"—is only found in chickens," Prasad said in his soft voice. "Ducks don't carry it."

"Back away," Vidya repeated. "I will press the trigger in three . . . two . . ."

The man fled into the crowd. Vidya watched until he was out of sight. Then she slid the whip into her belt, shrugged her shoulders in the harness, and continued on her way. Prasad followed. The crowd watched for a moment, then slowly closed about them.

"My wife has fine reflexes," Prasad observed. "It did not occur to me that our own people would wish to harm us or take our property."

"My husband is trusting," Vidya said, not sure at that moment whether she was annoyed at him or fond of him. The adrenaline rush was wearing off and her hands would have been shaking had they not been gripping the wheelbarrow staves.

Prasad reached over and squeezed her hand twice. She smiled at him. The gesture, born on their wedding night, had originally meant "I love you," but it had, over the years, become a more all-purpose signal of anything positive. Here, Vidya took it to mean "you did well."

Hours passed. Hunger pinched Vidya's stomach—she and Prasad had skipped breakfast to save food—and she was sweating even though a thick layer of clouds blocked the sun. It was warm for early fall. The world of Rust had an even, temperate climate because it had no moons to stir wind and water to anything greater than a balmy breeze or gentle rain. Vidya had dim memories of torrential rains and rushing winds, but after her parents emigrated to Rust, all her experiences with weather involved slow, easy swings from sun to clouds to rain and back again. Now the above-average temperature made her uneasy. Had the Unity done something to the weather as well as spreading the blight?

Vidya's stomach growled, and a hunger headache coiled behind her forehead.

"We need to eat," Prasad said. "Perhaps over there."

They guided cart and barrow to the edge of the road and into what had been a hayfield. Mushy stalks squelched under Vidya's shoes, and the fetid smell lessened her appetite. A waist-high stone wall divided the field in half, however, and this was Prasad's goal. Other people were taking advantage of the wall as a place to rest, but Prasad, Vidya noticed with satisfaction, warily kept his distance from them. They wheeled their respective conveyances to a likely spot and pulled themselves up to the wall's bumpy top. Vidya groaned as her weight left her aching feet.

"May I sit with you?"

The whip was already in Vidya's hand and pointed at the speaker. It was a woman with a pack on her back and two small children at her side. Vidya didn't lower the whip.

"Of course," Prasad said gently. "Do you need help?"

"Prasad," Vidya warned. "We can't—"

"Our old community was destroyed," Prasad replied. "If we wish to survive, we must build a new one."

"We can be three more pairs of eyes to watch for thieves." The woman nodded at Prasad's cart. "Or duck-nappers."

A laugh popped from Vidya's mouth before she could stop it. She motioned for the woman and her children to sit. The woman's name was Jenthe. The children were her sister's.

"My sister was Silent," Jenthe continued. "Her owner planned to hide just her—not her husband or children—in case the Unity won the war. I think she was planning to run away, but then she and her husband disappeared. Now we're traveling to Ijhan because they have food."

Vidya shot a glance at Prasad's cart. "Do the children belong to your sister's owner?" she asked bluntly. "Are they Silent, too?"

"Vidya," Prasad said. "We don't need to be rude."

"We need to know," Vidya replied. "If the children are Silent, they're valuable."

Jenthe pulled both children closer to her. They looked

at her with wide eyes. Vidya sighed. Jenthe's gesture had answered Vidya's question as clearly as a shout.

"I'm not going to take them from you," Vidya said quietly. "But someone else might. It isn't duck-nappers we have to worry about."

"I've worried about that since we left," Jenthe said, and changed the subject. "Have you heard if we've surrendered to the Unity yet?" She rummaged around in her backpack and took out half a piece of flat bread. She divided it between the children, but took none for herself. Vidya sighed and waited. On cue, Prasad offered Jenthe a piece of their own flat bread, which she finally accepted after minimal pressure from Prasad. Vidya mentally went over their tiny store of food, all that remained after six months of bombs and blights. It would take them three days to reach Ijhan, maybe four, and they could do it without slaughtering the ducks if they ate two small meals a day. If they fed three more mouths, though, they'd have to eat the ducks, and Vidya had been counting on using them as trade goods. She had a feeling that the money they carried wouldn't be worth much.

"I haven't heard of surrender," Prasad was saying. "Perhaps we're winning."

Vidya glanced at the river of refugees on the road and suppressed an acidic remark. There really was no point. Words wouldn't change their situation.

"May we sit with you?" said a cautious voice. Vidya sighed and chewed her bread.

It took four days to reach Ijhan. In that time, their group had grown to twenty people. Prasad's crate had four ducks left.

Vidya had visited Ijhan half a dozen times in her life. She remembered it as a sprawling city of trees and low buildings. It still was, but now a refugee camp had sprung up around it like a moat around a castle.

"They aren't letting anyone in," Mef reported. He was fourteen and on his own now. Prasad charged him with scouting ahead because he still had energy for it and he had a knack for gathering information. "They've built sandbag walls around the whole city. Trucks came out with food four days ago, but that's been it."

A murmur went through the group and Vidya bit her lip. Counting the ducks and Gandin's two geese, the group had enough food for two or three days. The filter on Vidya's water bottle would also give out soon, and she didn't want to think about what filth had accumulated in the ponds and streams. The area around the city already smelled like a sewer.

"They aren't letting *anyone* in?" Prasad asked. The desperate note in his voice made Vidya's heart lurch. The past several days had been hard on all of them, but it showed most on Prasad. The skin around his eyes sagged with hunger and fatigue and he spoke little. When they curled next to each other to sleep, she had felt the tension in his body grow with each passing night. She wanted to comfort her husband, this strong man, but she didn't know how to do it other than to stand beside him.

Mef shook his head. "No one goes in. The famine is just as bad in the city."

Vidya took Prasad's hand and squeezed twice. He squeezed back, but the gesture lacked any strength.

Vidya clasped her hands around her shins beneath the overturned handcart. Soft, gentle rain washed down from the sky to form soft, gentle mud. The latrine pits had already overflowed. Turds mixed with dirt and piss mixed with water until it was impossible to tell one from the other in a mix like sloppy pudding. Cholera and dysentery swept the camps. Babies and young children, already weak from lack of food, fell sick and died in mere hours. Vidya's last meal had been a handful of beans four—or was it five?—days ago. They had cost her and Prasad the tent. The only water Vidya had was what she could catch from the sky. Her skin was waterlogged and flaccid, with white sores Prasad said were a form of mold.

At first, all Vidya had been able to think about was food. Thoughts of tender goose, crunchy falafel, sizzling beef, and hot flat bread with sweet honey bombarded her until she thought she would go insane. Now she wasn't thinking of food, or anything else. Her stomach no longer cried out and it had long ago become a dull ache inside her. Prasad had left several hours ago on an errand he refused to discuss, but Vidya didn't have the strength to care. She stared into the rain from the scant shelter of Prasad's cart, not even wondering what would happen next.

"My wife," Prasad said.

Vidya looked up. Prasad stood in the rain in front of her up to his shins in mud. His skin was blotchy like her own and his frame had gone gaunt. A lump rose in her throat at the sight of him in such a condition.

"My husband," she whispered.

He reached for her hand and squeezed twice. She squeezed back and he tried to pull her up. His body lacked the strength, and she had to manage on her own.

"You must come with me," he said.

Vidya let him lead her away, leaving the cart behind. The energy whip made a lump in her pocket. She had tried to trade it for food, but there had been no takers.

Vidya and Prasad passed the pitiful shelters of the tiny community of twenty they had gathered, now shrunk to less than a dozen. Jenthe and her children had vanished days ago. Gandin had died of cholera. Mef was still alive, a coughing ball of misery beneath a scrap of wood. The boy didn't look up when Prasad and Vidya passed.

They moved through the camp, and it eventually penetrated Vidya's mind that they were heading toward the city. The sandbag walls were broken only by gates which were watched by guards who looked as hungry as the refugees. Prasad showed something to one of the guards, who waved them through.

All this barely registered with Vidya. The stupor that had fallen over her was unshakeable. She concentrated on putting one foot in front of the other beside Prasad without sparing a glance for the city.

Finally she realized the rain had stopped. She was sitting in a soft chair and Prasad was talking to a woman behind a desk. They were in an office, a large one with plush carpets and paneled walls. The woman was tidy and well fed, seemingly immune to war and famine. A nameplate proclaimed she was KAFREN JUSUF, VICE PRESIDENT OF ACQUISITIONS. She spoke. Vidya tried to concentrate, but simply didn't have the energy. Prasad said something, and she nodded automatically.

Something pricked Vidya's fingertip. Kafren Jusuf was standing beside her, holding a small med-comp. The lights flashed green. Kafren sat behind her desk again and passed Vidya and Prasad each a data unit. Vidya looked down. The screen showed a contract between Silent Acquisitions, Incorporated and Vidya and Prasad Vajhur.

"This is our offer," she said. "We will provide you with food, housing, and medical care. You will receive the sum of fifty thousand *kesh* in three payments—ten thousand upon signing, twenty thousand at the birth of the first child, and twenty thousand at the birth of the second. You also agree to have penile-vaginal intercourse at least three times per week until pregnancy is established. You will use no birth control."

"And if the children aren't Silent?" Prasad asked softly.

Kafren leveled him a glance. "Any child born of you and Vidya will be Silent. It's a medical certainty. Now, in section two, you'll notice . . ."

Kafren droned on. Vidya stared down at the contract. She had known this was coming, had known it from the moment she had seen Prasad slip the medical data chips into his possessions, had known it the moment he had left her with his completely empty cart.

She felt a twinge of conscience, but it was brief. The children she might have were theoretical, mere dreams. What was real was Prasad beside her and the famine in his face.

Vidya's eyes met Prasad's. They were sunken, fearful, and uncertain. In that moment she knew that if she refused this contract, he wouldn't fight her. He would starve without complaint or regret. Somehow, that made the decision easier. Vidya reached for her husband's hand and squeezed twice.

ONE

Planet Rust

Serenity is the slope down which the spirit flows into the Dream. Serene must you walk the paths, and serene must you ever remain.

—Irfan Qasad, *Pathways to the Dream*

"We *have* authorization!" Ara shouted. "I tight-beamed it ten minutes ago."

The ship shuddered. Kendi Weaver slapped the override on the gravity regulators. "Peggy-Sue!" he barked. "Load maneuver Yooie-One and execute!"

"Acknowledged," replied the computer. On the view screen, the stars yawed into white streaks. Everyone on the bridge leaned a hard left in their seat harnesses. Kendi's stomach bobbed down toward his feet, then leaped into his throat. A big red smear rushed by the screen and Kendi assumed it was the planet Rust. Then the stars straightened out and Kendi was able to swallow his stomach.

"Nice," growled Gretchen Beyer from the sensor boards.

"Dammit, stop firing!" Ara yelled from her position on the floor. "We're a Unity vessel!" She scrambled to her feet beside Kendi's chair and leveled him a look that would freeze beer.

"Sorry," he said helplessly. "It was all I could think of. If that charge had come closer—"

She waved him to silence. Ara was a short, round woman who could look Kendi in the eye if he was sitting. Her deep brown skin hadn't paled much after two weeks of ship lighting, and it was almost as dark as Kendi's. She had short black hair which displayed a round, open face with a hint of double chin, a face that looked like it should be smiling over a tray of fresh cinnamon rolls.

"Excellency, please respond," Ara said to empty air. "This is the *Post-Script*. We are a registered vessel with the Empire of Human Unity. Why are you firing?"

Silence.

"Are we still transmitting?" she murmured to Ben Rymar at communication. He nodded. Ara raised her voice.

"Excellency," she said, "we have no defenses against your firepower. I repeat—we are merchants come to trade. We received landing authorization via Silent courier fifty-five hours ago."

Kendi, meanwhile, reset the safeties on the gravity, then carefully aimed the ship away from the planet. He held his fingers over the thrusters, ready to punch them up to full speed if the satellites orbiting Rust readied another volley.

Static crackled over the speakers. "Glory to the Unity," said a different voice. "You did not transmit the codes."

Ara's neck muscles moved like a team of wrestlers. "Yes. We. Did. To whom am I speaking, please?" she added.

"Peggy-Sue, mute me," Gretchen said softer than the communications system could register.

"Acknowledged." A blue light winked at the sensor boards to remind Gretchen that her voice was currently screened from the communication system.

"They're stalling, Mother Adept," she told Ara. "I've snuck into their network, and they're checking out our story."

"This is Prelate Tenvar of the Empire of Human Unity Trade Commission," crackled the voice. "We have received no communication from you. Transmit the proper codes or be fired upon."

Ben's mute light flashed. "They're trying to track down the courier, Mother. I think I can jump ahead and drop a false transmission into their lines, but for now you'll need to keep them happy with what I've already given them."

Ara marched over to the captain's board and punched up the codes Ben had spent hours forging. Her purple trader's tunic rustled as she moved. Ara played the role of indignant trader well, and only the tightness around her mouth betrayed nervousness. Kendi's own heart was beating hard and he swallowed dryly. Escape into slipspace this far into Rust's gravity well was impossible, and he could almost feel the Unity lasers and charges trained on their ship's all-too-thin ceramic skin. Kendi goosed the thrusters a little and set the ship drifting casually away from the planet just in case.

Drift away, he told himself, *but don't* look *like you're drifting away.*

He stole a glance at Benjamin Rymar. Ben was bent over his boards. His bright red hair was disheveled and his trader's tunic was rumpled, even though he had just put it on. Ben always looked rumpled, even after a shower. Kendi wasn't sure how he managed it.

"Got it!" Ben whispered. He tapped a button and raised his voice. "It's done, Mother. I deleted their message before it was received and faked verification of who we're pretending to be."

"I just hope Tenvar isn't a drinking buddy of your mark's, Ben," Gretchen said. "Otherwise they'll fry us like an ant under a magnifying glass."

Ben bent his head back over the boards, but Kendi saw his blush. Kendi's fingers moved and the words *Lay off, Gretch, or you can forget about trading duty shifts* marched across Gretchen's screen.

Teasing, she sent back. *No need to snit.*

Ara, meanwhile, settled into her chair and pulled the harness around her. "Prelate Tenvar," she said, "I have transmitted our authorization. Again. Have you received it?"

Silence. Kendi held his breath.

"Prelate Tenvar, are you there?" Ara said, allowing a hint of exasperation to creep into her voice. "Prelate, please. I've transmitted our authorization four times to four Prelates. How long will—"

"Why are you traveling on a vessel built in the Independence Confederation?" Tenvar's voice demanded.

Ara sighed loud enough for the microphones to pick up. "You'll pay for this, apprentice," she said a bit too loudly.

Kendi recognized a cue when he heard one. "You agreed to it, Boss."

"That information, Prelate," Ara said, "is in our transponder code. Please read it. Our ship was salvage."

Another long pause. Kendi closed his hand over the gold disk that hung around his neck beneath his tunic and whispered, "If it is in my best interest and in the best interest of all life everywhere—"

"You are cleared for landing on field seven-eff-one,"

Prelate Tenvar's voice said. "Do not leave the ship until the quarantine crew has inspected your vessel. Glory to the Unity."

"Thank you, Prelate," Ara said. "Glory to the Unity."

Ben shut off the transmitter and the entire crew heaved a sigh. Ara sagged briefly in her harness, then unbuckled herself and stood up.

"Kendi and Gretchen," Ara ordered, "I want you on my turf in the Dream. Ten minutes. Ben, you pilot. Get Trish and Pitr up here to handle the other stations."

"Yes, Mother," Ben said.

"Ten minutes?" Kendi complained. "How fast do you think I am?"

"I heard," Gretchen drawled, already heading for the door, "that you were a two-minute man myself."

Kendi bounded to his feet to chase her, but Gretchen nipped into the corridor and punched the close button. Kendi flung his arms out and pretended to slam into the door. After hanging for a moment, he slid to the floor. Ben actually snorted, and Kendi couldn't suppress a smile.

"Kendi." Ara sighed. "We don't have time—"

The door slid open, revealing the solemn face of Trish Haddis. She stepped over Kendi's prone body and took up Gretchen's position at sensors. Behind came Pitr Haddis, her twin brother. The two of them looked nothing alike. Pitr was a blocky man, with close-cropped brown hair, oddly wide hazel eyes, and a firm chin. Trish, in contrast, was small and delicate looking, with a long brown braid and a build more like an adolescent boy's. She did share Pitr's eyes.

"We were on our way up when Ben called," she said, explaining their prompt appearance. "Was Kendi responsible for that u-turn? The galley's a mess."

"Kendi will clean up," Ara promised.

"Geez," Kendi grumbled from the floor. "Save the ship and all you get is KP."

"Kendi," Ara said sternly, "go."

"Going, going." Kendi rolled to his feet and trotted down the corridor.

The *Post-Script* was a small, wedge-shaped ship with only three decks. The narrow corridors were dingy and in need of paint. Dull gray ceramic showed through the beige. Kendi reached the lift, but the elevator had been rattling alarmingly of late, so he instead descended the ladder to the crew quarters on the deck below the bridge.

Third door on the left, Kendi reminded himself. Despite the ship's small size, Kendi still got confused. The *Script*'s doors and corridors were unmarked and they all looked alike. He chose a door and thumbed the lock. It slid aside, meaning he had found his quarters on the first try.

Ten minutes, he grumbled to himself as the door slid shut behind him. *Who does she think I am? Super-Aussie?*

Kendi's quarters were spartan. A neatly made bed took up one wall and a battered computer terminal occupied another. A dozen book disks sat in a rack above the terminal, while a very few clothes hung in the closet. A short red spear leaned against the wall in one corner. The bathroom was up the hall, though the room sported a small sink with a medicine chest and mirror.

Kendi pressed his thumb to the medicine chest's lock plate and the doors popped open. On the shelves inside lay several ampules all filled with amber fluid. A dermospray occupied the bottom shelf. Kendi racked an ampule into the cylindrical handle, pressed the flat end against his arm, and pressed the button. There was a soft *thump,* and a red light indicated the ampule had emptied. Kendi put the dermospray away and removed his purple tunic. Beneath it he wore nothing but sandals, a brown loincloth, and the neck chain with the gold disk that marked him as a Child of Irfan. The mirror showed him a spare, cleanly built body, with dark skin and short, tightly curled brownish hair. His nose was flat, and his eyes were so black it was hard to tell iris from pupil.

Kendi took up the red spear, which was the length of his leg from his knee to his foot, and checked to make sure the rubber tip on the spear's point was secure. Then, in one smooth motion, he bent his left leg and slipped the spear under his knee, as if the spear had become a peg leg. Under ideal conditions, Kendi would have thrust the spear into the earth to keep it from slipping out from under him, but that was impossible on a ship. Hence the rubber tip. A languid warmth stole over him—the drug at work.

It took a moment for Kendi to make sure of his balance. Then he closed his eyes, cupped both hands over his groin, and started a series of breathing exercises.

If it is in my best interest, he thought, *and in the best interest of all life everywhere, let me enter the Dream.*

As he breathed, the noises of the ship—the faint hum of various machines, the vague whisper of moving air, the steady drone of distant engines—faded away. Colors swirled behind his eyelids as the drug took effect. Kendi breathed. He imagined himself standing in a deep cave with a tunnel that spiraled outward. Carefully, he added details. Cool water dripped from stalactites and ran down stalagmites. The floor was chilly beneath his bare feet. Glowing fungi provided faint illumination, and their musty smell filled his nose. Slowly, Kendi walked out of the cave and up the spiral tunnel. With every step, the details of the cave became sharper. The floor pressed his soles and the chill air raised goose bumps on his skin. The rock took on color, rich shades of red, turquoise, and purple.

Light appeared ahead of him. Kendi moved toward it. A moment later, brightness blinded him and he squinted until his eyes adjusted. When his vision cleared, he found himself at the base of a cliff with a wide plain stretching before him. The earth was dry and covered with scrubby vegetation. Overhead, the sun burned in a cloudless blue sky. A falcon shrieked high on the dry wind. Every detail was clear and sharp.

It was the Dream.

Kendi surveyed the landscape around him. It never ceased to fascinate him. He wondered if Irfan Qasad, the first human to enter the Dream, had felt the same. A thousand years ago, before the discovery of slipspace, a colony ship had encountered the Ched-Balaar, an alien race intent on colonizing the same planet the humans wanted. Fortunately, the aliens proved willing to share. There was just one catch—the Ched-Balaar insisted the humans take part in a ceremony and drink a special wine to cement relationships between the two species.

The wine—drugged—and the ceremony's hypnotic chanting drew Irfan Qasad and several of her crewmates into the Dream. Amazed, the humans experimented and learned that the drug allowed them to enter this shared dream at will, though some were better at getting there than others. Some of these people began to "hear" voices of humans on Earth. Eventually these Terran humans were drawn into the Dream and were able to communicate with the Ched-Balaar, and their brethren humans, though they were separated by thousands of light years.

The colony ship carried in its hold thousands of embryos, both human and animal, to colonize each planet and keep the gene pool fresh. With the help of the Ched-Balaar, the humans experimented on the embryos, isolating favorable genes to produce people who could find the Dream. The first children produced by these experiments developed speech late, and even afterward spoke only rarely outside the Dream. They became known as the Silent.

On the hot, scrubby plain, Kendi spread his arms to the wind. His clothing and medallion had vanished. Naked, he took a few steps onto the plain and cocked his head to listen. Voices whispered in the breeze and rumbled through the earth. He sorted through them. Kendi recognized Ara's throaty alto, but all the others were strange to him. Gretchen must not have arrived yet. Cautiously he extended his senses, testing earth and air, ready to act if he felt the odd presence again.

There was localized babble some distance away. It was probably the Silent on Rust, but at this distance Kendi couldn't tell for certain. Further off, he felt thousands—millions—of firefly flickers as other Silent on other planets entered and left the Dream. Kendi felt no sign of the strange child.

Kendi put up his arm and whistled shrilly. The falcon dove like a feathered boomerang, pulling up in time to land on Kendi's forearm. Although the falcon's talons were capable of crushing bone, they only pricked Kendi's skin. In the real world, Kendi's arm would have been reduced to a shredded mess, but this was the Dream.

"Sister," Kendi asked the falcon, "can you learn for me who speaks in the distance?"

The falcon leaped from Kendi's arm. In mid-air she changed into a kangaroo that bounded swiftly away. Kendi watched her go, then strode purposefully across the scrubby vegetation. Spines from ground-hugging spinniflex plants tried to pierce his feet, but in the Dream Kendi's soles were covered with thick calluses. As he walked, he was aware of the living earth beneath him. Every particle was alive and breathing. Every piece was separate, and yet part of a whole. Just for the practice, Kendi narrowed his focus for a moment to a single particle. It was a human female, completely unaware that her mind made up a tiny part of the Dream. He thought she might be sleeping, but he couldn't be sure. Reaching out of the Dream to the non-Silent was difficult for him, and in any case it wasn't why he was here.

Then he felt it. A flicker at the edge of awareness. Someone was reaching not into the Dream, but *through* it, as if from one mind to another. Kendi pounced on the feeling, trying to pin down which direction it was coming from. It vanished before he could nail it.

Damn, Kendi thought, frustrated. *But at least we know the kid is still around.*

Kendi resumed his walk, following the sound of Ara's whisper. As he grew closer to her, he felt the shift where Ara's mind molded the Dream to her own perceptions. The only way to communicate with another Silent was to agree who would shape the Dream space they shared. Ara had said that she, Gretchen, and Kendi were to meet on her turf, so as Kendi walked, he released his expectations of reality and surrendered them to Ara.

The landscape changed with scarcely a ripple. The spiny spinniflex became soft green grass. Cool water tinkled softly in an elaborate fountain, and exotic perfumes scented the air. Tall shady trees blunted the sun's rays. Fat oranges and glistening pears hung heavily in their branches, and birds twittered among the leaves. Ara sat on the lip of the fountain. She wore a simple green robe of gauzy material. A close-fitting hood covered her hair and ears, and emeralds glittered across her forehead. Kendi wore loose red trousers and a long white linen shirt. His gold medallion had returned, and he now wore a silver ring set with a golden piece of amber. Ara wore a ring as well, though hers held a sparkling blue lapis lazuli.

"Where's Gretchen?" Kendi asked without preamble.

"Not here, obviously," Ara replied.

"Yes, I am." Gretchen emerged from behind the fountain. She wore the same outfit Ara did, except her robe was blue. Her gold disk gleamed brightly, and her amber ring matched Kendi's. Gretchen was a tall woman with fair skin, pale hair, and thick eyebrows. Her eyes were gray and her lips were a startling, heavy red. Kendi had always thought she would look good in a belly-dancing outfit.

"Good." Ara looked at Kendi. "Is the child here in the Dream?"

"I sensed a brief presence," Kendi said. "And as far as I can tell, no one else has sensed the kid at all. I'm the only one."

"Keep watching. If the child turns up again, try to narrow the trail. It'll take decades to search all of Rust. I want this wrapped up in a few weeks."

"Unfair," Kendi protested. "No one else could even narrow it down to a single planet in the time I did. You can't complain that—"

"It wasn't a judgment, Kendi," Ara interrupted. "Just an observation. You did well. Right now, I want you two to talk to the Silent on Rust. We need information, and they're our best bet."

"Way ahead of you," Kendi said, mollified. "I sent my sister to scout them out."

Gretchen shuddered. "That creeps me bad. If your little creature didn't come back, you'd be brain damaged." She sniffed. "Not that we'd notice."

"Enough, children," Ara said pointedly. "We have work."

Kendi bowed slightly, hand on his disk. "Yes, Mother Adept. This humble Child of Irfan begs your—"

"Shut up and listen," Ara growled. "You, too, Gretchen. I want you both to sniff around the Rustic Silent, find out what the current situation on the planet is. Kendi, did you read those files?"

Kendi looked sheepish. "I've been busy."

"Right. Gretchen?"

"The Empire of Human Unity invaded sixteen years ago," Gretchen replied primly. "It conquered Rust in seven months. It dropped a bunch of bio-weapons to soften the populace and generally shot the place up until some of the powerful governments cried 'uncle.' Those governments were allowed to keep power provided they stomped on their neighbors. Standard Unity tactic. The holdout governments got mad at the ones that caved, which made it easier for the Unity—the Rustics started fighting among themselves."

"I did read that much," Kendi said in a peevish tone. He perched on the smooth lip of the fountain. "I didn't see anything about Rust's economy, though. Have they recovered from the Unity takeover? If they haven't, the slave market will be really tight."

Gretchen shrugged. "They're still in a recession. The Unity imposes artificial restrictions on trade, and it's siphoning away resources through heavy taxes. That hurts. I'd bet a year of your stipend—"

"Hey!"

"—that we'll have to hunt for this kid in at least three fields."

"Free citizens, legitimate slaves, and black market slaves?" Ara hazarded.

Gretchen nodded. Behind her, an orange thumped softly to the grass. "I just hope this kid is a legitimate slave. It'd make everything a hell of a lot easier."

"Buying a slave would be easiest," Ara agreed. "But we may have to persuade a free person to come with us or even track a kidnap victim through the black market. That's where you come in, Kendi."

"I live to serve."

Ara rounded on him. "Kendi, I'm in no mood," she snapped. "I barely talked us out of being destroyed by Unity security, I have to impersonate a master trader, and we have to find this rogue Silent before the Unity or one of the corporations does. I have no patience for smart remarks and slapstick jokes. Is that clear, Brother Kendi?"

Her sudden fury hit him like a slap. Kendi nodded, abashed. Gretchen smirked.

"All right, then." Ara settled her robes. "Once we get down there, Kendi, I want you nosing around the seamier parts of town. But. Stay. Out. Of. Trouble."

"Yes, Mother," Kendi said meekly.

Another orange fell from the tree. It squished when it hit the ground. Kendi glanced at it in surprise. Black mold was growing on it. Kendi blinked. That was strange. He'd never seen anything like it in Ara's garden before.

"Gretchen," Ara continued, not noticing the orange, "I want you to check the legitimate slave markets."

Gretchen nodded. "What'll you be doing?"

"I need to report to the Empress," Ara replied. "Then I'll be pumping bureaucrats. You two get started while I'm doing that."

"Yes, Mother," Gretchen said.

Kendi, still staring at the orange, realized Ara was waiting for an answer and he had to scramble to remember what she had said.

"Kendi?" she said dangerously.

"Check the seamier parts of town," he said. "Get started while you talk to the Empress."

He was about to mention the orange when a falcon screamed overhead. Kendi held out his arm. The falcon landed, and new knowledge instantly flooded his mind. For a moment there were two of him, one sitting on the edge of a burbling fountain, the other perched on a wiry forearm.

"Did she—you—find the Rustic Silent?" Gretchen asked.

Kendi nodded, and the falcon duplicated the movement. For a moment he lost his balance, then regained it as the disorientation passed. He flung his arm up, tossing the falcon to the skies. She beat her wings to gain altitude, then circled overhead.

"I'll let her lead you to them," Kendi said. "We'll go through my turf, all right?"

"Why can't you just take us to them directly?" Gretchen grumbled.

Kendi shook his head. He knew that distance had no meaning in the Dream. He knew that the need to walk to other "places" through his own Outback was purely artificial. All this his conscious mind knew. It seemed, however, that his subconscious held more sway.

"Sorry," he said, rising. "That's the best I can do."

"Just make sure you conjure me some decent clothes, then," Gretchen told him. "I'm not going on a nude walkabout."

"Be careful," Ara cautioned.

"I'll make sure we're wearing clean underwear," Kendi

said solemnly, and trotted off before Ara could reply. Gretchen scrambled to follow while the falcon flew ahead. Kendi heard a heavy sigh from Ara before the fountain disappeared behind them, and he smiled quietly to himself.

A moment later, the landscape changed back to the scrubby plain. Hard heat and sunlight beat down from the cloudless sky. Kendi's clothes melted away until he wore only a loincloth, and that only because he knew Gretchen didn't want to see him naked. Gretchen's robe reformed itself into a khaki explorer's outfit, complete with pith helmet and hiking boots. They walked in silence, following the falcon toward the Silent on Rust. After a moment Kendi realized he hadn't mentioned the rotten orange to Ara. He paused to turn back.

"Now what?" Gretchen asked, annoyed.

Kendi glanced in the direction of Ara's garden, then resumed walking. Ara was already in a bad mood. There was no point in making it worse. He could ask her about it later.

TWO

The Dream

An empire is a prison to which not even the ruler holds the key.

—Emperor Bolivar I, *Musings of a Warrior*

Mother Adept Araceil sighed as Kendi and Gretchen vanished into the trees. Both of them were odd in their way. Gretchen had a mouth, and Kendi was, well . . . Kendi. He had some strange views. What she knew of the Australian aboriginal tribes of Earth did not quite paint a picture that resembled her best and most powerful student.

Ex-student, she reminded herself. Kendi had taken his vows to become a Brother almost a year ago, but Ara still hadn't made the mental adjustment. He was certainly powerful; she knew of no one else who could split his mind into two pieces in the Dream. But his attitude!

At least he's better than he once was, she thought ruefully. *It's hard to remember sometimes.*

Ara stood up and concentrated for a moment. Her mind cast out, searching for a pattern she had been given. When she found it, she willed herself to let go of her garden.

She found herself in a grand hall with polished floors of gray marble and soaring pillars. The pressure of someone else's Dream perceptions pushed on Ara's mind, ordering her not to dictate reality. With a deep breath, Ara forced herself to comply. It was like making herself let go of a life raft. Even after decades of Dream experience, it was hard for her to give up control.

It had been pure hell keeping this fact from Kendi.

A furious tapping of footsteps clicked toward Ara, and a clawed creature the size of a small bear approached. It had a flattened head and rounded body, with furry arms that ended in stubby fingers. A silver Seneschal's chain ringed its neck.

"Who are you and what do you need?" the creature asked. It wasn't speaking her language, of course. Language did not exist in the Dream. Here, the Silent communicated by direct exchange of ideas. Ara's mind, however, automatically transformed the concepts she received into language.

Ara bowed and gave her name. "I need to send a report to her Imperial Majesty. Is a Silent messenger available, Seneschal?"

The Seneschal clacked its claws on the polished floor. "I have instructions to convey you directly to her Imperial Majesty for any report, Mother Adept."

Ara blinked, then hurriedly followed the Seneschal, who was already clicking across the hall to a great set of double doors. Ara gathered her robes, wishing she had more time to prepare. She wasn't ready for another Imperial audience. Her knowledge of Imperial etiquette was limited, and the idea of looking the fool filled Ara with dread.

The Seneschal opened the great doors and guided Ara inside. The room beyond was midnight dark except for a dozen tiny lights that floated slowly about like fireflies.

"Choose anyone you like," the Seneschal said. "The Empress awaits."

Ara made herself reach for one of the lights at random. It—he—froze at her touch.

May I use your body, Silent brother? she asked.

I live to serve, came the reply. *Count to ten that I may position myself.*

Ara counted, then *pushed.* She found herself kneeling on a pillow. Green-blue grass covered the ground, and a fresh summer breeze wafted around her. Ara's head was bowed low, all but touching the ground.

"You may rise, Mother Adept," said a female voice.

Ara brought herself to a kneeling position and used the time to take stock of the body she possessed. It was a well-muscled male. Brown hair dusted his forearms, and his torso was lean and strong. He wore voluminous black trousers and a collar, the marks of a Silent slave. A thrill rippled through Ara. No matter how often she did it, she always found it incredible that her body was light-years away while her mind was here, on another world in the body of another Silent.

Ara snuck a glance at her surroundings. Her first audience with the Empress had taken place in a small room, when her Imperial Majesty had personally informed Ara, one of the Children's most successful recruiters, that she was to lead an expedition to find the body behind the mind Kendi had sensed in the Dream. This time Ara was in a white pavilion large enough to shade two or three acres. Several slaves stood poised with food and drink while a handful of others knelt on pillows similar to Ara's. Armed guards were posted all about the pavilion.

Directly before Ara was the Imperial Majesty herself, the Empress Kan maja Kalii. She sat on a pillow which sat, in turn, on a raised dais. The Empress was close to Ara's height, but angular and lean, with ebony-black skin and equally dark hair piled high on her head. Tiny jewels orbited her head in lieu of a crown. Silky blue robes cascaded down her shoulders. Ara couldn't even hazard a guess at her age. The air around both Ara and the Empress shimmered slightly, meaning Kan maja Kalii had activated a sound dampener to ensure their words remained private.

"Speak, Mother Adept," the Empress said. "You have a report?"

"I have, Imperial Majesty," Ara replied, and explained what had happened when the *Post-Script* arrived at Rust. The slave's deep voice sounded odd in her ears. "The government is surely suspicious of us, but we've already begun searching for the child," she finished. "I doubt the Unity Silent have uncovered its presence. My stu— that is, Brother Kendi will look for it in the underground slave market while Sister Gretchen and I explore the legal venues."

"Is it wise to send Brother Kendi along this path, Mother Adept?" the Empress asked. "As I recall, he is someone who sometimes—these are your words—'needs to be sat on.' "

Ara bowed to hide her startlement, though she didn't know why she was surprised. If Ara were in the Empress's sandals, she would have accessed every file she could get her hands on, too.

"Brother Kendi has grown in the months since I wrote those words, Imperial Majesty," Ara said. "He also has a knack for making underworld contacts, and his ability to locate people within the Dream is uncanny. He is still the only Silent who has sensed the child, after all, and he was able to narrow its location to a single planet. Not only that, he was the one who identified the child's ability to possess the non-Silent."

The Empress nodded. "Very well, then. I also want you to continue reporting directly to me, and not your superiors among the Children of Irfan. This child's existence must be kept a secret as long as possible. Your skill and discretion in similar matters is why I chose you directly, and I expect you will live up to your own high standards."

Ara bowed her acquiescence. The Empress rose and began pacing the dais. Everyone in the pavilion, including Ara, scrambled to rise as well. A small tickle at the back of Ara's mind told her that the drugs were wearing off. Soon she would have to return to the Dream, and from there to her body. Was it proper to tell the Empress this? Or was Ara expected to hang on until her mind was sucked back through the Dream and into her body? That would saddle her with a disorientation that might confine her to bed for days.

"I'm nervous, Mother Adept," the Empress said. "Brother Kendi claims he has felt this child reach through the Dream to possess other minds, willing or not. Such a child would have the power to topple empires, including this Confederation. What if this child possessed me? Or another ruler? The balance of power between the Independence Confederation and its neighbors is delicate. One mistake could mean war."

"Anyone would know instantly that you had been possessed, Imperial Majesty. The child would not have your knowledge or experience. It would be impossible—"

"We always thought it was impossible for the Silent to possess any but another willing Silent," the Empress pointed out. "Who knows what else this child can do? What if the wrong people gain control of this child?" She paused. "I've been thinking, Mother Adept, and I've decided that the safety of this Confederation is more important than the chance to . . . study this new form of Silence."

"Imperial Majesty?"

The Empress sank back to her cushions, though everyone else remained standing. Her regal face was blank as stone.

"If, in your opinion, this child would pose a threat to the Independence Confederation, I want you to destroy it."

"Impossible!" Ara blurted. Then she flushed. "I mean, I don't—that is—"

"I know, Mother Adept," the Empress said gently. "I understand."

Ara gathered her wits. "Imperial Majesty, I haven't so much as struck another person since I was a child. How could I—"

"It's no easy thing," the Empress agreed. "But it may be necessary."

Ara opened her mouth to protest again, etiquette or not. Then she noticed the hard brown Imperial eyes upon her. Those eyes represented over fifty billion lives. Thousands of those lives could be extinguished if someone made a bad decision. Millions of them would end if someone declared war. Ara snapped her mouth shut. One life against so many. The Empress met her gaze, let her look. After a long moment, Ara swallowed.

"Yes, Imperial Majesty," she whispered.

"Thank you, Mother Adept," the Empress said. Her voice was tired. "I have laid an onerous duty on your shoulders, and I take responsibility for the child's death, if it comes to that. You are but the scalpel that does the bidding of the doctor."

"Yes, Imperial Majesty."

The Empress nodded. "I'm sure you need to return to your body, Mother Adept."

A dismissal. Ara bowed and knelt on the cushion. As she let go of the slave's body, the Empress spoke again.

"If you have trouble making this decision, Mother Adept," she said, "think of this: What would happen if the general populace learned of a Silent who could control the unwilling and non-Silent?"

Ara found herself back in her garden. The slight dizziness was accompanied by a terrible chill. The desire to return to her body was growing steadily, but that need didn't shut out the Empress's last words.

What would happen . . . ?

Ara shivered. On most Confederation worlds, the Silent were either monks in the service of Irfan or slaves in the service of the Empress. On other worlds, the Silent were treated as potential threats and hunted down with ruthless efficiency. On still other worlds, the Silent were tolerated or even respected—as long as they kept their place. True, there were equally as many worlds on which the Silent were treated the same as other "normal" professionals, but even in these places, Ara always felt a measure of underlying mistrust.

What would happen if the general populace learned of a Silent who could control the unwilling and non-Silent?

Ara knew the answer. Riots. Witch hunts. Executions.

It had happened before, had been happening since the time of Irfan Qasad. Ara had been lucky, and she knew it. On Bellerophon, Ara's homeworld, Silence was considered a holy blessing, and most Silent ended up with the Children of Irfan. Their major striving was to train the Silent in the use of their gifts and to ensure that they followed ethical practices. Most stayed with the Children after completing their training. They taught or researched or administrated or performed the intersystem communication work that kept the order solvent.

After the discovery of slipspace, they also recruited.

Slipspace granted easy travel to non-Confederation worlds, letting the Children seek Silent who had been sold or were being persecuted or had remained ignorant of their gifts. Ara herself had bought and freed nearly three hundred slaves and outright stolen dozens of others.

The tickle nudged her again. Ara was about to leave the Dream when something landed at her feet with a *splat*. It was a pear, one so rotten it had turned black. Several others dotted the ground.

What in the world? Ara thought. She looked up at the tree above her. Every pear was rotting on the branch. So were the oranges in the other trees. She stared. The hunger to return to one's body often interfered with the concentration necessary to hold a Dream world together, but she had never experienced anything like this.

A roar boomed across the garden. Behind the wall rose a terrible monster with green skin and long fangs. It stepped over the wall with another roar and reached for Ara with a clawed hand.

"Hello, Kendi," she said amiably. "Did you do the pears, too?"

The monster melted and vanished, leaving a wide-eyed koala bear in its place. Kendi emerged from behind a tree. He was wearing the linen shirt and trousers Ara usually conjured for him. The koala sniffed at the rotten pear.

"Didn't even faze you, huh?" Kendi said, reaching down to scratch the koala's ears.

"No. It was a good monster, though." She nudged the pear with a toe. "Well?"

Kendi looked down. "Not me. I noticed it earlier, though, and figured I'd better come back after my sister"—he gestured at the koala—"lead Gretch to the Rustic Silent."

Ara stared at the trees and concentrated. She expected sweet oranges and firm pears. This was *her* Dream, and by Irfan she would have them. Nothing happened.

The ground dropped away. Ara lost her balance and fell several feet. Her breath slammed out of her lungs when she hit. The earth thundered beneath her and a thousand cracks tore the garden wall.

"Kendi!" she shouted.

"It isn't me!" he yelled back. "What the hell is—"

A pit yawned beneath him and he vanished with a shriek.

"Kendi!" Ara lunged for him, but he had already disappeared. A brown blur of movement leaped into the darkness. A moment later, the falcon, grown impossibly large, rose on laboring wings from the pit. Kendi hung by one arm in her talons. The ground vibrated, and clumps of earth dropped into the depths. Ara grabbed Kendi's free arm and helped the falcon haul him to solid ground. The moment his weight left her, the falcon flashed back to normal size and fled to the skies with a defiant scream. The earth continued to rock and rumble under their feet, making it a struggle to keep their balance.

"We've got to get out of here," Kendi gasped. Ugly welts and scratches marked his arm. Psychosomatic memory would carry them over into his real body. If he had fallen into the pit, his body would have perished with his mind.

"Where's Gretchen?" Ara asked. "Is she safe?"

"She's that way," Kendi gestured. Gretchen's exact location instantly came from Kendi's mind into Ara's, even though the words she "heard" were vague and imprecise. Quickly she grabbed Kendi's wrist.

"Mother, wait!"

But Ara had already moved them both. A wooden deck popped into existence beneath them. Cool, crisp air washed over Ara, filling her nose with the scent of salt and sea. White sails creaked above them. Beside her, Kendi's Dream form wavered like a bad hologram, then snapped into focus. He fell retching to hands and knees. Ara looked around. Although the ship was moving steadily up and down, everything looked stable. Kendi continued to retch.

"You aren't really sick," she said. "It's all in your head."

"Thanks for the sympathy," Kendi said, wiping his mouth with the back of one hand.

"What's going on?" Gretchen asked. She stood behind them at the helm, the giant spoked wheel held loosely in her grip. Gretchen wore a pirate shirt and sailor's cap, as did Ara and Kendi.

"Are you all right?" Ara said.

"Why shouldn't I be?" Gretchen asked suspiciously. "I talked to some Silent on Rust, but they won't say much. The Unity's got them scared shitless. You aren't checking up on me, are you? Because if you are—"

The tickle to return suddenly blew into full-fledged need. It was worse than having an overfull bladder. Gretchen was all right. The rest could wait.

"I'm leaving," Ara said. "Get out of the Dream, both of you. That's an order." And she let go of the Dream.

THREE

The Dream

The best spy hides in open day, where everyone can see.

—Kethan Majir, *Letters from Prison*

Kendi Weaver got to his feet, his stomach still lurching around his insides. His arm hurt, his drugs were wearing off, and he wanted nothing more than to call up hot, dry Outback. Gretchen's mind pressed in on him, however, keeping the Dream ocean washing up and down beneath him. The motion worsened his nausea.

"Let's go, Gretch," he said. "I'm about done in."

Gretchen caught sight of his arm and let go of the helm. "Jesus, what happened to you?"

"I'll explain on the ship, Gretch. I have to go." And he released the Dream.

Ship and ocean vanished, replaced by gray ceramic walls and a red spear under his knee. He disentangled himself and sank down to the narrow bed. Angry red scratches ran down his arm, and bruises were already forming. His shoulder was stiff, and faint pangs of nausea still oozed through his stomach. No matter how hard he tried, Kendi still couldn't master instantaneous movement through the Dream. The abrupt change from one world to another was just too much.

Another small wave of nausea. Kendi took deep breaths until the feeling passed. Both the nausea and his injuries were in his head. If he could keep his Dream and waking selves more separate, as Ara was fond of reminding him, his mind would stop creating counterparts to injuries he sustained in the Dream. Most Silent only sustained slight discomfort if they were hurt while Dreaming, though actual death in the Dream meant death in the waking world, no matter how finely tuned a Silent's control might be. This knowledge lessened neither pain nor nausea.

After a moment, Kendi pulled on a robe and went down

the hall to the bathroom. He took a hot shower, sprayed his arm with disinfectants and painkillers, and swallowed an anti-inflammatory agent for his shoulder. Feeling better, he headed back to get dressed and found Ben at his door. Ben's red hair was tousled as usual, though his purple tunic had been recently smoothed.

"Hey, Ben," Kendi said. "I was in the bathroom."

Ben turned. His blue eyes fixed on Kendi a moment before glancing away. "We've landed," he said. "Customs will board pretty soon, and I've got some bad news. Jack downloaded the latest illegals for Rust. I guess your . . . uh . . . your . . ."

Kendi groaned theatrically and entered his room. Ben followed with a certain reluctance, like a puppy trying to figure out if it was welcome or would be shooed out the moment someone noticed it. Kendi thumbed the lock on his medicine chest and gathered ampules.

"I would've called on the intercom," Ben continued, "but Peggy-Sue couldn't find you. Poor thing's old and full of bugs."

Kendi, still gathering ampules, stole a glance at Ben over his shoulder. He was shorter than Kendi, and stocky. His build, muscular but not intimidating, filled out the trader's tunic very nicely, and his face had an open, ingenuous look.

And so damned handsome, Kendi thought.

Kendi's injured shoulder suddenly spasmed. Ampules scattered over the floor. Instantly Ben was at Kendi's side, his hand on Kendi's good arm.

"Are you all right?" he asked.

"Yeah," Kendi grunted. "It's all in my head, but it still hurts. Guess my mind is stronger than the painkillers."

Ben guided Kendi to the bed, and Kendi let him. There was nothing wrong with his legs, but he couldn't bring himself to pull away from the gentle, familiar warmth of Ben's hand. He sat down and Ben knelt to gather up the ampules. Kendi felt a little empty when Ben let go.

"Ben," he said suddenly.

"No, Kendi," Ben said without looking up.

"But—"

"I'm sorry, Kendi. Just 'no,' all right?" Ben's knees

cracked when he got up, his hands full of ampules. A slight blush colored his face.

"Ben, I just want to know *why*. I mean, you all but pushed me out the door."

"Kendi, please don't. Not right now."

"I don't want to hurt you, Ben," Kendi said quietly. It was hard to keep his voice steady. "You've been avoiding me since I moved back to the monastery. This is the first time I've been alone with you, and on this ship, that isn't easy to avoid."

Ben looked away, then nodded. "I don't like avoiding you. I want to be friends, Kendi, but—well, we can talk later, I promise. Maybe we can be . . ." Then he shook his head and backed away. "Look, I'll put these in the smuggling compartments in the engine room, all right?"

Kendi nodded. His heart beat fast and his mouth was dry. Ben trotted into the hall and the door slid shut.

"Maybe we can be . . ." Kendi repeated aloud. Elation filled him and he wanted to leap to his feet in a dance of joy. He forced the feeling down, however. "Maybe" meant only "not no." Kendi lay back on the bed and sighed heavily. He could still see Ben's blue eyes, feel his firm hand, hear his quiet voice.

If it is in my best interest and in the best interest of all life everywhere, he thought, *please let "maybe" mean "yes."*

Another knock at the door made him sit up. "Come in."

Gretchen slid the door open. "Intercom's broken," she announced. "Ara told me what happened. She wants to brief everyone, but first—"

"Attention! Attention!" said the computer's voice. "Unity customs officials will board in five minutes."

Kendi stood up. "Guess the intercom's fixed."

"Do you think what happened has something to do with the child?" Gretchen asked as they headed for the door.

"Dunno," Kendi said. "But something that can do *that* to the Dream scares the hell out of me."

The quarantine and customs people only confiscated five shots of painkillers, a pair of goldfish Ara had warned Trish not to bring, and three heads of lettuce from the galley.

Some extensive clinking that passed from Ara's hands to the inspector's ensured that they confiscated nothing else.

After they left, Ara called a briefing in the tiny galley. Despite her earlier threat, Kendi didn't have to clean up the mess left by his abrupt u-turn. Jack Jameson, who held forth as ship's cook and quartermaster, had already taken care of that. Not everyone could sit down, even though the crew numbered only eight. Kendi—and the others, he was sure—would have preferred to meet somewhere else, but the customs inspectors had just left, and Ara was worried they might have planted listening devices. Trish had so far managed to sweep only the galley.

Ara, Kendi, Gretchen, Trish, and Ben got seats at the table. Jack, a thin, blond man in his late fifties, hovered in a corner. Pitr's solid bulk occupied the doorway. Abruptly he yelped and stood aside. Harenn Mashib slouched into the room, her dark eyes heavy above her blue veil. She was short, with an average build and olive skin. Kendi wondered what she had done to make Pitr jump. Harenn moved toward Jack's corner, and he vacated it immediately.

"Coffee?" she grumped.

"I'd like to get started," Ara interjected tartly, and launched into an explanation of what had happened in the Dream. Pitr, who was also Silent, went pale.

"So whenever you go into the Dream, I want you to be extra careful. Get out if something in your environment changes and you can't fix it," Ara concluded. She drummed her fingers briefly on the tabletop. "I also met personally with the Empress."

The group stirred at this, and Kendi stole a glance at Ben. Ben's eyes, however, remained locked on Ara.

"She wants the child at all costs," Ara said. "She's worried this kid might kill someone or even start a war. We are to find the child quickly. Highest priority."

Kendi shifted in his seat. Something didn't feel right. He looked closely at Ara's face, but found no help there. Like Ben, she wouldn't look at him.

She's holding something back, he decided. *What's with that?*

"Kendi will search the black markets," Ara continued. "Gretchen will check out the legitimate slaves. Ben, you and Trish see what you can find on the nets. Anything unusual might be a clue. Pitr, I want you to explore the Dream, see if you find anything funny. I'm going to shmooze with the bureaucrats. Jack, you deal with inquiries about buying our cargo. Harenn, you keep working on the damage we sustained when the Unity fired on us."

"I'll probably be a few days, Mother," Kendi said. "It takes time to make contacts. I'll check in when I can."

Ara nodded, still without looking at him. "Just remember—we are nothing more than humble confection traders. If you even poke your nose out a hatchway, make sure you're wearing a purple tunic. Questions? Then head out, troops."

Everyone except Kendi moved for the door. After the room cleared, he turned to Ara.

"I can't wear the tunic when I'm trying to make contacts," Kendi said. "I'd be better off posing as an out-of-towner instead of showing up as an off-worlder."

"You'd know better than I would," Ara said in a neutral voice.

The hell with it. "Ara, what aren't you telling me?"

"What do you mean?"

"I mean, you aren't telling me everything. Did the Empress say something? Something you left out of the briefing?"

"No."

Kendi blinked. "You know, I think that's the first time you've ever lied to me."

"Leave it, Kendi."

"Ara, I'm second in command here. If the Empress told you—"

"I said, leave it!" Ara snapped.

"Fine." Kendi rose. "Just don't get yourself killed or incapacitated, *Mother*, or I'll be commanding this shitshingle half blind." And he left the galley.

Ara shifted impatiently from foot to foot. She examined her fingernails. She counted the gray ceiling tiles. And she waited. Behind her, in the public clerk's office proper, low murmurs mixed with the clatter of computer keys and flat-voiced computer responses as people used the terminals.

Despite the computer access, however, a hefty line of people waited to talk to the half-dozen clerks behind the counter. Painted signs admonished, EVERYTHING FOR THE GOOD OF THE UNITY, YOU ARE YOUR NEIGHBOR'S KEEPER, and YOU HAVE A FRIEND IN THE UNITY. The room was cramped and dingy, with dirty white tile on the floor and cheap, lumpy walls. Ara had been waiting in line for an hour, and that gave her time to think. Words and phrases mixed in her head, and the office offered no distractions.

The safety of this Confederation is more important.

I think that's the first time you ever lied to me.

I want you to destroy it.

There's something you aren't telling me.

The line shuffled forward a pace. Ara sighed. She had wanted to tell Kendi what the Empress had said, but the words had stuck in her throat. How could she kill a child?

Maybe it won't come to that, she told herself. *Maybe the child won't be a threat.*

"Glory to the— Ara? Stars above, is that you?"

A chill stabbed Ara's bones. She glanced up sharply and realized she had reached the front of the line. Behind the counter was a man who looked about sixty. He was bald, heavily freckled, and thin. He didn't look the least bit familiar. Who was he? How had he recognized her? Should she brazen it out? Pretend he was mistaken? Run for it?

She settled on polite bewilderment.

"I'm sorry, sir," she said. "I don't think I—"

"It's me, Ara. Chin Fen."

Recognition dawned. "Fen?" Ara gasped. "What the hell are you doing here?"

Fen shrugged. "Everyone's got to go somewhere. What are the odds, huh? Looks like you didn't complete—" He halted for a moment, then leaned forward, lowering his voice conspiratorially. "Complete your Silent training after all."

Relief washed through Ara, though she didn't relax. Chin Fen had left the Children of Irfan when he and Ara were in their early twenties. She remembered him as quiet and shy. More of a hanger-on than a friend. He'd always been friendly, though, and now that Ara was over her initial shock, she realized his presence was a gift, a free contact.

"I didn't recognize you at first," she admitted. "But what should we expect after—"

"Don't say how many years it's been," Fen interrupted. "I don't want to hear it."

God, he's a year younger than I am, Ara thought, trying not to stare at the wrinkles and spots. *And I'm not even fifty. Is that what living under the Unity does?*

Fen lowered his voice again. "Look, don't tell anyone that you're Silent, even an untrained one. You'll be sold into slavery. You wouldn't believe what I went through to avoid being found out."

"I won't tell if you won't," Ara murmured.

Fen nodded. "So what made you leave the . . . university?"

"I had a change of heart," Ara replied. "It didn't turn out to be what I was looking for."

"For you and me both," Fen laughed. "How long did you last after I left?"

Ara thought quickly. She'd have to remember whatever lie she told. Best to keep it simple. "Two years. Maybe three? I haven't thought about the university in a long time."

"It was a good time. You, me, Priss, Dello, and—what was his name? The guy who limped."

"Benjamin," Ara supplied with a small twinge.

Fen snapped his fingers. "Benjamin Heller. Wouldn't let us call him Ben. Whatever happened to any of them? I never heard."

In a split-second, nearly thirty years fell away. Claxons blared again. The eerily calm computer's voice announced the hull breach. Benjamin shouted in frantic surprise.

"I don't know," she said. "I fell out of touch."

The man behind Ara pointedly cleared his throat. Chin Fen took the hint.

"Maybe we can have dinner later and catch up," he said. "What can I help you with right now?"

Ara drummed her fingers on the countertop. "Information. I'm selling chocolate, and I hear Rust is hurting for it."

"We are," Fen said, with a small laugh. "I can't remember when I last tasted the stuff. But we don't carry trade info here. You want the Commerce Chamber."

"I'm not worried about my current cargo," Ara replied.

"It's the future I'm looking at. I have a couple of standing contracts for slaves, and I need to know more about Rust's regulations. I tried to access the public terminals, but they won't let me in without a code. The error message said I could get one here."

Although it would be relatively easy for Ben to hack into Rust's nets again, Ara saw no point in risking arrest over information that could be gotten legitimately with proper paperwork. Best to save Ben for the high-powered stuff not available to the public.

Fen's face cleared. "Access codes I can help you with. I'll just need to download your papers. And there's a forty *kesh* charge."

"Forty *kesh*?" Ara yelped. "I could open my own store for that."

"Not on Rust," Fen replied. "Sorry."

Making a big show of grumbling, Ara paid the fee and let Fen download from her computer pad the identity papers Ben had forged for her. In the interest of keeping everything simple, he had used their real first names and falsified last names.

"I adopted my grandmother's name after she died," Ara breezed when Fen asked about the discrepancy. "I wanted to honor her memory."

"Did you ever marry?" Fen used a small scanner to verify her retina and thumbprints.

"No." She laughed. "Running a merchant vessel doesn't leave time for romance."

"It must be more interesting than working here." Fen's fingers flicked over his terminal. "All set. If your crew wants access, though, they'll each have to come down here themselves. Tell them to bring a good book."

"And a small fortune," Ara groused.

Fen leaned across the counter. "I'm supposed to go on break soon. Let's get something to eat, hey?"

Ara's initial instinct was to make excuses. She'd have to watch every word she said and remember every lie she told. A moment's thought, however, told her that this man was a friendly contact in unfriendly territory.

"I'll wait in the lobby," she said.

Chin Fen's face lit up like a puppy in love, and suddenly Ara wasn't so sure she'd made the right decision.

FOUR

Planet Rust, City Ijhan

The arm of coincidence is long indeed.
—Silent Proverb

Kendi Weaver wandered from stall to stall, pretending to browse and trying to keep the memories at arm's length. Voices, colors, and smells swirled around him. He wanted to run all the way back to the *Post-Script*. But most of the Silent on Unity worlds were slaves, and Kendi's knack for worming his way into the underworld made the illegal slave market his most logical assignment.

The black market for slaves was, as usual, hidden in the red-light district. On Rust, just like elsewhere, it was easy for black marketeers to tell inquisitive authorities that their merchandise was only for rent, not sale, and to pay the fines—or bribes—for violating antiprostitution laws. It had taken two hours to find Ijhan's red-light district and four days of "shopping" to get a feel for who was selling what. During that time, he'd picked up rent boys from three different places, thumped some illegal dermosprays, and paid for time in bed so word would get out that he was customer, not guard. The antidote strips Harenn had implanted under his skin kept Kendi from getting high, but there was no way around the sex. Kendi hoped Ben didn't find out.

Two of the rent boys had had red hair.

Kendi browsed the market. At first glance, the place looked like any other market near sunset. The area was closed to ground traffic, and stalls and booths were scattered up and down the street. Buyers crowded the sidewalk, and the street was full of bicycles and people pulling light passenger carts. Vendors hawked food, clothing, and cheap jewelry. Shouts and conversations mixed with smells of sizzling fat and human sweat. Signs and posters were everywhere, extolling HUMANS, YES! ALIENS, NO!, LOVE THE UNITY LIKE YOURSELF, and OUR CHILDREN ARE THE UNITY.

Kendi ignored all of this. He couldn't shake the feeling that he should hurry. His mind held no doubt that other Silent would soon feel the strange child's presence. When that happened, others would start looking, too.

Some stalls were large enough to be living rooms. Others were actually entrances to what looked like apartment houses. Prostitutes, male and female, were draped inside and in front of these stalls. Most looked bored, some looked scared, a few looked seductive.

"Hey!" called a familiar voice as Kendi passed one stall. "Looking for more fun?"

Kendi turned to the speaker, a young man with a long face and thin lips. Kendi put a knowing grin on his face and entered the stall. It was carpeted with threadbare rugs. Three attractive young men were stretched out on the ground. They glanced idly at Kendi as he shook hands with their pimp.

"Your man was pretty good yesterday, Qadar," Kendi said. "Worth it."

"Mine are trained," Qadar breezed. "These other places just throw someone into bed with you and take your money. I make sure my boys know what they're doing. You want a drink? Or a refill on your dermos?"

"Don't need the refill," Kendi said, patting a brace of dermosprays in one pocket, "but I'll take some wine."

He and Qadar made further small talk while one of the rent boys brought Kendi a glass of wine. When the timing felt right, Kendi leaned conspiratorially toward Qadar.

"I've got a friend," he said. "And we're in the market for something . . . permanent, you know? Someone we can have whenever we want. But we don't want to pay taxes and license fees and all that shit every year. You know anyone?"

Qadar hemmed and hawed until Kendi dropped considerable *kesh* on the table.

"Talk to Mr. M and to Indri. They'll set you up," Qadar said, and gave directions to their stalls.

Kendi winked. "I'll be back. Gotta keep your men in practice."

Out in the market, Kendi suppressed a shudder and paid to wash hands and face at a hot-water stall. When he emerged, he stopped abruptly enough to earn an elbow in the side from an annoyed passerby.

The boy was back.

Kendi's heart lurched. The boy slouched against a gray aerogel wall half a block up the street. His clothes were ragged, even torn, but he was quite handsome, with tousled black hair and a swarthy complexion that contrasted sharply with a startling pair of ice-blue eyes. He looked fifteen or sixteen.

Kendi looked away, then back, careful not to stare. He had seen the boy around the market several times. Something about him rang bells in Kendi's head, but he couldn't say what or why. Kendi doubted he was the kid they were looking for—that would be too much to hope for. The Children of Irfan had been planning to spend several weeks or months on their search. Finding their quarry in only four days would be a miracle. But the elusive Silent child wasn't the only person Kendi was seeking.

Kendi studied the boy's face as best he could in the gathering dusk. It was the eyes that drew him. Utang, Kendi's brother, had blue eyes just like them. They were rare among the Real People. Excitement gripped Kendi. His heartbeat sped up, and he found himself trotting briskly toward the boy. At that moment, the boy's gaze met Kendi's. Their eyes locked. Then a look of fear crossed the boy's face and he bolted. The crowd swallowed him up.

Dammit! Kendi gave himself a mental kick. He'd been walking with too much purpose. The boy had probably mistaken him for guard. Kendi should have let the crowd carry him toward the boy. He sighed heavily and headed for Mr. M's stall.

It was another entryway masquerading as a booth, though it was much plusher than Qasad's. Thick rugs covered the floor, and people lounged provocatively on comfortable-looking furniture. Several were talking to customers. Sweet incense perfumed the air. The proprietor bore down on Kendi the moment politeness allowed, computer pad in hand.

"Something I can help you find?" the man asked. He was older, and as round as Ara, though she had more hair.

Kendi drew himself up. "I represent an . . . interested person. We're looking to acquire a few things on a permanent basis."

The man hemmed and hawed just like Qasad had. Kendi dropped more *kesh* and mentioned the other places he'd patronized. "Check with them and they'll tell you I'm a good customer."

The man tapped some keys on his pad and spoke to it in a low voice. Kendi let his gaze wander around the booth, feigning boredom despite a dry mouth and sweaty palms.

"Do I hear fifteen? Fifteen for this fine— fifteen, thank you, sir. Do I hear twenty? I have fifteen, will someone give me twenty?"

"I'd be glad to show you what we have, sir," Mr. M said, breaking into Kendi's memory. "This way, please."

Kendi followed Mr. M through an opening in the back of the booth and into the tall, thin house behind. The round little man presented his thumb for verification, opened a heavy door, and descended a flight of stairs. Dampness mingled with faint murmurs from below. Kendi's stomach churned. The urge to run welled up, but he bit the inside of his cheek and went down the steps.

It was like descending into the past. Mr. M's words barely registered as he showed Kendi a long row of people. Each person wore a thick metal bracelet on wrist and ankle. On the concrete wall behind them glowed a series of disks. They were sensors that tracked the movements of the shackles. If any slave moved beyond a prescribed area, the shackle transmitted first a warning tingle, then a wrenching shock unless the slave immediately returned. If the slave somehow managed to stay mobile after a full shock, the shackles became electromagnets, instantly chaining ankle to wrist and hobbling the escapee.

The youngest slave in the basement was a girl of nine, the oldest a man of seventy. Kendi passed a teenage boy who looked up at him with frightened eyes, and memories rushed at him. He was twelve again, fettered to a hard white floor near his mother. A procession of people probed and pushed at him with rough hands. Anger mixed with hurt, frustration, and fear, and all of it turned to terror as he was lead away from his father and sister. His brother was already gone.

Kendi rubbed his wrists and firmed his jaw. He would find them—all of them. If he had to check every slave in the universe, he would do it.

". . . can produce Silent children," Mr. M said.

Kendi snapped his head around. "Say that again?"

Mr. M's eyes gleamed briefly. "I said, this particular cow"—he gestured to a seated woman—"can produce Silent children. She has already borne three."

The woman looked up at Kendi. Her brown eyes were empty, vacant.

"Each one comes with papers that will stand up to the closest scrutiny," Mr. M was saying. "Do you see anything that interests you?"

Any*thing*. As if they were discussing rugs or lamp shades instead of people. Kendi realized he was grinding his teeth. To cover his consternation, he bent down to touch the woman's shoulder. She tried not to flinch.

Nothing. Her children might be Silent, but she was not.

Kendi moved down the line, ignoring the slaver's chatter and touching the shoulder of every slave under the age of twenty. None was Silent.

"Nothing young enough for you?" Mr. M asked. "I do have contacts who—"

Kendi curtly waved the man to silence. "Nothing here interests me."

"I'm expecting more next week," the slaver told him. "Cows and bulls both."

"Then I may return." He strode up the stairs without another word.

Back in the busy, crowded market, he paused to lean against a wall. He wanted a shower, or a long soak in a tub. But there was Indri's stall to visit. Kendi wondered how long it would take to find the child and if his sanity could stand up to repeated visits like this one.

Deciding to get it over with as quickly as possible, Kendi started off, and halted. The ragged boy was back, slouched against the same wall, scanning the crowd with those oddly blue eyes. Kendi ducked between a pot seller and a noodle merchant and peered cautiously at the boy's face.

It wasn't just the eyes. The boy's skin tone and facial structure reminded Kendi strongly of Utang, the older brother he hadn't seen in over fifteen years. Kendi couldn't keep his excitement down. Was it possible? Had his brother escaped slavery and had a son?

Right, he told himself. *In a universe of who-knows-how-many trillion people, you just happen to arrive at the one market in the one city on the one planet where a nephew you didn't even know existed hangs out.*

But the resemblance was undeniable. Kendi bit his lip. More astounding coincidences were common enough. Why should this one be so unbelievable?

Steam rose from the noodle merchant's water kettles and the pot seller cried out to passersby about the fine quality of his wares. It was almost dark, but the market showed no sign of slowing down. Here and there, street lights flickered to feeble life. The boy didn't move.

Kendi wondered what he was doing. He couldn't be hustling—the local houses didn't put up with freelancers. Was he dealing drugs? Why had he run away when Kendi approached?

A heavyset man in a blue jumpsuit approached the boy and engaged him in conversation. Kendi noticed two other sharply dressed men drifting steadily toward the duo from different directions. The impending scenario was obvious from Kendi's vantage point. Kendi cracked his knuckles.

You don't need to get involved, he told himself. *Just walk away.*

But Kendi's feet refused to move. After more conversation—negotiation?—the heavyset man cocked his head toward an alley. The boy hesitated. The other two men sidled closer.

Don't do it, Kendi pleaded silently. *You don't need whatever he's selling.*

The boy nodded once at the heavyset man and trotted ahead of him into the alley. The man gestured to his compatriots, and all three swarmed in after him.

Shit, Kendi thought. *Shit shit shit. That kid won't even know what hit him.*

The alley gaped like the space between a lion's paws. This was none of Kendi's business. For all he knew, the boy was a drug dealer or serial murderer who deserved whatever the men were planning to deal out to him.

"Right," Kendi said. He dashed across the market, dodging shoppers and bicyclists and earning angry shouts from both. With a deep breath, Kendi plunged into the alley.

The alley was dark and smelled rancid. Kendi skidded on something slippery, caught his balance, heard a yelp of pain. Just ahead of him, the boy had been shoved up against one wall. The heavyset man held him there by the neck while the other two stood with their arms crossed. Snarling, the captor drew back a fist, and the boy squeezed his eyes shut.

Kendi flung himself forward. He barreled straight into the heavyset man. He went down, Kendi on top of him. Kendi leaped free and spun to face the other men who had already produced weapons. The boy's eyes popped open. One man carried a blade that crackled and snapped. The other aimed a pistol.

Operating on instinct, Kendi dove for the ground. Energy spat through the air above his head. He rolled to his feet and came face-to-face with the crackling knife. An arc flashed in the air and something slashed Kendi's arm. It went numb from shoulder to elbow. Kendi's foot smashed the man in the groin. The knife clattered to the ground, but Kendi could feel the other man's pistol trained on his back. Everything moved in slow motion.

Dodge dodge dodge, he thought. His legs pushed him sideways and warm, fetid air moved against his cheek. Kendi flattened himself against the alley wall, expecting pain to crash across his back. Nothing. He looked over his shoulder at the gunman. The man stood motionless, pistol in his outstretched hand. The heavyset man lay where Kendi had tackled him, and the man with the knife moaned on the ground. Kendi spared a glance for the boy. He was staring at the gunman. Puzzled, but deciding it would be best to take care of the immediate threat first, Kendi removed the pistol from the man's unresisting hand. Kendi pistol-whipped him and he fell.

"Are you all right?" Kendi said to the boy.

The boy stared at Kendi. "Who the fuck are you?"

"I was going to ask the same about them." Kendi gestured at the attackers. "What was that all about?"

The boy said nothing. Kendi stuck the pistol into his belt and tried to massage some feeling back into his arm. It was going to hurt like hell, he was sure. The man Kendi had kicked tried to get up. Kendi drew a dermospray from his pocket and pressed it against the man's arm. There was a muffled *thump*. The man sighed and fell silent. Kendi turned back to the boy.

"Did you stop that guy from shooting me?" he asked.

Silence.

"Look, I just saved your life, and I think you saved mine. Did you?"

Still no answer. Exasperated, Kendi tried to grab the boy by the shoulder, but the boy backed away. "Bump off. Don't touch me unless—"

"Hands in the air!" barked a voice.

Both of them spun. A man and a woman in the red-and-black uniforms of the Unity guard stood in the alleyway, pistols aimed and steady. Behind them was a sleek patrol cruiser, the only type of ground car allowed in the market. Kendi raised his good arm. The boy raised both of his.

"I said, hands up!" the woman snapped.

"I can't raise my other arm," Kendi said. "One of those guys hit it with an energy blade."

"Take the pistol out of your belt with your fingertips," the woman ordered. "Drop it on the ground."

Kendi obeyed. A pang shot through him as he remembered the dermosprays in his pocket. Even the most cursory search would turn them up. Tension made a cold knot in his stomach.

"These men attacked us, officers," he said. "The gun belongs to them."

The male guard snorted. His partner eased closer and kicked the gun away. Kendi saw sweat trickle down the boy's face.

"Both of you put your hands on the wall," the male officer said. "Now!"

Shakily, Kendi put his good arm on the wall. A dozen possibilities flickered through his mind and were just as quickly tossed aside. No fighting. Kendi had caught the boy's attackers by surprise. The same approach wouldn't work with alert Unity patrol guards. Running was out of the question. He'd be gunned down. He couldn't even call Ara for help—wearing a communicator while making underworld contacts would have spelled his death.

Hard hands landed on his shoulders, feeling his back and moving down his sides.

And then there was a strange jumping sensation, as if the world had leaped to one side. A dizzy spell made Kendi glad he was leaning against the wall. The feeling was the same one he got after he'd been . . . been . . .

Shit! he thought. *I was possessed! The kid possessed me! Did he possess the guards too?*

A harsh grip spun him around and he looked into the face of the Unity patrol officer. The boy was nowhere in sight.

"What the hell did you do?" he snarled. "Where did your little friend go?"

"I don't know," Kendi said. "I swear!"

The man smashed Kendi's face and he fell to his knees. A foot slammed into his stomach, and he vomited over the alley floor. Kendi wondered if Ara would find his body as pain exploded at his temple.

FIVE

Sejal's Journal

DAY 4, MONTH 10, COMMON YEAR 987

I turned my first trick today.

There. I said it. Or I wrote it down, anyway.

I've never kept a journal before. It's kind of weird. I'm typing because I don't want Mom to overhear me talking to the terminal. It's an old, clunky thing, and you have to talk loud to get its attention. We can't afford a new one, though.

Okay, I'm not a virgin anymore. Or does this not count? It's not like I let the guy screw me or anything. I'm not into men. Or does this mean I am? I don't feel any different, and I don't look any different. I'll write it all down and maybe then I'll know if something changed.

I'm kind of scared.

The voices haven't gone away. I was hoping they would when I lost my virginity. I don't know why I thought they might. Sometimes I think I'll go nuts. They whisper and whisper and I can't quite understand what they're saying. Grampy Lon says hearing voices is a sign of Silence, but I haven't said much about that to Mom. Every time I bring it up, she changes the subject or just clamps her lips together. I know I had the test—twice—when I was little and that it came up negative both times. They take Silent kids away, so I can't be Silent.

Anyway. I was talking about the other stuff.

I did it for the money. You don't make much busking, that's for sure, and there aren't any jobs for a sixteen-year-old who can't afford more school, not when slaves do the work cheap. No one gives a shit how many hours you spend studying on the nets, either. So I stood on the corner down by the kelp seller's with my flute. I've been playing since I was six, ever since Grampy Lon decided to give me lessons, and I'm pretty good.

Okay. The kelpies are at the edge of the market, almost into the business district, and there were lots of bureaucrats skulking around under the tall buildings the Unity sprayed up after the Annexation. The traffic was heavy, with both groundcars and aircars. Between them and the people on the street, it's almost claustrophobic—perfect spot for a busker, I thought.

I thought wrong. After three hours, my fingers ached and I had a quarter *kesh*—enough to buy lunch if I was careful. That was when Jesse wandered over.

I met Jesse six months ago at the market. He's not that good looking—scruffy black hair, heavy eyebrows, pointy nose, pretty good build—but he doesn't work for one of the houses, which means he's cheap and he can usually find a jobber. I think he lives on the street, dodging slavers and goons from the houses. One time the house goons caught up with him and beat him so bad it gave him a permanent limp. He started sucking a lot more jay-juice after that, and I think he tricks to feed his habit.

Anyway. Jesse looked at the two coins in my hat and tossed in fifty *kesh*. I stopped playing.

"Glory. What the hell is that?" I asked. I don't talk the same at the market as I do at home. Mom would have a moon fit if she knew how much I swear and how bad my grammar is when I'm on the street—or in this journal.

"Glory. It's your share." Jesse hooked his thumbs in his pockets.

I just gave him a blank stare.

"You see that guy across the street?" He jerked his head. "The one in the red shirt."

Automatically I glanced across the street. An older guy in red was leaning against one of the buildings. Traffic buzzed between us. The guy was lean and looked maybe forty, but for all I knew he had just left a fresh-up and was older than Grampy Lon. He looked nervous.

"What about him?" I asked.

"He asked if I knew anyone for a three-way. Pays fifty each. You in?"

I grabbed the *kesh* from my hat and thrust it at Jesse. "Forget it."

"Come on, guy," Jesse said. His thumbs didn't leave his pockets, so I was left holding the *kesh*. "I haven't had a jobber all day, and he won't do just me."

"No."

"It's not like he's gonna fuck you or anything," Jesse said. "All you got to do is lay back and relax. I'll do the work."

"I'm not into guys, okay?"

"What's that got to do with it? It ain't sex, Sejal. It's money. M-O-N-E-Y." He glanced at my hat. "You been busking here all day for that?"

"Yeah," I admitted.

Jesse sidled closer. He smelled like sweat and cheap leather and suddenly I flashed on him. I do that sometimes. It started about six months ago, and it isn't anything I can control or shut off. It scares me shitless. It's hard enough dealing with my own feelings without someone else's crowding in, and right then Jess was a real jumble-up. He was hungry for food and he was *really* hungry for jay-juice. He was nervous and he was hopeful. One thing he didn't feel was lust. The flash faded.

"Listen," Jesse said. "This guy'll give you fifty *kesh* for half an hour. He probably won't even last twenty minutes."

My mouth had gone dry and I snuck another glance across the street. The guy was still there. I tried to sense what he was feeling, but the flash didn't work. It never does when I'm trying.

"Fifty *kesh*, Sejal," Jesse repeated. "You ever earn fifty *kesh* in twenty minutes?"

"No," I answered, but not as loud as last time.

Jesse gestured at my flute. "You've been playing the wrong instrument, man."

I looked at him. In that moment I could have pushed him away with my mind. That's something else I can do, and it *always* works. It's like I'm reaching out and pulling strings that make the other person dance, and I can do it to a bunch of people all at once. I've been able to do that for about three months now.

The first time was by accident. I was on my way home

from busking with two *kesh* in my pocket when a big guy grabbed me and another one put a knife to my neck. A third one was with them. I was too scared to even think. I just shoved at them with my mind. I'm not sure how to describe it. It was like I could feel this . . . *place* around me, and I reached through it to them. I reached *hard* at two of them, and they just froze where they were. The third one got scared, and I reached through that place and flipped his switches and made him *really* scared. He ran away.

I haven't told anyone about that, either. Not Jess or Grampy Lon, and definitely not Mom. I don't know if it's related to flashing on what people feel. It probably is, but who can I ask?

"Listen, just help me this once, okay?" Jesse said. "You don't like it, you don't have to do it again, but you'll still have that fifty. Twenty minutes, man."

I looked at the guy. His hair was lighter than mine, almost brown. At least he wasn't ugly. Jesse had told me about some jobbers who were really fat or who didn't wash, but this guy looked okay. Fifty *kesh*. More than a month's rent.

"What's he want us to do?" I asked.

Jess grinned and led me across the street.

At least the guy didn't want anything strange. Jess was right—all I had to do was lay there with my eyes shut. I didn't know whose mouth was on me or who was making the bed shake. The hotel room was stuffy and musty smelling and the sheets were a little damp. The mouths and the motion seemed to go on and on, and I just wanted to get the hell out of there.

And then I reached out with my mind the way I did to those two guys. I didn't want to touch this guy like that, but I did. I reached through that place and found him all hot and horny. I flipped his switch and gave him the mother lode of all orgasms. He yelled, and something warm spattered my leg. Then he flopped down to the mattress. I kept my eyes shut. My teeth were clenched so tight my whole head hurt.

"Shit," Jess muttered. "He fainted."

Jess wet a washcloth from the bathroom, wrung some

water over the jobber's face, and then wiped my leg. When I opened my eyes, the guy was up and dressing. He had a big smile on his face.

"Any time you boys are up for that again," he said, "I'll pay double. Glory."

He gave me and Jess another twenty *kesh* each and left. I glanced at the clock. Twenty minutes. Seventy *kesh*.

"What the hell happened?" Jess almost whispered, staring down at the *kesh* in his hand. He was still naked.

"I don't know." I pulled my clothes on. "Look, is that it? Are we done?"

"We're done, man, unless you want to file for taxes."

I didn't laugh. I just left.

Now I'm in my room. Mom's getting ready to go to a meeting. Her whole life is meetings. She'll probably want me to go and take care of the little kids, but I think I'll tell her to fuck off.

Well, probably not like that. I love Mom, but sometimes she's a real pain. She's always dealing with some neighborhood disaster at some neighborhood meeting. She acts like the whole place will fall to pieces if she doesn't keep it up.

I wonder what she'd say if she knew what happened? I bet she'd throw a cat. So how the hell am I going to tell her about the money?

I'll save it. If I get enough, maybe I can buy us passage off this rockball and we can move someplace where the wind doesn't smell like fish.

Huh. The only way to get that kind of money is to keep tricking, and I'm not doing that again. Not in a hundred years.

Mom's coming. Better sign off.

DAY 8, MONTH 10, COMMON YEAR 987

I did it again. I shouldn't have, probably. What if I got caught? It isn't just the Unity, but the houses, too. The houses have it all staked out—who can trick where, what they can do. And they beat the shit out of anyone who bugs in on their territory.

Anyway. I started off down in the market with my flute, not planning to trick. It was a good day—got two *kesh* in less than three hours. But every time someone dropped a coin in my hat, I kept thinking about how I got seventy *kesh* in twenty minutes.

Jesse was tricking a ways up the street from me. He saw me and gave a little wave. A couple minutes later a guy—not the same jobber as before—walked up to him. They talked for a minute, then went off together, Jesse still limping. I looked down at the little coins in my hat. Then I thought, *The hell with this.*

I collapsed my flute and shoved it into my pocket, then sort of casually walked over to the spot where Jesse had been standing. I left my hat where it was. Someone grabbed it and ran, but I didn't care. My heart was beating hard enough to choke my throat. I leaned against the wall and hooked my thumbs in my pockets like Jess did. After a second I realized he did that to tighten his pants across his crotch. I felt like everyone was staring at my privates, but I didn't move my hands.

It ain't sex, I told myself. *It's money. M-O-N-E-Y.*

My mouth dried up like a raisin. I didn't know what the rules were. Do you look at people? Tell them you're for rent up front? I should've asked Jesse.

Just to make things harder, the voices started whispering at me again. I concentrated hard, tried to make them go away. I can never quite make out what they're saying, and it's scary. Sometimes they come at night, and that's the worst. It sounds like ghosts breathing on me.

And then this woman walked up to me as easy as you please and said, "Glory. You look like you're lost."

Whisper whisper whisper whisper.

I started to deny it, then realized the woman knew I wasn't lost. What should I say? What would Jesse say?

"Glory," I answered. "It's hard to find your way around this place."

"You need a ride somewhere?" She was about ten years older than me, a little heavy, with short brown hair. Her clothes looked really expensive.

Whisper whisper whisper.

"Um, sure," I said. "I could use a ride."

"Then let's go."

Her aircar—aircar!—wasn't that far away, but I was so

nervous I could hardly walk. I wouldn't get anything done if I was scared, so I started pretending I was Jesse. Jesse knew which way was up. I was Jesse, strong and smart.

The voices faded a little bit, and that made me feel even stronger.

In the aircar, the jobber put her hand on my thigh, but I was in control by then. "It's a hundred," I said, pulling the number out of thin air. She handed it to me.

Her place was a rooftop penthouse, which meant she was a high-placer in the Unity. She landed on the roof near a door. A maid let us in. The jobber treated the maid like she didn't exist, so I did the same. The maid ignored me, too.

I tried not to stare at the penthouse, but it was hard. Thick carpets covered the floors, paintings and statues were everywhere—real ones, not holograms—and her bedroom was bigger than my whole apartment. I figured she liked the color blue because everything in her room was done in it. Blue carpets, blue walls, blue bedspread.

The jobber shut the door and pulled me down on the bed without saying anything. I figured she wanted me to undress her, so I did. I was Jesse, who knew what to do. I opened up her shirt—she wasn't wearing underwear—and pulled off her skirt. She just lay back on the bed with her eyes shut and didn't move.

That sort of startled me. She didn't try to undress me or kiss me. She just lay there. Her breasts were like little pillows with spots of pink on each. I stared at them—I had never seen a woman naked before. I was hard as a rock. (See? I knew I wasn't into guys.) That was when she started talking.

She talked more dirt than a lot of the guys I heard on the street. Half of it was calling me names like "street whore" and "dick boy," and half of it was telling what she wanted me to do. I was glad because I didn't have to figure it out for myself.

She climbed on top of me. All of a sudden I wanted out of there in the worst damn way. I didn't like the way she smelled or looked or sounded, and I didn't want her skin touching mine. Before she could do anything else, I reached through that place and made her come hard and fast. She screamed and fell sideways onto the bed. I was scared the maid would come running in.

"What the hell did you do?" the jobber panted.

I shrugged. Then I noticed the voices had faded completely.

"Can you do it again?" she said.

The words popped out before I even thought. "For the right money."

She gave me another hundred *kesh*, and I did it again. It was easy, and I didn't even have to touch her much. So much for getting out of there.

After that, the jobber went into the bathroom. I pulled my clothes on and looked around. She had four closets and her dresser was the size of a freight truck. It occurred to me that I could probably hoik something worth a lot more than a couple hundred. And if the jobber walked in, I could just freeze her in place until I was done and she'd never know the difference. I even reached for her dresser. Then I stopped.

Okay, fine—I'm a rent boy. Hooker. Prick for hire. But I'm not a thief. One thing you don't do back in the neighborhood is steal, and I wasn't going to do it here, either.

The jobber came back in kind of a hurry, as if she'd remembered she'd left a potential thief in her bedroom. So fuck her. Less than an hour later, I was back at the market with two hundred *kesh* in my pocket. I felt pretty good. I was smooth, in control. People would give me money for easy work.

I got home a little while ago. Mom isn't here, of course, and I don't know where she is. She doesn't have a regular job. Like I said, the neighborhood takes up a collection to pay our bills and rent in return for all the organizing she does. Mom's really the queen around here. No crime, no drugs, no wife-beating, and you keep a clean house or you're out. Mom can't legally make anyone move, but the Unity doesn't give a shit what we peons do to each other, and when two dozen people show up to haul your furniture out to the street, you can't do squat.

Mom's good at banding people together. Something in her voice forces you to listen to her. Besides, everyone likes living in a place where you don't have to worry about jay-heads breaking in looking for stuff to steal and where there aren't any gangs cruising the streets. Who's going to win, a bunch of addicts hyped up like hummer fish or a group of organized, motivated patrollers?

So we're all poor but honest folk around here. Mom got people to grow vegetables on roofs and in window boxes to sell down at the market for community money to pay for doctor visits and stuff. Some people raise small animals—chickens and rabbits and pigfish—and we sell them, too. Everyone contributes around here. If you don't, the furniture committee shows up.

Anyway. I tried to take a nap when I got home. My room is tiny, with a bare wood floor and a lumpy bed that creaks. There's a little dresser and an even littler closet. Good thing I don't have very many clothes. I thought about the jobber, who was probably sitting in her big blue room, sipping a drink brought in by her maid, and my room seemed even smaller.

I got out my flute and played for a while. Sad songs. I don't know what it is. When you're depressed, you want depressing music. You should want happy music to make you feel happy. When you're depressed, though, happy music makes you want to puke.

I want off this rockball. Only one way to do that, isn't there?

Mom's coming. Signing off.

SIX

Planet Rust, City Ijhan, Patrol Guard Station #4972

Stone walls might a pris'ner make,
But psyche binds the slave.
—Travil Garr, *Poems from a Merchant*

The door fell shut with a crash. Ara glanced around to take in her surroundings—tiny room, two chairs bolted to the floor on either side of a table, and probably no end of hidden surveillance devices. A sign read THE UNITY PUNISHES ONLY THE DESERVING. Kendi sat in one of the chairs, head in his hands. Ara sat down across from him.

"Are you all right?" she asked.

"Get me out of here," he whispered hoarsely.

Ara nodded. "I've arranged to pay the fines. It won't be long." She reached across the table and grasped one of his hands. Kendi's skin looked like it was coated with ashes. His eyes were bloodshot, a half-healed cut slashed one forearm, and the hand that Ara wasn't holding shook slightly. He squeezed her hand with a thin smile before looking down at the table again. Outrage filled Ara's heart at the condition of her student.

The last two weeks had been filled with anxiety. When Kendi had failed to check in, Ara had waited twelve tense hours before initiating a search. Trish and Pitr tried scouring the Dream for his presence on Rust, but an active search through the Dream for Kendi's real-world mind and body ran the risk of alerting Unity Silent to their presence—a bad idea for a group of undercover monks trying to snatch up a Unity citizen—and the need for stealth hindered their movements. In the end, Ben and his hacking skills had met with success. Even so, it had taken ten days to locate Kendi in jail and six more to negotiate the Unity's bureaucracy and arrange to pay his fines. Chin Fen and the connections he had made over the years had been a great help, Ara had to admit, and she had lied her way through several lunches with him. Now Kendi sat before her, bruised and beaten. His hand was cold in hers.

They sat like that for a long time, wordless, teacher and student, until the door finally ground upward.

"Let's go," boomed the guard.

Kendi got up and shuffled toward the door, head down. Ara followed, gritting her teeth and trying not to glare at the guard.

Don't get anyone angry, she told herself. *You're getting what you want. That's all that counts.*

They made their way through the chilly prison. The corridor was windowless and only dimly lit by heavily shielded bulbs in the ceiling. Ara kept her eyes resolutely ahead. She refused to glance at the tiny cells crammed with people or acknowledge the heavy smell of poor sanitation, of men, women, and children all thrown in together. There was nothing she could do for these people. There was no point in looking at them. But she couldn't block out the heart-rending sounds they made, the pleading cries that filtered between the bars.

Another door led them out of the prison area and into the office area, a huge open place filled with regimented rows of gray metal desks. A constant rumble of voices, clattering keys, and metallic-voiced computers pervaded the background, and the air smelled of disinfectant and body odor.

At one of the desks, Ara thumbed more paperwork and listened grimly as an official informed them that as a convicted criminal, Kendi would be assigned a spot on a work detail list for the Unity as part of his sentence. Two hundred *kesh* ensured that Kendi's name would be mysteriously absent from the work list.

At last they reached the main desk. Four receptionists directed traffic, and on a long row of benches sat various people in emotional states ranging from agitation to apathy. Ara's jaw was sore from grinding her teeth and biting back harsh words. A familiar figure waited on one of the benches for them, and Kendi's bruised face brightened immediately.

"Ben!" he said, and Ara laid a hand on his arm.

"Wait," she murmured. "We aren't out of this until we've cleared the building."

Kendi checked himself, but Ara didn't miss the look he shot at Ben, as if the young man were a rescue pod in hard vacuum. Part of Ara bristled. Although Ben had tracked Kendi down on the nets, Ara had arranged for his release, and now Kendi was all but ignoring her.

On the other hand, I don't feel about Ben the same way Kendi does, she thought wryly. *I wonder if Kendi knows how transparent he is?*

Ben gave Kendi a small smile and patted his shoulder as the three of them exited the patrol station.

Outside, hazy clouds covered the sun, but the air, as usual, was mild. The sidewalk was crowded. A pair of slaves washed windows near a pile of broken concrete. Another group of slaves dug into the exposed earth beneath the cement. They did not, Ara noticed, have power tools, and their clothes were ragged and filthy. An overseer in a red uniform watched them, energy whip in hand.

The little group trotted quickly up the street. After they turned a corner, Ara ran a small scanner over all three of them.

"No bugs," she said. "We can talk."

"Thank all life!" Kendi burst out, ignoring the odd stares he gathered from passersby.

"Are you hungry?" Ben asked.

"Starving."

Ara looked at him, and then, with a glance at the crowded street, drew him into an empty doorway. "You're looking awfully cheerful for someone who was so depressed a minute ago."

"That was an act," Kendi replied. "Mostly. In order to keep other . . . people off my back, I acted crazy. Manic-depressive. Most of the people in there are afraid of lunatics. You showed up during my depressive phase."

"And now you're manic?" Ben commented dryly.

Ara shook her head, still worried. Despite his explanation, she didn't like Kendi's cheerfulness. It was too sudden, even for him. Kendi was a child of open spaces, someone who coped with extended voyages by spending long hours in the Dream. A fortnight in a Unity prison must have been a nightmare of the worst kind.

"Let's get you something to eat," she said. "And you can tell us what happened."

"I found him," Kendi said.

"Who?" Ara asked.

"The kid. The one we're looking for. I found him."

Ara caught her breath. "How? Where is he? What's he—"

"Mother," Ben interrupted firmly. "You just said that Kendi needs to eat. I agree."

Ara's first impulse was to ignore Ben and ask more questions. A glance at Kendi's ashen face, however, destroyed that idea.

"You're right," she said. "I got carried away. Food first, questions later."

"Back at the ship?" Ben asked.

Ara nodded. "Safest place to talk."

An hour later, Kendi, newly showered and in clean clothes, sat on his bed. Harenn sat next to him, methodically probing his wounds with fingers and medical scanner. Ara occupied the room's only chair and watched intently. Kendi winced under Harenn's ministrations, but didn't cry out.

"You're barbaric," he growled.

"The Australian aboriginal tribes," Harenn said, "are reputed to have a superhuman ability to withstand pain. I assumed this is why you refused painkillers. You do not have this ability?"

"That was before the whites tainted us," Kendi said. His voice was still too cheerful for Ara's taste.

Harenn ignored him. "Your concussion has healed, as have the bruises and the cut. You have cracked no ribs. There is really nothing for me to do except give you pain medication, and you do not wish this."

"What about the boy?" Ara said from her chair. Her worries about Kendi would have to wait.

Kendi explained about the alley, the fight, and the Unity patrol. "So I was arrested," he finished. "The kid must have taken the time to search my pockets and grab the drugs. Otherwise I would've been in really deep cabbage."

"And you were not before?" Harenn muttered.

"I want to be clear on this," Ara said. "The boy possessed you."

Kendi nodded. "I felt that little shift you always get after someone else leaves your mind, but I hadn't let him in. It was a possession—or something very close to it. What's amazing is that he must have hit the patrol at the same time. Otherwise he wouldn't have gotten away. That's three people all at once, and two of them weren't Silent."

Ara gnawed her lower lip. The situation frightened her more with every passing moment. There was no recorded instance of a person with such an ability in the entire history of the Dream. How many people could this boy control? Six? A dozen? An army?

If, in your opinion, this child would pose a threat to the Confederation . . .

"Why did he not possess the men who attacked him?" Harenn asked. Her dark eyes were half-closed above her opaque blue veil. It made her look sleepy.

"I think he was going to," Kendi said. "Then I showed up."

A knock came at the door and Ben entered with a tray. Kendi's head jerked around and Ara almost rolled her eyes. She knew about Ben and Kendi's breakup, of course. She knew that Ben had done the breaking. But when she'd pressed for details, Ben had refused to give them. Ara gave a mental sigh. Ben was like his mother—too tight-lipped for his own good.

Ben handed Kendi the tray. Delicious smells of spiced beans and honeyed bread wafted up from the dishes. "Jack's talking to a buyer," he said. "So I made you lunch." He looked around for a place to sit and, seeing none, took up a spot on the floor.

"You cooked?" Kendi said, genuinely impressed. "Wow."

Ben shrugged. "Someone had to. I hope it's okay."

Kendi tried a bite and smiled. "It's great. Though anything would be better than the slop I've been eating lately. Not," he added hastily, "that this is anywhere close to that. I mean—"

"Shut up and eat, Kendi." Ben laughed.

"Have there been other disturbances in the Dream?" Kendi asked.

"Yes," Ara said. "Silent all over the galaxy are frightened. Gretchen also managed to strike up a conversation with two Unity Silent without letting them know who she was. They've felt the boy's presence, and they suspect his power goes beyond normal Silence."

"Hell," Kendi muttered.

"They haven't narrowed his location to Rust," Ara concluded, "but they are looking."

"How do we find this boy, then?" asked Harenn. "Before the Unity does?"

"I'll go back to the red-light district," Kendi said, mouth full. "None of you knows what he looks like."

Bad idea. Bad idea. "The guard will be watching for you," Ara warned.

"So?" Kendi countered in that maddeningly cheerful tone. "My fines are paid. I'm not on a work list. They can't do anything to me."

"Except follow you, harass you, and re-arrest you under trumped-up charges like they did the first time."

"I don't see any other way," Kendi breezed. "In fact, I can start looking tonight. I feel fine."

The hell you say, Ara thought.

"Make a composite drawing on the computer," Harenn said. "That would be simple enough. Ben could put this image into our implants and set the computer to scan for the child. Then more of us could start looking."

"Good idea," Ara said, shooting Harenn a grateful look.

"But—" Kendi began.

"Get to it as soon as you can." Ara got up and moved for the door. "We can all fan out tonight. If anyone finds him, I want you to follow him. Find out where he lives. If you can get close enough, plant a tracer on him. It'll be easier to persuade him to come with us if we know something about him. Kendi, you stay here and rest after you do the composite. That's an order."

"But—"

"I thought getting the child into our hands was highest priority," Harenn interrupted. "Why aren't we simply snatching him off the street?"

"The boy can possess the unwilling and non-Silent, Harenn," Ara replied levelly. "How far do you think a kidnapping attempt would get?"

"Stun him," Harenn countered. "Once he is on the ship—"

"He could possess the entire crew," Ara finished. "Wouldn't that be fun? He needs to come of his own free will. Let's move out. Kendi, composite. Then rest."

She left, all but towing Harenn behind her.

Kendi watched the door slide shut. It didn't clang like the . . . other doors. Ben moved to the chair and Kendi kept a wary eye on him. After a moment he realized it was because he was afraid Ben would steal his food.

"Was it bad?" Ben asked.

Kendi looked up. "Was what bad?"

"The prison."

"It was what you'd expect."

"What happened in there?" Ben pressed.

"Nothing important," Kendi replied. "Don't worry about it."

"Kendi, don't you think you should talk about—"

"Suddenly you're an authority on talking?" Kendi snarled. Ben flushed and Kendi felt instantly contrite. "I'm sorry, Ben. I'm not angry with you. Thanks for finding me."

"I couldn't leave you in jail." Ben ran a hand through thick red hair. "You think the boy's a relative, don't you?"

Startled, Kendi swallowed a mouthful of beans and gave a shrug. "Maybe."

"Don't lie," Ben admonished. "The only time I see you this excited is when you think you're on the trail of your family. Kendi, please don't get your hopes up. You know what the odds are, don't you?"

"I always get my hopes up," Kendi said, more sulkily than he'd intended. "Sometimes it's all that keeps me going."

"I just don't want to see you hurt, okay?"

"Don't get on my back, Ben," Kendi warned.

Ben got up. "Fine. You should make that composite." He pulled a dermospray from his pocket. "I brought this up from the smuggling compartments. I figure you'd want it. Do the composite first, though."

He set the spray on the bed next to Kendi and left.

Why had he snapped at Ben like that? Stupid, stupid, stupid.

Maybe I can make it up to him, he thought. *Send him flowers? And chocolates, too, fresh from the hold.*

An image of Ben surrounded by thousands of red roses and with satin boxes of chocolate piled at his feet popped into Kendi's head. He began to laugh and found he couldn't stop. Guffaws echoed about the spartan room. With a great deal of snickering and snuffling, he got himself under control. Kendi wiped his streaming eyes, feeling strangely tired. His ribs ached.

Better do the composite, then, he thought.

Kendi got to his feet. A headache was gathering, and the thought of a fat dermospray full of painkillers was unbelievably tempting. Painkillers, however, would interfere with the drugs he needed to enter the Dream later. Gingerly he sat down at the terminal, called up an artist's program, and set to work. Half an hour later, the kid's startling blue eyes stared at Kendi from the screen beneath loosely curled black hair.

As he finished, he became aware of the unyielding ceramic walls around him. The ship seemed to wrap itself about Kendi in a confining cocoon. The Outback and its wide-open spaces called. He uploaded the composite into the ship's computer and sent Ara notification that he was finished. Without waiting for a reply, he shut down the terminal and picked up the spray Ben had left him.

Slowly and painfully, Kendi undressed, got out his spear, positioned it under his knee, and set the dermospray against his arm. *Thump.* Colors swirled behind his eyes, and he found himself in the cool darkness of his cave. He was about to begin dancing around the spiral that would carry him to the surface when he paused. Another cave entrance lay off to one side. After a moment's consideration, Kendi plucked a burning torch out of thin air and went in.

The second cave was enormous, large enough to contain a good-sized ship. It made an empty space around Kendi that swallowed the slight sound of his footsteps. A pile of wood lay in the center of the cave, and Kendi tossed the torch onto it. The wood caught and blazed brightly. Far overhead, a hole let the smoke out.

The fire illuminated smooth, dry walls. This was not a living cave with water dripping from walls and ceiling. Water would have ruined the paintings.

The walls were covered with them. Livid colors leaped

gracefully across stone and traced history as they went. At the bottom of one wall squatted a pregnant woman in labor. Farther along, an infant that bore a strong resemblance to Kendi crawled across a floor. In other pictures, the baby crossed into childhood and adolescence. In the background, various adults made worried faces about their steadily declining contact with their ancestral traditions. They pooled their resources to buy passage on a colony ship to reestablish tribal ways on the planet Pelagosa. Kendi and his family went into cryo-sleep.

A thousand marks painstakingly scratched into the stone stood for the passage of a thousand years. Kendi also felt it stood for the loss of a thousand Real People. The next picture showed slipships, invented while Kendi's family and the other colonists slept, overtaking the slower-than-light colony ship and landing at Pelagosa to set up colonies of their own. Governments rose and fell back on Earth, and people forgot about the dozens of colony ships still patiently coasting through space.

Another picture. A slipship crept up to the colony vessel. Slavers boarded and took control. A line of chained Real People trudged up to the auction block.

Another picture. Kendi's owner gave him a blood test and discovered Kendi was Silent, a term Kendi had never heard before. The woman put Kendi up for resale at a quick profit.

Another picture. A short, round woman touched Kendi's shoulder. Kendi entered the monastery on Bellerophon, entered the Dream, studied navigation and piloting.

Met Ben.

Kendi gave himself a shake. He hadn't come down here to meander through the past. A pile of roots and other plant material lay near a water bag. Kendi chewed different roots and mixed the resulting paste with water on a flat stone until he had a palate of several colors. Using his fingers, he drew figures on the wall with the cooling paint. He detailed his arrival on Rust, the time in the market, his encounter with the strange boy.

The Unity guard.

Kendi's hands trembled and he faltered before he could draw the details of his arrest. The cave wall was chilly beneath his fingertips. Abruptly, he felt restless, hemmed in by the cave. He had to get out, get out *now*. He shook the paint from his hands, trotted out of the side cave into the main cavern, and danced his way up the spiral to the outside world.

The Outback spread before him, free and wide and open. Hot air moved over his body. The falcon screamed a greeting and Kendi waved. Voices, many more than normal, buzzed and whispered on the wind, but Kendi ignored them. The falcon plunged to earth and changed into a kangaroo. Kendi whooped and took off running, long legs flying over the sandy earth. The kangaroo bounded alongside, easily keeping pace. Kendi ran and ran beneath the pure golden sun.

A slight vibration tremored under his soles. Kendi instantly halted. The earth was shaking. The kangaroo shifted back into falcon shape and took off screaming for the skies. Tiny stones danced around Kendi's toes and his bones vibrated. Before he could react further, the ground ahead of him cracked and split with a sound like a hundred thunderstorms. Earth dropped down into the crevice, as if the supporting ground had vanished. Kendi backpedaled, heart pounding, adrenaline singing through his veins. He should leave immediately, but letting go of the Dream took a certain amount of concentration, impossible to achieve when the earth beneath his feet was crumbing into nothing. Kendi managed to spin and sprint. The crumbling ground followed him. Earth loosened beneath his soles, and Kendi forced himself to put on an extra burst of speed.

He felt the minds as he ran.

Thousands of mental voices cried out as the earth shifted and fell away. Each particle of earth, each stone and pebble, was Kendi's symbol for the minds that made up the Dream, and so many of them plummeted into the cracked ground. Kendi had no time to wonder what was happening to them. He could only run.

The tremors stopped. Kendi slowed his pace and cautiously turned. Earth and air lay perfectly still. The falcon circled in the sky above Kendi's head. He caught his breath in stunned amazement. About fifty paces behind Kendi stretched a wide canyon, one so wide, Kendi could barely make out the opposite side.

Warily, Kendi crept on hands and knees to the edge of

the canyon and peered downward. Nausea rocked him, and he flung himself flat on his stomach so he could feel the solid ground beneath him. The bottom was far away, and it was a seething black. Kendi couldn't tear his eyes away. The canyon had no floor. Instead, a roiling blackness shifted and quivered. Uncertain tendrils crawled up the canyon walls like hungry tentacles before sliding back down again. The smell of rotting meat and moist graveyard dirt wafted upward. Then a long, low wail made of a hundred voices keened upward. The sound tore across Kendi's nerves like icy fingernails. He clapped his hands over his ears and forced himself to roll away from the canyon's edge. The wail and smell faded, but the canyon remained.

Kendi lay panting on his back. The heat pressed down on him, and he let it bake the fear away. He could never cross that canyon, even if he could manage to create a bridge long enough. Not with that reaching, wailing blackness below.

"In the name of all life," he whispered to the sky, "what is it?"

He rolled to a sitting position at what he hoped was a safe distance from the canyon. This was not good. Travel and distance in the Dream were based completely on the perceptions of the Silent. This meant that Kendi would not be able to talk to any Silent who, in Kendi's mind, lay on the other side of the canyon. Kendi's forehead furrowed. The canyon did not exist. There was nothing ahead of him but rough Outback terrain.

The canyon remained.

Voices of other Silent babbled on the breeze, and Kendi knew they were experiencing the same thing he was. He considered trying to contact someone to ask if they knew what had happened and why, but he couldn't bring himself to do it. Instead, he stretched his senses, searching for signs of the boy.

Nothing. Kendi drummed nervous fingers on his thigh. That didn't seem right. The canyon was still there, which meant that the person who had created it must still be in the Dream. If the boy—Kendi's nephew—was causing the problem, he should still be in the Dream, and Kendi should be able to feel his thought patterns. But he felt nothing.

Kendi picked up a handful of dirt and let it trickle hypnotically through his fingers. They had to find the boy and Kendi had to know if he was a relative. The idea that his family was still out there somewhere, treated as property and denied their place as free citizens used to make him frantic with worry. Over time, that had become a part of him, a desire carved into his soul like a stream carving its bed through rock. Kendi reached for another handful of earth, and his hand closed over something hard and cylindrical. Startled, he looked down.

It was an iron bar.

"Tattoos! Color yourself with a tattoo!"

"Come see my dresses! You, madam—I have just the thing for you!"

A crate of chickens clucked at passersby and a baker's pans clattered as she set out her sweet-smelling wares. A light haze over the sun kept the air balmy and pleasant. In the center of an intersection stood a marble statue of Premier Yuganovi, leader of the Unity. Ara stood out of the flow of traffic, ignoring merchants and scanning faces. Somewhere out in that mess were Trish, Pitr, Gretchen, and Harenn, all armed with Kendi's composite. She wished they could show the boy's picture around and make inquiries, but she didn't want word to reach the kid that someone was looking for him. He'd probably drop into a hole somewhere and they'd never find him.

Ara flicked another glance at the image on her ocular implant. Kendi's composite was good, and it shouldn't be hard to spot this kid. On the other hand, they were talking about a city of several million people, thousands of whom were in the marketplace. Ara tried to scan the faces in her immediate vicinity without appearing to stare. Even though there was a good chance the computer would spot the boy before she did, Ara couldn't help but look. Around her swirled the sounds and smells of the crowded market. Meat sizzled on open-air grills, chains clattered on old-fashioned pedal bicycles, and people shouted to one another in a cacophony Ara would have found delightful if she hadn't been so worried.

It wasn't just that the boy's power had been proven beyond any doubt or that Ara would have to decide whether he should live or die. She was also worried about Kendi. He had spent two weeks in a Unity prison and it was clear the experience had been horrifying. And in behavior that came straight from a psychology textbook, he refused to discuss it.

And as Irfan said, "The real world becomes the Dream," Ara mused.

Maybe Ben could worm it out of him. She'd have to talk to him later about it. Right now, she had a job to do.

Ara patrolled the market, quickly establishing a pattern. She would find a vantage point and examine passing faces for several minutes, then move on to another spot. After three hours of steady walking, she paused to wolf down something bland and crunchy wrapped in soft bread for supper. Her calves and feet ached from all the walking, and she was sure bruises were forming on various parts of her body from elbows and knees of passersby. One of the disadvantages of being short was that people tended to run over you if you weren't careful. It was also damned difficult to get a good look at faces without standing on tiptoe.

Her implant flashed for her attention. Ara jerked her head to the right, and her implant drew a red outline around a figure just up the street. She caught her breath. Facial features, eyes, hair. He was even slouching against a wall like Kendi had reported. Ara tapped her earpiece.

"I've found our friend," she subvocalized. "I'm looking right at him."

"Where are you, Mother?" Pitr's voice replied in her ear.

Ara looked around. She had no idea. There were no street signs or landmarks. "Not sure. There are a lot of people selling clothes and cloth around here, and I just passed several electronics merchants. I saw a statue of the Premier a while ago."

"Hold on," Pitr said. *"Let me link up with Ben so we can figure out where everyone is."*

"I was just down where you are now, Mother," Trish piped up. *"You're about four blocks from the red-light district. I can be there in twenty minutes, if the crowd lets me."*

"I've got you all triangulated," Ben's voice broke in from

the ship. *"Gretchen's closest. Go to your ocular implant, Gretchen, and I'll overlay directions for you."*

Brief pause.

"Got 'em," Gretchen said. *"Give me ten minutes."*

"Hold it," Ara said. "He's moving. Stay linked everyone."

The boy meandered down the street, hands in his ragged pockets. Ara dodged around an old man with a basket and hurried after him, her lips pursed with determination. She wasn't going to let him out of her sight no matter what.

"You're moving south, Mother," Ben reported. *"Gretchen, you're coming in from the east. If you hurry, you might be able to get on the street ahead of him."*

"Dammit!" Gretchen snarled. Ara winced and put a hand to her ear. *"One of those passenger bikes collided with a wheelbarrow. A crowd is gathering and I can't get through."*

Ara twisted and ducked her way through the crowd and up the street. The boy had long legs, and his casual saunter was Ara's brisk trot.

"You're almost at the edge of the market, Mother," Ben said. *"You should be seeing regular streets soon."*

Ben was right. Up ahead, Ara made out groundcars zipping through an intersection. The boy reached the corner and stopped there. He took up his customary slouch against a wall. Ara halted as well and scrutinized the boy more closely. No electronic shackles clamped his wrists or ankles and he wore no collar around his neck. Ara cursed silently. Unless his master was extremely permissive, the boy was free. He would have to be persuaded, not bought.

A pair of guard marched by and Ara faded back. The boy seemed to ignore them completely, but she saw he was watching them from under half-closed eyes.

Ara tried to think. How should she approach him? She didn't want to frighten him off, but she didn't want to lose him, either. Two tiny transmitters nestled in her pocket and she could probably plant one by "accidentally" bumping into him. On the other hand, if he figured out what she was doing, it would probably destroy all hope of a working relationship. Maybe she should just try to strike up a conversation. But how?

Ara sighed. It was so much easier to do this in a slave market. You pointed, paid, and took the person home. It took awhile to convince some slaves that the Children of Irfan were actually setting them free, but all in all it wasn't that hard.

And how would Irfan have viewed this? she thought tartly. *A Mother Adept whining to herself that the job will take some effort.*

Chastised, Ara decided to simply watch the boy for a while to see if she could gain any clues about how to approach him. It would also give Gretchen and the others time to catch up.

A long, dark groundcar drove up to the curb and one mirrored window lowered itself a few centimeters. The boy sauntered up to it. The window lowered farther and he leaned inside. Ara noticed that his ragged clothes were definitely on the tight side and many of the rips seemed strategic.

"Uh-oh," Ara said.

"What happens, Mother?" Harenn asked. *"I have met Gretchen and we are coming."*

"Ben," Ara subvocalized hurriedly, "hack into the nets and find out who owns a groundcar with registry number"—she squinted—"H14 dash 35J. Hurry!"

"On it."

"What is it?" Gretchen asked.

Ara stepped up to the street. The boy was still leaning into the car and couldn't see her, though she was barely three meters away. For a brief moment she considered trying to plant a transmitter on him and almost instantly decided against it. He might notice. Plant one on the car? No. Any car that expensive had disruption devices for just such an occurrence. She scanned the street instead.

"Ben, are there any cabs in the area?" she asked.

"I can't check that and find the registration number at the same time, Mother."

"Mother Adept, what's happening?" Gretchen demanded.

"I think our boy is a . . . working lad," Ara murmured. No cabs were in sight.

Harenn spoke up. *"So pick him up and offer to pay for an hour or two. What is such a problem?"*

The boy backed out of the window. The car door opened and he climbed inside.

"Shit," Ara muttered.

"The car is registered to Melvan and Xava Yshidra," Ben said. *"Do you want their address?"*

And then, by a miracle, a cab turned a corner and buzzed up the street. Ara waved frantically and it stopped. The other vehicle slid smoothly into traffic as Ara leaped into the cab.

"Glory to the Unity. Stay behind them," she said, pointing. There was no way in hell she was going to say *Follow that car.*

The driver, a rawboned woman with blond dreadlocks, obeyed without a word. As they drove off, Ara caught a glimpse of Gretchen and Harenn emerging breathlessly from the market.

"Do you want the address, Mother?" Ben repeated. *"And do you still want me to find a cab?"*

"Not yet and no," she subvocalized. "Gretchen and Harenn, I'm in a cab and I'm following the boy. He's in another car."

"We saw," Gretchen said. *"What do you want us to do?"*

"Stay where you are," she ordered.

The electric engine on the cab was nearly silent, meaning the driver could probably tell that Ara was carrying on a quiet, one-sided conversation. However, she gave no sign she heard or understood. Ara liked that. She peered forward, never letting her gaze stray from the car they followed.

The car made a right turn, then another right, and another. Her quarry was going in a big circle. Ara imagined the car had a soundproof partition between driver and passengers to afford a certain amount of privacy for their . . . activities. Ara wondered whether it was Melvan or Xava who was in the backseat with the boy. For all she knew, it was both.

They passed the original street corner and Ara resisted the urge to wave at Gretchen and Harenn. Ara settled back in her seat to think. The boy was obviously a prostitute. This didn't bother Ara. It made her job easier. As Harenn had pointed out, she could simply proposition him and use the opportunity to talk. But Kendi had said the local houses didn't tolerate freelancers. How had he gotten away with it?

Ara drummed her fingers on the gritty arm rest. The cab's interior was worn and dirty. A small sign informed her that a network link was available for a surcharge, and a muted vidscreen set into the back of the driver's seat showed a local newscast. A second sign said that slaves must prove their owners had granted permission for them to ride in a cab and they must pay in advance. A third sign said, YOU ARE SAFE WITH THE UNITY.

What if the men in the alley had been enforcers? That would make sense. One of the houses may have gotten wind that the boy was turning tricks and sent a couple of goons. Ara wondered if they were still in prison.

The groundcar drove up to the same curb and the boy exited. Ara told the cabbie to pull over and let her out. Ara paid the fare and climbed out just in time to see Gretchen bump heavily into the boy. Harenn, a few steps away, watched from behind her veil.

"I'm so sorry," Gretchen said with uncharacteristic politeness. "Goodness me, I almost knocked you over. Are you all right? Glory to the Unity."

"Yeah, yeah, glory," the boy replied. "Don't touch me, lady." And he hurried away.

Ara trotted up to her. "You didn't touch him flesh to flesh, did you? Did you plant a transmitter?"

"No, and what do you think?"

"Got him," Ben said. *"You don't have to run now."*

Ara gestured to Gretchen and Harenn. "Fan out. Harenn, since he hasn't seen you, I want you to cross the street and get ahead of him. Gretchen, you stay a little farther behind, and I'll get closer. Pitr, follow as best you can and be ready to stand by. Trish, either grab a hotel room or go back to the ship and get into the Dream. Find us and follow us so you can whisper at people. Watch for the boy there, too, and for anything else that's strange."

"On my way, Mother," Trish said.

"Got it, Mother," Pitr said.

"Yes, Mother," Harenn and Gretchen said in chorus. The three of them took up their positions and headed up the street in silent pursuit.

SEVEN

The Dream

[A] dream taught me this wisdom, and . . . I still fear I may wake up and find myself once more confined in prison.

—Pedro Calderon de la Barca

". . . all right?"

Kendi tore his eyes away from the iron bar in his hand. Trish was standing above him. She wore a strap of brown cloth across her breasts and another across her loins. The outfit looked strange on her white, sticklike figure. How long had he been staring at the bar? He should have felt Trish's presence instantly.

"Did you hear me, Kendi?" Trish said. "I asked if you were all right."

"I'm okay." He scrambled to his feet, bar in his hand. Where had it come from? He hadn't called it up. Did it have something to do with the canyon or the kid?

"Mother Ara told me to watch the dream for signs of the kid," Trish said. "I think that thing"—she gestured at the canyon—"qualifies. Did it almost open up under your feet, too?"

"Yeah. And there's something in it that screams at you."

"I heard." Trish shuddered. "Is it the kid, do you think? Can you sense him?"

Kendi closed his eyes and stretched out his senses. Nothing. The ground showed no further signs of shaking, the scrubby vegetation was alive and healthy, and the tiny tickle that told him his drugs were wearing off began to itch behind his eyes.

"I don't feel anything," Kendi admitted.

"What's the bar for?"

Kendi hefted the bar without answering. It didn't belong here. It would disappear. One . . . two . . . three.

The bar remained, cool and heavy, in his hand. It was just like the bars across his cell in—

Kendi flung the bar away. It spun off and vanished into the distance.

"What was that about?" Trish asked.

"Nothing," Kendi said. "Look, my drugs are wearing off. I'd better go, all right?"

Trish gave him an odd look. "Sure. I've got scouting to do. See you on the ship later." And she vanished.

Kendi gathered his concentration. *If it is in my best interest and in the best interest of all life everywhere, let me leave the Dream.*

His room on board the *Post-Script* snapped into being. Kendi disentangled himself from the spear under his knee and dressed with care, wincing at his bruises and the pain in his ribs. Well, there was no reason not to use painkillers now. After a quick visit to the infirmary, Kendi felt much better and had decided to discuss the situation with someone.

"Peggy-Sue," Kendi said, "locate Mother Ara."

"Mother Adept Araceil is not on board the *Post-Script*," the computer reported.

Doing merchant stuff, he wondered, *or tracking the kid with my composite*? "Peggy-Sue, locate Brother Pitr."

"Pitr Haddis is not on board the *Post-Script*."

"Peggy-Sue, who *is* on board?"

"Benjamin Rymar, Sister Trish Haddis, and Jack Jameson are now on board."

"Peggy-Sue, locate Ben Rymar.

"Benjamin Rymar is on the bridge."

Kendi headed up to the bridge. Ben wasn't Silent and he didn't understand the intricacies of the Dream, but Jack wasn't someone Kendi had spent a lot of time with, and Trish was busy in the Dream.

Or you're just looking for excuses, he thought to himself.

Ben was at the communication board. His fingers danced over the console and his soft voice muttered commands to the computer. As usual, his red hair was tousled and his purple tunic was wrinkled. The main vidscreen showed a map of the city of Ijhan. Different colored dots and a single gold star flashed on it. Ben turned as Kendi entered.

"You're supposed to be resting, aren't you?" Ben said.

"I can rest up here." Kendi flung himself into the captain's chair. "What's going on?"

"We're tracking the kid. Hot on the trail."

Kendi's stomach panged. He bolted to his feet and rushed over to Ben's board. Without thinking, he put a hand on Ben's shoulder and leaned over to look at the console. "And no one told me? Where are they? How long would it take me to get there?"

"They're up on the map." Ben's dextrous fingers continued to move like dancing spiders. "Gretchen bugged him. And you aren't going anywhere. Mother's orders."

"Neighborhood's getting worse," Ara's voice said from the console. *"Careful, everyone."*

Ben shifted, and Kendi suddenly became aware of the firm muscle bunching beneath his hand. He self-consciously took his hand away.

"Uh, why are you working so hard?" Kendi asked. "All you have to do is keep an eye on the transmitter."

"And mask the signal from the Unity," Ben said. "And keep an open link to the net. And track down—"

"I get it, I get it," Kendi said. "Want some help?"

"It's covered," Ben replied absently.

Kendi nervously sank back down into the captain's chair to watch Ben work. Ben had rolled up his sleeves, and fine red-gold hairs gleamed on his forearms. Kendi could see Ben's collarbone, sharply defined above the wrinkled collar of his tunic. On the vidscreen the multicolored dots chased the gold star over the map of Ijhan. A silence fell on the room, and Kendi didn't try to fill it despite his churning stomach. The odds against his hopes were high, laughably so, but that didn't stop his nerves from screaming at the thought that he might have found a part of his family again. Kendi watched the vidscreen and tried to calm his too-brittle nerves. His mouth was as dry as salt.

Ben continued to work. Silence stretched across the bridge.

"Ara's hiding something," Kendi said, suddenly desperate to fill the quiet.

Ben looked up, a puzzled expression in his blue eyes. "Sorry?"

"Ara's hiding something," Kendi repeated. "I think it's to do with the kid. I asked her, but she denied it. She lied."

"She doesn't lie," Ben said stoutly. "At least, she never has to me."

"Not to me, either. At least, not until now. It makes me angry, Ben. I'm second in command, but I don't know all the details."

"What am I supposed to do about it?"

Kendi leaned toward him. "Talk to her, would you? Find out what's going on."

"Me? What makes you think I'll have any sway?"

"You've known her a little longer than I have," Kendi replied dryly. "Please?"

Ben sighed. "I'll try. But if she gets mad at me, I'm taking it out on you."

The sun was setting and the neighborhood was getting worse. A trio of toughs watched Ara as she passed and she wished she had some sort of weapon, despite Unity law. Almost anything more powerful than a knife was strictly forbidden, and Ara had decreed pistols too risky. Now she wished she had taken the chance.

The crowd on the sidewalk was light, though battered groundcars hummed up and down the crumbling pavement. Trash littered the streets, and the people had a more haggard look. Most of the buildings were older, made of brick and mortar instead of aerogel. Many of them were cracked, and quite a few lay in ruins—victims of the Unity bombing years ago. Another time she passed a vacant lot filled with rickety shacks. Ragged people looked at Ara over open cooking fires. The marketplace, she realized with an odd clarity, was meant for the more affluent citizens of Irfan. This must be how the majority of the population lived.

A Unity guard groundcar, red and black, cruised slowly down the street. The people quietly vanished into their shacks, and Ara forced herself to keep an impassive expression as it went by. Were they looking for the boy? Ara assumed the Unity didn't know who he was yet—they would have already snapped him up—but that could change at any moment.

Something tapped at Ara's mind. *~Don't worry about the guards, Mother,~* came Trish's voice. *~I'm whispering to them. They don't want to stop anyway, so they're taking my advice.~*

~Good work,~ Ara replied, grateful for the reassurance. Trish was very talented at whispering and knew her job well. All Silent could reach out of the Dream and contact other Silent, though many could do nothing more than alert the receiver to their presence. "Knocking," as it was called, was a widely accepted signal for the receiver to drop into the Dream for full conversation or to open themselves up to full possession by the sender, as the Empress's slave had done for Ara. Most Silent, including Ara and Trish, could push the communication a little further and transmit words from the Dream to the real world, and a few could actually brush the minds of non-Silent. Full possession of the non-Silent was impossible—or so Ara had thought—but the truly skilled could nudge non-Silent minds, enhancing a latent emotion or suppressing an existing idea. Trish was good at both.

Ara continued up the street, eyes glued to the boy. Her calves ached again. She'd been on her feet all afternoon, and it was now well into evening. Every so often she glanced back and caught a glimpse of Gretchen behind her. Harenn remained ahead of the procession, following cues supplied by Ben whenever the boy altered course. The boy himself, hands stuffed in his pockets, strode onward.

~I have news, Mother,~ Trish said.

~Can it wait?~ Ara asked almost petulantly.

~The Unity Silent have narrowed the kid's presence down to Rust.~

A chill rippled Ara's skin. *~It was inevitable. What else do they know?~*

~They think he's powerful. That means we—yike!~ Her voice cut off.

"Trish? Trish, what's wrong?" Ara didn't realize she'd spoken out loud until she saw the odd looks from the ragged people passing her on the street. With a double pang she noticed she'd lost the boy. She sped up a bit and caught sight of him again. His head was down and he was still using his ground-eating pace.

~Trish!~ Ara said urgently. *~Trish, can you hear me?~*

~I'm all right, Mother,~ came Trish's Dream whisper, and Ara wanted to go limp with relief. *~The ground went shaky again. I had to move fast.~*

~Don't stay in the Dream if it's going to risk—~

~I'm fine, Mother,~ Trish interrupted almost sharply. *~I know what I'm doing.~*

Ara took the hint. *~Sorry. Sometimes I'm half Mother Adept and half mother hen.~*

The boy turned another corner, automatically losing Harenn, and Ara stirred her tired legs to a trot. When she turned the corner, Ara found a strange barrier. It was about half a block up the street and had been formed out of a variety of materials—old bricks, chunks of concrete, even old furniture. The wall spanned the street, though a gap in the center would allow a groundcar to slip through. Ara's quarry had already passed through the gap and she hurried to catch up. Through the gap she could see that the neighborhood on the other side looked much the same as this one, except the gutters and sidewalks were clear of trash.

"Hold it!" snapped a voice. Ara halted. A man armed with some kind of staff was standing guard just inside the wall. The staff was tipped with a wicked-looking metal ball. "Glory to the Unity. I don't recognize you. What's your business here?"

~I'm on him,~ Trish whispered. *~He's stubborn and a bit afraid, though. It'll make things difficult.~*

Just up the street, Ara saw the boy disappear into one of the apartment buildings just as Gretchen caught up. Ara put on a disingenuous smile and shot Gretchen a look that told her to keep quiet.

"Glory to the Unity," Ara said. "My daughter and I are looking for an apartment."

The guard frowned. "In here? Where?"

Ara pulled out her computer pad. She pretended to check the screen, then squinted up the darkening street. "There," she said, pointing at the building the boy had entered.

The guard narrowed his eyes. "You sure? I don't remember anyone saying they wanted to move."

"That's the address from the ad. Who are you?"

"Neighborhood patrol," the man said. "And we don't allow certain kinds of people in here."

"Oh? People like who?" Gretchen asked.

"Drug dealers, gangs, hookers, other riff-raff," the man said.

~He's strong, Mother,~ Trish said. *~He doesn't want to let you pass and I don't think I can change his mind.~*

Ara raised her eyebrows. "Are you sanctioned by the Unity?"

"No," the man replied carefully. "We're unofficial. We wanted a clean neighborhood, and the Unity doesn't seem interested in giving it to us. So we made one."

~Good move, Mother,~ Trish put in. *~Keep acting authoritative.~*

"I see," Ara said briskly. "Well, if you aren't Unity, you don't have the power to keep me out, do you?"

The man shifted. "You can pass through the streets," he admitted. "But no one moves into our neighborhood without Vidya's okay."

"And where does this Vidya live?"

"There." The man pointed to the boy's building.

"Well, then," Ara said, still in a brisk tone, "I guess that'll kill two birds with one stone. We shall pass now."

"Wait!" shouted another voice, and Harenn hurried up to them. Her veil fluttered with her breathing. "I'm here."

"My other daughter," Ara supplied before the guard could ask. "You're late, my dear. Shall we? Glory to the Unity."

They strolled past the guard and into the neighborhood.

~That was good, Mother,~ Trish chortled. *~You sounded like a queen.~*

"Daughter?" Harenn asked.

"I'll explain later," Ara said.

"Mother, what's happening?" Ben said in Ara's earpiece. *"The kid has stopped moving and I think he's indoors."*

"He's in an apartment house," Ara said. "We're going in. We'll probably be out of touch for a while, so hang tight."

"What about me?" Pitr asked. *"I'm about half a kilometer away."*

"If you can, find a place to wait for us," Ara instructed. "If not, head back to the *Script*."

The apartment house was a block away from the wall. The neighborhood buildings, while in poor repair, were at least clean. Windows gleamed. No papers or other detritus clogged the gutters. Walls were cracked, but any loose bits of mortar had been cleared away. Window boxes made of scrap lumber sported flowers and herbs. People sat on porches, enjoying the cooling night air, and flute music floated from a window.

"Interesting," Harenn murmured. "Inhabitants in the other neighborhoods we passed would not dare to be sitting outside in such a manner."

Ara nodded in agreement as they arrived at the boy's building. No one sat on the steps but the entryway door was locked. When Ara tried the old-fashioned knob, a speaker whirred to life.

"Glory to the Unity. Please state your name and your business," a scratchy computer voice said.

Ara ignored it and tried the door again.

"Glory to the Unity. Please state your name and your business."

"Can you get this open, Gretchen?" Ara asked.

"Probably," Gretchen said. "But the gate guard is watching us."

"Damn. Ben, can you get a list of residents for this building?" Ara recited the address.

"The directory lists eighteen," Ben replied. *"Do you want all of them?"*

"Can you tell what floor the boy is on?"

"The first," Ben said promptly. *"I think you should know Kendi's here and he's biting his nails like corn on the cob."*

"Glory to the Unity. Please state your name and your business."

"What are the names of the first floor residents?" Ara said.

"Keeren and Jace Muhar, Nara Oliva, and Vidya and Sejal Dasa. Nara is an old lady, Keeren and Jace are listed as spouses. Vidya and Sejal are listed as mother and son."

The boy was named Sejal, then. The Empress and her orders loomed in Ara's mind. She may have to ensure the death of someone named Sejal. Ara faltered. She had never been easy with the idea of deciding whether this boy would live or die, and the fact that he now had a name and a mother made it even worse.

"Glory to the Unity. Please state your name and your business."

Hunger rumbled in Ara's stomach. Her legs ached, and

she was bone tired. Suddenly the idea of seeing the boy—Sejal—up close was nothing but repellent.

"Let's get out of here," she said.

"Leave? But we're so close," Gretchen protested.

"I'm tired, I'm hungry, and the boy isn't going anywhere," Ara said with more firmness than she had intended. "The Unity won't find him by tomorrow. We'll come back later. Let's go."

Ara marched off, not waiting to see if Harenn and Gretchen followed. At the gate, she nodded once at the guard. "Glory. No one home," she said without stopping to care about the transparent lie. And with that, Mother Adept Araceil strode swiftly back toward her ship.

Benjamin Rymar stood uncertainly outside Ara's door. Kendi had been right—Mother Adept Araceil wasn't quite herself. It wasn't just that she had gone straight to her quarters without speaking to anyone after she, Harenn, and Gretchen returned from the city. Ben also knew Ara well enough to see the signs that something was bothering her—a certain tightness around the mouth, certain tense gestures—and these signs had shown up after her conference with the Empress. The problem was obviously something to do with the Silent, and Ben wasn't Silent. It was therefore none of his business.

Of course it's your business, said a small inner voice. *You're a member of the crew. Her problems have an impact on you.*

But Ben shrugged the voice away. The Children of Irfan had problems and dealt with situations that the non-Silent couldn't even comprehend. None of his business. That had been made abundantly clear to him from childhood.

So why was he now standing outside her door with the promise he had made to Kendi fresh in his mind?

Kendi. Ben closed his eyes. It hadn't been easy avoiding Kendi aboard the ship. When Ben had been forced to go alone to Kendi's quarters to gather the dermosprays, he'd been sweating bullets. He remembered the jolt he'd experienced when Kendi's arm spasmed and the look of pain that had crossed his face. He remembered the warmth of Kendi's arm when he'd helped Kendi sit on the bed. He remembered words bubbling up and he remembered barely swallowing them in time. Kendi always took the tiniest mole hills and from them built mountains to rival Everest. It was bad enough Ben had said "maybe." He was sure Kendi had gotten a lot of mileage out of that one by now.

So why had he said it?

Ben shook his head. That was easy enough to answer. Love. The two weeks Kendi had gone missing had been pure, unadulterated hell. Trish had had to pry Ben away from the consoles for food and rest, and he had taken risks hacking the nets that made him shake in retrospect. Once Kendi had been located, Ara ran paperwork and Ben lay alone on his single bed, feeling guilty that he was free and wondering what was happening to Kendi. Was he being beaten? Raped? Murdered?

Ben had barely slept. And then, when Kendi had walked into the foyer, looking pale and ashen, Ben had wanted to grab him and never let go. He had restrained himself just in time. It wouldn't do any good. Their relationship wouldn't work. Ben had let himself stay in it for too long as it was.

Ara's door still stood in front of him, and Ben realized he was stalling. Firmly, he pressed the door chime.

"Who is it?" came Ara's tired voice over the intercom.

"It's me, Mother. Can I come in?"

The door slid open and Ben entered. As Captain and Mother Adept, Ara commanded quarters larger than anyone else's, but, in contrast to Kendi's spartan room, all available space was filled. Bookshelves were crammed with thousands of book disks. Two large desks, each with its own high-powered terminal, lined opposing walls. Someone had managed to squeeze a tiny galley off to one side. Rugs and weavings hid the gray ceramic walls and floor with bright colors and designs. A pair of easy chairs had been tucked into the corners, and the air was tinted with the sweet smell of lingering incense. Ara was seated at one of the desks. The terminal was active, but Ara had swivelled in her chair to face the door.

"Hi," she said. "I was meaning to tell you—good work on the search today. We couldn't have tracked Sejal without you."

Ben shrugged and sat in one of the easy chairs. "When are you going to go get him?"

"Soon," Ara replied, and turned back to her terminal.

"Mother," Ben said, deciding just to plunge in and get it over with, "what's bothering you? You haven't been yourself lately."

"It's a tense situation. The Unity Silent are aware of the boy, and we need to move quickly tomorrow." Ara tapped at the console. Numbers and text flashed by too quickly for Ben to read, but he got the impression it wasn't anything important, that Ara just wanted to appear busy.

Ben switched tactics. "Kendi's worried about you."

"And I'm worried about him." Ara blanked the screen and turned again. "Has he said anything to you about prison?"

"He won't talk about it. I've tried once or twice, but he always changes the subject."

"Keep trying, would you?"

Ben's red eyebrows lowered. "This wouldn't be a subtle attempt to get us back together, would it?"

"It's not subtle." Ara smoothed her purple tunic. "I worry about you, too, you know. It's obvious to me you've been unhappy without him."

"Mother—"

"And that's another thing. It's always *Mother* now. It sounds like you mean *Mother Adept*. Whatever happened to *Mom*?"

Ben shrugged. "Everyone else calls you 'Mother.' It's just easier, I guess. People might think the only reason I'm here is because I'm your son."

"Everyone on board knows you're my son, Ben," Ara chided gently. "They also know you're one of the most talented people on this ship. Communications, forgery, hacking. And you have your pilot's license now. I chose you for this crew because there isn't anyone else who can do what you can."

Except enter the Dream, Ben thought. His eyes strayed for a moment to one of the small holograms on the desk behind his mother. The small round projector that formed the base was old and worn, older than Ben, in fact. It showed the head and shoulders of a man in his early twenties, a little younger than Ben. He had neatly combed dark hair, smiling green eyes, and a dimple in his chin. On the base was inscribed BENJAMIN HELLER. When Ben was little, he used to fantasize that Benjamin Heller was his father. He had been named for the man, after all. Ara had told him a few stories about Benjamin Heller, that he was handsome, laughed easily, and had a penchant for puns and practical jokes. Ben's little-boy imagination had added to the picture. Benjamin Heller would be strong and caring, and he would swing Ben through the air or wrestle with him on the floor. He wouldn't spend endless hours in a Dream trance or leave Ben with relatives while he tracked down more important people—Silent people—who had been enslaved on other planets. It was all just a fantasy, though. Benjamin Heller had died years before Ben's implantation in Ara's womb.

"Can we go back to *Mom*?" Ara asked. Her voice was almost pleading, and Ben couldn't help a small smile.

"How about *Mother* in public and *Mom* in private?" he suggested.

"It'll do." Ara gave a small smile of her own, then got up and went over to the miniature galley. "Would you like some tea? We can talk about you and Kendi. You never did explain why you broke it off with him. Peggy-Sue, raise tap temperature to boiling."

Ben opened his mouth to give an evasive answer, then closed it. She'd done it again—manipulated the conversation away from herself. Ben had seen her do it with her authority as a Mother Adept. Now she did with her authority as a mother. Abruptly, Ben had had enough.

"I came in here to talk about you, Mom. Not me."

Ara blinked, a tea mug in either hand. "Well, *that* was . . . direct."

"I want to know what's bothering you, Moth— Mom. Was it something the Empress said?"

"No."

"There—you lied again."

"I did not."

"Mo-om." Ben gave the word two exasperated syllables. "I have to agree with Kendi. If you're holding back some-

thing important and something . . . happens to you, he won't know everything he needs to."

Ara silently handed him a steaming mug. It smelled of raspberries. "Strong with no sugar," she said. "Just the way you like it." She paused a moment, stirring her own tea. The spoon made a light clinking sound. Ben waited.

"It's something I have to deal with," she said finally. "No, don't interrupt. You were right. I lied. It's something I can't bring myself to talk about yet."

"Something about finding Sejal." He took a hot, raspberry sip and set the mug down.

"Yes."

An idea stole over Ben. "Is it that he's really related to Kendi?"

"What?" Ara looked startled.

"Kendi thinks Sejal is a relative of his."

"Oh no," Ara groaned. "If I know Kendi, he's already worked out how Sejal is related to him and where his relatives must be. Now what do we do?"

"Don't try to change the subject. If the Empress didn't mention Kendi's relatives, what did she say?"

Ara blew on her tea.

"Mom. You're going to have to tell us eventually. Why not now?"

"I might have to kill Sejal," Ara said into her mug.

Ben stared. Ara drank, then cupped her hands around the tea mug as if they were cold.

"Kill him?" Ben said at last. "Why?"

"If, in my opinion, Sejal would, quote, 'pose a threat to the Confederation,' " Ara said quietly, "the Empress wants me to kill him."

"She gave us an order like that?" Ben said incredulously. "What does she mean by 'a threat'?"

"I'm not completely sure," Ara said. "She left it up to me."

"God." Ben got up to pace the rug. "How could she order us to do something like that? What does she think we are?"

"She ordered me, Ben. Not you. Or anyone else."

Ben stopped. "That's why you've been so upset?"

"Yes."

"God," Ben repeated. "That's cold-blooded of her. How could one boy with a freak ability threaten the entire Confederation?"

"If he possessed the right person or people at the right time, he could start a war, or assassinate an important person, or any number of things. Not to mention that if word of a Silent with the power to possess unwilling non-Silent gets out to the public, witch hunts will start all over the place. No one would be safe then."

Ben was still pacing with agitation. "So the Empress chooses *you* to decide whether or not Sejal should die and then she says you have to pull the trigger, is that it? Who the hell does she think she is?"

"She thinks she's Empress."

Ben whirled on her, ready to make a sharp reply, when he noticed the tears standing in Ara's eyes. Immediately he swallowed the remark and knelt by her chair to put an arm around her shoulders. She hesitated, then leaned her head against him. Ben remained very still. He had been an adult for several years now, but a handful of years didn't erase a lifetime of expectations. Parents comforted their children, not the other way around.

"It's all right, Mom," he said softly. "All you have to do is decide that Sejal isn't a threat and you're off the hook."

Ara was sniffling now, looking not at all like a firm, decisive Mother Adept. Anger rose in Ben's chest. Kan maja Kalii might be the Empress and her word might be law, but Ara was Ben's mother. In that moment, he would have socked Kalii on the jaw cheerfully and without hesitation.

"It isn't that simple, Ben," Ara said. "The Empress—and now I—have to think of literally countless lives. If I make a mistake and don't . . . and I let Sejal live, thousands or even millions of people could die in his place. I'm afraid the Empress might be right, and I don't know if I'll be able to do what needs to be done."

Ben didn't know what to say to that, so he stayed quiet.

A moment later, Ara sat up and reached for a tissue to blow her nose. "Thanks, Ben. I feel better now."

"Do you want me to tell Kendi about . . . about this?" Ben asked hesitantly.

Ara shook her head. "It's my job. I'll do it tomorrow."

EIGHT

Planet Rust

The universe is unfair. We can merely hope it will be unfair in our favor.

—Ched-Balaar Proverb

Kendi tried to run, but there was no room. Unyielding stone hemmed him in. Shadows flickered like dancing trolls.

"Keeeeennnnnddiiiiii," rasped a voice. "Keeeeennnd-diiiii."

A dark puddle spilled across the floor, reaching for Kendi's feet. He couldn't see, he couldn't move, he couldn't cry out. A bright object flashed. Kendi screamed and bolted awake.

He was sitting up. Sweat ran in tiny rivulets down his bare torso and darkened the sheets. He sat there a moment, panting. He was on the *Post-Script*, in his quarters, in his bed. The lights were on—he couldn't bring himself to darken the room. He slumped a bit. The nightmare was already fading.

"Attention! Attention!" Peggy-Sue said. "The time is now seven a.m. Attention! Attention! The time is now—"

"Peggy-Sue, halt alarm," Kendi said with remembered excitement. He swung his legs over the side of the bed and reached for his bathrobe. Today, Ara had promised, they would talk to Sejal.

Ara entered the galley, coffee cup in hand, last night's resolve firm in her mind. At the sight of Kendi's grinning face, however, she completely lost her nerve.

"Sejal today, right?" he said. "Trish says the Unity knows about him, so we have to move fast."

Ara sat and hid behind a sip of coffee. The others had already breakfasted, so she and Kendi were alone in the little galley. The smell of rice meal and toast hung on the air. Despite her exhaustion and the fact that she had unburdened herself to Ben last night, Ara had slept fitfully and she felt heavy circles under her eyes.

"Yes," she said, forcing herself to sit erect. "We're going to see Sejal today. But I don't think you should come, Kendi."

"What? Why the hell not?"

"You've got too much invested in this. I don't know how objective you'll be if you think he's a relative." Ara poured thick brown honey over crisp toast. "You'll scarce him off."

"Who told you I think—" Kendi began, then caught himself. "Ben."

Ara bit into her toast, hoping Kendi would agree just this once. No such luck. Kendi leaned forward, elbows on the table.

"I need to come with you," he said. "I saved Sejal from those goons. He owes me, and he'll be more willing to talk to me than to a total stranger."

Ara didn't have the energy to fight. She threw up her hands. "Fine. Come along, then. But if I signal you to shut up, you shut up. Clear?"

Kendi saluted.

"That wasn't an answer."

"All right." Kendi sighed. "Your wish is my command. When do we leave?"

Ara rose. "Right now."

The taxi door slammed shut and the vehicle zipped away, leaving Ara and Kendi at the gate. The neighborhood was as Ara remembered it except for a different guard at the gateway. Ara decided not to mince words. Her stomach was tight, and she didn't feel like bandying about.

"Glory. We're here to see Sejal Dasa," she said.

"Glory. What for?" the guard, a husky, dark-haired woman, said.

Ara stepped on Kendi's foot before he could speak. "It's a private matter. May we pass?"

~I don't have to do anything, Mother,~ Trish said from the Dream. *~This one isn't very suspicious.~*

Trish was right. The woman looked at them for a moment, then wordlessly stepped aside.

"Nice lady," Kendi observed. "Polite."

"She's doing her job. And stop dragging your foot like a hunchback. I didn't step on it that hard."

"So *you* say."

Ara smoothed her trader's tunic, unable to help a small smile. Kendi could be exasperating, but he knew how to lighten a mood. She pointed. "Sejal's apartment building is over there."

"Clean neighborhood," Kendi said, admiringly. "Better than those other places we passed through. You could eat off the street here."

~There's a thought,~ Trish said.

No people sat on the porches, and Ara assumed most of the adults were at work. A group of children ran up and down the sidewalk, yelling and giggling in some game or other. Their clothes were patched but clean. About a kilometer ahead of them, Ara could make out another wall and gateway. She wondered how extensive the wall was and what kind of neighborhood patrol Vidya had set up. Whatever she had done, it had apparently worked.

Ara and Kendi climbed the short flight of steps to the apartment building's front door and Ara tried the knob.

"Glory to the Unity. Please state your name and your business," said the scratchy-voiced computer.

"We're here to see Vidya and Sejal Dasa," Ara told it.

Whirr, click. "Please repeat your request."

"We're here to see Vidya and Sejal Dasa," Ara repeated, louder this time.

Whirr, whirr, click. "Please repeat your request."

"Ancient hardware," Kendi muttered.

"Dasa!" Ara shouted at it. "We want to see Vidya Dasa!"

"Why are you looking for her?" said a voice beside them.

Ara turned. A woman was leaning out one of the first-floor windows. She looked to be in her late forties, with white-streaked dark hair, brown eyes, and an oval face. Worry lines left tracks across her skin.

~She's nervous,~ Trish reported.

"My name is Ara," Ara said. "This is Kendi. We're actually trying to find Sejal Dasa. Are you his mother?"

"Why are you looking for Sejal?"

Ara sized the woman up. It was a sure call she was Vidya

Dasa, and it was an equally sure call that she wasn't very trusting. Ara's instincts told her to go for brisk and businesslike.

"We have an offer for him," she said. "A business proposition."

"Who are you with?"

"Not the Unity," Ara replied. "Could we come in, Ms. Dasa? It'd be much easier to talk about this in private."

Vidya paused for a long moment, then nodded once. "Door," she said, "open."

She actually had to say it twice more before the computer would release the lock. Vidya withdrew through the window, and Ara and Kendi strode up the dingy hallway to the apartment door. Vidya ushered them inside. The apartment was, like the neighborhood, threadbare but tidy. Scuffed throw rugs covered a pocked wooden floor and an ancient terminal sat in one corner. The windows were open, and pale blue curtains fluttered weakly in the breeze. The place smelled of curry. A swaybacked sofa and two ancient chairs were arranged around a coffee table made of packing crates. Vidya gestured them to sit, though when Ara made for one of the chairs, Vidya blocked her way. Ara took the sofa instead and Kendi sat beside her. Vidya took the chair. Kendi, Ara noticed, was fidgeting.

"I need you to tell me who you are and what you want with my son," Vidya said.

Ara settled herself before beginning. "My full name is Araceil Rymar do Salman Reza. I am a Mother Adept of the Children of Irfan. This is Brother Kendi Weaver."

"Silent monks," Vidya said in a neutral voice. "I have heard of your people."

"Then you know we aren't here to hurt you or your son," Ara said.

"Can we talk to him?" Kendi asked.

"Why?" Vidya asked evenly.

~She's getting angry,~ Trish said. *~It's clouding her up. I can barely read her.~*

"He's Silent," Ara began, "and we want to ensure the Unity doesn't—"

"He is not Silent." There was an edge to Vidya's voice. "I know this for a fact."

"Who's his father?" Kendi burst out.

"Kendi!" Ara snapped.

"His father is dead," Vidya said. "He was my husband."

Kendi's mouth worked silently for a moment, then he asked, "Was your husband born on Rust?"

"Yes, as was his father before him."

Kendi deflated on the hard sofa and Ara's heart ached in sympathy. He might have brought it upon himself, but the deep disappointment on his face was so clear that Ara couldn't help but feel sorry for him.

"Could we speak to Sejal?" Ara asked.

"He is not Silent," Vidya repeated with more heat.

~Careful, you two,~ Trish said, *~I don't like this.~*

"Ms. Dasa," Ara said, "we have . . . information to the contrary. We aren't here to take him in as a Unity slave. I should tell you, though, that the Unity is aware of him, too. They just haven't tracked him down yet. We can smuggle him into the Children of—"

"Sejal is *not Silent*," Vidya hissed. Her hand came up holding a short rod she had pulled from the space between the cushion and the chair. A blue spark crackled at the end. "Leave my house."

Ara drew back on the sofa. "What in—?"

"An energy whip," Kendi supplied. "It annoys cows but might kill a person."

"Especially when it is set to full power." Vidya's hand was steady. "I will activate this whip in ten seconds. Nine . . . eight . . . seven . . ."

~She means it,~ Trish warned. *~I'd get the hell out if I were you.~*

With a wordless glance at Kendi, Ara rose and strode for the door. Kendi followed. Neither of them spoke until they had left the building and cleared the guard at the gate. People passed them on the street without a second glance.

"What was that all about?" Kendi burst out when they were a safe distance away.

"I don't know," Ara said, puzzled. In all the years she had been recruiting for the Children of Irfan, no one had ever reacted quite like Vidya. Most people were overjoyed to earn the attention of the Children. It meant a guaranteed career, even a certain amount of wealth. And for slaves it meant freedom. Vidya's response made no sense.

"So what do we do?" Kendi asked. They were standing in the shadow of a crumbling building not far from the neighborhood wall. Cars buzzed up the street, leaving whiffs of ozone in their wake.

Ara thought a moment. "I want you to find Sejal when he goes out, see if you can catch him alone."

"Find him how? I'll bet you a hundred *kesh* that Sejal's going to change his clothes and that bug Gretchen planted will be worthless."

"You know what part of the market he hangs out in," Ara replied. "Like you said, Sejal knows you, and if he feels he owes you, you may have better luck."

"And what are you going to do?"

"I'm going to have lunch with an old friend."

The restaurant was cheap and low key, with food Ara had learned to tolerate, if not enjoy. Ara would have preferred to meet somewhere more upscale, but she had been forced to admit that such would have drawn unwanted attention to herself and to Chin Fen.

The menu scrolled across the table and Ara tapped what she wanted—plankton stew, fishtail salad ("fishtail" being a variety of Rustic kelp), and algae bread. Then she checked the calendar. Rust kept a ten-day week, and today was the third day. By now, Ara had shared enough lunches with Fen to know his food choices never varied from week to week. Ara tapped in his order—brown rice, peat shrimp, and a salad made of seapad pulp. According to Fen, the calm, tranquil seas of Rust gave rise to plants with huge red leaves that floated on the surface and covered several square kilometers. Seapads were sturdy enough to walk on, and the pulp from their leaves was a major food source for the Rustics. The leaves and the rich plankton filling the seas around them were red, giving Rust its name.

Fen had also hinted broadly that he might like to take a walk with her across a seapad some time. Ara had fallen back on playing stupid, pretending to miss the implied invitation.

"Glory," Chin Fen said, cheerfully sliding into what he termed "their" booth. "Did you order yet?"

"For both of us," Ara said. "Glory."

"Thanks. Did you get your friend out of jail?"

Oops. Ara had forgotten to update Fen. "Yes. I'm sorry—in all the stress and excitement, I forgot to let you know."

"I understand. No problem."

It was a problem, Ara could see it in his dark brown eyes. "I really am sorry, Fen. It's been so hectic. That's a weak excuse, I know. We couldn't have gotten him out without your help. I really owe you."

"I'm not angry, Ara," Fen said. "Really. How could I get angry at you?"

Ara suppressed the desire to compress her lips. Fen was nice, but for all his aged appearance, he still reminded her of a young puppy—eager to please, frightened of alienating anyone, unable to deliver even a justified rebuke. It was a personality that annoyed her. She was also growing more and more certain that Fen was entertaining romantic ideas, but Ara had never been attracted to the short, spineless type.

"Well, I'm still paying for lunch," she said.

"You always pay for lunch," Fen said. "I mean, I think that maybe I should—"

Ara waved a hand to cut him off. "I need every tax deduction I can get. Don't worry about it."

"Sure, fine." Fen swirled his water glass, leaving a glistening trail of condensation on the tabletop. "So how did your friend do? In prison, I mean."

"It wasn't pleasant for him," Ara said, "but he won't talk about it."

A server brought their order, temporarily halting their talk. Once the food was tasted and proclaimed acceptable, Ara managed to steer further conversation away from Kendi and keep it light and meaningless, laughing at any even vaguely witty remark Fen made. She drew the line, however, at batting her eyelashes. When the timing felt right, Ara dropped her little bombshell.

"I need another favor," she said.

Fen cocked an eyebrow, and Ara supposed he meant to

look archly seductive. She sighed internally and wished Pitr or Trish could slip into his mind from the Dream and dampen his attraction to her. Fen, however, was Silent, if only half-trained, and would notice even subtle tampering.

"I need information on a woman named Vidya Dasa," she said. "I've looked in the nets and can't find anything on her but an address and the name of her son. Can you dig deeper?"

"I suppose," Fen said. He pulled a computer pad from his shirt pocket. "What's the son's name?"

Ara gave it, along with Vidya's address. "Thanks, Fen. Anything you can get will be a big help. It's worth a dozen lunches and a big box of chocolate."

"I don't do this for the paybacks, Ara." His fingers edged toward her side of the table. Ara picked up her fork and took a salty bite of plankton so he wouldn't try to take her hand. The motion seemed to effectively spoil the moment for Fen and he reached for his water glass instead.

"What do you need to know for?" he said.

Ara leaned forward conspiratorially. "It's a secret. I can't tell you right now, but I promise I'll explain later."

Gretchen would have rolled her eyes at the melodrama. Kendi would have made a smart remark. But Fen merely nodded compliantly. Ara began to understand why he had never been promoted.

The rest of the lunch passed without incident. Pleading a business meeting, Ara paid the bill and left before Fen could ask her to dinner. Lunch was businesslike. Dinner had romantic implications Ara would rather avoid.

"Mother Ara," came Jack Jameson's voice over her earpiece, *"I need you back at the ship for a minute. The buyer I've been negotiating with has agreed to a price on the dark chocolate and we need you for the finalizations."*

"On my way," she subvocalized, flagging down a cab. It seemed like she was always involved in commerce of some kind or other. If she wasn't dealing in information or humans, it was chocolate.

Ara had to admit she preferred the chocolate.

Kendi sucked up the last sweet noodle and thrust the bowl back at the vendor. "Again."

The food seller gave him a wary look. "That was your third one," he said. "Don't you think you've had enough?"

"I'll decide when I've had enough. Just fill the bowl."

"If you throw up, do it somewhere else," the seller warned. But he filled the bowl.

Kendi slurped up the sweet, floppy confection. Still more sugar rushed into his system and he was starting to feel like a hummingbird on caffeine, but he didn't care. He had started lunch with three sticks of beef shish kebab and followed them with grilled hot peppers, a plate of tangy red kelp, and two cups of plankton-in-broth. His stomach was aching and bloated, but he ignored it. He also ignored the little internal voices that told him he wasn't acting a proper member of the Real People, who practiced balance and moderation in all things.

We knew of the Dream long before Irfan Qasad and her ilk, they said, *and we knew of it because we lived in balance.*

Kendi stared down at the bowl, then left it on the noodle seller's counter and walked away. The sounds and smells of the market rushed around him like a dirty wind. Sejal was not his nephew. Utang was not on Rust, had never been on Rust. He had failed to find his family again, Ben remained distant, and Ara was still keeping him in the dark about something. Kendi wandered through the market, sugar singing through his veins, rebukes of his ancestors ringing through his head. What could happen next?

Naturally at that moment his implant flashed and outlined Sejal ahead of him in the crowd. Like Kendi, Sejal was wandering through the market, hands thrust into his ragged pockets. This time, however, no excitement thrilled through Kendi. Sejal was an intellectual exercise now, a puzzle to solve. Some instinct told Kendi to hang back and watch instead of approaching Sejal directly. Obeying it, Kendi faded back and followed.

"*Post-Script,*" Kendi subvocalized. "Are you there?"

"*Communications are currently unmonitored,*" answered Peggy-Sue. "*Do you wish to alert someone or leave a message?*"

"No. End communication."

Kendi continued shadowing Sejal. This time, however, he paid less attention to where Sejal was going and more attention to how Sejal interacted with his environment. The boy earned admiring glances from several people and a look of open greed as he passed the stall of Mr. M, the man who had the long row of slaves in his basement. There was no denying Sejal was handsome, with those blue eyes that contrasted so sharply with his black hair and brown skin. His clothes were a bit small for him, and they showed off a well-shaped body that would continue to develop as Sejal drew closer to adulthood. If Sejal was aware of his looks, however, his walk didn't show it. He stayed hunched into himself, ignoring everything around him. Kendi slid through the crowd of shoppers. Sejal paused at a corner, then took up a position against one wall. Kendi moved out of the people stream to observe him.

Sejal underwent a minor transformation at the corner. He stood straighter and a look of cool indifference dropped onto his face. A slight smile stole across his lips, and he hooked a thumb in his pocket. Kendi furrowed his brow and halted between two stalls. What did Sejal do on the corner all day? And what had the goons in the alley been after him for? Wasn't Sejal afraid they'd come back?

Most of the passersby ignored Sejal, as he ignored them. But finally a man who looked to be in his late forties approached Sejal. They conversed at length, and Kendi's heavy stomach tightened. This was how the encounter in the alley got its start. This time, however, Kendi didn't see any heavies moving in.

Sejal and the man walked up the street together and Kendi followed, more curious than ever. Eventually the pair entered a seedy building Kendi recognized as a cheap hotel. Kendi, in fact, had brought rent boys here to establish underworld "credentials," and the place rented rooms by the hour for those who were so inclined.

The implications for Sejal's presence there were obvious.

"He can't," Kendi whispered. But even as he said it, he knew Sejal could. It explained the two-small clothes and the time spent posturing at the corner. The alley goons must have been representatives from the local houses wanting to "discipline" a freelancer who was moving in on their territory. Kendi stared at the hotel in shock, wondering how he could have missed something so obvious. Why hadn't Ara told him? He couldn't imagine she didn't know. Maybe she'd figured Kendi already knew about it or had forgotten to mention it after his arrest. A lot had happened and it may have slipped her mind.

Abruptly Kendi's gorge rose, and he barely managed to make it to an open sewer grating before the contents of his stomach came up. The crowd made a hole around him, but kept on with business.

After the nausea passed, Kendi hauled himself to his feet and managed to stagger to a spot on the sidewalk where he could watch the hotel. He still felt a little sick. He also felt a great deal of outrage.

Balance, he thought. *Balance and moderation. Anger will not help here.*

And why was he so angry? What was it to Kendi? It wasn't as if he hadn't seen this sort of thing before. He had paid for rent boys himself.

Yes, but they had been adults, consenting and willing. And they had been before Kendi's arrest and his sentence—

Kendi pushed the thoughts away. According to the Unity records Ben had conjured up, Sejal was sixteen, old enough to be considered an adult on many worlds. The man had not forced Sejal into the hotel, and Sejal was, presumably, being paid.

Still, it bothered him. He sat on the sidewalk and fidgeted. He was considering seeing if a nearby stall owner would sell him something to take the sour vomit taste out of his mouth when Sejal's client emerged from the hotel. Kendi blinked and checked the time on his ocular implant. Only thirteen minutes had passed.

That was fast, he thought. *Most people want to take their time with—*

Kendi's stomach abruptly tightened. What if the man was one of those sick monsters who got his erotic kicks out of strangling or stabbing people? What if Sejal was lying dead or injured in that hotel room?

Kendi was scrambling to his feet when Sejal emerged from the hotel. As Kendi watched, Sejal took up his customary position on a nearby corner. Within moments, a woman approached and they went into the hotel together.

Business is good today, Kendi thought, suddenly cynical.

The woman left twenty minutes later with Sejal exiting a few minutes behind her. Sejal went back to the corner and, ten minutes after that, went back inside with another woman.

Okay, this is weird, Kendi thought, curiosity piqued despite his other emotions. *What's his game?*

Six men and three women in Unity guard uniforms pushed their way through the market crowd and stormed toward the hotel. Kendi bolted upright. It was a raid.

"Mother, a call's coming in for you," said Ben's voice over the intercom. *"It's Chin Fen."*

Ara sighed and tapped the console in her quarters. "Thanks, Ben. Patch him through."

A moment later, Fen's wrinkled face appeared on the console screen. His expression showed suppressed glee. They exchanged greetings, and Ara was a bit surprised when Fen got straight to the point.

"I did some checking on Vidya and Sejal Dasa," Fen told her. "And I thought you might like to know what I found."

"Definitely," Ara replied. "What'd you dig up?"

Fen briskly cleared his throat. His manner was no longer that of a lovelorn puppy. He had instead become an efficient colleague. Ara wondered briefly if he had realized that she didn't find obsequiousness attractive and was now going for professionalism.

"Vidya Dasa doesn't exist much of anywhere," Fen said. "The earliest record I could find of her goes back only sixteen years ago, when she moved into her current apartment. She registered a birth certificate for one Sejal Dasa. That's pretty much it—no tax forms, no employment listings, not even a shopping excursion. I only found a few sporadic mentionings of her in other people's records—mostly her son's—but no real information on her. She's lived at her current address for sixteen years, she pays her rent on time, and that's it."

"Doesn't she pay access charges for the network?" Ara asked. "What about utility bills?"

Fen shook his head. "Network and utilities are part of her rent. If she logs onto the nets, she does it with a pseudonym that I haven't been able to track. I'd say she's going out of her way to make herself as invisible as possible. And there's more."

"What?"

"I said there isn't a record for her that goes back further than sixteen years. This isn't *too* unusual. The Unity annexed Rust twenty-odd years ago, and a fair number of records were partially wiped or destroyed during the . . . transition."

Nice way to put it, Ara thought sarcastically.

"However, Vidya is an unusual name, so I ran it. Twenty-eight women, counting *your* Vidya, are or have been registered on Rust with that name. All but five have continual records that go back before the Unity Annexation. One of those five is listed as no longer living on Rust. Two of the five are listed as dying several years after Vidya Dasa's earliest record, so they aren't her unless your Vidya kept up a double life. One more of the five Vidyas was sold into slavery and her current owner is still paying taxes on her. The fifth one—Vidya Vajhur—disappears from all records about seven months before Vidya Dasa pops up." Fen leaned forward. "It looks like Vidya Vajhur decided to disappear and become Vidya Dasa. She kept her original first name, I think, in case she ran into someone who knew her. It's easy to explain a change of last name, but a change of first name is more awkward."

Ara flashed back to the time she ran across Chin Fen in the registry office and the relief she felt that Ben hadn't changed her first name for her forged Unity paperwork. For a dreadful moment she thought Fen was on to her, but she quickly discarded the idea. If Fen knew she was a spy, he would have reported her by now.

"I can see that," Ara said aloud. "Do you know why she changed her name, if that's what she did?"

Fen hesitated. "I'm not sure," he said, reluctant to admit that he had failed on this point. "But I can tell you more about Vidya Vajhur. She's a lot more interesting than Vidya Dasa."

He paused, and Ara, restraining her impatience, gestured for him to continue.

"It's going to cost you," Fen said slyly.

Alarm bells went off in Ara's head, but she kept her face calm. "Fen," she said carefully, "I'm doing all right, but I'm not rich. I can probably come up with—"

"Not money," Fen interrupted. "Time."

"Time?"

"On a seapad leaf." Fen grinned mischievously. "I'll tell you what I found if you agree to one walk at sunset on a seapad leaf. Deal?"

Ara tapped her feet on the floor. She hadn't expected this, not from Chin Fen. Did he have a backbone after all? Ara thought a moment. She didn't really need Fen's information at this point, now that she had what was probably Vidya's real name. Ben could probably learn more than Fen had. On the other hand, using Fen to search didn't carry a prison sentence, and it really wouldn't do to waste what had turned out to be an excellent contact within Rust's bureaucracy.

"Deal," she said with a forced smile. "What'd you learn?"

Fen matched her smile. "Vidya Vajhur was a cattle farmer. She was actually born on Earth, though her parents emigrated to Rust when she was a toddler. She married a man named Prasad Vajhur. You'll notice 'Dasa' is part of 'Prasad' spelled backward."

Ara nodded.

"Anyway, the full records of her farming survived Annexation, but they're pretty boring reading. How about I hit a few high points and you tell me if you want more detail, all right?"

Ara got the feeling Fen was enjoying stretching this out. "All right."

"Vidya Vajhur was under contract to breed Silent children for the Unity."

"What?"

"Well, her contract wasn't originally with the Unity," Fen amended. "It was with a company called Silent Acquisitions, Limited. They traffic in Silent slaves."

"I've heard of them," Ara said, trying to regain her composure. "Dreamers, Inc., is a paragon of virtue compared to them."

"According to their medical records," Fen said, "any child Vidya and Prasad had would be Silent, and they apparently negotiated a contract with Silent Acquisitions just before the Unity came. After the Annexation, the Unity took over the contract. Vidya and Prasad produced and gave up two healthy babies, fulfilling their contract."

"How could she do such a thing?" Ara blurted. "I've heard of it, of course, but I can't sympathize."

Fen shrugged. "No idea. Anyway, a year after that, records show she had a third child, a daughter. Silent, of course."

"And?" Ara prompted.

"Here's where records get spotty. Katsu—the daughter—disappeared when she was barely a year old. A guard report lists her as kidnapped, presumed dead. When she was ten, Katsu would have been taken to be raised in Unity service, of course, and the guard assumed the kidnapping was staged as a way for Vidya and Prasad to keep her hidden somewhere. But the report lists the case as closed, with a link to another report."

"Another report?"

"The next day, Vidya reported Prasad as missing. And that is the last record I could find of Vidya Vajhur anywhere."

Ara chewed her lower lip. "It looks to me like Prasad ran away with Katsu."

"He got away with it, too."

"And then Vidya decided to disappear as well," Ara said, thinking aloud. "But why? She hadn't done anything wrong."

"Maybe she wanted to escape further scrutiny," Fen ventured. "The Unity was probably pressuring her to 'confess' to the whole thing when actually Prasad took off and left her holding the bag."

"Possible," Ara conceded. "She then moves to another part of the city and changes her name—not too hard with so many records damaged or destroyed in the Annexation. Now she can start over free and clear."

"With her son Sejal."

Ara thought for a moment. "Fen, when was Sejal born in relation to Prasad's disappearance?"

Fen glanced at something in front of him. "Eight months afterward. Ah! There it is."

"Yes." Ara nodded. "Vidya was already pregnant again when Prasad vanished. She made herself disappear because she knew the child would be Silent and that the Unity would take him away. She didn't want to lose him like she'd lost her husband and first three children."

"Except," Fen said, raising a finger, "I have Sejal's medical history here. She couldn't avoid doctors completely, and his gene scans indicate he is not Silent."

Ara had to force herself not to jump to her feet. "What? I thought you said any child Vidya and Prasad had would be Silent." Her mind raced. If Sejal wasn't Silent, how had he possessed people? Had Kendi been wrong?

"Obviously Prasad isn't Sejal's father."

"Or someone changed the records. Or bribed the doctor."

Fen shook his head. "Extremely doubtful. Those records are strictly guarded. The best hackers on the planet couldn't touch them. I also doubt Vidya could come up with a bigger bribe than the bonus doctors get for discovering Silent children."

"You have a point," Ara conceded. "It's a puzzle, though. Can you netmail me copies of what you found, Fen?"

"Already did," Fen answered. He leaned forward again, an anticipatory look on his face. "Now, tell me what you want all this for. You promised to explain later. It's later."

There was a hint of whine in his voice that suddenly annoyed Ara terribly. She wanted to comb Fen's records herself and set Ben to finding what Fen had missed. She wanted to find Sejal and talk to him face-to-face. But Fen was staring at her from the view screen.

"I'm trading in genetics," she said. "Viable embryos and such. Vidya and Sejal seem to be prospects."

Fen whistled. "The paperwork on that must take you months."

"It does," Ara said shortly. "But it's high profit, low volume. Can't ask for more. Look, Fen, I have to—"

"This wouldn't also have anything to do with that Silent everyone's talking about around here, would it?"

Cold goose bumps rose on Ara's neck. She went stock-still. "What Silent?" she asked casually.

Fen folded his arms. "The one they've posted a big reward for. Haven't you been watching the news?"

"No," Ara said faintly. "I haven't had time."

"There's a powerful rogue Silent somewhere on Rust," Fen said. "And the Unity wants him. Bad. Problem is, they don't know what he looks like, or even if it's a he. All they know is that he's young and he's somewhere on Rust. And now you're here sniffing around this boy Sejal Dasa. A connection?"

Shit shit shit. Ara struggled to remain calm. "Coincidence, Fen. You just told me yourself Sejal isn't Silent. I'm interested in his genetic potential."

"I see." Fen's tone made it clear he didn't believe her. Ara's heart lurched. Would he turn her in? She couldn't leave Rust without Sejal. And time was growing short. They had to get Sejal off Rust, and fast.

"Look, Fen, I have to go," she told him. "What you told me about Sejal and Vidya changes things, and I have people to contact. I really appreciate your help."

"So when do we take our walk?"

Ara blinked at him. "Walk?"

"On the seapad. Remember? My price for helping you? How about tomorrow?"

Ara felt genuinely flustered. Not because Fen was pressing her for a romantic interlude, but because of its timing. So much was happening now and so quickly, the question felt out of place. Once she got Sejal on board, Ara intended to hurl the ship into slipspace as soon as humanly possible.

So promise him, she told herself. *Even assuming you're around long enough for him to cash in on it and if he lays a hand on you, all you have to do is give him one hard push and he's sea monster meat.*

"Tomorrow it is," Ara agreed. "Why don't we meet at the restaurant at seven?"

A huge smile spread across Fen's wizened face. "See you then. Glory to the Unity." And he signed off.

Ara was getting immensely tired of that phrase.

"Peggy-Sue," she said. "Open intercom to Ben Rymar. Ben, can you raise Kendi?"

"I'm not on the bridge, Mother," Ben replied. *"Let me get up there first."*

Ara sat back and thought while she waited. Stress tugged at her gut, but she pushed it firmly aside. They were doing all they could to find Sejal, and the Children still had the best chance of getting to him first.

Vidya "Dasa" Prasad had voluntarily given up her children. Ara shook her head. How could she do such a thing? Unbidden, Ara's mind flicked back to Ben's implantation. Five years after Benjamin Heller's death, Ara had become aware of a growing desire—need—for a child. She had told herself she was being ridiculous. She was Mother Araceil Rymar of the Children of Irfan, youngest person ever to attain that title, with a clear shot at also being the youngest to make Mother Adept. She was powerful in the Dream, had personally taught half a dozen students, was a widely recognized expert in transcendental morphic Dream theory. Her life was full, she was busy, her friends and students loved her. She didn't need anything.

But Mother Araceil Rymar of the Children of Irfan wanted a baby.

Still, Ara put off the idea another year, until a casual conversation with Mother Adept Salman Reza, Ara's own mother, changed her mind.

"I don't need a baby right now," Ara complained. "But—oh, Mother—I *want* one like you wouldn't believe."

"Well that's the key right there," Salman said. "Those who need children make poor parents. Those who *want* them make fine ones."

It seemed as if the universe were siding with Ara's mother. Two days later, Ara and her compatriots were encased in vacuum suits, inspecting a derelict ship they had found while tracking down rumors of an illegal Silent slave ring. The ship orbited the moon of a gas giant and appeared to have taken heavy damage in a firefight. It was Ara's guess that the ship had been transporting Silent slaves and had run afoul of other pirates. The ship was completely empty. Cargo and crew had either been evacuated, captured, or blown into space. Ara had just been about to leave the cargo hold when she came across a star-shaped metallic object the size of a basketball. It lay forgotten in a corner. She caught her breath, recognizing it as a cryomodule for embryos. The readout said they had been frozen in the same year Benjamin Heller had died.

Back on her own ship, a medical scan revealed that the module contained eighty-seven embryos, a dozen of which were still viable, and all of which carried the genes for Silence. Grandfather Melthine, Ara's superior, was uncertain what to do with the embryos once Ara returned with them to Bellerophon. They could not be placed in artificial wombs and grown to maturation—it was well established that Silent fetuses invariably withered and died under such conditions. And were they Silent children waiting to be born, or simple clumps of cells? Hundreds of years of debate hadn't changed—or solved—the issue. In the end, Melthine ordered the embryos placed in storage until someone could come up with a solution he liked.

Ara decided to end the debate for at least one embryo.

"Do you want a daughter or a son?" asked the doctor on the day of implantation.

"Let the universe decide," Ara replied, and grinned as the doctor dramatically covered his eyes with one hand and plucked a tube from the module. Nine months later, Benjamin Rymar was born, red hair, blue eyes, and all. Ara held him tight and whispered happy greetings in his tiny ear.

As time passed, Ara discovered motherhood wasn't exactly what she had expected. In some ways it was more, and in other ways it was less. She exchanged fieldwork for teaching and was surprised at how little she regretted it. There was laughing and singing, night feedings and toilet training, sleep overs and bullies. Ben's speech developed late, as was expected of a Silent child, but Ben's tenth birthday came and went, and Ben showed no awareness of the Dream, no ability to hear the little whispers from the minds that created it. A worried Ara ordered batteries of tests. The monks who conducted them, however, could only shake their heads. Genetically Ben was Silent, but some unknown factor of environment kept him from expressing that trait.

Guilt had weighed Ara down for months. Had she done something wrong while she was pregnant? Was it something she had done or said to him? In the end, she'd been forced to accept that there was no way to tell. For all she knew, it was a side effect of being frozen as an embryo for so many years. She supposed that it didn't really matter. Ara wouldn't have traded Ben for a truly Silent child, nor would she have given him up. Not after she had fought so hard to have him in the first place.

So how could Vidya give her babies to the Unity? And would her history make her easier or harder to persuade? The memory of a crackling energy whip played across Ara's mind, and she had the sinking feeling it would be harder.

NINE

Planet Rust

The policeman and the terrorist are birthed from the same womb.

—Anonymous

Kendi burst into the hotel lobby barely thirty seconds ahead of the guard. The desk clerk, a short man with a horsey face, looked up, startled.

"What room is the hustler in? The kid with blue eyes," he snapped.

"Uh—"

"There's a raid right behind me," Kendi said. "What room?"

The clerk was already heading for the back door. "Room one-oh-two," he called over his shoulder. Then he was gone.

Kendi dashed for the hallway. He had reached the door to the first room when the front door smashed open and armed guard poured into the lobby. "Everybody freeze!" one shouted. Kendi kept on moving.

Room 102 was only a few steps farther up the hall. Without stopping, Kendi rammed his shoulder into the door. The cheap plastic gave with a crack like a gunshot. Kendi stumbled into the room. Inside, Sejal jumped away from the woman he had entered the hotel with. They were standing next to the sagging bed. The woman's blouse was open, and she yanked it shut with an outraged screech.

"The guard's right behind me," Kendi gasped. "We have to get out!"

Without a word, Sejal rushed to the grimy window. It wasn't made to open. Footsteps and shouts rumbled from the hallway.

"Who the hell are you?" the woman demanded. She was in her thirties, with brown hair and eyes. Kendi ignored her and snatched up a lamp, intending to smash the window with it.

"Freeze!"

Two guards framed the shattered doorway, one leveling a pistol, the other pointing a camera. It flashed just as Kendi flung the lamp at them. The guard fired just as the lamp struck his arm. Energy cracked through the air and burned a hole in the wall. The smell of burnt aerogel filled the room. Sejal didn't move. The guard with the camera abruptly balled up a fist and socked his partner on the jaw. With a startled grunt, the man went down. The woman screamed again.

Still operating on autopilot, Kendi kicked the window as hard as he could. The tough plastic cracked. One more kick and it shattered. Sejal dove out of the room. Kendi followed. If the woman wanted to follow suit, that was her business. Kendi refused to worry about her.

The alley behind the hotel was dark and smelly. Kendi wondered if every alley in the Unity was the same as he and Sejal scrambled to their feet and sprinted for all they were worth. They emerged from the alley and threaded their way through the market crowd. After a few meters, Kendi grabbed Sejal's shirt.

"Slow down," he hissed.

Sejal obeyed, and the crowd obligingly closed around them. Without hurrying or looking back, Kendi strode briskly up the street, towing Sejal with him. After he was sure they weren't being followed, he hauled Sejal into a restaurant and sat him down in a booth.

"Hey!" Sejal growled. "Just who the hell do you think—"

"I *think*," Kendi growled back, "that I saved your ass. Twice. And I *think* that means you owe me some of your precious time. Or do you want to complain to the guard?"

Sejal said nothing.

"All right." Kendi settled back into his chair, trying to get his pounding heart back under control and folding his arms across his chest so his hands wouldn't shake. He had acted purely on impulse, and only now were the possible consequences catching up with him. If he had been caught, he'd have been thrown back into the Unity prison. The memory of a writhing figure and a muffled scream flashed through his mind, and he shoved them away.

"So what do you want?" Sejal asked warily.

"A beer," Kendi muttered, and punched up the table's menu. He ordered the first alcoholic beverage that appeared under his fingertips, and sweetened kelp juice for Sejal. "Look, Sejal—"

"How do you know my name?"

"We talked to your mother."

Sejal leaned across the table. "You stay the hell away from my mother," he hissed. "Lay one finger on her and I'll cut off your—"

"Hey, I'm on your side," Kendi interrupted. "Look, let's cut the tough street kid act. If anyone asks, I'll tell them you flashed a knife at my balls, all right?"

Sejal grudgingly leaned back again.

"All I want to do is talk," Kendi continued. "I have some questions."

"Like what?" Sejal asked warily.

"Did you possess those cops in the alley? And the one in the hotel?"

Sejal's blue eyes shifted. He didn't answer.

Kendi sighed. The kid was distrustful, but probably with good reason. He glanced around. The booth afforded them a certain amount of privacy, and there weren't any other patrons within hearing range.

"Look," Kendi said, "I'm not a Unity guard or a spy or a slaver. My name is Kendi Weaver. I'm a Child of Irfan."

"Who's Irfan?" Sejal asked.

"We're an order of monks." Kendi met Sejal's gaze square on, willing himself to look trustworthy and honest. "We find people who are Silent and we train them."

A strange look passed over Sejal's face. "I'm not Silent. I was tested for it at birth."

"Sejal, only the Silent can possess other people like—well, not like you do, but similar to the way you do."

"I'm not Silent," Sejal repeated stubbornly.

"Listen." Kendi leaned forward. "Do you sometimes hear voices whispering at you? Voices you can't quite hear?"

Sejal's eyes went wide. "How did you know that?"

"When you dream at night, is it sometimes so real, you wake up and it feels like you're still dreaming?"

"Yes," Sejal almost whispered.

"You're Silent."

Sejal bit his lip. The shifty arrogance had left his face and he looked like a frightened twelve-year-old instead of a streetwise teenager. "The Unity ran tests when I was born. If I was Silent, I'd be a slave right now."

Kendi held a hand out over the table. "Try this," he said.

Looking even more bewildered than ever, Sejal took Kendi's hand. A jolt banged through Kendi's arm and crashed down his spine. Sejal gasped and yanked his hand away. Kendi sat stunned. A serving tray scuttled up to the booth and placed their drinks on the table. Both Sejal and Kendi ignored them.

"What the fuck?" Sejal said hoarsely.

Kendi shook his head. It felt as if every vertebra in his spine had fused for a split second. He had never felt a jolt that strong before.

"What the hell was that?" Sejal demanded.

Kendi cleared his throat. "The Silent touch," he said. "It happens when you touch flesh to flesh with another Silent old enough to reach the Dream."

"Every time?" Sejal asked, eyes wide.

"The first time," Kendi clarified. "And once you touch another Silent, you'll usually be able to find them when you're both in the Dream."

Sejal stared. "That's being Silent? That and the voices?"

"That's part of it," Kendi said.

Sejal blinked hard and remained quiet for a moment. It took Kendi a second to realize that Sejal was holding back tears. Kendi's chest welled with sympathy. Poor kid. His childhood had obviously been hard, he'd been selling himself on the street, and now Kendi was scaring the life out of him.

"Hey, it's all right," Kendi soothed. "Being Silent is a gift. We can teach you—"

"It's not that," Sejal said in a thick voice. "I'm relieved. God, it's a fucking *relief.*"

Now Kendi blinked. "A relief?"

"About six months ago," Sejal said, swiping at his eyes with quick fingers, "I started hearing voices whispering in my head. Some days they got so loud I couldn't even hear myself think. I couldn't tell anyone—they'd think I was crazy. I thought I was. Now you pop up and tell me—show me—that I'm not."

"You're not crazy," Kendi said with an emphatic nod. "But you *are* Silent."

"So if *I'm Silent,*" Sejal emphasized the two words as if he were tasting them, "why didn't I show up on the Unity gene scans?"

Kendi shook his head. "That I don't know. It may be an old-fashioned mistake."

"Maybe," Sejal said dubiously. "So what do we do now?"

"Now we—"

"Kendi," came Ben's voice in his ear. *"Kendi, are you there?"*

Kendi held up a hand to Sejal. "I'm here," he subvocalized. "What's going on?"

"Trouble," Ben said. *"You and Sejal are on a wanted list for the Unity guard."*

"What? Shit!"

"Was there a raid on a hotel in the market?"

"Yeah. I almost got caught in it. Why?"

"One of the guards had a camera. Standard Unity procedure on a vice bust in case someone gets away—like you did. Your and Sejal's pictures are on the nets. You're wanted for unlawful solicitation, breaking and entering, malicious destruction of property, assault of a guard officer, and resisting arrest."

"What's going on?" Sejal asked. "Who are you talking to?"

"We've got to get moving," Kendi said, rising and throwing a *kesh* on the table for the untouched drinks. "The Unity's looking for us."

Without a word, Sejal followed Kendi out of the restaurant. Kendi eeled through the crowd outside, trying to glance in all directions at once. Every muscle was taut with tension. The crowd, however, seemed content to ignore them. If anyone recognized them as fleeing felons, no one gave any indication. Kendi refused to relax. The general populace may not be up on the latest wanted pictures from the guard, but the guard itself was, and the guard would have ocular implants just like Kendi's that would alert them if any wanted criminals passed through their line of sight.

"Where are we going?" Sejal asked.

"Kendi, what are you doing?" Ben asked almost simultaneously.

"I'm heading for the ship," Kendi replied to them both.

"He *what?*" Ara screeched.

"He interfered in a Unity raid," Ben replied calmly. "Kendi got Sejal out of there before they would have been arrested."

"That *idiot.*" Ara fumed, nearly knocking her coffee cup off the console in her quarters. Ben stood in the doorway.

"Idiot?" Ben echoed, confused. "Kendi saved Sejal from the guard."

"And caused us a hell of a lot of trouble." Ara closed her eyes, trying to bring her temper under control. Once, just once, she wished Kendi would think before he acted.

"I don't see how—"

"If the Unity had arrested Sejal," Ara said in a level voice, "we could have bailed him out. Sejal would be grateful. Vidya would be grateful. Sejal would want to come with us. Everybody wins. Now they're both wanted and we're in up to our necks."

"Well, in any case, he's headed back here with Sejal."

Ara bolted to her feet, and this time the coffee cup went crashing to the floor. "He's what? Shit! Ben, get on the transmitter and tell him to stay the hell away. Go! Hurry!"

Ben fled. Ara rushed into the corridor behind him, pulling her purple trader's tunic over her clothes as she went.

"Peggy-Sue," Ara barked, "open intercom channel to Brother Pitr. Pitr, grab two sets of slave shackles and two brother's robes. Meet me down at the main hatchway on the double! Move!"

"All right, Mother," Pitr's voice said. *"But what—"*

"Peggy-Sue," Ara interrupted, "close channel and open intercom to Harenn Mashib. Harenn, emergency. Meet me down at the main hatchway with a medical kit, and I mean yesterday!"

"Obeying," Harenn replied instantly.

"Peggy-Sue, close channel and open intercom to Ben Rymar." Ara reached the lift, decided not to wait for it, and started down the ladder instead. Ceramic clanged beneath her hurrying feet. "Ben, have you gotten hold of Kendi yet?"

"Yes, Mother. He and Sejal are in the spaceport. Kendi wants to know why—"

"Where's the first place the guard will come looking for Kendi?" she snapped. "God, I can't believe that boy's stupidity today. Tell him to find someplace to hide. We'll be there shortly. Peggy-Sue, close channel and open intercom to Jack Jameson. Jack, we're going to have company pretty soon and they're going to ask a lot of questions. I want you to keep your mouth shut. You don't have any idea where Kendi is, or where I am."

"But I don't *have any idea where Kendi—"*

"Meanwhile, I want you, Gretchen, Ben, and Trish to get the ship ready for takeoff. You might only have a few seconds' warning, so I want the bridge staffed at all times. Clear?"

"Clear. But—"

"Peggy-Sue, close channel." Ara reached the bottom of the ladder and all but flew down to the main hatchway. On the way she met up with Harenn. Harenn's veil was slightly askew, and she carried a briefcase-size medical kit.

"What happened, Mother?" Harenn asked in a breathless voice.

Ara was about to explain when Pitr's solid form hurried up, his arms piled with cloth.

"Slave shackles?" Ara asked.

"Under the robes," Pitr replied.

Ara opened the hatchway. "Peggy-Sue, activate magnetic locks ship-wide and open them for no one but me or Brother Kendi."

"Acknowledged," the computer said.

Ara waved Pitr and Harenn through the hatch and shut it. A faint hum indicated the magnetic locks were active. The landing field, carefully gridded with precise yellow lines, stretched around them in all directions. Ships of varying shapes and sizes rested like giant insects, one to a square. Transports carrying fuel and cargo zipped over the aerogel asphalt. Overhead, the sun burned in a cloudless sky.

"Ben," Ara subvocalized, *"where's Kendi hiding?"*

In response, a red trail overlaid itself on her field of vision as Ben uploaded directions to her ocular implant.

"What happens, Mother?" Harenn demanded again. "We need to know."

"It's Kendi," Ara said, and strode off along the trail. She explained with short, terse phrases as they went. Pitr whistled under his breath.

"Are any Unity guard coming now?" Harenn wanted to know.

"They're demanding entrance at the ship," Ben said. *"They said Kendi and Sejal are wanted for assaulting an officer. That makes them high priority."*

"Stall," Ara ordered. "Tell them the locks are malfunctioning."

"Acknowledged."

The red trail led Ara into the spaceport proper, a large, flat building filled with customs offices, air traffic controls, and who-knew-what. The air inside was cool, and the volume of voices rose considerably when they entered. Ara followed the trail to a private restroom that offered showers as well as toilet facilities.

"Well, that's one intelligent decision he made," Ara muttered, and thumbed the chime.

"It's occupied," said a strange voice, and it took Ara a moment to recognize it as Sejal's.

"Let us in," Ara snapped. "Quick!"

The door slid open. Ara, Pitr, and Harenn ducked inside. Kendi and Sejal sat on narrow benches within. The cubicle was tiny, too small for five people, so Ara turned to Pitr.

"Wait outside and play guard," she said. He set down his bundle of cloth and left.

"Ben told me what's going on," Kendi said. "And I don't want a lecture, Mother. I'd do everything exactly the same way if I had to do it again, so don't waste your breath shouting."

"Who the hell are you?" Sejal broke in.

Ara drew herself up, trying to rein in her temper. "I'm Mother Adept Araceil of the Children of Irfan."

"Okay," Sejal grunted. "What's that mean to me?"

"It means," Harenn said, "that she can take you off this planet."

"I'm not going anywhere if she"—Sejal pointed a finger at Ara—"gets Kendi in trouble."

Kendi shot Ara a smug look, and it took all her willpower not to smack him. *Later,* she told herself. *We'll hash this out later.*

"Sejal," she said in a calm voice, "you and Kendi are both at grave risk. We have to get you off Rust, and quickly, before the Unity gets hold of you. Harenn—your kit."

"What about my mom?" Sejal said as Harenn opened her medical kit. "I can't just leave her."

That stopped Ara dead. She had been concentrating so hard on Sejal, she had completely forgotten about Vidya.

"We can come back for her later," Ara said. "The Children of Irfan usually offer relatives work at—"

"Just leave her? What are you, nuts?" Sejal said incredulously. "She's my mother!"

"Hey, it's all right," Kendi said, laying a hand on Sejal's shoulder. "We'll send another team later."

"No!" Sejal shook off Kendi's hand and scrambled to his feet. He was almost a full head taller than Ara, and she was forced to look up at him. "I'm not leaving without—"

"All right," Ara broke in quickly. "We won't leave until we talk to her. Ben, how are things at the ship?"

"Who's Ben?" Sejal demanded.

"Jack's still stalling," Ben reported. *"Trish is in the Dream helping him by whispering at the guard to keep them calmed down."*

"Good. Can you patch me through to the Unity communication system and connect me with Vidya Dasa?"

"It'll take a minute," Ben said doubtfully. *"The Unity's monitoring us pretty closely right now. I have to change channels and masks every few seconds."*

"You're wonderful, Ben," Ara told him. "Let me know when you have her on."

"What are you doing?" Sejal asked.

Ara wedged herself next to him on the hard, narrow bench. "I'm setting up a call with your mother. Meanwhile, I want you to put these robes on and let Harenn work on you."

"Work on me?" Sejal echoed, looking a little bewildered. Now that Ara had promised to contact Vidya, most of his belligerence had faded. Ara herself had also calmed down a little, and it came to her that she was sitting next to the person she might have to kill. She swallowed, wanting to edge away from him on the bench, put some distance between them, but there was no room.

"I will change your face, Sejal," Harenn said. "Hair and eyes, perhaps your nose and forehead. Come by the mirror. There will be no pain."

Sejal glanced at Kendi, who nodded. Everyone remained silent while Harenn worked. She lumped coagulant paste over Sejal's nose and forehead and worked it like a sculptor. The material was normally used to seal cuts and other wounds, but in sufficient quantities, it could be used for short-term cosmetic alterations. When Harenn took her hands away, the paste faded and matched itself to Sejal's skin color. His profile had been altered significantly, with a longer nose and thicker forehead. Next, Harenn had Sejal cover his face while she sprayed his hair with a strong disinfectant. She waited one minute, then told him to rinse off in the sink. When he was finished, his hair was several shades lighter, almost blond.

"Now you, Kendi," Ara said.

Kendi wordlessly submitted to Harenn's ministrations, though he refused to look at Ara. Before Harenn finished, Ben came on over Ara's earpiece again.

"The Unity guard are demanding entrance," he said. *"They're going to damage the ship if we don't get the door open."*

Ara gritted her teeth. "Peggy-Sue, are you monitoring?"

"On line," the computer said.

"Peggy-Sue, release hatchway magnetic locks. Then initiate file lockdown and scramble, priority one."

"Working."

"Mother!" Ben yelped. *"What are you doing?"*

"Kendi and Sejal aren't on board, Ben," Ara explained. "Let the guard look. Tell Jack to spread some chocolate and *kesh* around if he thinks it'll help. I just wanted to stall."

"Acknowledged. Vidya Dasa is on the line. Keep it short, Mother. I'll have to terminate the connection once the guard reaches the bridge, assuming your file scramble doesn't do it first."

Ara ran a lead from her earpiece to a speaker set into the wall for just this purpose. "Ms. Dasa?" Ara said.

"Where's my son?" Vidya demanded without preamble.

"I'm here, Mom," Sejal said. "Can you hear me? I'm all right."

"Release him now," Vidya snapped. *"Harm one hair and you will pay."*

"Ms. Dasa, we're trying to help," Ara said as calmly as she could. She could already imagine the black-booted feet of the guard tromping through her ship, turning the rooms upside-down, flinging possessions to the floor. "There isn't time for long explanations. Your son is in trouble with the Unity. So is my appren—so is Brother Kendi."

Out of the corner of her eye, Ara saw Kendi's expression darken. Her verbal slip hadn't been lost on him.

"We need to get Sejal—and you—to safety," Ara concluded. "Can you meet us somewhere?"

"Mom, it's okay," Sejal interjected. "Kendi helped me out of a tough spot. I trust him."

Pause.

"Where are you?" Vidya asked.

"I'd rather not say on this channel," Ara said.

"Then how can we arrange a meeting?"

"Mom," Sejal put in, "meet us at the monster building. You remember where that is?"

Another pause. *"I remember. I'll be there in fifteen—"*

"Guard's coming," Ben cut in. *"Good luck."*

The com line went dead.

"Monster building?" Kendi asked.

Sejal grinned. "It's an office not far from here. They built it when I was little. Mom and I were walking past when they sprayed it up, and I thought it looked like a monster coming up out of the ground. We always called it the monster building after that."

"Then let's go," Ara said, disconnecting the lead. "But first put these on."

She handed Sejal and Kendi each a brown robe. After they put them on, Harenn sprayed some of the cloth with disinfectants to discolor the fabric while Ara tore holes. Then she held up sets of shackles. Each set was made of one large collar and four smaller ones.

"This one's for the neck," she told Sejal, indicating the large collar. "The others are for wrists and ankles."

"I know how they work," Sejal said. "What are they for?"

"No one looks twice at poor, bedraggled slaves," Kendi said in a bitter voice. "Come on."

Sejal swiftly donned the shackles. Kendi put his on more slowly. Ara clipped the master unit—a box the size of a fist—prominently to her belt.

"It isn't activated," she said. "But stay close."

Ara braced herself for a smart remark from Kendi, but he said nothing. The lack was surprisingly jarring. Hiding her consternation, she slid open the door and greeted Pitr. He raised an eyebrow at Kendi and Sejal's changed appearance but said nothing. They set off through the port, Kendi and Sejal walking humbly to the rear, heads low beneath their ragged hoods. Ara's heart jumped every time she saw a guard, but they ignored the little group as they processed to the exit.

"Now where?" Ara murmured.

Following Sejal's quiet directions, they proceeded up the crowded street. Groundcars honked, flit cars swooshed, and starships rumbled. The heavy air smelled of sweat and fuel. A pair of Unity guards stood silent watch by the door, and Ara casually turned her face away from them. Her back felt exposed, and she had to force herself to walk at a normal pace.

The monster building looked much like all the other buildings around it—tall, gray, and blocky. Vidya, tight-faced, was standing near the main entrance. It took her a moment to recognize Sejal. She started forward, apparently intending to grab her son, then aborted the motion, opting instead to wait for the group to approach.

"A small courtyard is in back of the building," Vidya told them. "It remains empty at this time of day."

Ara nodded and followed Vidya around the office building to the rear, where a little cobblestoned area occupied space between the buildings. Little sunlight reached the place, and a tired-looking tree drooped over a wooden bench. Food containers littered the stones. Kendi and Sejal started to take the bench until Pitr caught Kendi's arm.

"Slaves sit on the ground," he said gruffly.

Kendi's eyes went icy, but he nodded and sat. Sejal joined him. Vidya stiffly took the bench between Ara and Pitr.

"Are you all right, Sejal?" she said. "What have you done to yourself?"

"I'm fine, Mom. It's a disguise."

Ara blinked. Sejal's manner had changed. Gone was the tough street kid she had met in the tiny restroom. His posture was less belligerent, his voice quieter. Even his word choice was different. Was the street persona a mask? A personality he had created while working the streets? Or was the street kid the real Sejal and this one the fabrication?

"Why is the Unity looking for you?" Vidya asked. "What did you do, Sejal?"

A red flush crept up Sejal's face.

"He's Silent," Kendi said quickly.

"He is *not* Silent," Vidya snarled.

"Yes I am, Mom," Sejal said. "Kendi showed me. He proved it."

"Impossible!"

"Mom—"

"Ms. Dasa," Ara said in a soft voice, "your son has a very powerful form of Silence. He already has abilities I've never even seen before. Why are you so sure he isn't Silent?"

Vidya glared at Ara. Her jaw worked back and forth for a long moment.

"I know about the other children," Ara said, voice still soft.

"What other—" Pitr began, but Ara raised a hand and hushed him.

"Ms. Dasa—Vidya," Ara continued, "I know about your contract with Silent Acquisitions. I know about your other babies, and I know your husband disappeared."

"Prasad," Vidya whispered. Her brown face had paled.

"Who's Prasad?" Sejal asked from the stony ground.

"He's your father," Ara said.

Vidya's face abruptly twisted into a mask of rage. "How *dare* you? How dare you come into my life like this? After I have worked so hard to make everything safe? How dare you tell us these horrible things?"

"You're not denying them," Ara pointed out. "Vidya, we don't have a lot of time. It boils down to this: The Unity guard is looking to arrest your son. We can take him—and you—off-planet to escape. We need you to decide."

"The Unity guard doesn't arrest the Silent," Vidya snapped. "Slavers do. Why is the guard looking for him?"

"He is a prostitute," Harenn said bluntly.

Vidya's mouth fell open. Her expression said Harenn's remark had been worse than a slap. After a moment, she whirled on Sejal.

"Is this true?" she demanded.

"Mom, I—"

Vidya reached down and grabbed him by the shoulders. "How can you do such a thing?" she cried. "When I have worked to make our neighborhood a safe place for you? How could you be so ungrateful?"

A dozen emotions washed across Sejal's face. "Is that all you care about? It's always about the neighborhood. 'You have to be a good son of the neighborhood, Sejal. You have to be a model for the neighborhood children, Sejal. The neighborhood must be safe. The neighborhood must be clean.' The neighborhood, the neighborhood. Who gives a shit?"

Vidya slapped him. Sejal fell silent. "The neighborhood let you grow up, boy," she hissed at him. "I built the neighborhood for *you,* so you would always be safe."

Something clicked in Ara's head. "Because it wasn't safe for Katsu and Prasad?" she said. "Because it wasn't safe for your husband and your daughter?"

Vidya snatched her hands back and folded them in her lap. Her head bowed.

"What daughter?" Sejal asked. A red mark from Vidya's slap was darkening on his face. Sejal's jaw trembled, and Ara couldn't tell whether it was from anger or tears. "Mom, what's going on? Who are Prasad and Katsu? Why can't I be Silent? You have to tell!"

Vidya remained motionless for a long moment. When she finally spoke, her voice was steady. "You can't be Silent, my son, because I arranged it to be so."

"What do you mean?" Sejal whispered.

"Your father's name is Prasad Vajhur," Vidya said.

"You also have two brothers, but I don't know their names. We had to give them to the Unity."

"What about Silent Acquisitions?" Pitr asked.

"Our original contract was with them," Vidya answered. Her voice was flat, emotionless. "It was hard. When the Unity blighted Rust, there was no food anywhere. Prasad and I were starving, and we knew we would die soon. Both of us, however, carry the genes for Silence. We are not Silent ourselves, but any children born between us will be. This includes you, Sejal."

"But—" Sejal began.

"Let me," Vidya said. "Silent Acquisitions offered us food, shelter, medicine, and money in exchange for two babies. The condition was harsh, but at the time it seemed a better choice than painful death. If I had known then how difficult it would one day be, I would have let myself die with Prasad beside me."

"But you didn't know," Ara said.

"I was young and we were dying." Vidya's hands twisted in her lap. "Less than a week after Prasad and I signed the contract, the government surrendered to the Unity, and the Unity took over our contract. It dictated new terms, and we could do nothing. The money was reduced to a fraction. The first contract promised we would have housing and medical care for a year after the second child was born, but a month afterward, we were on the street. I don't know how, but Prasad found work as a garbage collector. We had two tiny rooms in a half-ruined apartment building, a single small income, and I was pregnant again."

Vidya fell silent again. Sejal stared at his mother as if hypnotized.

"That must have been Katsu," Ara nudged.

"Yes. She was a beautiful baby, and all ours. The Unity knew she was Silent, but I managed to convince myself that the ten years I would have with her before they took her away would be a far, far better thing than losing babies I never had the chance to hold."

"But you eventually realized that wasn't the case," Ara said. "So you arranged a fake kidnapping, hoping to hide Katsu someplace safe."

Vidya looked at Ara, genuinely surprised. "The kidnapping was very real. When she was nine months old, someone broke into our rooms. They took my little Katsu. I woke up in the morning and realized she hadn't cried all night. My first thought was that she had slept through the night, but then I found her empty bed." Vidya's voice had gone flat again. "Prasad was . . . I don't think I can describe it. He wanted to run in a thousand directions at once. I begged him to let the guard find her, but Prasad insisted that he had a better chance, that he knew the neighborhood better. He left, and he didn't come back. I reported him missing as well. A week later, he was still missing, and I realized I was pregnant again."

"Me?" Sejal said.

Vidya nodded. "You. I was sure whoever had kidnapped Katsu had killed Prasad, and that they would come next for this baby and for me. So I ran."

"You changed your name to Vidya Dasa," Ara put in. "Easy to do, since the Annexation damaged so many records."

"Yes. I took part of Prasad's name and made it mine and his son's. Perhaps that was a mistake."

"But if your genes make every child you and Prasad have Silent," Kendi asked, "why were you so sure Sejal wasn't?"

"I arranged it to be so," Vidya said.

"What?" Sejal said. "How?"

"When you were less than two months in the womb," Vidya told him, "I found a . . . man. A genegineer. He said he could make a retrovirus. The virus would alter your genes and render you non-Silent."

"A lie," Harenn said flatly. "Such changes are only possible for an embryo less than two weeks old. For a fetus, it is not."

"This was a new procedure," Vidya said. "He wanted a test subject, but could find none. Making a valuable Silent into a worthless non-Silent would be highly illegal in the Unity. Because of this, he was willing to perform the procedure without payment. And it worked. When Sejal was born, the Unity doctor scanned him for Silence and found none. I was so happy."

Sejal shifted on the cobblestones. "But I'm Silent, Mom.

I touched Kendi, and something exploded in my head. He said only the Silent feel that."

"We'll have to figure that out later," Ara said.

"I didn't want my son to disappear," Vidya continued as if no one had spoken. "The genegineer gave me secret money in exchange for permission to examine Sejal from time to time, which let me stay away from tax collectors, but the only place I could afford to live was a neighborhood as bad as the one where Katsu had disappeared. Drug dealers, gangs, and thieves were everywhere, and the Unity did nothing to stop them. But one day I realized the good people in the neighborhood, the ordinary ones, outnumbered the bad, and I remembered a thing Prasad had told me when we were walking to Ijhan during the famine. He said that our old community had been destroyed. To survive, we had to build another.

"I talked to my neighbors and united the building I lived in. Then the building next to us joined us, and the next and the next. We threw out the gangs and built a wall out of scraps and ruins to ensure they would stay out. We repaired everything we could and cleaned what we couldn't. Our neighborhood was a proud place, and it was as safe as I could make it."

Vidya stopped speaking and looked at Sejal. "Though I didn't make it safe enough," she added, voice heavy with sadness instead of anger. "How could you do this thing? I thought you were a good son, a son I could be proud of."

Sejal flinched as if he'd been dealt a physical blow. "And you were a great mother?" he snarled. "Do you know what my first memory is? Sitting on the floor at a damn neighborhood meeting. You were talking to other people and ignoring me. You're always talking, Mom, and it's always to someone besides . . . besides me. You talk, but you sure as hell don't listen."

"I talked and I worked," Vidya cried, "so you would never have to worry about being attacked in the street or stolen away from your family."

"What family?" Sejal shot back. "All my life, you were doing something for the neighborhood. When were you home to make us a family?"

"I was home always," Vidya said, looking shocked. "The

neighborhood was my job. The collections paid our rent. The neighborhood—"

"I don't give a shit about the neighborhood," Sejal shouted. "Don't you know anything?"

"I know my son has been selling himself on the street."

"I was doing it for *us,*" Sejal said, voice cracking. "I was trying to earn enough money to get us off this slimy rockball. Just *us.* Not the neighborhood, not anyone else. For once I wanted something for just *us.*"

Tears ran down Sejal's face. Ara squirmed on the bench, acutely wishing she were somewhere, anywhere, else. The looks on Pitr's and Kendi's faces proved they felt the same way. Harenn was hidden behind her veil, and suddenly Ara realized how handy such an item must be. She cast about for something to say that could end the argument, but for once she was at a loss.

"What you did was a form of slavery," Vidya replied in a cold voice.

"It was either that or deal drugs, Mom."

"It was a terrible thing," Vidya said stubbornly.

"I only sold myself, Mom," Sejal snapped. "You sold your children."

Kendi gasped. Vidya fell silent. Her hands stopped twisting in her lap, as frozen as her face. Sejal froze as well. His words hung in the air. Time and silence stretched unbearably. Ara wanted to crawl under one of the cobblestones.

"Take him," Vidya whispered.

"What?" Ara said.

"Mother?" Ben asked in Ara's earpiece. *"Mother, are you there?"*

"Take him with you," Vidya repeated, still whispering. "I have failed as a mother. Take him and train him and do whatever else you do."

"Mom—" Sejal began.

"No, Sejal," Vidya interrupted. "You are right, and you must go."

"Mother?" Ben said.

"What is it, Ben?" Ara subvocalized.

"It took me a while to get everything back on line after your file scramble, or I would've called earlier. The guard have left the ship. They didn't find anything, but they've

posted half a dozen officers outside. I don't know how you're going to get in."

"We'll worry about that in a minute," Ara replied, and was suddenly filled with an impulse to rush back to the *Post-Script* so she could hug Ben hard. "Stand by."

"You can come with us, Vidya," Kendi said. "You don't have to stay here."

Vidya shook her head. "I have . . . responsibilities I must attend to."

"The neighborhood," Sejal spat.

"No, Sejal." Vidya got up. "I have to talk to the man who . . . made you what you are. There are questions he must answer. And none of you can wait for me." She reached down and pulled Sejal to his feet. He rose reluctantly.

"Sejal, I love you, and you must go," she said, and embraced him quickly. "And I am not leaving you forever. I will find a way to join you when I am done here."

"The monastery is on a world called Bellerophon in the Independence Confederation," Ara said, rising to her feet. "Once we get out of the Unity, I'll leave notices about you. When you get out yourself, ask in any public place or on any public network how to contact me—Mother Adept Araceil—and the Children of Irfan. Eventually one of our people will hear of you and take you to us."

Vidya nodded.

"And now," Ara finished, "we must leave."

Sejal and Vidya hugged once more, and a lump rose in Ara's throat. She had said good-bye to Ben often enough, and more than once had wondered if she'd ever see him again. Kendi led Sejal away, leaving Vidya at the bench. Sejal's face remained rigid, and Ara didn't try to speak to him—she was sure he was controlling tears he didn't want to shed.

As they were leaving the courtyard, Sejal suddenly stopped. "Mom, there's a loose floorboard in the back of my closet," he said over his shoulder. "Put your finger in the knot and pull it up." Then he stiffly started walking again before Vidya could reply.

TEN

Planet Rust

I seen my duty and I done it.
—Anonymous

A very subdued group made its way back toward the spaceport, knowing that their problems were just beginning. Ara activated her earpiece.

"Ben, what's the status on board?"

"Unchanged," Ben said in a broadcast that encompassed Pitr, Kendi, and Harenn. *"Six guard outside the ship that I can see, possibly more I can't."*

"They figure Kendi has to come back eventually," Pitr said as they walked.

"What's the matter?" asked Sejal, who didn't have an earpiece and could hear only half of the conversation. Ara quickly explained.

"So?" Sejal said. "I can hold off six people, no problem."

All four monks halted on the sidewalk and stared at him. "You can?" Ara said.

"Sure."

"Why didn't you hold off all the guards at the hotel then, instead of just making one punch the other?" Kendi demanded.

Sejal shrugged. "I can't do more than one off the top of my head. I need some time to concentrate. Hard to do that when people are throwing lamps and crashing through windows."

"Sejal," Ara said carefully, "how many people can you . . . *handle* at once?"

Another shrug. "I don't know. The most I've ever done is eight."

Ara's stomach went cold. What was Sejal's maximum? Ten? A dozen? A thousand? An army? Ara imagined a troop of grim-faced soldiers all unafraid to die because someone else was controlling their very thoughts. Could this boy who had cried at his mother's feet do something like that?

But he was a boy, Ara reminded herself, who had been selling himself on the streets for money. A boy who grew up without a father and felt neglected by his mother. The perfect recipe for trouble.

Their disguises were still in place, so getting into the spaceport proved relatively easy. The place was crowded, as usual, and guard were everywhere, though none gave Ara and the others a second glance.

"How close do you need to be, Sejal?" Ara murmured over her shoulder. Sejal's collar and shackles were still in place and he walked a pace behind her.

"I need to see or touch them," Sejal replied in an equally low voice.

They made their way to the landing field. Harenn trotted off ahead and returned to report that the six guard were still there and that she had found a vantage point that might work.

They ducked and weaved their way across the field. The harsh smell of fuel hung in the humid air, and the sun had fallen low in the sky. Eventually, the familiar gray wedge of the *Post-Script* became visible ahead of them. They stopped behind an empty loader and peered around it.

"Is that it?" Sejal asked, pointing. A half dozen guard were waiting by the ramp that extended up to the hatchway, their black-and-scarlet uniforms unmistakable.

Ara nodded.

"All right." Sejal strode toward the ship.

"What's he doing?" Pitr gasped.

"Don't move," Ara ordered. A small cynical part of her wondered if the guard would open fire. That would certainly solve her problem. In any case, there wasn't anything she and the others could do but watch, unless they wanted to take on six armed guard with their bare hands. Sejal, in his shackles and ragged robe, stopped fifteen or twenty meters away from the guard and stood with his arms folded.

"What are you doing there?" a guard shouted, but Sejal didn't answer. "You, slave! I said, what are you doing there?"

Sejal remained silent. The closest one, energy rifle at the ready, came forward.

"Listen, boy, when the guard asks you a question, you better—" The guard stopped, frozen in place. Behind him, the others' faces went slack. Sejal's gaze was fixed, unmoving.

"Go!" Ara said. "Kendi, you get Sejal."

The group needed no urging. They sprinted past the motionless guards and all but tumbled into the hatchway when it opened at Harenn's touch. Ara glanced over her shoulder. Kendi was leading Sejal across the aerogel asphalt. The boy moved slowly, as if in a daze. Ara wanted to scream at them to hurry up, but she kept her mouth shut. It took forever for Sejal to cross the threshold of the hatchway. Ara was starting to slam it shut when another voice shouted, "Wait!"

Reflexively Ara stopped. A figure darted through the hatchway. On the asphalt beyond, the guard hadn't moved once. The figure slammed the hatchway shut, and Sejal blinked myopically.

"Who—?" Pitr asked.

The figure turned. It was Chin Fen.

"Fen!" Ara gasped. "Why the hell are you here?"

Fen smiled. "Because you owe me a walk on a seapad leaf?"

"Mother," Ben's voice said over the intercom. *"The guard know something's up, but they don't know exactly what. They're demanding entrance to the ship."*

Ara gestured, and Pitr grabbed Fen from behind. The moment he touched Fen's bare arm, Pitr gasped, though he didn't let go. "He's Silent, Mother."

A knife appeared in Harenn's hand, and she flicked it to Fen's neck. The blade made a scraping sound on his skin. Fen's brown eyes went wide.

"Who are you working for, Fen?" Ara demanded.

"Mother, what do we do?"

"I don't work for anyone!" Fen squeaked. "I swear! I hate the Unity. That's why I came to you."

"Mother, they're going to open fire on us. Rifles won't do much to the ship, but they've already radioed for heavier artillery."

"Take off, Ben," Ara said.

The floor rumbled beneath them. Harenn's knife didn't waver from Fen's neck and Pitr remained as motionless as a hazel-eyed block of granite.

"Kendi, get to the bridge and take over piloting," Ara said. "We've got everything covered here. Fen, you'd better talk fast or I'm going to shove you out the airlock once we make orbit."

"I got sucked into the Unity right after I left the monastery," Fen said hurriedly as Kendi ran off. Harenn's knife remained at his throat. "I thought it would be something good, humans first and all that, but by the time I realized how repressive it was, I couldn't get out because I had no resources and I was too afraid and then you walked into the office and I knew you weren't just a trader because it just felt wrong and then when you wanted all that information about Vidya and Sejal I figured you were up to something big."

"You paid him to spy on me and Mom?" Sejal asked incredulously. The glazed look had left his eyes.

Ara ignored him. "Why did you choose this particular moment to show up, Fen?"

"I really did come about our date," Fen said. "We were supposed to meet at seven, remember? You didn't show up and there was no answer when I called your ship, so I came down. Then I saw the guard and they froze like statues and I saw you rush past them. All of a sudden I saw how cowardly I'd been all these years and that this might be my last chance to get out of the Unity, and oh, please believe me, Ara. It's true."

Ara clenched a fist in exasperation. This wasn't anything she wanted to deal with right now, but she had to make a decision.

"Sejal," she said, "remove your shackles and put them on Fen. Be ready—you'll feel a jolt. Pitr, once he's set up, take him and Sejal down to the galley and explain to Jack what's going on. Give Jack the master unit"—she handed it to Pitr—"and tell him to keep an eye on Fen. I don't want him out of Jack's sight for a second, got it?"

"Yes, Mother," Pitr said.

Fen yelped when Sejal touched him. "Holy mother! I was right. He's the one. You found him!"

Ara didn't respond to this overly obvious statement. "After you've taken Fen down to Jack," she continued to Pitr, "I want you and Trish to go into the Dream. Whisper to anyone who follows us and get them to make mistakes. Harenn, you get down to engineering in case we get hit. We're in for a rough ride, so be ready."

Fen accepted Sejal's shackles without protest. Ara headed for the bridge. Kendi had arrived well ahead of her and was already at the helm. Ben was back at communications, and Gretchen was running sensors. Ara took her customary chair. The ship shuddered slightly, and it made an odd rattling noise.

"What is it with your boyfriend?" Kendi asked.

"Boyfriend?" Gretchen said.

"He's chained up in the galley," Ara replied, glancing at the vidscreen. It showed nothing but red sky. "And he's not my boyfriend. What's going on up here?"

"We've cleared the spaceport," Kendi reported. "A couple of cargo ships were caught off-guard since we didn't have clearance or a flight plan, but I managed to dodge them."

"The Unity's screaming bloody murder," Ben added. "We've been ordered to return to the port immediately or they're going to fire on us."

"Do you think it's because of Kendi or do they know about Sejal?" Gretchen asked.

Ben shrugged. "They're not saying."

"How long before we can slip?" Ara asked.

"Not sure," Kendi admitted. "I still have to calculate a course. I could do a random slip, but I have no idea where we'd come out. The odds of popping out in the middle of a star or something are small, but it's still a risk."

"Anywhere would be better than here," Gretchen said.

"Go," Ara told him.

"I'm not done," Kendi said. "Before I can do even a random slip, we have to clear the atmosphere and get out of Rust's gravity well, and how fast we do that will depend on—"

The ship shuddered hard. A thunderous crash echoed through the bridge, and an alarm blared.

"—on how often they hit us," Kendi finished.

"Four ships in pursuit," Gretchen said. "They're armed with lasers and missiles."

"That hit caused some light damage," Harenn's voice said from the intercom. *"Do not allow such a thing more than once again or there will be some serious difficulties."*

"Thirty seconds until we break atmosphere," Kendi reported.

"I'm picking up two missiles," Gretchen said. "Intercept in fourteen seconds. Thirteen . . . twelve . . . eleven . . ."

"Evade!" Ara snapped.

"I'm trying!" Kendi shouted. The vidscreen sky swooped and dipped as Kendi frantically maneuvered the ship. "The missiles are using visual locks and I can't break them. And this tub doesn't have anything to throw."

"Eight . . . seven . . ."

"Ben!" Ara yelled.

"No good." Ben's fingers worked the console like hyperactive junebugs. "I can't find their guidance systems."

"If they hit us, we will die," Harenn said dispassionately.

Ara didn't know what else to do. There was no time to think. "Brace yourselves, people!" was all she could think of to say.

"Four . . . three . . ."

Ara looked over at Ben. If she died, she wanted to be looking at her son. Ben was still working the console, and she knew he'd keep working it until it came apart under his hands. Her heart swelled with pride.

"Two . . . one . . ."

WHUMP!

Ara's head snapped downward under the impact. The ship yawed sideways, and the image on the view screen swooped sickeningly. Alarms blared all over the ship and something on the bridge started to smoke.

"We're still functional!" Kendi shouted over the noise. "I think I can—there!" The darkening sky righted itself, though the bridge was still filled with noise. A few stars scattered themselves across the vidscreen image like salt crystals.

"Can we still clear the atmosphere?" Ara shouted.

"I think so!" Kendi yelled.

"Peggy-Sue!" Gretchen screamed. "Mute alarms!"

The alarms went silent, leaving a ringing in Ara's ears. "Why are we still alive?" she demanded.

In answer, Ben hit a key. The speakers came to life, though recent damage made the transmission hiss with static.

"Attention *Post-Script,*" said a voice. "This is Rell Hafren of the warship *Star's Doom.* We know you have the boy Sejal Dasa. He is the property of the Empire of Human Unity. Hand him over at once and you will not be harmed. Repeat: hand over the boy and you will not be harmed."

"We aren't transmitting," Ben said. "They can't hear us."

"They figured out who Sejal is," Ara breathed. "Dammit! I was hoping we could get away before—"

"Mother, the warships are powering up imp guns," Gretchen reported. "If they hit us with an electromagnetic pulse, we'll lose main power and they'll be able to grab us with a gravity beam at their leisure."

"Sixteen seconds to slipspace," Kendi said, "and that's if I push."

"Push, dammit!" Ara said.

"Ten seconds to power disruption," Gretchen said.

Ara swore. "Harenn, is there anything you can do to shield us?"

"Not in ten seconds."

"Five . . . four . . ."

"Nine seconds to slipspace," Kendi reported.

"Attention, *Post-Script*—"

". . . two . . . one . . . zero."

Ara braced herself—

—and nothing happened.

"Report!" she said.

"They should have zapped us," Gretchen replied, obviously confused.

The answer popped into Ara's head like a cork from a champagne bottle. "Trish and Pitr," she said gleefully. "They're whispering to the weapons officers from the Dream and making them hesitate."

"We have slip!" Kendi smacked his console. A screech of stressed ceramic ripped through Ara's ears and the vidscreen stars dissolved into a rainbow wash of nauseating color.

"Hull breach in sections six and seven alpha!" Harenn said. *"We are venting atmosphere."*

"Can you deal with it?" Ara asked.

"Not in slipspace."

"Attention! Attention!" the computer interjected. "Hull breach in sections six and seven alpha. Atmosphere at ninety-five percent."

"Suits!" Ara yelled, already moving for the bridge's storage locker. "Move it, people! Kendi, how long before it's safe to come out of slipspace?"

"Gimme three more minutes," Kendi said, not leaving his console.

Ara handed out silvery suits and helmets, then donned her own. A breeze drifted through the bridge. "Ben, once you're suited, take over for Kendi. Gretchen, head below and help Jack get Sejal and Fen set up with the spare suits."

"Who the hell is Fen?" Gretchen asked.

"Attention! Attention! Hull breach in sections six and seven alpha. Atmosphere at ninety percent."

"I'll explain later," Ara said. "Harenn, seal off the lower deck. We can at least save some atmosphere on the upper one."

"I have already attempted this," Harenn's calm voice replied. *"The doors are not responding. In addition, I have lost forty percent of main power, and emergency reserves are off line. I must shut down the gravity generators to compensate."*

"Attention! Attention! Hull breach in sections six and seven alpha. Atmosphere at eighty-one percent."

Ara sealed her helmet, muffling the sounds from the bridge. Her own breathing echoed loudly in her ears. Suddenly the deck left her feet and she was falling. Gretchen yelped and snagged the storage locker door. Ara resisted the impulse to windmill her arms and instead grabbed the back of Ben's chair. The velcro patch sewn there for exactly this purpose snagged her palm. Colors washed nauseatingly over the vidscreen, making Ara's gorge rise. The view of slipspace made most humans ill, and Ara was no exception, especially in zero gee. Gretchen pushed off and drifted over to her console, where she punched a few keys. The vidscreen went blank.

"Thank you," Ara said. Gretchen shoved herself toward the door without replying. She still had to check on Sejal and Fen.

"Attention! Attention! Hull breach in sections six and seven alpha. Atmosphere at sixty-four percent."

"Kendi," Ara said, "suit."

"Almost done." He was panting. "We'll be in normal space in less than two minutes."

"You'll be unconscious in less than one," Ara said. "Move!"

Kendi looked like he was going to protest, then apparently changed his mind. He pushed out of his chair and swam to the storage locker. Ben waited until he had landed, then took Kendi's place while Ara assisted her gasping ex-student into a suit. He was already in a half faint. His face was flushed from blood summoned to the surface of his skin by the low pressure. Quickly Ara sealed his helmet and heard the welcome hiss of oxygen from the tanks. Kendi's breathing steadied and his eyes opened.

"I'm good," he said over the suit's communicator. "Thanks."

"Attention! Attention! Hull breach in sections six and seven alpha. Atmosphere at fifty-one percent."

"Take your console, Kendi," Ara said. "Have Harenn check you for bruises and capillary damage later—you're going to be sore."

"Yes, Mommy."

"Peggy-Sue, open intercom to Gretchen Beyer," Ara continued. "Gretchen, is everyone suited up down there?"

"Sejal got his on," Gretchen replied. *"That Fen guy fainted, but Jack and I got him into his suit. Did you know Fen is Silent?"*

"Yes. What about Trish and Pitr?"

"I have no idea. They aren't down here."

Kendi swam over to the pilot's chair. "Take us out of slipspace, Ben. We should be safe by now."

The ship shuddered and boomed.

"Attention! Attention!" Peggy-Sue said. "Hull breach in

sections six, seven, and nine alpha. Atmosphere at thirty-eight percent."

"We're leaking like a sieve," Ara groused. "Harenn, can you repair all that, or are we going to be wearing these suits all the way back to Bellerophon?"

"I am still assessing the damage," Harenn replied. *"I will report the moment I know more."*

Ara shoved herself into her customary chair and belted herself in place. The suit's thin material was slightly rough, catching the chair's fabric and preventing her from sliding off while she did so. Then she took several deep breaths to quell her roiling stomach. Zero gee had never been Ara's personal favorite.

"Where are we, boys?" she asked to distract herself.

"No idea," Kendi said. "I was concentrating too hard on getting us into slipspace to program any coordinates. There's a K-class star within easy reach, though, if Harenn wants a power source."

"Head for it." Then Ara remembered she hadn't checked on Trish and Pitr. "Peggy-Sue, open intercom to Sister Trish and Brother Pitr Haddis. Are you two suited up?"

"Suited up and heading down to help Harenn," Trish said.

"Pitr?" Ara said. No answer. "Pitr, please respond."

Nothing. A chill slid up Ara's spine.

"Attention! Attention! Hull breach in sections six, seven, and nine alpha. Atmosphere at thirty-one percent."

"The intercom might be damaged," Ben pointed out.

"Peggy-Sue," Ara said, "where is Pitr Haddis?"

"Brother Pitr Haddis is in his quarters," the computer replied.

"I'll go down and check on him," Ara said to Ben and Kendi in a carefully light voice. "He's probably fine. You two stay here and figure out where we are."

She unbelted herself and pushed toward the door. Pitr was fine. The intercom had just been damaged. He was not hurt, he was not dead.

So why was he still in his quarters?

"Attention! Attention!" the computer said. "Hull breach in sections six, seven, and nine alpha. Atmosphere at twenty-seven percent."

Ara reached Pitr's quarters and tried the door chime with a gloved finger. No response. The door, when she tried it, turned out to be locked. Abruptly, she'd had enough of being in suspense.

"Peggy-Sue," she snapped, "captain's override for the lock on Pitr Haddis's quarters."

"Voice print verified. Override accepted." The door slid open, revealing a darkened room. Pitr, Ara remembered, always shut the lights off when he went into a Dream trance.

Ara floated in the hallway for a moment, then grasped the doorsill with both hands and hauled herself in. She immediately rebounded off something big and floppy. With a shriek, she shoved herself away from it. The motion sent her spinning, and she couldn't see. Darkness swam past her faceplate. One of her arms connected with something solid, and she collided with a . . . wall? Ceiling? Whatever it was, it halted her. Her suit made a hissing noise as the fabric brushed the ceramic bulkhead. Ara finally got her bearings. She was pressed against the floor.

"Lights!" she hollered.

The room sprang into brightness. Ara turned. Pitr's corpse, the thing she had rebounded from, drifted toward the ceiling. His arms floated outward from his body, his legs were splayed, and his face was red and bloated. Across the room, a dermospray flipped slowly end over end.

Pain and sorrow crushed her against the floor. Ara tried to hold back the tears. Crying in zero gravity was difficult enough—blobby tears gathered in the eyes, blurring vision until they broke free and drifted away. In a helmet, they splashed everywhere. But Pitr was dead. He had been in the Dream holding back the Unity when the ship started losing atmosphere. Trish had left the Dream in time, but Pitr's body had probably fallen unconscious and he hadn't made it to a suit. Now he was dead. What was she going to tell Trish?

"He died saving us," she whispered to see how it sounded.

It sounded fake.

"Mother Ara," Harenn's voice said, *"we have patched the breaches. We are venting no more atmosphere. Trish and I*

will continue to augment the repairs until it is safe to re-enter slipspace."

"How long will that take?" Ara asked, surprised at how steady her voice was.

"Three or four days. Less if others help. After that I can fix main power and reinstate gravity."

"Understood. Peggy-Sue, close intercom."

Pitr's body bumped the ceiling. Someone should secure him—it?—before the gravity came back on. It wouldn't be right for the body to come crashing to the floor. And there would be funeral arrangements, and burial, and a Dream ceremony, and—

Pitr was dead, and he had died for her.

Zero gravity or no, Ara put her helmeted head in her gloved hands and cried.

ELEVEN

Sejal's Journal

DAY 4, MONTH 11, COMMON YEAR 987

My old journal got left behind when we left Rust, so I'm starting a new one on the ship. Everyone's pretty upset around here, so I'm staying out of the way. That means I pretty much stay in my room and mess around on the computer like I'm doing now.

The ship's called the *Post-Script* and it's pretty cool, though Kendi says it's a piece of junk, even when they have gravity. Being weightless made me sick as a dog for an entire day. It feels like you're falling, but when you look around, the walls aren't moving and you never hit anything. A tiny push sends you spinning, but it seems like you're holding still while the ship spins around you.

At least I didn't throw up like Fen did. He barfed in his helmet, and it floated around his head like chunky fog. It would've been funny if it hadn't been so disgusting. Gretchen—she's big and blond and kind of pretty and she seems kind of familiar—turned on some kind of vacuum that sucked most of it away, but bits and pieces still clumped in his hair. He couldn't take his helmet off to clean up, either. No atmosphere.

Anyway. Kendi took me to a room and set me up. He told me to stay in it until all the repairs were made. I do tricks in zero gee and hunt through the computer database for stuff to read. We got atmosphere back a few hours after Harenn made basic repairs, though Fen still couldn't shower. No gravity. As for me, between monkeying around with zero gee and the computer, I haven't gotten bored yet. I play the flute a lot, too. I can sit cross-legged in the air upside-down and play. And the room I'm in is a lot nicer than my room back ho— back on Rust.

I'm trying not to think of Rust as home. I don't live there anymore. It's weird. For years all I could think of was getting off Rust. But now I'm not so sure. I don't know what's going to happen next. Kendi says we're going to a monastery on Bellerophon, which is in the Independence Confederation. They'll train me how to use my Silence.

I'm Silent.

I said that aloud while I was typing it.

I'm Silent.

Those words make me feel so free! I hadn't realized just how scared the voices and dreams made me until Kendi touched me in the restaurant and jolted me all the way down to my feet and told me I was Silent. The voices and the vivid dreams are all normal, he says. I'm normal! It makes me feel like I could fly, even without zero gravity.

I like Kendi. And not just because he saved my ass, what? Two times? Three? He *listens* to me, believes me. I don't know about Ara, though. *Mother* Ara, I guess I'm supposed to call her. I mean, she was *stalking* me? And she has this way of looking at me, like she's sizing me up. It kind of reminds me of the look some jobbers get, jobbers that make me want to run far and fast because they want something I don't want to give them. Other times she seems nice and caring. When she's like that, she reminds me of Mom.

I don't know what to think of Mom. She dumped a lot of stuff on me just before we left, and there's no way to talk to her about it. I want to know more. I mean, I have two brothers out there somewhere? And a sister who was kidnapped? And then there's my dad. I mean, Mom always said he was "gone" whenever I asked, and I just kind of assumed she meant he was dead. But now I hear he (and my *sister!*) just disappeared one day. I've got a whole family out there somewhere, but now I'm leaving Rust, and I'll never find out any more about them. How could Mom not tell me this stuff? And who the hell does she think she is getting mad when that bitch Harenn told her I was tricking? Like Mom has any right to be angry after she sold her own kids!

Sometimes I get so mad I want to pound something, but I'm not going to ruin anything for myself on the *Post-Script* by flapping off. I'm even polite to that bitch Harenn.

I hope Mom found the money okay. I'm worried about her.

Anyway. The hull's almost fixed. It broke open when we were running away from the Unity. I thought we were dead for sure, and I still get nightmares about it. One of the guys who came to get me when Kendi and I were at the spaceport—Brother Pitr was his name—died making sure we'd get away. I didn't even know him, barely talked to him, but he gave up his life for mine. Mother Ara held a service for him and jettisoned the body into space. Then everyone who was Silent—Mother Ara, Kendi, Sister Gretchen, and Sister Trish—went into the Dream. Kendi told me later that they hooked up with a whole bunch of other Silent and had another service. Then they all went back to work repairing the ship.

Anyway. Like I said, the ship's almost completely repaired, and that's good news. A redheaded guy named Ben helped get main power restored so they could turn the gravity back on. I felt heavy at first, but now everything feels normal again. Fen's a lot happier, anyway.

I remember where I've seen Gretchen—Sister Gretchen—before. She bumped into me when I was getting out of a jobber's car. Kendi said she planted a bug so they could follow me easier. When I got mad, he said they did it because they wanted to be able to keep an eye on me in case something bad happened. I still don't know. I can't get pissed at everybody. Can I? This whole situation is screwed up.

Anyway. I still like Kendi, I guess. He sits next to me at meals and cracks jokes that almost make me wet my pants from laughing so hard. And he knows what it's like to be scared about being Silent.

He told me about the Children of Irfan, who they are and where they came from. Now I'm going to be one of them. I'm excited and nervous at the same time. And I'm normal!

TWELVE

The Dream

Poverty won't force you to steal, and neither will wealth stop you.

—Padric Sufur

Padric Sufur peered carefully through the branches of the pear tree. The round-bodied Mother Adept sat on the lip of her fountain, hands in her lap. At her feet was placed a cabana chair. A male human Silent reclined in it and a tall glass with a pink umbrella sticking out of it hovered within his reach. The Silent had blond hair and wore an arrogant expression. Padric swallowed his distaste and forced himself to pay careful attention. He needed to find out if his information had been correct.

Beyond the garden wall, a section of sky remained blacker than a thunderstorm. Occasional flicks of red lightning streaked across the darkness. Even from this far away, Padric could feel the misshapen-ness of it. The area had cropped up yesterday over the giant canyon, and Padric hadn't dared get close to it yet. Silent everywhere kept a wary eye on it and speculated on what it meant in frightened whispers. Meanwhile, however, Dream business had to continue. Padric carefully settled his wings about his tiny hummingbird body and listened.

"It'll take another day to repair the hull to Harenn's satisfaction," Mother Adept Araceil Rymar said in her harsh human voice. "After that, it should take us about ten days to arrive at Bellerophon."

The Silent sipped his drink and said nothing. His eyes, however, carried the rapt concentration of a trained Silent bent on absorbing every word. Once he left the Dream, Padric knew, the man would recite every word Araceil had said into a recorder. Good Silent always had highly trained short-term memories.

"I have not yet evaluated Sejal's . . . destructive potential," Araceil continued. "As Brother Kendi predicted, he seems able to possess the unwilling and non-Silent, though the exact extent of this ability we don't yet know. I'll conduct more tests back on Bellerophon."

Every nerve in Padric's body snapped to attention and his feet clenched the pear twig so tightly the bark dug into his skin. So his information had been correct. It was suddenly very hard for him to sit still, and Padric forced himself to remain motionless only with great effort of will. Although the form he had taken was tiny, his slightest movement would send weak ripples through Araceil's portion of the Dream and she might notice him.

Araceil shifted on the lip of the fountain. "In anticipation of your Imperial Majesty's next question, I don't know how long it will take to determine if Sejal is dangerous enough to require . . . elimination. However, I am prepared to"—her voice faltered slightly—"to follow through on your wishes and will keep you informed. End classified transmission."

Padric almost blinked. Araceil had orders to kill this boy? But of course. Humans were all alike in so many ways.

"The message will be delivered," said the blond Silent in a toneless voice. He and his chair vanished without another word.

Araceil stared at the spot where he had been. Then a long sigh escaped her. The expression on her face was full of uncertainty, and Padric wondered if she was going to burst into tears.

"Dammit!" she suddenly yelled, and smacked the fountain water with one hand. Liquid sprayed everywhere. "And damn *you!* Damn you to a hundred hells, you damned Imperial bitch!"

Padric watched tensely from the tree as Araceil conjured up a vase and hurled it against the garden wall. It shattered with what Padric assumed was a satisfying crash. A hot wind rose, fluttering the green leaves and waving Padric's twig up and down. Araceil raised a fist, and a lightning bolt cracked down from the clear blue sky. It split an orange tree from top to bottom. The concussion thudded against Padric's fragile bones, and smoking splinters flew in every direction. He smelled burning wood.

"Damn you!" Araceil howled.

Another lightning bolt destroyed another tree. Nervously wondering if his might be next, Padric shot out of the tree, wings blurring, creating tiny ripples in Araceil's Dream fabric. It was a risk, but Araceil was probably too distracted to notice right now. Besides, Padric was good.

Padric was one of the few Silent who could change his shape in the Dream. He could take the form of something small and innocuous, such as a mouse or a bird. He had experimented with stones and blades of grass, but rocks and plants can't see or hear, so he had instead concentrated on animals. In these other forms, Padric could creep into another Silent's territory, eavesdrop on conversations or meetings, and creep back out again with none the wiser.

As far as Padric knew, his talent was unique. Other Silent were subconsciously and firmly attached to their shapes. They expected their own form in the Dream, and that's what they got. The first time Padric had come into the Dream, however, he hadn't been able to take a shape at all. He had hung about as an amorphous blob. It had taken his instructor KellReech several months to coax him into a shape, and he had early on taken to shifting forms like quicksilver.

As a teenager, he had used the talent for his own amusement, spying on Silent who came into the Dream to play or sculpt Dreamscapes or have private talks. As a young man, he had used the talent for personal gain. Overhearing a few privileged conversations had allowed him to make some very wise investments over the years. Very wise indeed.

Another lightning bolt crashed downward, splintering the pear tree Padric had been using for cover, and Padric decided he was far enough away to make a real run for it. Although Padric was as adept as any other silent at teleporting from one Dream location to another, the abrupt lack of his presence would cause an inward rush of Dream energy, much like water would hurry in to replace a rock that suddenly disappeared, and that would definitely be noticed.

The hummingbird skimmed low over the ground and shifted into a small feline creature with orange-brown fur. Padric tore soundlessly across the ground faster than a groundcar, muscles bunching, claws extended for maximum purchase.

A distinct rumble emanated from the dark area behind Padric as he ran. He risked a glance over his shoulder and saw more red lightning suffuse the strange blackness. Instead of vanishing, however, the lightning left streaks behind, as if the darkness were cracking. Padric skittered to a halt and stared. Around him lay a flat, featureless plain; he hadn't bothered to create anything more specific once he cleared Araceil's realm. He sat back on his haunches and stared some more. The red cracks glowed like lava. What was happening?

Padric spread his whiskers with a *whiffing* noise, uncertain what to do. After a time, he became aware that someone was treading close to his Dream space. A feathery touch asked permission to approach his domain. It was KellReech.

"Approach," he called. Although sprint-cats from Rothmar couldn't make speech sounds, Padric managed it. His subconscious might continue to reject the idea of a rock that could see or a leaf that could hear, but an animal that could talk didn't seem to bother it overmuch.

KellReech appeared next to him with a soft *pop,* and Padric felt the ripples in his Dream space. KellReech was a Villor, bipedal and short, perhaps a meter tall. Her skin was covered in a rainbow shimmer of greasy scales, and her face was flat, with a wide mouth and two small brown eyes. Her fingers were long and graceful as grass stems.

"Have you looked closely yet?" she asked without preamble.

"No." Padric raised an orange-brown paw. "Shall we?"

KellReech wordlessly wrapped his paw in her graceful multi-jointed fingers. The Dream *twisted,* and they were standing at the edge of darkness.

The wail hit Padric first. His ears flattened on his skull and he gave an automatic hiss. The wail was harsh and discordant, raking Padric's nerves. KellReech released his paw and he forced himself to look at the scene more closely.

It wasn't just the sky that was dark. It was every scrap of earth and air. Everything ahead of them was three-dimensional blackness cracked by scarlet. It stretched from horizon to horizon. Inside the darkness, Padric could dimly make out movement, but no exact shapes, not even the canyon that had opened below it. This place had no form, and Padric wasn't strong enough to force one on it. He didn't dare walk through it or even stab a claw into it.

The wailing continued. Other Silent in a range of races and species were scattered up and down the long boundary between the darkness and the Dream. Some conversed in pairs or groups. Others simply stared. No one crossed into the wailing black. Whispers murmured in the background, somehow still audible over the noise. The Dream was always full of whispers. Padric noted several humans among the Silent and carefully turned his head so he couldn't see them.

"It grows," KellReech murmured. "I don't know what to make of it."

"Has anyone tried to cross it?" Padric asked.

"I have heard nothing of such an attempt," KellReech replied. She reached down to touch his head, unusual for her. "On the other side are nineteen planets with Silent. They are either surrounded by this or they are inside it. I can't sense them, this much I know."

Padric concentrated for a moment, but it quickly became obvious that he wouldn't be able to sense anything beyond the boundary either. For a moment he thought he heard a faint cry under the wailing. He peered ahead, trying to see better. There was a brief flicker, like something flitting at the corner of his eye. Padric craned his neck. For a second he was sure he had seen a human woman amid the chaos. He caught a glimpse of long black hair and an impression of youth. She was . . . dancing? Then she was gone.

"Did you see that?" he asked KellReech urgently. "The human girl?"

"I saw her," KellReech replied, her hand still on his head. "What does it mean?"

"I don't know."

"I will go consult with others." KellReech took her hand from Padric's head and vanished without another word. Padric backed farther away from the red-streaked darkness, then gathered his concentration. Obediently his mind conjured up a picture of a spartan stone hall with pillars and a satin reclining couch. He was *here,* but he wished to be *there.*

A small wrench, and he was standing in the pillared hall, exactly as he had imagined it. The blackness was far away, a smudge on the horizon visible through one glassless window, and from this distance he couldn't hear the painful wail. Padric forced himself to set aside thoughts of the ongoing disaster for the moment, knowing KellReech would tell him of anything she found. There were other things he had to consider. He jumped onto the satin couch and worked at the soft cloth with his paws.

So his information had been right—Mother Adept Araceil was a person to watch and it had been worth every moment spent spying on her. Another wave of excitement washed over Padric and he actually began to purr. He had heard the rumors of a powerful Silent, of course, and his information had told him the boy was on a planet within the Empire of Human Unity. However, the idea of a Silent who could control the unwilling and non-Silent was . . . well, it was a dream come true.

A thought struck him. Was the boy responsible for the black place? He considered the idea for a moment. Doubtful. The disturbance had the feel of many minds, not just one. Was it his project, then? Padric would have to get hold of Dr. Say on Rust and find out quickly. Meanwhile, it would be best to get his hands on the boy. It would spell disaster if the Unity got hold of—

Padric was sinking into the couch. Startled, he tried to stand up, but the cushions pulled him down as if they were made of quicksand. He panicked for a moment, then struggled free of the couch with a sucking sound and flopped ignominiously to the cool marble floor. Beside him, the couch melted into black mush. Padric scrambled to his feet and leaped away from it, claws scrabbling on the smooth floor. The remains of the couch hissed and bubbled like a pitch cauldron, spreading dark ooze across the floor. The ooze ate into the floor, chuckling to itself as if it were alive. It threw up a dank, moldy smell redolent of rotten vegetables.

Then came the screams. A dozen, perhaps a hundred

voices, all in pain, all wailing like a cold wind. It came from every direction, tearing at skin and nerves. Padric had to leave the Dream, and quickly, but the screams made it hard to concentrate. A column pressed cold against Padric's side. He leaned against it, trying to take in its solidity and ignore the chuckling that oozed steadily toward him. The horrible wail keened louder. Suddenly Padric was back in the camps, hearing the screams of the other inmates, their cries for help and mercy. He flattened his ears again and yowled in sympathy.

The column shifted against Padric's fur. He jumped away with a hiss and spun to face it. The white stone bulged with odd shapes. Distorted human forms moved within the rock, stretching and twisting in impossible directions. Eyes bulged and contracted, skin and muscle contorted. An arm broke free with a wet sound and reached for him. Padric scrambled backward. Cold slime washed over his hind feet, oozed between his toes. Padric tried to leap free, but the blackness held him fast. Still chuckling, it crawled up his haunches. A tendril snapped upward and wrapped around his shoulders like an icy snake.

Padric shut his eyes. He was not in danger. He was not going to die. He was Padric Sufur, and he was a master in the Dream. The ooze climbed, engulfing his front legs. Padric forced himself to shut out the horrible keening, the cold slime crawling up his body. It reached his chest and shoulders. Padric inhaled deeply, ignoring the rotten smell and the fact that he couldn't feel his feet. He was calm. He was in control.

The icy ooze rushed over his head. Padric automatically tried to inhale and choked. He couldn't breathe. He couldn't see. He couldn't—

Padric Sufur's eyes snapped open and he sat up with a gasp. He flailed wildly about his bed for a moment before realizing that the slime was gone, the wailing was silent. He had successfully left the Dream.

Padric wrapped long, thin arms around his chest, acclimating himself to his real shape. It was bony and inefficient. KellReech had a lower center of gravity and more dexterous fingers. Chipk had many legs and eyes and soft brown fur. Padric's body was mostly hairless and his hands were awkward. His face was lean and hawklike, with a long nose and thin lips. His body was equally lean, with long limbs and hands. Out of the Dream, Padric had allowed a few wrinkles to creep across his face to remind him that, despite appearances, eighty-eight wasn't young, even for a human.

The bedroom had already raised the temperature to the toasty warmth he preferred upon awakening from the Dream, but a chill suffused his bones. Padric's room was large and spare, furnished with only a bed, end table, and wardrobe. Like each room in the rest of his home, this one was a clear dome with, in Padric's considered opinion, the most beautiful view in the universe.

The estate occupied most of an asteroid, and it consisted of a series of above-ground half-bubbles blown from the rock and sand of the asteroid itself and reinforced with clear polymers. Thick carpets went right up to the edge of the dome, where the floor became the pocked surface of the asteroid. If Padric dimmed the lights, making the dome effectively invisible, it looked as if the room were standing in the middle of a vast desert beneath a soft black sky and steady, shining stars. And the gas giant, of course.

The ringed gas giant, which Padric had named Gem, dominated the heavens, and her rainbow surface was often chased by raging storms large enough to engulf entire planets. Padric's asteroid currently skated the giant's icy ring, making it look as if a glittering, blue-white road stretched past the horizon. An entire team of what Padric called his "gardeners" did nothing but scan the asteroid's projected orbit for ring debris and remove anything that might punch a hole in, or even scratch, the domes. It was terribly expensive, especially when the asteroid's orbit carried it through the ring itself, but the view was well worth it.

Padric sat tailor-fashion on his bed and drummed his fingers thoughtfully on one thigh. His heart had slowed, but a certain tension remained in his gut. The Dream was becoming more and more dangerous. He would have to arrange a meeting with Dr. Say, and quickly.

The bedroom door opened and a large spiderlike being scuttled in. A silver tray was balanced expertly on its back, and the delicious smells of sweet rolls and coffee filled the dome. Padric shivered with Dream cold again and all but snatched the coffee mug off the tray. He sipped the bitter warmth gratefully. The spider, meanwhile, set the tray on the nightstand, then stepped back and waved its forward legs and antennae. Padric, adept at the sign language, didn't need to activate the translator.

"Will you require anything more, sir?" Chipk, the spider, was asking. He was a Kepaar who had lost status on his homeworld. Padric had hired him, though Chipk had the unnerving habit of referring to it as "buying my soul."

"The newest reports about the Dream, please," Padric replied in his own language. He couldn't speak Kepaarin—not without multi-jointed legs—but Chipk knew Padric's language perfectly well. It was an equitable arrangement.

"The news has already been downloaded into the room, sir," Chipk said, and withdrew.

Padric sipped from the mug again. Although coffee was originally a human discovery, it had taken the ministrations of more evolved races to produce the best results, and Padric's staff always ordered beans that had never touched human hands or soil.

"Meth-pa," he said, "news. Text format."

A holographic view screen obediently appeared in front of him and words scrolled down it. There were several stories about Silent who had been caught in strange accidents or fought terrible monsters. Per Grill, a Silent from Bell Star Station, had nearly been swallowed by a giant worm. A pair of Silent involved in a delicate stock market transaction had been hit by a tornado. They described the whirlwind as "screaming at us."

Nileeja Vo was dead.

Padric gasped and hurriedly reread the article. Nileeja Vo was—had been—a field recruiter for Dreamers, Inc. Her husbands had found her dead on her couch, a look of terror on her face. According to the newspaper, she had finished a mail transfer within the Dream, and the other Silent, the one receiving the information, had left the Dream just fine. Moments later, something had killed her Dream form, and her body had quickly died.

Padric put a bony hand over his mouth as he read. A small bit of sorrow clotted his throat. He had met Nileeja

Vo at the same time he had met KellReech. Padric remembered squatting in the filthy camp barrack when a strange being entered, flanked by two guards. The being was short and scaly, with long graceful fingers. It moved through the room, touching each inmate and moving on without speaking. Padric watched in wary fascination until the creature came to him. When its fingers brushed his bare shoulder, a jolt flashed down his spine.

"This one," the being said.

The guards took Padric by the upper arms, and full-blown terror burst upon him. He struggled and fought until one of the guards cracked him across the head with a baton. The world went dark.

When he awoke with an ache in his head and nausea in his stomach, the short creature was standing next to him. It occurred to Padric that he was lying on a bed, a soft one. The creature pressed something against his arm. There was a soft *thump,* and the headache and nausea vanished.

"Who are you?" Padric asked.

The creature smiled with its wide mouth. "My name is KellReech," it said.

The door opened, and another being walked in. This one was over two meters tall and willowy with enormous black eyes, a shock of wild white hair, and rough brown skin. It carried a food tray. An appetizing smell filled the room and Padric's mouth watered. He sat up and saw that he was dressed in clean pajamas. His body also felt clean, though he hadn't bathed in months. The willowy creature set the tray in Padric's lap. He instantly shoveled food into his mouth, not even stopping to examine or taste it.

"This is my colleague, Nileeja Vo," KellReech said. "And we represent Dreamers, Inc."

While Padric bolted his food, KellReech explained further. New Prague, Padric's planet, had been invaded and taken over by the One World Regime without any formal declaration of war. New Prague was now an official protectorate of the Regime, and random segments of its population were alternately enslaved or put into the work camps. That much Padric knew, though he didn't stop eating long enough to say so.

KellReech went on to explain that Dreamers, Inc., was a

separate entity, a private corporation that provided Dream communication at competitive prices to anyone who had the means to pay for it. Dreamers, Inc., was always on the lookout for more silent, and they had bribed the regent of the camp for the privilege of combing the inmates for any Silent the Regime might have missed. They had found Padric.

Padric took a long pull from a large glass of milk, though he listened carefully to every word. There would be a catch somewhere, he was certain of it. In the camps, no one did anything for free.

Nileeja sat on the foot of Padric's bed, and he spared enough attention to see what his surroundings were. He was in a small room with metal walls and a carpeted floor. A ship? The room contained only his bed, an end table, and a single chair. Nileeja smelled faintly like crushed grass.

"You to be free now, Padric," Nileeja said in a soft, soothing voice. "This mean you to have choices. You to tell us you to want walk away right now, and we to take you wherever you want to go. No obligation. Or you to join Dreamers, Inc."

She went on to explain that Dreamers, Inc., would train Padric to use his Silence at their extensive and highly advanced facility, though not for free. Upon completion of his training, he could either work for Dreamers, Inc., with living costs paid and salary going to pay off debts, or he could strike out on his own and give a portion of his earnings to Dreamers, Inc. until the debt was paid.

Padric sucked crumbs off his fingertips and promptly chose to join. What other choice did he have? KellReech and Nileeja Vo nodded their approval and told him to sleep.

Padric later learned there were no other humans aboard the *Quiet Dreamer,* though there were a dozen other aliens, all different, all Silent. The *Dreamer* was on a long-term recruiting mission and wouldn't return to headquarters for several months. During that time, it became obvious that something had to be done about Padric. He suffered terrible nightmares. He stole from the crew and new recruits. He told lies, and once he even set fire to his mattress. Eventually, KellReech started meeting with him on a daily basis to talk. Padric later learned that KellReech had been reading books on human psychology, though she admitted to Nileeja that some of it was hard to grasp. Still, she did her best.

"Of course," KellReech said during one session. "You are angry. You are in pain from what your fellow humans did to you. You hate them for it, and you hate yourself."

At first, Padric didn't want to talk to her at all, and KellReech wisely did not threaten to withdraw Dreamers, Inc.'s offer if he didn't behave. Eventually, after much coaxing, Padric did talk to her. He told her about the camps and the guards, talked about how he had stolen from other inmates and informed on them to get better treatment for himself.

"You feel guilty about what you did," KellReech said. "But the urge to survive is a strong instinct among humans. You did what you had to do, and it's normal to feel guilt and hatred. It's normal to hate yourself and other humans."

When the ship reached the moon that served as the headquarters for Dreamers, Inc., Padric's training began. Once he finished, Padric elected to go freelance and send a portion of his wages back to Dreamers to pay off the debts and interest incurred by his rescue and training, but he still retained several contacts with the company, including KellReech. He had fallen out of touch with Nileeja Vo, however, and hadn't laid eyes on her in over thirty years.

Now she was dead.

Sorrow washed over Padric. He sat silent for a moment, then ordered the computer to make a sizeable donation in her name to whatever charity Nileeja's family might deem appropriate. The computer would route the order to Padric's own team of Silent, who would go into the Dream, contact his bank—literally Padric's bank—and authorize them to transfer the funds to a bank on Nileeja's world. The Silent who worked for Padric's bank would contact the Silent who worked for the bank on Nileeja's world, and they would accept the transfer. Padric's bank would deduct the amount of money from his account, and the other bank would add the amount to theirs. Transaction completed.

Padric, meanwhile, still on his bed, swallowed his sorrow a bit more easily than he thought he should. On the other hand, he hadn't seen Nileeja Vo in three decades. With a heavy sigh he turned back to the news. Several articles mentioned the blackness. Dreamers, Inc., and the Children of Irfan, among others, had declared the situation a full-blown emergency and had set task forces to studying the problem. Padric reached thoughtfully for a sweet roll. If this was indeed the result of the project, he would need to keep the fact under wraps for a while longer. Maybe he could put some quiet pressure on Dreamers, Inc., to slow their investigation. The Children of Irfan would be harder to deal with, but he'd come up with something.

Meanwhile, he needed more information.

"Meth-pa," he said, "search for 'Empire of Human Unity' or 'Unity,' capital *u,* and 'Silent,' capital *s.* Exclude news released by the Empire of Human Unity itself."

"No matches," the computer reported.

"Meth-pa, search for names 'Sejal' and 'Araceil Rymar.' Include Unity news releases."

"No matches."

Padric nodded. These were telling facts. The Unity was keeping its mouth shut about Araceil and Sejal. That either meant the boy was so worthless he wasn't worth mentioning, or that he was so valuable the Unity didn't want word of his existence to leak out. Considering what Araceil had said, Padric took the latter point of view. Padric would have paid serious money to see the expression on Unity Premier Yuganovi's face when he learned a ragtag bunch of monks had gotten the better of him.

Another sip of coffee, and some of the chill left Padric's bones. Sejal was an incalculably valuable asset to whoever controlled him. Besides, if one project failed, it was best to have another.

"Meth-pa, begin transcript of Dream session. Label 'Sejal' and cross-reference by date and time."

"Recording."

Padric set down his coffee, took a deep, calming breath, and slipped into a light trance. Word for word, he dictated the conversation he had overheard between Araceil and the messenger to Empress Kan maja Kalii.

"Meth-pa," he said when he was done, "how long would it take my slipship to reach the planet Bellerophon?"

"Approximately six days, two hours."

And Sejal would reach Bellerophon in eleven days. That gave him five days to plan. Padric picked up his cup, which had kept the coffee hot for him, took a sip, and quite literally stared into space.

THIRTEEN

Planet Rust

You'll never find it if you don't look.
—Maternal Proverb

Vidya Vajhur stared through the grimy window. A pocked, gray aerogel wall was the hotel room's only view, but she didn't really see it.

She had failed. All the visions, the work, the planning. Failed. True, Sejal was still alive, was still out there somewhere on a world called Bellerophon. But he had first been sold, used, chewed up by the slums. The proof lay in his words and in the coins that lay heavy in her pocket.

He is a prostitute.

The blunt, hateful words were burned indelibly into her brain. Those words were why she couldn't go with the monks to Bellerophon. Vidya needed time away from Sejal. Whenever she looked at him after hearing that terrible sentence, Vidya could only see Sejal in bed with . . . women? Men? Both? She didn't want to know. Perhaps once she had been apart from Sejal long enough to start missing him, the images would change. But now she couldn't bear to look at him.

Vidya forced the images away. The room was stuffy and smelled of dust, but Vidya hadn't been able to open the window. Conversations from neighboring rooms filtered in through the thin walls. Mounted on the wall was an ancient terminal that, after some coaxing, grudgingly produced a newscast. Vidya skimmed it, looking for news of Sejal and the Children of Irfan. Nothing so far. Vidya allowed herself a small sigh of relief.

After bidding Sejal good-bye, Vidya had gone home, only to be stopped at the guard station outside the neighborhood. Enyi, the neighborhood guard, had warned Vidya that two Unity guard were waiting for her in the apartment.

Kicking herself for not realizing this would happen,

Vidya had gone to the apartment building across the street and set watch from the lobby. Less than two hours later, two Unity guard left her building and hurried away. Vidya's heart lurched. If they were leaving, Sejal had obviously been located, but there was no way to know if he had escaped or been captured. Trying not to think about the latter possibility, Vidya dashed across to her apartment and went into Sejal's closet. The knot and loose floorboard were exactly where he had said they would be. She pulled up the board and fished out a small cloth bag. It was heavy with *kesh*.

Vidya didn't stop to count it or think about where it had come from. Instead, she flung clothes, toiletries, and a few other items into a carryall and left. She'd told the startled gate guard that she didn't know when—or if—she would be back. Then she hurried away, putting failure behind her.

Now in the stuffy hotel room, Vidya flicked off the terminal. If Sejal and the Children of Irfan had been captured or killed, the news would have been full of the story so everyone would see the futility of defying the Unity. The lack of news meant they had escaped.

Vidya knew she herself could probably never go back to the neighborhood. The Unity guard would want to question her, see if she knew where Sejal had gone. Vidya had no intention of letting the Unity get its hands on her again.

Taking a deep breath, Vidya dumped the coins out on the bed and counted them. Over two thousand *kesh*. A small fortune. A whore's wages. Suddenly Vidya wanted nothing to do with the money and she was seized with an impulse to throw it away. Then practicality intervened. She would need money to live on. If she were careful, two thousand *kesh* would let her eat for two weeks and maybe still have enough to bribe passage off Rust.

But first she needed some questions answered.

Vidya rummaged through the carryall and removed a wide scarf that she expertly twisted into a loose hood around her head. It was a minimal disguise, but she doubted the guard would be looking for her that hard. Sejal was clearly gone, so there was no need to scour the streets for him. There was almost certainly a warrant out for Vidya's arrest. But it was doubtful the guard would conduct house-to-house searches or cordon off streets. As long as she avoided showing her face and paid hard currency for her purchases, she should be all right.

Tucking the energy whip into her pocket, Vidya left the hotel and gratefully inhaled the fresh night air. Salt breezes mixed with the scent of old plankton, and an overwhelming sense of déjà vu stole over her. For a moment she was seventeen years younger, her husband and daughter were newly missing, and she was looking for someone who could ensure the baby growing in her womb would not be Silent, would not disappear. She had failed at that, too. But that was then. Eighteen years of forging a new neighborhood and battling Unity bureaucracy had given her skills and contacts she hadn't possessed before, and she was more adept at dealing with people. First she would find the genegineer who had altered Sejal. Vidya had been too young, too grateful to ask specific questions before. But that, too, was then.

Vidya squared her shoulders and strode off into the night.

A data pad clattered to the kitchen table. The screen glowed serenely, indifferent to the rough treatment, and the black letters of the message continued to march across the clear plastic. Prasad Vajhur steepled brown fingers beneath his chin. He had known this day would come. It had been inevitable. A part of him, however, had put off thinking about it, hoping it wouldn't happen. Now he wished he had thought about what to do when he had had more time to plan.

Prasad left the pad where he had tossed it and wandered out of the tiny kitchen, through the equally tiny living room, and down the corridor toward the bedrooms. Prasad commanded a two-bedroom apartment with a den—luxurious quarters on a base where space was at a premium, but that had been part of the deal. Prasad had definitely had his fill of cramped living quarters.

He eased open the door to the first bedroom and peeped inside. A figure lay curled up under the blankets, breathing heavily in sleep. Night-black hair spilled over the pillow and hung over the edge of the bed. The walls were lined with aquariums of varying sizes, and a rainbow assortment of fish darted, floated, or lazed about their tanks. The soft burble of water and steady hum of filters filled the room.

The door squeaked slightly under Prasad's hand. Prasad tensed, then shook his head with a small smile. He could smash a dozen ceramic plates against the wall and Katsu wouldn't waken, and that was assuming her sleep was normal. When she was in the Dream, Prasad could probably set off a small explosive and she would never notice. Other Silent could be jolted out of the Dream with the proper physical stimulus but not his Katsu. For the hundredth time he wondered if he should speak to her about that. In the last few months, Katsu had been spending more and more time in the Dream. He didn't know what to make of it, and it worried him.

Prasad closed the door, went back to the living room, and stared out one of the small round windows. At this time of day it showed nothing but blackness. Prasad tapped a button next to the glass and a floodlight instantly illuminated the immediate area outside. Half a dozen colorful fruit-fish froze, their fins splayed out in fear. Then they fled into the dark depths. Prasad stared at the bed of red kelp and peat that framed his window and carpeted the ocean floor as far as the floodlight reached. The base was hidden under a peat-covered pile of rock, meaning windows were few and carefully hidden. The fact that Prasad and Katsu's apartment had three of them showed his importance to the project.

At times like this Prasad longed for the days before the Annexation, when he and Vidya took long walks together in the balmy night air. Katsu had grown up completely indoors. An arboretum was no substitute for real weather and wind. Prasad also feared Katsu was lonely, though she had never complained. The only people her age on the station were definitely not suitable companionship.

And now the researchers wanted to harvest her eggs.

Prasad leaned against the cool glass. Soft currents rippled the waving kelp. At times like this he missed Vidya so much it was a physical pain. The worst was not knowing what had happened to her. Was she even alive?

Prasad shut the floodlight off and turned away from the

window. He felt restless. Although it was full night, he left the apartment and wandered up the empty corridor.

All the corridors were painted in bright, cheery colors. Murals and holograms in strategic places gave the illusion of space, and both were changed erratically to ease some of the day-to-day monotony. The base itself was a nest of domes and corridors that snaked in all directions. The layout followed no definite pattern, which had initially confused Prasad, but also served to keep monotony at arm's length. And after seventeen years and a fair amount of silver hairs, Prasad knew every step. His footsteps were hushed by carpet, and the only sound was the faint creaking of ceramic bulkheads as they expanded and contracted under fluctuations in water temperature and density. Prasad ambled aimlessly, not really paying attention to where he was going.

A few minutes' walk up several corridors and down two staircases brought Prasad to a door labeled PROJECT LAB: AUTHORIZED PERSONNEL ONLY. Prasad hesitated. He had more or less intended to visit the arboretum. His feet, however, had led him here. Hesitantly, he touched his thumb to the plate mounted next to the door.

"Authorization accepted," said the computer. "Good evening, Mr. Vajhur."

Prasad stepped inside. Unlike the base itself, the lab was laid out more sensibly—a small grid of offices at the front, larger grid of locker rooms and labs behind them, and the Nursery behind that. Prasad passed his office and the laboratory area. Several of the lab doors were actually airlocks that bore such labels as BIOHAZARD, ANTIVIRAL PROTOCOLS IN EFFECT, and CLEAN-SUITS REQUIRED FOR ENTRY.

Prasad continued back to the Nursery. The door was triple-locked and fully a meter thick. He stared at it for a moment, then pressed his thumb to the plate and held it there. He heard the customary tiny hiss.

"Thumbprint and DNA verified," said the computer. "Welcome, Mr. Vajhur."

With a soft hum, the locks disengaged and the door swung open. Beyond lay a single long corridor. Prasad stepped inside and the door swung shut again.

The word "nursery" always conjured up wooden cradles,

colorful books, and smiling rocking horses in Prasad's mind. The Nursery, however, thoroughly failed to live up to this image. A main corridor, gray and uncarpeted, branched into several rooms. Prasad glanced into the first. A clear plastic barrier broken only by another heavy door divided the room in two. Four bassinets lined the wall on the other side of the barrier along with a changing table stocked with diapers and other infant supplies. No decorations or pictures graced the stark gray walls. No toys took up space beneath the beds. Instead, a cryo-unit lay below each, ready to receive the child in case of an emergency such as a bulkhead breach.

A collared slave woman sat in a rocking chair with a white bundle in her lap and a bottle in her hand. Prasad nodded to her, and she nodded back. He gestured at the bundle. The slave, who was in her late forties and dressed in a bright orange coverall, gently disengaged the bottle and held up the baby.

It looked perfectly normal for a newborn, though Prasad knew better. Somewhere in the lab's network computer lay more information on that baby and its nursery-mates than on any other humans in history—DNA, RNA sequencing patterns, mitochondrial structure, brain development, source of DNA. Prasad would never, ever look up that information. He didn't need it to perform his job, and he didn't want to know which of the children had sprung from him.

The baby opened its mouth in protest at the interrupted feeding. The barrier would have kept Prasad from hearing anything if there had been anything to hear. These babies never made a sound when they cried. The slave brought the infant back to her lap and plied the little bottle. Prasad moved on.

Further down the corridor was another room-and-barrier combination, though this one had five hospital beds in it with the side-rails raised. Toddler-sized bundles made lumps under the sheets, and Prasad had to look closely to see the motion of their breathing. Another female slave dozed in another rocking chair. A large medical supply cupboard lined the back wall, and various pieces of medical equipment lay waiting in the corners.

Prasad continued down the cool corridor, footsteps echoing slightly. At this hour no one bustled about. Dr. Say and Dr. Kri were almost certainly in bed, probably together. They pretended that there was nothing between them, but everyone knew. The only ones up and on duty were the Nursery slaves. Prasad had initially been startled at the presence of slaves. Dr. Say, however, had explained that they could tell only as few people as possible about the lab's location. Free people often had families and they wanted much higher payment to stay on an underwater base for months at a time. Slaves, however, cost the same whether they worked above the water or under it, and they didn't have to be given time away from base. Shock collars ensured they didn't revolt, and even if they did, there was no place for them to go unless they could hotwire a submarine.

Prasad's feet carried him past four more rooms containing barrier, beds, and nurse, then halted at the last room of the Nursery corridor. With a grimace, Prasad realized this was where he had been intending to come all along. This room was the largest yet, with eighteen occupied beds. Five slaves, burly and muscular, stood careful guard. The black-haired figures on the beds were strapped in. Atrophied muscles and tendons shortened from disuse made their limbs thin and withered looking, with clawlike hands that curled under their chins. The fingers twitched like epileptic insects. Prasad stared at them, expressionless, and even as he watched, one of the children opened its eyes. Its head and shoulders came forward as far as the straps would allow, and its mouth twisted open. The neck spasmed, jerking the head about, and a dark tongue quivered between stretched lips. Saliva dribbled down its chin. The barrier was soundproof, though Prasad knew that despite the fact that the child looked like it was screaming, it was absolutely silent.

Silent. Prasad stared, ignoring the sidelong glances of the guards. The children were silent and Silent. They—Prasad, Dr. Say, and Dr. Kri—had made them that way. Everyone knew that a Silent fetus had to come to term in a living mother's womb. It didn't matter what species that being might be, and it didn't matter what technology anyone tried as a substitute for a living mother's voice or heartbeat. Silent fetuses grown in artificial wombs invariably withered and died. Most people assumed that the Silent were, on some level, aware of the minds around them, and the presence of the mother's mind was crucial.

Until the lab came along. When Prasad first met them, Dr. Say and Dr. Kri had barely begun their research, but they had already made several advances. It was simply a matter of brain chemistry. A developing fetus did not actually have to have its mother's mind nearby—it only needed to *think* its mother was nearby.

"All sensation and memory," Dr. Kri had said in his rich, mellow voice, "is nothing but a series of chemical patterns stored in the brain. All we have to do is figure out which chemical pattern the brain of a live-womb fetus creates when it senses its mother nearby, create that chemical sequence ourselves, and transplant it into the brain of a machine-womb fetus."

It hadn't been that simple, of course. Genetic codes—and therefore chemical patterns—varied from fetus to fetus, which meant creating a series of genetically identical embryos. There was also the fact that some gene combinations seemed to thrive better than others. Learning these combinations had taken several years and many failed fetuses. There was also the problem of chemical delivery. They experimented with direct site delivery using microscopic chemical packs slipped into hijacked white blood cells, but in the end, it had been easiest to produce a retrovirus that would bond with—and change—the neural DNA itself, forcing the cells to create their own memory codes.

Prasad had spent his days cutting and splicing genes, many of them his own. Katsu, meanwhile, spent her time in a small nursery area set up within Prasad's lab. A slave woman looked after her needs, but Prasad had wanted his daughter nearby.

Several fetuses were already gestating by the time Prasad had arrived, and it wasn't long before the babies were born. Very early, however, it became clear that something was wrong. The subjects didn't respond to outside stimuli. They rarely moved, and they never, ever cried.

After some study, Dr. Kri came to the conclusion that their brains hadn't developed quite properly. The subjects were barely as intelligent as a fish or a bird. They were certainly not sentient. He had advocated destroying them and starting over. But Prasad had argued vehemently against it. He knew it was because he looked at the infants, perfectly formed but so very quiet, and in them he saw Katsu, but he argued on scientific grounds. Why destroy them when there was more to learn? Dr. Say had agreed and persuaded Dr. Kri.

Other batches of subjects were removed from the machine wombs, but none of them seemed to be intelligent or self-aware. They spent most of their time with their eyes closed and responded only to intense stimuli, especially pain. On the rare occasions when their eyes opened, they were blank and staring. The experiments continued.

Katsu, meanwhile, grew into a toddler and then a child. To Prasad's pride, she seemed to be extremely intelligent, though she was also very quiet. She seemed possessed of a strange patience, perfectly happy to while away the hours completely by herself. Oddly, she rarely asked questions about the world outside the research base. Katsu seemed to accept the fact that trips to the surface were difficult and rare.

The moment she was old enough, Prasad ensured she could access the computer networks through a disguised link that the Unity would not notice, and she seized on it with an almost startling hunger. Not a social child to begin with, Katsu became even more withdrawn with the addition of network access to her life, and Prasad had to limit the amount of time she spent there. He also kept an eye on what she did with her computer time, and discovered she had a passion for marine biology. He arranged trips for her on the base's submersible, a small, bubblelike vehicle, so she could collect samples of fish and plant life.

She was also fascinated by the experimental subjects. Although they did little but lie still in their beds on the other side of the plastic barrier, Katsu would watch them for long periods with her unreadable dark eyes. At first Prasad and the others had tried to shoo her away to her play area, but Katsu always drifted back. Eventually Prasad gave up trying. It was either let her look or lock her out of the lab, and he just couldn't bring himself to leave her completely in someone else's care.

Prasad did worry about Katsu's social development. The

base had little over a dozen other people in it—Drs. Kri and Say, Prasad, a research virologist named Max Garinn, and eleven slaves who cooked, cleaned, and took care of the research subjects. And Dr. Say avoided Katsu. Prasad had never seen her near his daughter. But Katsu didn't seem to mind. She spent time with her computer, her fish, and her father. Except for the test subjects, the other people on the base barely seemed to exist for her.

Just before Katsu's ninth birthday, Prasad and other scientists noticed a change in the lab subjects, the ones from the first batch that Dr. Say had wanted to destroy. At times, they expressed agitation, twitching movements that bordered on convulsions. One day when Prasad was observing, one of them sat up and screamed. Or at least, that was what appeared to happen. The subject opened its mouth wide and had a look of fear on its face, but not a single sound emerged from its throat.

Prasad and the other researchers didn't know what to make of it. Max Garinn, a tidy, blond man with a long mustache he liked to twirl, was especially fascinated. He offered several theories, none of which sounded plausible. Then Katsu, at her customary place near the barrier, spoke up.

"They're in the Dream," she said in her soft voice.

And no matter how much Max Garinn and Prasad urged her, she refused to say more.

Dr. Say immediately reset the medical sensors to read neural activity among the subjects, something she hadn't done before because human Silent never showed direct awareness of the Dream without training. She found increased activity in each subject's right hemisphere, consistent with normal humans in REM sleep and with Silent humans in the Dream. The pons of each subject was also sending a multitude of signals to the thalamus and cerebral cortex, again indicating dream—or Dream—activity.

Excitement reigned in the lab for weeks as the phenomenon was studied. Obviously the early batch of subjects had met with some success—they were able to reach the Dream, and without training. Prasad tried several times to entice Katsu into telling him how she had known, but she continually refused to say.

The same thing happened when the next set of subjects reached their eleventh year, and the next set, and the next. At this point thirty-five subjects were reaching the Dream on a steady basis.

So was Katsu. At age thirteen, two years after the first subjects entered the Dream, she had lain down on her bed and, without help from any drugs Prasad knew about, gone into the Dream herself. She had reported the fact to Prasad at dinner that night in the same tone of voice that she might have used to report the acquisition of a new fish. Astounded, Prasad pressed for details, but Katsu avoided giving them. All she would say was, "They taught me."

And Prasad had to be content with that.

Dr. Say had wanted Prasad to be more persistent, to the extent of forcing the information from her if necessary, but Prasad couldn't bring himself to do it. Katsu's presence in his life was a delicate, fragile thing, something to be honored and cherished. He couldn't bear to raise his voice in her presence, let alone wring information from her.

As time passed, Katsu spent more and more time in the Dream and less on the computer. Prasad had no idea what she did in the Dream, but she seemed none the worse for the time she spent there. At age seventeen, Katsu was a beautiful, serene young woman. Nothing seemed to bother or even startle her, and Prasad could not imagine her any other way.

And now they wanted her eggs.

Prasad's genes were conducive to creating Silent subjects, and Dr. Kri had determined that Katsu's were as well. Not only did she carry both Vidya's and Prasad's rich genetic structures, Katsu additionally carried a bonus—Vidya's mitochondrial DNA. The mitochondria, a tiny cell structure that converts sugar into energy, contains a strand of DNA separate from the cell's nucleus. Mitochondrial DNA, however, is passed down from mother to child. The father contributes nothing to it. This meant that Katsu's mitochondrial DNA was a clone of Vidya's and that Katsu would pass it on to her children one day. Dr. Say wanted to incorporate just Vidya's DNA into more test subjects, and this was a way to do it.

On the other side of the barrier, another subject opened

its mouth in a silent scream. Their blood pressures skyrocketed during these episodes, and their brainwave activity indicated a seizure reminiscent of epilepsy. Prasad still didn't know what to make of it, though Dr. Say claimed to be working on a theory.

They are not sentient, Prasad told himself over and over. *The mental capacity is not there. They aren't aware that they exist any more than a fish or a chicken is.*

But lately Prasad had begun to wonder. How could something nonsentient have so much brainwave activity? How could something without a mind enter the Dream? And how was all this helping Dr. Say and Dr. Kri figure out how to let Silent gestate outside a mother's living womb?

Prasad continued to stare through the barrier. His breath fogged the plastic with warm white mist. Some of those subjects were his children, just as surely as Katsu was his daughter. Were they suffering? Did they feel fear and pain? Lately, he had become more and more sure that they did.

A great restlessness filled Prasad. How long had it been since he had visited the surface? Three years? Four? Suddenly he felt caged in. How had he let himself go on this far?

Then he thought of the surface. It was the surface where wars were waged, where Silent children were ripped from their parents' arms, where innocent people starved because a foreign government desired more resources. Down here everything was safe and hidden. Food was plentiful. His daughter was free to pursue whatever interest she desired.

And what would happen if she desired an interest that took her above the surface? he thought. *What would Dr. Kri say to that?*

Prasad left the lab and walked the quiet corridors back to the apartment. The entire place felt wrong to him now, and he felt a growing restlessness, as if something were coming for him and for Katsu, something that had nothing to do with her eggs or her genes. Should he and Katsu leave the complex? Get out right now? But how could he arrange it?

Prasad Vajhur checked on his daughter one more time—she was still asleep or in the Dream—and went to bed, where he spent a fruitless night trying to sleep.

FOURTEEN

Ship *Post-Script*

The greater your knowledge, the smaller your risk.
—Silent Proverb

"He's going to need a teacher, Ara," Kendi said, trying to keep his temper.

"Not a good idea at this stage," Ara replied firmly.

"What the hell is that supposed to mean?" Kendi demanded. "Sejal has a new form of Silence, and someone needs to teach him how to use it. He's already sixteen years old. He should have started lessons years ago."

Ara set her tea on the small table next to her armchair. Kendi sat across from her in a matching armchair. Ara's quarters always seemed overstuffed to him, with their preponderance of furniture, rugs, bookshelves, and desk space. The place felt stuffy and humid, a far cry from the spartan quarters he himself kept.

"You've answered your own question," Ara said. "Sejal has a new form of Silence. How can anyone teach him how to use it?"

"Silence is Silence," Kendi shot back. "He needs to learn meditation and concentration, no matter what his abilities are. And he needs to start now."

"Have you been in the Dream lately?" Ara asked.

"I've been too busy. Harenn kept us all jumping, trying to get the ship back in order. You're the only one who's been in since . . ." Kendi licked his lips, trying to suppress the lump of sudden sorrow in his throat. "Since Pitr's funeral."

"The Dream has gotten more dangerous since then," Ara said flatly. "There have been more incidents like that pit opening up and that canyon appearing, and now there's some sort of . . . I don't know what to call it. A storm, maybe. It's swallowed up nineteen planets, and their Silent have gone incommunicado. This is not a good time to bring a novice into the Dream."

"I won't be bringing Sejal into the Dream," Kendi shot back, though Ara's description of danger had piqued his curiosity. "He has to learn breathing and meditation, and then we have to figure out what drug cocktail will get him the rest of the way. We have to get started now."

"Kendi," Ara said, switching tactics, "you've never taught anyone before. You're inexperienced."

"So were you at one time. Look, I've had all the courses on how to teach the Silent, and I've reviewed the material. I have to start somewhere. If I get stuck, I'll call for help."

"Kendi—"

"Why are you being so stubborn about this?" Kendi interrupted. "Ara, what's going on? I know there are things you haven't told me. Is this related to any of that secrecy bullshit?"

"There's no need to swear," Ara said primly.

"The hell there isn't," Kendi snapped. "You've been leading us by the nose for days and telling us next to nothing. You even kept quiet about this new thing in the Dream until now." His voice softened. "That isn't like you. The Real People—my people—have a saying: 'It's far easier for people to do what's necessary when they understand why it must be done.' "

"Irfan said that," Ara murmured.

"She got it from us," Kendi said without missing a beat. "Look, the point is you know I'm right. Keeping information from us—from me—isn't helping here. What has the Empress been telling you?"

"Did I say this had anything to do with the Empress?"

"Dammit!" Kendi slammed his fist on the arm of his chair, but the padded surface muffled the noise and crippled the dramatic impact. "Fine. Keep your secrets. But I'm taking Sejal as a student."

Ara gave him a cool stare. "You can't do that."

"Oh yeah? Try this. *The Law of the Children,* section four, subsection six, paragraph two point one, and I quote: 'Any Silent who has achieved the rank of Sibling or higher may begin instructing students.' I'm still a full Brother, last I looked. Section eight, subsection twelve, paragraph four point one: 'Any Sibling who locates and brings a fellow Silent to the ranks of the Children has the option of becoming the new Silent's teacher, provided such an arrangement is agreeable to both parties.' "

"Just looked it all up, I take it."

"Look," Kendi said. "Sejal wants me for his teacher. He said so when I asked him this morning. The regs are on my side. For once."

"There are too many unknowns here, Kendi. I won't let you."

"You can't stop me," Kendi countered, "unless you throw me in the brig. Oh, wait—we don't have one. Shucks."

"I'll confine you to quarters."

Kendi almost countered with the fact that he could press charges against Ara for breaking protocols. But, he realized, that would probably only spur Ara to dig in and become even more stubborn, and the fight would only escalate from there. Five years ago he would have fought, but despite what Ara liked to think, Kendi had learned at least a few things about human nature and the art of diplomacy.

"Ara," he said, "the law is very clear here. I found Sejal, I get to teach him. You know that's the case. If there's something you haven't told me that might change my mind, now's your chance."

"Why are you so interested in this boy?" Ara asked. "You do know he isn't related to you."

Kendi shrugged, ignoring the stab of disappointment awakened by Ara's words. "I like Sejal. He's a nice kid. We click when we're together."

"And are you sure you want to change that relationship? Being a teacher is different from being a friend."

"I want to show him the Dream," Kendi said simply.

"And you want the advancement opportunity."

Kendi gave her a hard look. Although he was a full Brother among the Children, Kendi didn't intend to remain a Sibling forever. As a Father, he would be allowed to scout on his own for other Silent outside the Dream. As a Father Adept, he would be able to lead a crew of recruiters as Ara did. It was a strict rule among the Children of Irfan, however, that new monks had to pay back all that the Children had done for them—education, room, board, and Silent training—and no one advanced beyond Sibling before this debt was repaid.

Repayment was partly accomplished through performing the intersystem communication work that remained the stock in trade for Silent everywhere and was the primary source of income for the monastery. Another rule, this one unwritten, stated that one paid back by paying forward. Taking on a student was the primary way of doing this, though finding and recruiting was another method. A fair number of Siblings were unsuited to recruiting or teaching, and remained Brothers and Sisters—field agents, communication experts, and researchers in the main. Brother Kendi, however, had his own agenda. Father Kendi would have the freedom and resources to search for his family on his own. Father Adept Kendi would be able to commandeer others to help him.

And successfully teaching a student with a heretofore unknown form of Silence would bring him a certain amount of notoriety, meaning the unofficial pay-forward period would be shortened considerably.

"I can't deny I'm looking to advance," Kendi said calmly. "But that isn't the main reason I'm doing this. You know me better than that, Ara."

Ara sighed. "I guess I can't stop you. Teach him, then. Just be careful."

Kendi rose and turned to go.

"And Kendi," Ara said. Kendi paused and looked back. "I've taught over a dozen students. I'm here if you need advice."

Kendi nodded his thanks and left.

Mother Adept Araceil Rymar emptied her teacup into the tiny sink. Kendi had learned a great deal, she had to give him that. Not long ago, he would have dug in his heels and kept on fighting, which would have only made her want to fight back. Now, however, he had learned how to sidestep this problem. Still, he hadn't noticed how she'd steered the conversation away from herself and levered it back on him.

Youth and beauty will forever lose to age and treachery, she thought wryly.

Ara stared down at the little brown trickles left in the bottom of the sink. She'd had the perfect opportunity to tell Kendi about the Empress's order, and still she found herself dodging the issue. Before that, there had been the excuse of needing to repair the ship and taking care of Pitr's memorial service and it had been easy to tell herself she'd take care of the situation as soon as all that was done. Now, however, she still found she couldn't do it.

Why burden him? she thought. *It's my problem, and there isn't anything he can do to solve it. He'll have his hands full with Sejal.*

She had hoped to talk Kendi out of teaching the boy. Not only was Sejal's Silence an unknown, it wouldn't be a good idea for the two of them to get too close. Not if Sejal might . . . die. Unfortunately, Kendi had been correct about the law. If she had continued to refuse him—and as Captain of the ship, she could technically refuse any request she wanted—her refusal would be overruled the moment they arrived back at the monastery. Besides, Kendi was, in many ways, another son to her, and she hated fighting with him.

Ara rubbed a hand over her face. The strain was starting to tell on her. She felt tired all the time, and she barely ate. It was difficult to summon the concentration necessary to enter the Dream, and she found herself avoiding the Dream in any case because lately it always seemed to involve messages to the Empress.

Her chime sounded. "Come in," Ara said automatically.

The door slid open, revealing Chin Fen. Behind him stood Harenn, eyes half closed, veil covering her lower face. Ara had ordered that whenever Fen left his quarters, he was to be accompanied by a crew member. He had no computer access, and no door on the *Post-Script* would respond to his voice or thumb. Electronic shackles still adorned his neck, wrists, and ankles, and everyone on board except Sejal carried a master unit.

"Harenn says the repairs are finished," Fen said. "Does that mean you have time to talk to me?"

Ara met Harenn's eyes over Fen's shoulder. She nodded and withdrew.

"I can clear space on my calendar." Ara sat. "Have a chair. Would you like some tea?"

Fen obeyed, choosing the seat Kendi had just vacated. "The only thing I'd like is some information. Nobody on this ship will tell me anything but their names. I've been cooped up in that tiny room for four days, and I'm going insane."

"Ask away, then."

"What organization are you with?"

"The Children of Irfan."

"I *knew* it," Fen howled. "I didn't believe for a second that you'd left them, or that if you did, you'd become a Unity trader. It just didn't fit."

"I didn't figure on running across someone I knew," Ara told him.

"Good thing you did," Fen pointed out. "Otherwise you would never have found Sejal and his mother. All those lunches. You were playing me for a sap."

Ara shrugged again. "You got free meals."

"Bitch," Fen said affably. "So what happens to me now?"

"Frankly, I have no idea," Ara said. "I can't trust you, Fen. You must know that."

"Why not? I helped you. I stuck my neck out for you."

"But I don't understand why you did it."

Fen looked faintly puzzled. "Because I *like* you, Ara. I've always liked you." He gave a small smile that deepened the wrinkles around his mouth. "And because you were my chance to get the hell out of the Unity. I had this half-baked idea that if I was nice enough to you, you'd get me off-planet. My motivations were selfish. Is *that* believable?"

"I'm still not sure," Ara said, ignoring his attempt at humor. "Listen, Fen—all I know is that you came barreling out of nowhere and jumped aboard my ship just as it was about to take off. Your timing was too perfect. How do I know you're not a Unity spy?"

"Look," Fen pleaded, "I knew you were looking for Sejal and his mother a long time before you left Rust. If I were a Unity spy, I would've reported you to the Unity right away. You'd have been arrested, I'd have been promoted, and they'd have gotten Sejal."

"You have a point," Ara admitted grudgingly. "But I still don't know what to do with you."

Fen shrugged. "Take me back to Bellerophon."

"Well, obviously. I'm sure the Grandparent Adepts will take you off my hands. I meant that I don't know what to do with you *now.* We're still eleven days out."

"How about taking the shackles off me and giving me access to entertainment programs or something? I'm going crazy with boredom."

Ara wordlessly pressed a button on the master unit. Fen's collar and shackles opened and thumped softly on the carpet.

"Thanks." He rubbed his wrist. "Nice quarters, by the way. You're ranked at Mother Adept these days? Or have they changed the rules about crewing a ship since I left the order?"

"Mother Adept Araceil Rymar at your service."

"I'm impressed," Fen whistled. "I'll bet lots of things have changed around the monastery in"—he coughed pointedly—"years."

Ara snorted in spite of herself. "Not as many things as you might think. Vasco Beliz is still head of the research division."

"Beliz?" Fen said incredulously. "He was older than refrigerator mold when I left. He must be ancient by now."

"He says he hasn't seen a refresher," Ara said wickedly, "but you know he has."

"What about Nowma Reed?"

"Retired. Long time ago."

They continued to talk, and to her surprise, Ara found she actually enjoyed it. She didn't have to remember previous lies or try to steer the conversation in any particular direction, and that was a tremendous relief. It was also nice putting off going back into the Dream. Now that Sejal's existence was pretty much common knowledge, at least among the Silent, the Empress's requirement of secrecy was no longer necessary, and Ara would have to report to the Council of Irfan everything that had happened—the discovery of Sejal, his odd powers, Kendi's adamant desire to teach him. Ara wasn't looking forward to it. So far she'd used the excuse of having to repair the ship and consult with the Empress as reasons to put it off, and Fen was a good excuse to put it off yet again.

Fen seemed different, too. Gone was the fawning, puppyish attitude that she had found so irritating. He was far more engaging when he wasn't hitting on her or going out of his way to impress.

"Is that Benjamin's holo?" Fen said at one point, nodding toward Ara's desk.

Ara automatically twisted in her chair to look at it, though she knew it was there. "That's him, yes."

"You told me you fell out of touch with him," Fen said. "What really happened?" He paused. "Is it bad?"

Emotions welled up in Ara's chest. For a brief, odd moment Pitr's face flashed before her, and all she could do was nod at Fen.

"I'm sorry," Fen murmured. "God. How did it happen?"

"Hull breach," Ara said, barely managing to keep her voice flat. "Some clueless idiot didn't perform the inspection properly and missed a weakened section. After a week in vacuum, the plate blew and took Benjamin with it. The inspector was charged with negligence, but that didn't help Benjamin any."

Fen looked stricken. "God," he said again. "I haven't seen him in years, but all of a sudden I feel like shit. It must have been horrible for you."

"It was," Ara said. "But we cope. I named my son after him."

"You have a son? Now this one you need to explain. I can't imagine you've got a husband who lets you keep a holo of your . . . former fiancé out in plain sight."

"Ah. Well, that's a story. You want some tea now?"

"Not if you have anything stronger. I suspect I'll need something to cushion my system against more shocks."

FIFTEEN

The Dream

True love, like a cough, cannot be long concealed.
—Ched-Balaar Proverb

Grandfather Adept Melthine always held Council meetings in a medieval stone hall. Brightly woven tapestries hung from the walls to hush echoes, and two enormous fireplaces stood at either end of the hall. Shuttered windows opened on a lovely green garden. One of the walls was purposefully blank: as a result, the cracked chaos on the horizon was not visible to anyone present. Kendi, however, could feel its wrongness, just as he could hear the muffled whispering of millions of Silent in the Dream.

The meeting hall had no doors because the Silent didn't need them in the Dream. A circle of fifteen sitting places made a ring in the center of the room. Some seats were common padded chairs for humans. Two other chairs were only large enough to seat a human child, and one chair was tall enough that Kendi's feet wouldn't touch the floor if he sat in it. Still other seats were simple cushions piled on the floor.

Grandfather Melthine, as head of the Council of Irfan, occupied a thronelike chair just in front of one of the fireplaces. He looked like his title—tall and silver haired, with kind blue eyes, and a lined face. A twisted walking stick leaned against his chair, and he wore a somber brown robe embroidered with fine gold thread. An amethyst ring, the symbol of his office, gleamed on his right hand.

Kendi sat next to Ara a quarter-turn clockwise around the circle from Grandfather Melthine. Because Kendi could not teleport within the Dream, Ara had been forced to bring him into the Council chamber, and it had taken Kendi a great effort of will not to throw up at the Grandfather Adept's feet. The pangs of nausea were only now wearing off. He and Ara were both dressed in the formal brown robes and gold disk medallions that marked them as Children of Irfan. Kendi wore a ring with a stone of yellow amber, indicating his rank as a Brother. Ara's ring was blue lapis lazuli, for her rank as a Mother Adept.

Despite his tension and the recent nausea, Kendi suppressed a yawn. He couldn't seem to get a good night's sleep lately. Every night he bolted awake at least once, slicked with sweat and breathing hard. He supposed he should talk to someone about it, maybe a doctor, but so much was going on lately, it didn't seem likely he'd be able to.

One by one, other Silent appeared in the center of the circle. The first four were human, two women and two men. They were followed by a Ched-Balaar, the species that had beat humans to Bellerophon almost a thousand years ago. They were a centauroid race, tall and wide. The Ched-Balaar, a male, blinked a moment to get his bearings. His body was covered with short blond fur, and his forelegs were longer than his hind legs. All four feet were heavily clawed, suitable for digging dirt and ripping logs. His neck was almost two meters long and flexible, topped with a round head impressed with two wide, round eyes and a single round hole in the forehead. He had wide, shovellike jaws and broad flat teeth. A pair of muscular arms were set below the neck. They ended in four-fingered hands. An indigo fluorite ring graced one finger, meaning he was a Grandfather in the order.

The Ched-Balaar settled in among a pile of cushions next to Grandfather Adept Melthine just as another Ched-Balaar appeared, and another. In all, four Ched-Balaar showed up, all ranked as Grandparent or Grandparent Adept.

The remaining four chairs were taken up by other races—a short, furry Grandmother Adept who was the same race as the Empress's Seneschal, a ponderous elephantine Grandfather with wrinkled red skin, a multilegged Grandmother who resembled a cat-size centipede, and an upright, lizardly Grandfather Adept who came to Kendi's waist.

Kendi fingered the amber ring he had conjured for his own finger, realizing with some nervousness that he was the lowest-ranked member of the order present. Then he shook his head. The Real People taught that there was no need for rank and order. Such things were artificial and arbitrary. Only the individual knew how well one's talents had been developed or how much one had learned. But Kendi had spent over half his life among people who took rank and order very seriously, and it was difficult to hold the concepts at arm's length.

Once everyone had settled in, Melthine rapped his twisted walking stick on the floor, and all eyes turned to him.

"Well, we all know why we're here," Melthine said. "No point in wasting time and drugs. Brother Kendi, Mother Adept Araceil reports that you have located a new Silent who has some unusual abilities. She also reports that, against her better judgment, you wish to take this Silent as your student."

Kendi glanced at Ara. Her face remained expressionless. When she had first told him that Melthine was convening this Council meeting, Kendi had wondered if Ara had gone to Grandfather Melthine to tattle on him, complain that he was acting against her wishes. But then he had realized that Ara would have been lax in her duties if she didn't report something so clearly unusual as Sejal Dasa. He also realized that he had begun to think of Ara as an adversary, and that disturbed him. They had certainly had their share of disagreements, but he would never have suspected her of trying to sabotage his career until now. He didn't like it.

"I want to make it clear, Brother Kendi, that you're not in trouble," Grandfather Melthine continued. "I think it's best if we hear what happened directly from you instead of through a recorded report. That's why you're here."

Kendi relaxed a bit. "Yes, Grandfather. Where should I begin?"

"When you first noticed something odd in the Dream, if you please."

The monks in the hall turned their full attention on Kendi. Eyes of varying sizes, shapes, and colors focused on him, and Kendi's mouth dried up. Public speaking had never been one of his strengths. Ara conjured up a bottle of water and handed it to him. He sipped from it, grateful for both the water and the gesture. Without a word, Ara had told him that she still knew him as well as any mother, and that her support lay firmly in his corner.

Kendi told the story. He left out a few details, such as the rent boys and the fact that he had suspected Sejal was his nephew. He also glossed over the Unity prison, though his heart sped up noticeably when he mentioned his arrest. Occasionally Melthine or one of the other Council members asked him to clarify a point, but for the most part they listened in attentive silence. Kendi ended with a summary of his conversation with Ara about teaching Sejal.

"I *am* within my rights to take him as my student," he concluded with a note of defiance in his voice. "The law is very clear."

The Ched-Balaar Grandfather who had first appeared in the circle spoke up in a deep, thrumming voice. "Such are unusual circumstances, Brother Kendi. You are new to instruction, and the young man requires special training for this Silence most unusual. Perhaps someone with greater experience is more appropriate."

"Mother Adept Araceil has offered to advise me." Kendi's insides felt shaky, but his voice remained firm. "I know I'm new to teaching, but I'm not foolish. I have no problem with shouting for help if I get in over my head."

"Is Sejal causing the disturbances in the Dream?" asked the Ched-Balaar Grandfather.

Kendi slowly shook his head. "I don't know. I'm not an expert in Dream mechanics. But I don't think he is. Tremendous pain and suffering emanates from the disturbance. Sejal doesn't seem to be in enough agony to cause anything like it."

"Isn't it possible that it's subconscious?" Grandfather Melthine said.

"I suppose," Kendi said, still dubious. "But it doesn't feel right. Anyone in that much subconscious pain, it seems to me, wouldn't be able to function well in the solid world either, and Sejal seems perfectly fine to me."

"Does the Empress know of this boy?" the centipede asked.

"She does, Grandmother Nik," Ara put in. Was that a quaver in her voice? "I have been in constant contact with her Imperial Majesty since we arrived on Rust. She has been receiving from me the reports that I've only recently made to the Council because her original orders were for me to keep Sejal's existence a secret. That order has been rescinded."

This brought on a storm of startled whispers among the Councilors. Melthine let it continue for a moment, then rapped his walking stick on the stone floor for attention.

"What is the Empress's assessment, then?" he asked.

"She wants him watched carefully and she wants me to continue reporting to her."

"What is her attitude toward the boy?" Grandmother Nik asked. Her Dream speech was high-pitched and full of little clicks. Kendi knew that in the solid world, he wouldn't even be able to hear her voice, let alone understand her language. "Did she give you any instructions regarding him?"

Ara hesitated. "With respect, Grandmother, this would not be . . . an appropriate venue to answer that."

Kendi glanced at her. She was doing it again—hiding information. He considered pressing her here in the Dream where it was impossible to lie, then discarded the idea. Pressing her was a good idea, but not here before the entire Council. He had the feeling that it would be best for him and Ara to appear united when it came to Sejal.

"Very well," Grandmother Nik said gravely. "I respect your judgment, Mother Adept. But I will require the information at a more appropriate time."

"Yes, Grandmother," Ara said quietly.

"Does anyone else have any questions for Brother Kendi or Mother Ara?" Melthine asked. No one did. "Then I adjourn this meeting. Mother Ara and Brother Kendi, I do want to discuss this further with both of you when you arrive on Bellerophon. Please alert me to your arrival and let me know if anything more happens."

"Yes, Grandfather," Kendi and Ara replied in unison.

Melthine vanished and the room went with him, leaving behind a flat, featureless plain. In the distance, no longer hidden by the castle wall, lay the deep canyon that had opened almost beneath Kendi's feet and the cracked darkness that covered it. Ara had said there were nineteen planets hidden by the chaos, either inside it or surrounded by it, no one knew for certain which. No one had been able to communicate with the Silent on those planets, which were part of a government that called itself the People's Planetary Democracy. The Independence Confederation, the Empire of Human Unity, and the Hadric Kingdoms had sent courier ships to investigate, but the fastest of the slipships wouldn't arrive for at least another week, and it would take further time for them to come back. Until then, the planets remained incommunicado.

One by one, the other Council members vanished. Ara and Kendi faced each other on the blank plain.

After a few heartbeats, both of them said, "My turf?" and laughed.

"We were at your place last time," Kendi pointed out. "Come on. The Outback isn't far."

"It would be even closer if you'd learn to transport yourself," Ara grumbled, but fell into step beside him. They walked in companionable silence, and Kendi carefully called to his Outback. After a short time, the terrain changed. The plain became sandy soil dotted with scrubby plant life. The sky deepened to a stunning blue, and the gold sun shone with glittering brilliance above them. Kendi welcomed the dry heat after the cool, stony castle. His clothes melted away, leaving him barefoot in a loincloth. Ara's robe changed into a white cloth strip over breasts and loins. The outfit worked well on Ara's round form and dark skin.

A high, free scream overhead announced the presence of Kendi's falcon. He put his arm up, and she dove down to land on it. He set her on his shoulder and continued walking. A short time later, they reached the cliff and the entrance to Kendi's cave. They entered together and sat down on the sandy floor just inside the cave's mouth. The walls were dry, and the air was cooler. The falcon leaped off his shoulder to perch on one of the rocks and preen.

"*Is* Sejal causing the disturbance?" Ara asked without preamble.

"I've thought about that a lot," Kendi answered, "and the idea just doesn't feel right. I can feel the pain in that blackness all the way over here, and I just don't get the feeling that Sejal is hurting like that. Not even Harenn hurts that much."

Ara nodded, her dark hair melding with the cave shadows. "I feel the same. And you can hear more than one voice wailing in the disturbance."

"What kind of group could cause such a thing?" Kendi asked. "And why?"

"No way to tell right now." Ara sighed. "Unless someone is willing to risk going inside the disturbance to look around."

Kendi shook his head emphatically. "Not me."

"My sentiments exactly." Ara shifted position and sat cross-legged. "All right, let's get this over with. Ask me what you *really* want to know."

"Are you going to answer me this time?" Kendi said warily. "No evasions? No changes in subject."

"I'll try, Kendi." Ara sighed again. "This will be hard for me, and I want you to keep that in mind."

The obvious pain in her dark eyes made sudden sympathy well up in Kendi's chest. The topic was painful for her. Why hadn't he seen that before? He could only have been making it worse, pushing at her the way he had. Shame made him fidget uncomfortably. Impulsively he reached out and took her hand the way she had so often taken his during his early, daunting excursions into the Dream.

"I don't want to hurt you, *Mother* Ara," he said. "Look, if it'll be that painful to—"

"No. It needs to be over and done with." She wet her lips. "Kendi, the Empress told me to watch and evaluate Sejal. She said that if, in my opinion, Sejal poses a threat to the Confederation . . ." She trailed off.

"Yes?" Kendi prompted, leaning forward. "The Empress said?"

"If Sejal poses a threat to the Confederation," Ara said again, forcing the words out one by one, "I am to kill him."

Kendi blinked, uncertain he had heard correctly. He turned her words over in his mind, not quite comprehending.

"Kill Sejal?" was all he could say.

"Yes," Ara said softly.

The simple word crashed over Kendi like a tidal wave.

He dropped Ara's hand. "You can't mean that," he sputtered. "*Kill* him? He hasn't done anything."

"I don't have to kill him," Ara said, "if he isn't a threat to the Confederation."

"How are you going to decide?" Kendi snapped. "And how are you going to kill him? Have you thought about that?"

"Every night since she gave me that damn order," Ara cried. "I don't want this responsibility. I didn't ask for it. But it's mine, Kendi. I can't do anything to change that."

"So tell the Empress that Sejal isn't a threat," Kendi yelled.

"It isn't that simple." Ara was wringing her hands now, but Kendi's earlier sympathy had been swallowed up by anger.

"Yes, it is," he said fiercely. "Choose not to kill him."

Ara closed her eyes. "Kendi, weren't your people vegetarian until they were forced into the desert by invaders?"

"What? What's that got to do with—"

"Just answer, Kendi. It relates."

Kendi nodded reluctantly. "Well, yeah. The Real People inhabited the coasts of Australia until the European whites forced them inland. The Outback didn't have enough edible plant life to support the tribes, so they ate meat for the first time. But animals aren't . . . aren't . . ."

He trailed off, unable to finish the sentence. Here in the Dream he couldn't lie. The Real People thought of animals and humans as equals. Taking animal life was no different from taking human life, but sometimes sacrifice was necessary on the road of survival. Sometimes the sacrifice was animal, and sometimes it was human.

"Help me, Kendi," Ara said in a soft voice. "You can help me—and help Sejal in the bargain."

"How?" Kendi demanded.

"You're Sejal's teacher. Make sure he understands what his power means and how to use it wisely. And make sure he follows the precepts of Irfan. If he does that, he won't be a threat to anyone." She paused. "But don't tell him about the Empress. If he knew, he would hate us, and that *would* make him a threat."

Kendi had opened his mouth to disagree, then snapped it shut. Ara was entirely correct. Again.

"Well then," Kendi said, rising. "I guess I'd better get to it."

Ara nodded and vanished, leaving brief Dream ripples in her place. Kendi was about to do the same when an odd patch of shadow farther back in the cave caught his attention. He peered closely at it. Cold fingers trickled down the back of his neck and made his hair stand on end. Was someone there?

Kendi held out his hand. There would be a burning torch in his hand, the shaft rough, the flame bright. A soft pop, and it was so.

The torchlight flickered and danced, but the patch of shadow retained an angular, motionless regularity. Kendi cautiously moved closer. Behind him, the falcon continued to preen.

"Who's there?" Kendi waved the torch forward, a definite tremble in his hand. Perhaps he should conjure up a weapon. Perhaps he should—

Kendi inhaled sharply. The shadow was a black iron grating that stretched across the back of the cave.

a scream and a cry and the knife flashed silver, then red

Kendi's throat thickened and he backed away. It wasn't real. This wasn't part of his reality. The black iron did not, would not, exist.

It remained stubbornly where it was. The falcon suddenly took off with a harsh clatter of wings that made Kendi jump. She fled out the cave's mouth.

a tiny cry quickly silenced

Kendi flung the torch down and ran. Sand and soil rushed beneath the soles of his feet, but always he knew the black iron lay behind him.

If it be in my best interest and in the interest of all life everywhere, Kendi thought, *let me leave the Dream.*

And he was standing in his room aboard the *Post-Script,* spear propped beneath one knee. Sweat drenched his body and salt stained his cheeks. Slowly, Kendi disengaged the spear, dried himself off, and got dressed. Already the image of the iron bars was fading from his mind, and he firmly decided to let it go.

* * *

The cave vanished, taking Padric's rock with it and leaving an empty plain. Padric Sufur uncoiled himself and flicked his tongue. His scaly body felt limp with relief. That had been close. Kendi was sensitive, powerful, and it had obviously been foolish to try to hide in his Dream. Padric didn't understand the significance of the iron grating that had frightened Kendi off, but he wasn't going to question a gift. If Kendi had explored the cave any farther, Padric would certainly have been exposed.

He coiled back up into a tight spiral and rested his head on his own back. So the orders of the Empress were still in full force, and Ara wanted them kept secret from Sejal. It was good strategy, if simplistic. Like Ara said, Sejal would almost certainly hate the Children of Irfan if he learned one of them had been ordered to kill him. Yes, he certainly would.

Hissing happily to himself, Padric Sufur summoned up his concentration and vanished from the Dream.

The ancient rhythm was slow and soothing. Kendi could have had the computer play a recorded loop, but it was more authentic to have the drum thud and vibrate in his hands. Sejal sat propped up on his bed, the position he had found most comfortable for meditation—and one that did not allow him to nod off. His legs stretched straight in front of him and his hands were folded in his lap. A gold ring with a ruby stone encircled one finger. The ring, which had once been Kendi's, indicated that Sejal was now officially Kendi's student. A strange sense of *déjà vu* stole over Kendi as he beat the drum's ancient rhythm. For a moment, he was a student again and Ara, his teacher, was beating the drum.

Kendi glanced at the readout monitor on the floor, which interpreted data from the band around Sejal's right wrist. According to the brainwave patterns, Sejal was deep in a trance. The young man was a quick study.

Sejal, of course, had been overjoyed five days ago to hear that the Council had approved and acknowledged Kendi as his teacher. Kendi, still a bit shaken from the Dream, had put a wan smile on his face and forced himself to concentrate on his student.

The student Ara might have to kill.

Abruptly Kendi shifted the drum rhythm to a jarring 7/4 rhythm. Sejal's brain patterns didn't change. Kendi halted the drum altogether. Still no change. Kendi put two fingers into his mouth and whistled so shrilly his own ears rang. No change.

Kendi nodded, impressed. Five days of steady practice had done their job. Sejal could trance so deeply that nothing short of pain or a double snap of Kendi's fingers—a prearranged posthypnotic signal—could disturb him. Sejal had definite talent. It had taken Kendi over two months of practice before he was able to achieve that level of trancing. Within a couple of months, Sejal might be ready to enter—

The monitor beeped for Kendi's attention. He glanced at it, and his eyes widened. His heart jumped. According to the brain monitor, Sejal had entered REM sleep, but his physiological signs indicated he was awake.

Sejal had entered the Dream.

Kendi bolted to his feet and fled the room. His shoes made slapping sounds on the floor and he sprinted for his own quarters.

"Peggy-Sue!" he shouted as he ran. "Open intercom to Mother Ara, Sister Gretchen, and Sister Trish. We have an emergency here!" He skidded around a corner, stabbed the entry plate by his door with one thumb, and shoved the doors open when they didn't slide fast enough. "Sejal's entered the Dream."

"What?" Trish asked.

"How the hell did he do that?" Gretchen said.

"You didn't give him any drugs, did you?" Ara demanded.

Kendi yanked open the medicine chest in his quarters and snatched up a dermospray. "I'm not stupid, Ara. He got in there by himself. Meet me on my t—"

The room spun and Kendi staggered. The dermospray clattered to the floor as he flung out a hand to steady himself on the sink. It felt as if he had been shoved from behind.

!KeNdi!

"Sejal?" he gasped. The voice had come from all around him.

"Meet you on your turf?" Trish asked, finishing his earlier sentence. *"I'll be there as soon as I can."*

!!keNDI!!

There was a sharp jerk, and Kendi found himself on an empty street. Nausea washed over him and he dropped retching to his knees. His hands wavered, and for a moment he saw the paving stones through them. The sensation was exactly what he felt whenever he moved instantly through the Dream. He closed his eyes and concentrated. He was *here,* everything else was *there.* He was in *this* spot at *this* time.

The nausea abated. Kendi got slowly to his feet and glanced around. Where the hell was he? Colorful stalls lined the pavement, but not a single person was in sight. It was the market on Rust. The place was completely, eerily quiet except for barely audible whispering. In the distance above and beyond the buildings was an area of blackness that looked like it had been cracked with a hammer. Red light glowed through the cracks.

This was the Dream.

"All life." Cold stole over Kendi. He hadn't visited the Dream since the . . . incident in the cave. It wasn't that he'd been afraid. What was to fear? He'd just been too busy with Sejal.

So why was he cold?

!!kendI!!

The world *twisted* and suddenly Kendi was in the apartment Sejal had shared with his mother. Dry heaves forced him to hands and knees, and it was several moments before he regained his equilibrium. Outside the windows, the sky was dark and streets were empty. Kendi staggered to his feet. It had to be Sejal. There was no other explanation. Except no Silent could snatch someone else into the Dream. It was impossible.

Impossible, he thought in wonder, *doesn't seem to apply to Sejal.*

Like the street, the tiny apartment seemed to be completely empty. The air was humid and stuffy and the place smelled of curry. Kendi glanced around uncertainly.

"Sejal?" he called. "Are you here?"

!!KeNDI heLp ME!!

The voice seemed to come from everywhere and nowhere.

"Sejal," Kendi said, forcing himself to keep a calm tone of voice, "listen carefully. I need you to relax. Relax and breathe."

No answer. Kendi was pretty sure what the problem was. Sejal's mind had not yet learned how to form a body for him in the Dream, and he was wandering discorporate. If he stayed in that state long enough, the Dream would stretch and thin his mind like the wind dispersing a thread of smoke.

"Imagine yourself, your body," Kendi said carefully. "Think about your feet and legs, how they connect and how they move. Think about your stomach and chest, how they feel and how they breathe. Think about your arms and shoulders, where they are and what they do. Think about your neck and head, how they look and what they see. Your body is *here,* everything else is *there.* You are *this,* the world is *that.*"

Kendi realized he was pacing and made himself stop.

"I am going to count. When I say *three,* you will be standing next to me. One . . . two . . . *three.*"

With a soft *pop,* Sejal appeared in the room with his eyes tightly shut. He was wearing the tight, ragged clothes Kendi had first seen him in. The Dream rippled briefly around him, but he seemed to be fine. Kendi's knees went weak with relief. Sejal's blue eyes popped open. He stared at Kendi for a moment, then burst out crying.

"God!" he sobbed. "God, I was . . . I was *everywhere.*"

Kendi, ready for the reaction, put an arm around Sejal's shoulder and guided him to sit on the couch. "Don't worry now," he soothed. "You're safe."

After a time, Sejal calmed down. "I'm all right," he said. "Sorry."

"It's okay," Kendi told him. "That's what I'm here for. I freaked out on Ara's shoulder plenty of times."

Sejal looked around. "Where are we? How did we get back ho— back to Rust?"

"We're here because you created this place," Kendi told him. "This is the Dream."

"The Dream?" Sejal echoed. "How?"

"I was going to ask you," Kendi said. Now that the initial crisis was over, Kendi had time to think about other matters, and his earlier tension remained. Sejal had yanked Kendi into the Dream and Kendi wondered if that meant he would be unable to leave it again.

"What's the last thing you remember before everything got strange?" he asked, keeping his voice calm.

Sejal shifted and the couch cushions creaked. "I was in a trance. You were beating the drum." He paused. "Then I heard something. It sounded like someone was calling me. You changed the drum rhythm, and I heard it again. I sort of . . . reached for it, and suddenly everything went crazy. I don't know how to describe it. It was like every place I'd ever been was rushing around me and voices were pulling at me and the wind was ripping me apart."

"Then what?"

Sejal furrowed his brow. "I needed help, and I called for you. I could kind of feel you. I knew where you were, and I called to you."

"I heard you," Kendi said. "We call that *knocking.*"

"Then I got really scared and I wanted you there. Like I said, I could feel you, so I reached for you and . . . and I *pulled.* Then I heard your voice telling me what to do. I did it, and next thing I know I'm standing in the living room. Are you okay? Did I do something wrong?"

Kendi shook his head. "I'm not sure how to answer that."

~Kendi?~

It was Ara's voice.

"We're here," he called. "Can you find us?"

The Dream rippled, and Ara popped into existence. Sejal drew back from her slightly.

"What happened?" she demanded. "Is everyone all right?"

"We're fine," Kendi said, and explained what had happened. Just as he was reaching the end of it, Trish and Gretchen appeared, meaning he had to repeat everything. Then Sejal told his version. Kendi noticed that even in the Dream Trish had dark circles around her eyes. She obviously hadn't been sleeping well since Pitr's death.

"How," Gretchen asked, "did Sejal pull you into the Dream, Kendi?"

Kendi shook his head. "I don't know. It might be an offshoot of his ability to possess people. I mean, we send our minds out of the Dream to take another Silent. In a way, he's doing something similar."

Sejal said nothing.

"We shouldn't talk about this here," Ara said decisively. "The instability has grown, and it's too dangerous to stay."

Gretchen turned to Sejal. "Are you creating it?"

"Creating what?" he asked, bewildered.

"The black cloud," Trish said. Her voice was quiet. "Didn't you see it?"

Sejal nodded. "Yeah, but I thought it was just . . . part of the landscape or something. I don't think I created it. I don't even know how I created all this." He gestured at the apartment.

"Reflex," Kendi explained. "When most Silent first visit the Dream, they create familiar, safe places. Eventually you'll be able to make whatever environment you want, but for now—"

"Let's discuss it later," Ara interrupted. "Kendi, can you get back out of the Dream?"

"I don't know," Kendi admitted nervously.

"Try," Ara urged. "We'll guide Sejal out."

Kendi closed his eyes and gathered his concentration despite a pounding heart. *If it is in my best interest and in the best interest of all life everywhere,* he thought, *let me leave the Dream.*

A falling sensation. Kendi flailed about, but he felt nothing, saw nothing. A scream tried to tear itself from his throat, but he didn't have a throat.

Abruptly he was looking at a misty gray thing. Kendi didn't move. After a moment, the gray thing resolved itself into the ceiling in his quarters. He was lying on his bed. The position was a bit disconcerting—usually he came out of the Dream with his spear propped solidly under his knee. He felt disoriented and dizzy.

A head moved into his field of vision. Worried blue eyes looked down at him from beneath tousled red hair.

"Ben?" Kendi asked, and noticed his mouth was dry as

Outback sand. Disorientation made his mind wander like the needle on a dropped compass. He needed something solid to hold on to, something to bring him back to earth. Without thinking he reached up a hand and touched Ben's cheek. It was warm and slightly raspy. This wasn't right. He wasn't supposed to do that, though he couldn't remember why. He pulled his hand back, feeling foolish.

"Are you all right?" Ben asked, ignoring Kendi's gesture.

"Thirsty," he croaked.

Ben left and returned with a glass of water. He helped Kendi to a sitting position. Kendi felt the quiet strength in Ben's arm and, sighing, let himself lean against the other man. The room settled a bit. Ben was solid, reassuring, unlike the changeable Dream. Oddly, Ben didn't pull away. Kendi's unfocused mind tried to analyze the situation for a moment, then gave up and just drank in Ben's presence. They sat there on the bed, Ben's arm encircling Kendi's back and chest. Kendi could feel Ben's breathing. Thirst burned in Kendi's throat and he knew he should check on Sejal, but he didn't want to move and lose Ben's embrace. Eventually thirst drove him to reach for the water, but his hands were clumsy. Ben held the glass and helped him drink. Kendi concentrated on the physical sensation of the cool water slipping down his throat, and his focus slowly returned. Briefly he considered playing up the muzziness to keep Ben's arm around him, then discarded the idea. He didn't like lying to Ben, even in that small way.

"Thanks," he said. "I'm okay now."

As Kendi expected, Ben moved away, though he didn't get off the bed. He turned sideways to face Kendi. Kendi could still feel the warm stripe of Ben's body heat on his back and side.

"What happened to you?" Ben asked, his voice carefully neutral. For a third time, Kendi explained. As he spoke, it dawned on him that this was an historical event. No one had ever been pulled into the Dream like this. It would probably be best to write a report or something so other people could read it or he'd end up repeating it, even on his deathbed. The Grandparent Adepts back on Bellerophon would certainly want the details, and Kendi should record them before they faded, even from Kendi's trained memory.

"Kendi, do you hear me?" came Harenn's voice from the intercom as he finished.

"I'm here," he said. "And even in one piece. Are you with Sejal?"

"Yes. He woke up a few minutes ago. So I am assuming Mother Ara and the others showed him how to exit the Dream. Physically he seems to be fine."

"Thanks," Kendi said, relieved. "I'll come down and check on him as soon as I can. Peggy-Sue, close intercom."

Silence fell over the room.

"Can you stand up?" Ben asked.

"I don't want to try yet," Kendi said. "I don't know why I'm so . . . off-balance. I shouldn't be."

"Psychosomatics?" Ben hazarded. "You usually use drugs to reach the Dream, but this time you didn't. Something's different, so you figure you should be off-kilter and that means you are."

"Maybe." Kendi inhaled deeply, exhaled hard, experimentally waved a hand in front of his face. Everything seemed to be working all right, but his knees felt a little weak. "Thanks for coming by. I really appreciate it."

Ben shrugged. Another moment of silence passed.

"Ben—" Kendi began.

"No, Kendi."

Kendi started to protest, then halted. He looked away, his jaw working in and out. His throat felt tight. He dropped his eyes and picked at the bedspread.

"You promised we'd talk later," Kendi said softly. "It's later, Ben. I know you still . . . care. I can tell. So tell me why you made me leave."

Ben remained stonily mute, though he made no move to get up. Kendi didn't look at Ben's face, afraid Ben would bolt if he did, though he could see Ben's hands resting on his crossed legs.

"Is it something to do with Ara?" he asked. "Something she said?"

No answer.

"Have you found someone else?" This question was hard to ask, and Kendi kept his eyes down.

Still no answer. Small relief.

"Is it because I'm a Child of Irfan?"

One hand made a shrugging motion.

"You don't like that I'm a Child?"

Smaller shrugging motion.

A knot grew in Kendi's stomach, but he said the words. "Ben, if you asked me to, I'd leave the—"

"No you wouldn't," Ben interrupted, and this time Kendi did look up. Ben's blue eyes were flat, and a thread of anger touched Kendi.

"What do you mean by that?" he demanded.

Ben exhaled sharply. "Look Kendi, do you know why I work for the Children? Even though I'm not Silent?"

"Because your mother's an Ad—" Kendi started, then stopped. "You're going to say that's not the reason why."

"You're right." Ben licked his lips. "Have you got any idea what it's like growing up the only non-Silent member of a Silent family?"

Kendi mutely shook his head.

"It means you're alone a lot." Ben's blue eyes drifted. "Mom was always running here and there, tracking down or saving Silent. Nana and Papa were busy, too, even though they're supposed to be semiretired. Aunt Sil and Uncle Hazid and my cousins—they're all Silent. I'm the outsider. The freak who can't reach the Dream."

Kendi grabbed Ben's pale hand with his dark one. "Hey—you aren't a freak. If anything, the Silent are freaks."

"Not in my family," Ben said bitterly. "When we were younger, my cousins made fun of me behind the adults' backs. My aunt and uncle and grandparents treated me like I was semiretarded or something. When I got older, my cousins looked—still look—at me with pity or contempt. They're always in the Dream or planning their next trip into it. Mom, too."

Kendi realized Ben hadn't pulled his hand away and took it as a good sign. "So why work for the Children?"

"At least this way I can do *something.* You want a computer hacked? An engine repaired? A ship piloted? I'm your man. You want a Dream, call someone who counts."

"You count to me," Kendi said seriously. "And you count to your mom. I love you and need you, Ben. You keep me grounded in the real world. You stay serious when I get stupid."

"I can't follow you, Kendi," Ben said in a flat voice. "The Dream calls and you have to answer. So does Mom and everyone else."

"And you think you can't compete," Kendi finished with sudden insight. "Ben, that's bullshit. You're more important to me than—"

"It doesn't matter, Kendi," Ben said. He set Kendi's hand aside. "I can't wait for you on the sidelines. I won't be the spouse who waits for you to come home from something I can't understand."

Ben got up and started for the door, leaving an empty space on the bed. Kendi's stomach lurched. He knew that once Ben walked through that door, any hope of a future with him would end. He wanted to grab Ben, snatch him back and hold him. The yearning filled him until it was a physical pain. The door slid open.

And then Kendi knew what to say.

"What if you could go into the Dream?" he said.

Ben halted and turned. "What?"

"Sejal pulled me into the Dream," Kendi said. "What if he could do the same for you?"

"I'm not Silent, Kendi." But a haunted look stole over Ben's handsome face. Excitement rose. Kendi scooted to the edge of the bed and got to his feet. His legs were steady now. It was going to be all right. Sejal would take Ben into the Dream, and Ben would finally see what it was like. His family problems would be over, and he could move back in with Kendi. They would be together again. Kendi's heart sang with joy.

"Genetically you are Silent," Kendi reminded him urgently. "What if all you need to reach the Dream is a jump start? I'll bet Sejal could do it. You could start training, even be a Brother. What about that?"

Ben stared wide-eyed, like a deer frozen in a spotlight. Then he turned and fled the room.

SIXTEEN

Sejal's Journal

Day 5, Month 11, Common Year 987

After Mother Ara got me out of the Dream, Harenn showed up at my room to examine me. I could hardly sit still for her on the bed. I had entered the Dream! I was pumped full of energy and I wanted to do it again and I didn't want Harenn around spoiling the feeling for me. I hadn't forgotten that she was the bitch who'd told Mom about me tricking, and now she was sitting on the chair in my room with Kendi's readout unit on her lap.

"You have done something unprecedented," she said. "There will be much excitement when we arrive at Bellerophon. You must be ready for that."

That set off an alarm bell. I saw myself standing in front of a big crowd of Silent who all stared at me like some kind of freak.

"What kind of excitement?" I asked, angry at her. "Are you going to tell them about the tricking? You sure couldn't keep your mouth shut around my mom."

"Your mother was being uncooperative," Harenn said. "We had little time, and I took the route that would convince her most quickly that you needed to come with us."

"It was none of your damn business," I snapped.

Her hand moved so fast I didn't even see it. Suddenly my wrist was trapped in a hard grip. It hurt. "Don't be a fool," she hissed behind her veil. "You are *everyone's* damned business."

I didn't like her hand on me. I was going to reach out with my mind and force her to let go when suddenly my empathy talent switched on and I flashed on her. A mix of emotion washed over me, and the topmost one was fear. I gasped. Harenn was afraid of me? Under that I noticed a sorrow and pain so deep and penetrating I was afraid I'd be sucked in. And she was also eager, so eager I was surprised she wasn't climbing the walls.

"You can possess the non-Silent," she said, still hissing. "Do you know what that means?"

Still awash in her emotions, I couldn't do anything but stare at her and shake my head.

"You could assassinate any ruler you choose by making him jump off a building or swallow poison. You could take the mind of any official and use her to spy on her own government. How much do you think anyone will care that you traded simple sex for mere money?"

The emotions switched off as abruptly as they'd switched on. Harenn let go of my hand.

"The Empire of Human Unity knows of you," Harenn continued, "and they sent a squadron of battle cruisers to take you back. Do you think a backwater gigolo rates that sort of attention?"

"I'm not a gigolo," I snarled at her, angry again.

"No," she returned, still calm. "You are far more than that. The problem is, you have been thinking as one."

"That's not true!" I snapped.

"Is it not? Tell me, then, why you left the planet that birthed you."

I felt like my head was blowing up like a balloon. "It was a backwater slimehole," I yelled. "We lived in a slum and there was no way out of it."

"You lived in a clean, safe neighborhood," she countered. "You lived in wealth and comfort compared to many of those around you. But you wanted more. So you sold your body."

"You're twisting it. You're making it sound—"

"And then, when we Children of Irfan arrived and offered to take you away, you accepted without hesitation because we promised to give you what you wanted. How is this different from what you did on the streets?"

"It's completely different!" I yelled. "It's not the same at all. I wanted to get Mom off Rust, too. I did it to help her!"

She stayed so calm I wanted to slap her. "If we had offered to take your mother off-planet on the sole condition that you remain in your slum on Rust, would you have accepted?"

"I—" I halted, unable to say anything. I should have said *yes,* but I wasn't able to—

Okay. I'll say it: I wasn't able to *lie* that fast.

Harenn nodded. "You were selfish. And it is easy to take advantage of selfish people, Sejal. You are fortunate that the first ones to do so of you were the Children of Irfan."

My thoughts were swirling around like a pinwheel and I couldn't do anything but nod.

"Many people will want you," she continued. "They will seek you out and try to use you. They will tempt you and entice you, and if you continue to think only in terms of a prostitute—and by that I mean in terms of what you can gain—then they will use you indeed, just as they would use a whore. And then they will cast you aside."

Harenn fiddled with the readout unit on her lap, the first fidgeting I had seen her do. Her words rang through my skull like a headache and it occurred to me that I had never asked why Kendi and the others had come to Rust in the first place. Everything had happened so fast, and I had just sort of assumed that Kendi had first found me by accident. A cold finger crept up my back.

"Did all of you go through all that shit on Rust just to find me?" I asked.

Harenn nodded. "Kendi was the first to feel you in the Dream, but the Unity Silent sensed you as well. Even before we found you, we knew you could perform impossible feats. Now you have pulled someone else into the Dream, and this too was thought impossible."

"Why is it impossible?" I said. "It wasn't hard."

"For you, perhaps." She paused. "Could you do such a thing for a non-Silent?"

Her eyes looked like hard brown glass. I wanted to squirm. It felt like she was examining me under a microscope. I remembered her eagerness.

"I'm not sure," I said.

"This is my selfishness, then," she said, as if to herself. Then she took a deep breath. "Could you do it for me?"

I blinked. After her long lecture about my thinking—and I have to admit she hit close—I wasn't sure how to react.

"You want to enter the Dream," I stalled.

She closed her eyes briefly. "I am not Silent, but my husband is. I wish to find him."

"You're married?" I blurted stupidly.

"I am. I was. My husband visited a Silent son on my body ten years ago. One day I arrived home and saw he and my son Bedj-ka were gone. I have since learned many things about the husband I thought I knew. He was a criminal who hadn't even told me his real name. I am his fourth wife and his fourth victim."

"Victim?"

"Yes. My husband carries strong Silent genes. He marries non-Silent women, beds them until pregnancy, then steals the child away for sale into slavery." Her voice was soft and poisonously calm. "I wish to find him. Other Silent have not been able to trace him in the Dream, but I am certain I could do it if I could only find a way there. I know his mind. I could track him. And then—"

She made a gesture at my crotch that made me cringe.

"Oh," I said, not sure what to tell her.

"If you learn to take non-Silent into the Dream, please alert me," Harenn said, getting up. "I have little to offer you except friendship and gratitude, but I hope you will consider it." And then she left.

I still have no idea what I'm going to tell her.

Day 8, Month 11, Common Year 987

Kendi won't let me back into the Dream. He says I need more controls, more people to watch me in case something goes wrong. But I *know* what I'm doing. I can feel it. Kendi's got me doing more meditation exercises now, but I don't need them. I can breathe and trance like it's second nature. I don't even need the drugs he says everyone else needs.

The whispering started again. Kendi says that the Silent are always at least a little aware of other minds in the Dream. That's the whispering I hear. Traditionally, it means the Dream is calling. Some people are more sensitive to it than others, and I guess I'm pretty sensitive. When you answer by entering the Dream, the whispering ends. For a while, anyway.

Kendi says no one knows how or why this works, though some people say that a Silent's brain is structured to *need* other minds around it. The Dream fills that need.

If it's a need, then why shouldn't I go?

Day 15, Month 11, Common Year 987

We're one day out from Bellerophon, and I did it. I went back. I'm shaky now, but I'm okay. For a minute I thought I was going to die, but—

It was easy, actually. I just went to bed, tranced as deep as I could, and reached for the Dream.

I opened my eyes in my room back on Rust. For a brief second, I thought I had fallen asleep and was dreaming. Then I realized that this place was too real, more real than a regular dream ever is. I half-expected Mom to come walking in. Suddenly I missed her and I hoped she was safe.

I pushed the feeling aside and went exploring. The whispering was still there, but it wasn't scary. It was comforting, a soothing presence in the background.

I left the apartment and trotted out to the street. It was empty. Kendi says that you can create animals in the Dream, but not people. Again, no one knows why. It may be a subconscious taboo that no one's been able to overcome.

Maybe I'll be able to do it one day.

Anyway. At the end of the street was that blackness I saw the other time, the one Sister Gretchen asked me if I was creating. Angry red cracks showed through it, and it felt *powerful.* It seemed bigger than last time. I stared at it. It felt like any minute the darkness was going to roll up the street like a thunderstorm.

And something in the darkness called to me. It was a strong voice, familiar and lonely. It didn't call to me by name, but it did call. I wanted to be there, next to the darkness. The desire filled me and pulled at me. And then it happened. The city vanished around me, and I was standing on a flat surface with darkness an inch from my nose. I jumped back, lost my balance, and fell flat on my ass.

I scrambled backward. My heart was beating fast. This close to the darkness, I heard a deep thrumming, a vibration that set my teeth on edge. And the darkness wailed. It cried and screamed. My hands shook. The whole thing scared the shit out of me, but I also wanted to go into it. It's like the way you want to pull a scab off a sore—you know it's going to hurt, but you can't resist.

There were other people around, some in clumps, others alone. Lots of them weren't human. I stared. The Unity doesn't allow non-humans, not even as slaves, and I'd only seen aliens in pictures or holograms. Most of them had too many legs or eyes or were weird colors or actually had tentacles. After a second I realized I was staring and I made myself stop.

The humming and wailing continued, like a nail dragging across glass. Something moved inside the dark, and that desire to go in filled me. I moved toward it again, ignoring an alien standing only a few yards away, and slowly put my hand out. My fingertips crept closer and barely entered the black area.

Instant cold swept my hand and arm. Some kind of force grabbed my hand and yanked me forward. I screamed. I dug in my heels and fought, but whatever it was had me good. I tried to leave the Dream the way Mother Ara had taught me, but I couldn't think straight enough to concentrate. The force dragged me in up to my elbow.

And then two other people were beside me, pulling me back. They grabbed hold of me hard. All three of us dug in and pulled. It felt like my arm was coming off, but we didn't stop pulling. Finally my arm wrenched free. We toppled backward into a pile with me on top and lay there breathing hard. After a second, we all rolled apart. I got up and turned to help the others up and thank them. That was when I noticed only one of them was human. The other had four legs, two arms, and a long neck with a big head. The other was a human woman with dark hair and eyes. She wore a brown robe and a gold disk on a chain. A Child of Irfan.

"You are uninjured?" the alien asked.

I tried to answer, but only squeaked. Whether it was from what had just happened or from the fact that I was facing a real alien, I'm not sure. I cleared my throat and tried again.

"I'm all right," I said. "Thanks."

"What possessed you to do something so foolish?" the woman asked.

I shook my head and gestured at the darkness. "What *is* that?"

"Is this the first time you view it?" the alien said. "You must be new in the Dream."

"Kind of." It suddenly occurred to me that if the woman was a Child of Irfan and she recognized me later, I might get into trouble for entering the Dream without permission. I thanked both of them again, pulled my thoughts together like Mother Ara taught me, and suddenly I was back in my room on the ship.

I sat up and looked at my arm. It still ached, and I felt bruises forming where the alien and the woman had hauled on me. Kendi had warned me this would happen, that any injury I received in the Dream would carry over into my physical body. I went down to the bathroom and took a hot shower, and that helped. I can't ask for painkillers without Harenn asking why.

Speaking of Harenn, she hasn't asked me again if I would take her into the Dream, though she nods when I meet her in the corridor or at meals. Part of me says I should do it and make her owe me, but then I realize I'm thinking like a gigolo again. Part of me says I should do it because it would help her. And part of me says I should just stay out of the whole thing.

When I was little and saw Mom making big decisions for the community, I thought it must be great to boss people around. I couldn't wait to be an adult so I could make big decisions too. Now that it's happening, I don't want it.

Sometimes growing up really shits.

Kendi tapped the final keys that brought the *Post-Script* into orbit around Bellerophon. Ara was engrossed with receiving last-minute landing instructions, Gretchen was relaying sensor information to Kendi's boards, and Ben—

Ben bent over his console, not looking in Kendi's direction. It was as if he and Kendi had never spoken. Ben had gone right back to avoiding Kendi, refusing even to speak to him except as ship's business required. It was driving Kendi insane. He'd tried to push Ben out of his mind by putting all his energies into teaching Sejal. It didn't work.

On the view screen, Bellerophon showed dark green continents and bright blue oceans beneath dramatic spirals of sweeping white clouds. Kendi sighed. After so much time on red Rust, the green, cool forests of Bellerophon called to him, making him long to vanish into emerald leaves and silver mists.

"He's doing it again, Mother," Gretchen said from her boards.

Ara looked up. "Who's doing what?"

"Kendi. He's making cow eyes."

"I never made cow eyes in my life," Kendi protested. "I'm just glad to be home."

Gretchen snorted. "Uh-huh. In a month, you'll be complaining about the humidity and how the trees get in the way of the view."

"You need to shave your mustache more often, Gretchen," Kendi said. "You're coming across all prickly."

This argument would have gone further, but Ara firmly put an end to it and Kendi turned his full attention back to piloting. Ben had already put the sound-dampeners on full, and the power drain made the ship sluggish. The Unity didn't care how much noise a ship made, making the spaceport a deafening place. Things were different on Bellerophon.

After only a tiny bit of wrangling with customs, the *Post-Script* crew was given official permission to disembark. Kendi, who had stuffed his few belongings into a single satchel, stood at the hatchway with Sejal beside him. Sejal's possessions consisted of a single computer button with his journal on it and the collapsible flute in his pocket. He was fidgeting restlessly as Kendi opened the hatchway.

A breath of cool, damp air redolent of moss and green leaves wafted over Sejal. He inhaled deeply. His first alien breath. Kendi had landed the ship at the edge of the airfield, and the wide brown trunk of a tree dominated the view from the hatchway. It was so tall, Sejal couldn't see the top. Between the ship and tree was a transparent chain-link fence, probably to keep unauthorized people off the airfield. A light fog hovered lazily among the trees like a tattered white cloak.

"Let's go, let's go," Gretchen ordered from behind them. "Some of us have lives, you know."

Sejal took another humid breath, then stepped forward with an oddly stiff gait. He almost paraded down the ramp, then hesitated.

"What's wrong?" Kendi asked beside him. Gretchen pushed past them, satchel in hand, and disappeared around the ship.

"This is the first time I've ever been on another world," Sejal said. "It seems like . . . I don't know . . . like it should be something special."

"Take a look around you." Kendi laughed. His white teeth shone against his dark face. "Does this feel ordinary?"

Sejal looked. Ships of all shapes and sizes rested on reinforced gray aerogel just as they did in the Unity, but beyond them loomed the forest. The trees stretched as high as Unity skyscrapers, and they were so wide that thirty humans couldn't join hands in a circle around one. Green ground-hugging vegetation misted the ground beneath them. The lowest tree branches were several stories above the ground. Sejal, a child of streets and skyscrapers, had never been outside the city, and though he had seen images of forests, he had never imagined them as looking like this.

"It's amazing," Sejal said, awed. "And it's so quiet."

As if on cue, a booming roar shattered the air. Sejal jumped. The sound was echoed by another in the far distance.

"What was that?" Sejal whispered.

"A dinosaur," Kendi told him absently. He kept throwing glances over his shoulder as if he were looking for someone.

"A dinosaur?"

"A prehistoric lizard from Earth. The dominant animals on Bellerophon are big lizards, so the first colonists started calling them dinosaurs."

Sejal peered nervously toward the trees. "Do they hurt people?"

"That's what the fence is for. It keeps the dinosaurs from squashing the ships—and vice versa."

Kendi led Sejal across the airfield, into the spaceport, and through another customs check. Kendi had to invoke his authority as a Child of Irfan to get Sejal, who didn't have any sort of passport, through this stage, but Sejal barely noticed. Like the Unity port, the Bellerophon port was extremely busy. Small carts and platforms zipped by. Speakers blared announcements. Restaurants filled the air with food smells. None of this was what distracted him, however. It was the aliens. They were everywhere, walking, lurching, or slithering in shapes and sizes Sejal had never imagined. More than once he saw the creatures like the four-legged one that had saved him in the Dream. He couldn't help staring, and Kendi had to yank him forward several times.

"I'm not used to all these aliens," he said in apology. "Do they live here?"

Kendi shook his head. "Most of them are just passing through. Humans and Ched-Balaar—the four-legged aliens—are the main people on Bellerophon. There's a fair chunk of other races at the monastery, though."

"Aren't the Ched-Balaar the ones who showed humans the Dream?" Sejal said, again awed.

"That's them. Come on. There's a train to the city leaving in a few minutes, and I don't want to miss it."

He hustled Sejal out the port's main entrance. A monorail train waited on a track, and the last people from the platform had boarded. Kendi and Sejal leaped aboard just as the doors were sliding shut. The train slid soundlessly forward, then uphill. Vegetation blurred into a green wall.

"Why are we going up?" Sejal said.

"The monastery—and the rest of the city—is built in the talltrees."

"How come?"

"Easier on the ecology—and easier to avoid getting eaten by a dinosaur."

A few minutes later, Kendi and Sejal disembarked on a wooden platform high above the ground. The track and platform were partly supported by the massive branches of the talltree and partly supported by thick cables drilled into the trunk itself. The monorail slid quietly away and vanished into the leafy branches. Between the cracks of the boards under his feet, Sejal could see the empty air that dropped several hundred meters straight down into gray mist. Green leaves and brown branches surrounded them. Behind him lay the station, a building that curved around the talltree. Platforms, ramps, ladders, and staircases formed a network farther up the trunk, connecting the tree to others in the forest.

"Where's the city?" Sejal asked.

"You're in it," Kendi said. "This is the town center. Over there's the town hall."

Sejal blinked. Now that Kendi had pointed it out, Sejal could make out other structures built into other tree canopies. They were all but hidden by thick foliage.

"Come on," Kendi said, plucking at Sejal's elbow. "We need to go up a couple more levels to catch the shuttle back to the monastery."

Sejal tried to obey, but it was difficult. Everything was so strange. He had no idea where he was or how to get around. With a pang he realized that if he and Kendi got separated, he wouldn't have the faintest idea where to go or what to do.

They trotted up a wide wooden staircase. All the buildings and platforms, in fact, seemed to be made of the wood instead of aerogel. When he asked about this, Kendi replied that talltree wood cured hard as steel, making it an ideal building material.

Humans and Ched-Balaar strolled the platforms. In contrast to the spaceport, no one here seemed to be in any hurry. The Ched-Balaar, in fact, were particularly slow moving and graceful. They moved in pairs or small groups, often with humans. An odd chattering noise followed them, and Kendi explained that the Ched-Balaar spoke by clacking their teeth together. Classes in the Ched-Balaar tongue would be part of Sejal's education at the monastery, though the instruction would be limited to understanding the language; no human could produce Ched-Balaar sounds.

They arrived at another platform and boarded another monorail. A while later, they disembarked along with a dozen or so other passengers. Sejal couldn't keep his eyes off the Ched-Balaar in the group. Their long, mobile necks made a slow sort of dance when they moved their heads, and their hand gestures were smooth and languid.

A chattering sound brought Sejal's head around. A Ched-Balaar stood next to them, apparently saying something, though Sejal had no idea what it was.

"Ched-Hisak!" Kendi said, and grasped both the alien's hands enthusiastically. "Great to see you! Let me introduce my student Sejal Dasa. Sejal, this is Ched-Hisak."

The Ched-Balaar turned to Sejal and held out its hands. Nervously, Sejal took them in his own. The palms were smooth and soft, like fine suede, and they engulfed Sejal's hands. As they did, a jolt shot down Sejal's spine and he gasped. Sejal had almost forgotten what happened when two Silent touched for the first time. Ched-Hisak chattered at him, unfazed by the sensation.

"He greets you as one Silent to another," Kendi said. "You can answer—he'll understand."

"Hello," Sejal said uncertainly. "Pleased to meet you."

Another monorail pulled up, and Ched-Hisak released Sejal. Chatter, chatter, chatter.

"Thanks," Kendi said. "We should get moving ourselves."

They both bid Ched-Hisak good-bye. Ched-Hisak boarded the monorail, and Kendi led Sejal up the platform.

"He was one of my first instructors at the monastery," Kendi explained. "You'll probably have him, too."

Sejal's stomach tightened. "I thought you were going to be my teacher."

"I can't teach you *everything,*" Kendi said with a small laugh. "You need to learn history and literature and computers and mathematics and a bazillion other things."

"Music?" Sejal said hopefully. The monorail doors started to slide shut, then paused as a man darted into the car. Kendi and Sejal found seats in the nearly empty car as the train slipped forward and the leaves outside made an emerald blur. The man who had boarded at the last minute stood blinking by the door. He had snowy hair and a few wrinkles. Sejal met his eyes for a moment. The man looked away.

"You mean your flute?" Kendi said. "Sure. 'The greater your knowledge, the smaller your risk,' as Irfan said. Once you complete the basic requirements for your degree, you can study anything you want."

Sejal's head was suddenly swimming. "My degree?"

"Without a degree, you can't work in the Dream, at least not for the Children."

Sejal fell silent for a moment. He was going to college? The idea hadn't occurred to him, not with everything else that had been going on. Excitement filled him.

"When do we get started?" he demanded.

"As soon as you get settled in," Kendi said. He crossed his legs at knee and ankle and suddenly Sejal wondered what it would have been like if Kendi had come on to him as a jobber. An image of the two of them in bed together with Kendi handing Sejal a fistful of *kesh* flashed through Sejal's mind. He grimaced. That was behind him. He didn't need to do that anymore.

The white-haired man settled himself in the seat next to Sejal despite the plethora of empty seats elsewhere in the car.

"Excuse me," he said. "Does this train go to the monastery of Irfan?"

"Sure does," Kendi replied. "And it's the last stop, so you can't overshoot."

"Is that where you youngsters are going?"

Kendi nodded and stuck out his hand. "Brother Kendi Weaver. This is Sejal Dasa."

The man flicked a glance at Sejal, then stared at Kendi's hand as if it were a piece of rotten meat. With a curt nod, he rose and changed seats. Sejal noticed he sat close to a pair of Ched-Balaar who sat chattering on their haunches in an open space farther ahead in the car.

"What the hell was that about?" Kendi said, dropping his hand. "Rude son of a bitch."

Sejal shrugged. People were always rude at the market. Why should anything be different here? He shot a glance at the old man, but he didn't seem to be paying any attention to Sejal.

Kendi continued to chat, but Sejal only listened with half an ear. It seemed like every time he looked away, he could feel the old man's eyes on him. Whenever he checked, however, the man was invariably staring out the window or at his fingernails or at the ceiling.

After several stops, the monorail halted one more time and Kendi got up.

"We're here," he announced.

The old man was still on the train and he rose as well. As they and the other passengers moved to the door, the old man stumbled and reflexively caught Sejal's bare elbow. A small shock traveled up Sejal's spine.

"Sorry," the old man muttered. He hurried off the train and disappeared. Sejal narrowed his eyes. The move had clearly been calculated. If Sejal had been in the market, he would have suspected a pickpocket. Sejal, however, had nothing in his pockets to steal except his flute and computer journal. A quick check showed both were still there. So what was the old man up to?

"Who *is* that guy?" Kendi grumped, hoisting his satchel.

"He's Silent," Sejal said. "I felt it when he touched me. I think he did it on purpose."

Kendi looked at him as they exited the train. "On purpose? What for?"

"I don't know." Sejal scanned the platform for signs of the old man, but he was gone. "He didn't want to touch you, but he wanted to touch me. Is he a Child?"

"Doubtful. He didn't know this train goes to the monastery. If you see him again, say something."

The platform was like the others—wooden, wide, and surrounded by leafy branches. The station was also like the other buildings Sejal had seen—a wooden half-circle that curved around the tree. Between the leaves the sky was gray, and the breeze had turned chilly. Sejal, still dressed in thin clothes fit for Rust's gentle climate, shivered and clasped his arms around his chest. From the platform spread a network of staircases and walkways. The stairs lead to other levels in the tree, while the walkways connected the platform to other talltrees. Buildings of many sizes nested among the branches like roosting birds, and the wooden walkways clomped and thumped beneath the feet of human and Ched-Balaar alike. Other races were visible here and there, and almost everyone wore the simple gold medallion that marked the Children of Irfan. The atmosphere was relaxed and unhurried, and Sejal began to relax into it.

"Come on," Kendi said. "We need to get you settled in."

Kendi selected a walkway seemingly at random. Sejal was a bit nervous at first—the walkway was made of wide boards suspended by cables overgrown with ivy, and it swayed beneath the rhythm of the feet that traveled it. What happened if someone tripped? It'd be all too easy to slip between cable and board and plummet to a mossy death below. When he got closer to the walkway, however, he saw that the empty spaces were covered with the same nearly invisible netting that had made up the fence around the airfield. Still, looking down made his head swim.

Kendi started fearlessly across the walkway. Sejal swallowed and forced himself to follow, one hand firmly on the cable. The walkway lurched and swayed beneath, the gray sky swooped above. It was wide enough for four humans to walk side by side, so Sejal's hesitant pace didn't halt traffic, though Kendi gained quite a bit of ground before noticing Sejal was no longer right behind him. He slowed and let Sejal set the pace.

"I'd forgotten how weird the walkways are if you've never done it before," Kendi said. "Once you get used to them, you won't even think about them."

A Ched-Balaar galloped past. The walkway lurched and swayed sickeningly, and Sejal clutched the cable with white fingers until the boards settled down again. "Why don't they make these things solid?" he asked hoarsely.

"Flexible walkways withstand the weather better." Kendi grinned a wide grin. "You should try getting around during a big storm. The walkways are a real challenge then."

Sejal didn't want to think about that. Instead he worked on simple walking. After a while, he found he was able to forget the drop and walk a little more briskly if he didn't look over the side.

As they walked, Kendi stopped several times to exchange greetings with other pedestrians, both human and alien. Kendi shook hands, exchanged hugs, and slapped palms with at least a dozen people. Although he introduced Sejal as his student, he didn't let anyone touch him, explaining that a Silent greeting would only add to Sejal's vertigo.

Sejal merely nodded, suddenly shy under the blur of names and faces. Back in the neighborhood, he had known everyone by sight and name. Here, he knew no one, and it was disconcerting. He felt like a balloon anchored by the thinnest of threads.

Eventually, they reached what Kendi said was the student dormitory. Sejal, engrossed in watching the boards as they went by beneath his feet, looked up and gasped.

The place was enormous, several stories high with balconies jutting out like dozens of cupped hands. Warm brown wood and clinging green ivy made the place seem friendly and homelike despite its size. Stairs, ramps, and even climbing ropes and sliding poles ran every which way. Even as Sejal watched, a teenage boy dropped from one balcony to the one below.

"They're not supposed to do that," Kendi said wryly. "But everyone does. Just don't get caught, all right?"

Sejal could only nod. He wouldn't get caught, largely because there was no way in hell he was going to do that.

A great curving balcony held the main entrance of the dormitory. Kendi took Sejal inside. Sejal's thin shoes came down on freshly scoured wooden floors. The ceiling of the entry area was high, with bare beams and a great many windows. Two humans staffed a wide desk near the front door. Kendi introduced Sejal, and they registered his thumbprint and voiceprint. Kendi had apparently sent word ahead that Sejal was coming, for there was no hemming or fumbling for paperwork.

"Linens and such are already in the room," one of the clerks said. "The computer will let you in. Its name is Baran."

Sejal's room was on the third floor. On the way up, they passed other students, all human. They nodded at Sejal and pressed fingertips to forehead at Kendi. When Sejal looked at Kendi in surprise, Kendi explained that it was a ritual salute from any student to any Child. Sejal would be expected to do the same, except when it came to Kendi.

"Your fingers would eventually fall off if you saluted every time you saw me," Kendi said.

They came upon a corridor faced with several doors. Kendi gestured at one, and Sejal pressed his thumb to the lock plate. The lock clicked and Sejal opened the door. The room beyond was cozily small, with the same scrubbed wood floor as the dorm lobby. A bed piled with white linens sat across from a desk which had a computer terminal set into it. An easy chair sat next to the closet. The room's white walls had been freshly painted and a pair of French doors opened onto a wide, sweeping balcony. Beyond the balcony was the by now standard view of heavy branches and thick foliage.

Sejal stared. He had been expecting a closet-size room with bunk beds and half a dozen roommates. He poked his head out the French doors. The balcony, it turned out, serviced several rooms, like an outdoor hallway.

"Bathroom's up the hall," Kendi said. "You'd think with all the billions brought in by our Dream communication work, they'd spring for individual facilities."

"This is great," Sejal said. "It's a lot better than my room back on Rust."

"We also need to take you clothes shopping," Kendi said. "Then we'll get you enrolled in classes."

"I don't have any money." Sejal tested the bed by sitting down hard. It was springy but firm. "How do I pay for stuff?"

"The monastery gives all its students a small stipend. A lot of people get here with little or nothing, especially Silent who used to be slaves, so you also get a little bonus when you first arrive. Don't get excited, though—you have to pay it all back when you graduate and start working for the Children."

"It beats . . . other work," Sejal said.

"That it does," Kendi agreed. "Let's go."

SEVENTEEN

Planet Bellerophon Blessed and Most Beautiful Monastery of the Children of Irfan

It is impossible to please the entire world and also one's family.

—Ched-Balaar Proverb

Benjamin Rymar flung himself back on his bed and stared at familiar beams of his raw wood ceiling. The floor around him was littered with bag and baggage. He should unpack. He should check his messages and his mail. But instead he stared at the ceiling.

Outside the French doors leading to the balcony lay the talltree forest. Green leaves and strong branches cupped themselves around Ben's tiny house, and the breeze carried the welcome fragrant scent of talltree bark. He wondered what Sejal thought of Bellerophon.

Sejal. Ben got up and strode into the living room toward the weight machine in the corner. The room was uncharacteristically tidy. Book disks were neatly shelved, the carpets were vacuumed, the furniture dust free. The second-year student Ben had temporarily hired to keep the place up was actually responsible for the cleanliness. Now that Ben was back, he gave it a week.

Other doors led to Ben's study and to the kitchen. The study was crammed with computer equipment in various stages of repair, but the kitchen was mostly empty. It was a running joke with Ara that if Ben wanted to cook he had to dust the stove first.

Ben lay back on one of the benches for some presses. Although a gravity enhancement machine took up less space, Ben preferred to exercise with bulkier metal weights. He found greater satisfaction in adding another chunk of metal to the pile than in tapping a keypad. To his consternation, however, he could barely move the current stack.

Ben grimaced. He should have realized. There had been no weight machine aboard the *Post-Script,* and he had gone without lifting for weeks.

He reset the machine to a lower weight and went to work. Arms, then chest, then back, then legs. Weights clanked and thumped. Sweat trickled down Ben's face and back. He hated lifting. It was boring, it was sweaty, and sometimes it hurt. But Ben did like having a well-defined frame, and he wasn't likely to get it sitting in front of a computer all day.

Ben let the weights thud to the floor and sat up. That was enough for the day. His arms, legs, back, and chest burned with the good feeling that always followed a satisfactory weight session. He went through a few stretches, then headed for the bathroom, peeling off sweaty clothes as he went. After weeks of enforced closeness on the *Post-Script,* it was a luxury to drop his clothes wherever they fell and walk naked to the shower. The practice annoyed Kendi, who was always—

Ben scrubbed harder with the soap and ended the shower with his customary blast of cold water. He wandered into the bedroom, leaving a damp trail on the carpet. Droplets glistened on his skin and the chilly air raised goose bumps. He rummaged through the tangle of unpacked luggage, searching for a towel.

Sejal had yanked Kendi into the Dream. All the questions Ben had been avoiding came crowding into his head. Would it work for any Silent? Would it work for non-Silent? Would it work for Ben?

Ben gave up the search and sat on the bed instead. It was a large bed, one he had bought at Kendi's insistence back when they had been together. Ben liked to sprawl in his sleep, and he had a tendency to crowd Kendi even after—

Dammit. He was not going to think about Kendi. He was not.

A cool draft wafted through the open window and across Ben's wet, bare skin. In response he grabbed up the bedspread and wrapped it around himself like a giant cloak. Pillows tumbled unheeded to the floor. Kendi's logic had been flawless. If Ben's lack of Silence was the reason Ben couldn't stay with Kendi, then making Ben Silent was the obvious solution.

Ben shuddered within the bedspread as it clung wetly to his body. The Dream always took people away from you—Ara, Kendi, Pitr. The idea of entering it himself made him sick.

And yet . . .

Ben unwound himself from the bedspread, found some clothes, and pulled them on. Just as he was fastening his shoes, the doorbell chimed. Ben scrubbed at damp red hair with both hands to hurry the drying and trotted toward the front door.

"Albert, who's here?" he said.

"Sister Gretchen Beyer," the computer replied.

Ben stopped. What the hell was Gretchen doing here? Already he could feel his face turning hot and he hated himself for it. Gretchen could make him blush even from the other side of a wall. She reminded him of his cousin Tress—loud and bossy. Ben sighed and opened the door.

Ben's house was high up in this particular talltree. Three stout branches as thick as a Ched-Balaar's body formed a sort of tripod to support the floorboards. A long staircase made a tight spiral around one of the branches to the main walkway below. Gretchen stood on the little front porch, flushed and breathless from the climb. She held a small package, and a few strands of hair had escaped the blond braid that hung over her shoulder.

"You need," she puffed, "to find a house on a lower level."

Ben shrugged. "The climb keeps me in shape. Come on in. What's going on?"

Gretchen entered the living room and flung herself casually down on the sofa, dropping the brown-wrapped package on one cushion. "You aren't seeing Kendi anymore, so I thought I'd make a play for you. You up for it, handsome?"

Ben's mouth fell open and his face grew so hot, he was sure he could fry an egg on one cheek. Then he realized that Gretchen was joking. He sat on the weight bench and simply looked at her until she snorted.

"The expression on your face." She grinned. "You need to lighten up, big boy." She glanced at the trail of sweaty clothes, including Ben's underwear. "Didn't take long for this place to explode, did it?"

"Gretchen, what do you want?" Ben interrupted, face growing hotter by the moment.

"Don't have a stroke," she scoffed. "I'm just joking around. I brought this." She held up the little package. "It's the drive to my house computer. When I got back, it started acting weird, and then it just went *foom.* I can't turn anything on or off, the trash isn't making records for the grocery store, and the toilet flushes every eight minutes on the dot. The repair shop said they can't get to it for at least a week. Can you fix it? I'll pay you."

He should have just told her to get the hell out. Instead, he found himself saying, "I'll have a look. Bring it into the den."

Gretchen did so and leaned against the door frame as Ben, silently berating himself for being a doormat, cleared some space next to his main terminal. He hooked the drive to his own system, uploaded a scanning program, and skimmed the data.

"No wonder the poor thing crashed, Gretchen," he clucked. "It's ancient. Where did it come from? Irfan's ship?"

"A joke!" Gretchen hooted. "My god, the man does have a sense of humor."

Ben flushed yet again, and a spark of anger flared. "Look, if you don't want my help—"

"No, no," Gretchen interposed hurriedly. "Sorry. My mouth runs away with me sometimes. Can you fix it?"

Surprised at how quickly Gretchen backed down, Ben said, "I doubt it. You'd be better off buying a new one and selling this thing to a museum."

"Another joke! You're a real—sorry." Gretchen waved a hand. "Look, Ben, I'm a little strapped for money right now. I can't afford a new house drive. Can you . . .?"

Ben sighed. "Give me a couple hours and I'm sure I can cobble something together."

"Yes! Ben, I adore you."

The words slipped out of Ben's mouth before he could stop himself. "Then why do you give me such a hard time?"

Silence. Ben found his face was still hot and he cursed himself for it.

"Because I like you," Gretchen said. "I don't talk this way to just anybody. I like Kendi, too."

Ben turned toward her. "Is that another joke?"

"Nope. Cross my heart." Gretchen drew an *X* over her chest, then slid casually to the floor to sit cross-legged in the doorway. "I used to have a big crush on you, you know."

"On *me*?" Ben almost squeaked, too startled to blush this time.

"Absolutely." Gretchen nodded. "Years ago, back when we were both students. I asked—okay, begged—Trish to set us up on a date, and she died laughing. I asked what was so funny, and she told me you were already seeing Kendi. That killed that."

Ben didn't know how to react, so he said nothing.

"Uh-oh. I've upset you." Gretchen pulled her knees up under her chin. "Ben, this was, what? Six years ago? Seven? When Mother Ara selected me for her recruiting team and I found out you were on it, I was glad because I figured I'd get to know you better. You're good, Ben, and I like working with you."

"Oh," Ben said, still uncertain. "I, uh, like working with you."

"No, you don't." Gretchen laughed. "You hate me. I'm not easy to get along with."

Ben managed a small smile. "Well . . ."

"See?" Gretchen shrugged. "It all goes back to my tragic childhood, of course."

"Where *did* you grow up, Gretchen?" He twisted sideways in his chair to rummage through a box on the floor. "You've never said."

"Earth. My family was from South Africa. Old money, but not much left by the time I was born." She shook her head. "No one would dare be Silent in *that* family. Genetic freaks, all of them."

"The Silent or your family?" Computer parts clattered and clunked as Ben sorted through them.

Gretchen laughed. "Another joke! You're getting better at this. The freaks were—are—the Silent. So I got to grow up in a lovely house with a lovely family who thought their lovely daughter was a freak. My brothers were total shits, especially when Mom and Dad's backs were turned." An expression of pain briefly crossed her face. Then she shook her head. "Anyway, I eventually signed up with the Children, so here I am in a treehouse asking a cute guy who has no interest in me whatsoever to fix my house hard drive. Who'd have thought?"

Ben came up with the partially repaired drive he'd been looking for. Multicolored wires dangled from the ports, and the housing was streaked with dust. To his surprise, the *cute guy* remark didn't redden his face.

"Fate is weird," he said solemnly. "If Mom's doctor had moved his hand a little more to the left, I'd still be in the freezer and you'd be asking someone else to fix your computer."

Gretchen cocked her head. "That was cryptic. Explain."

Ben did, surprised at how easily he was telling the story to Gretchen, a woman he had thought he disliked. "So somewhere in a laboratory," he concluded, "I've got eleven siblings."

Gretchen shuddered. "Creepy. Not you," she added hastily. "Just the idea that you could've easily been someone else."

"Anyone could," Ben said in philosophical tones. "When you think about how many millions of your father's sperm competed for one—"

"So how's that hard drive?" Gretchen interrupted. Ben noticed *she* was blushing and laughed. He laughed hard, unable to stop. Ruefully, Gretchen joined in and all tension left the air.

"All right, all right," she finally muttered. "Score for you."

Gasping, Ben decided to change the subject. "How do you get along with your family now?"

"I don't." Gretchen stretched. "I go back to Earth every so often to rub my success as a Child in my father's face. It was hard to give up being different when I came here, though."

"What do you mean?"

Gretchen shrugged. "I hated being different when I was a kid, so after a while, I turned it into a badge of courage.

'Look how strong I am, everyone. I'm different. I'm special.' But at the monastery, I'm not different or special at all." She gave Ben an idle, heavy-lidded glance. "It was hard to give up being special, even though it made my early life hell. Really hard. Happens to a lot of people, I guess."

Ben didn't respond.

"Well," Gretchen said, rising, "I'd better let you work in peace. Give me a call when the drive's done, all right? You're a doll."

And she left.

Ben stared down at the drive in his hands for a long time before he picked up a soldering iron and set to work.

EIGHTEEN

Planet Rust
Middle Ocean

If we do meet again, will we smile?
—Empress Kan maja Kalii

Prasad rose later than usual, feeling sandy-eyed and groggy. He hadn't slept well ever since he had received the news about Dr. Kri and Dr. Say wanting to experiment with his daughter's eggs. So far he'd managed to stall them for two days, but now they were likely to become more insistent, and he didn't know what to do next.

The sweet smell of frying honey bread filled the air, and Prasad inhaled deeply, trying to wake himself up. He belted on his robe and shuffled into the kitchen, where Katsu gave him a half-smile from the stove. Before he could greet her, however, the door chime sounded.

"Who in the world . . . ?" Prasad muttered. He opened the door—

—and froze. Standing in the corridor was Max Garinn, the blond virologist. He was twirling his mustache with fast, furious twists of the fingers. Prasad staggered, his knees weak.

Behind Garinn stood Vidya Vajhur.

Prasad stared. Vidya stared back. Her clothes were scuffed and dirty, and she wore a wide scarf around her neck. A battered carryall hung from her shoulder. Her expression was shocked.

"So you do know each other," Max Garinn said, still twirling his mustache.

"Vidya," Prasad managed to croak.

"I thought you were dead," Vidya said, her voice just as strained.

"Father?" came Katsu's voice behind him. "Who is at the door?"

"Your mother," Prasad murmured.

"Perhaps we should go inside and talk?" Garinn offered.

Vidya rounded on him, eyes flashing in exactly the way Prasad remembered. "Perhaps you should leave us in private."

Garinn took a startled step backward and Vidya strode into the apartment. Prasad made way for her, and she shoved the door shut in Garinn's face. Katsu backed into the living room, a confused look on her face. Prasad faced Vidya in the entryway and found himself unable to do anything but stare. She had changed. His memory had preserved Vidya in her youth, with night-black hair and a smooth, oval face. A part of him knew that this was ridiculous. Of course, she would age, just as he had. Her dark hair had wide white streaks in it and lines were etched in her face and neck. Her eyes, however, were the same deep brown. Those eyes stared at him, and he wondered if she was thinking the same thing, that he had aged.

What a ridiculous thing it was to be thinking! He hadn't laid eyes on his Vidya in seventeen years, and all that crossed his mind was how she looked? Emotions churned inside him. He wanted to snatch her into his arms and hold her. He wanted to run away, and that surprised him. He wanted to introduce her to Katsu, but wasn't sure how to go about it. In the end, he did nothing.

Vidya slapped his face. "Bastard!" she snarled.

Prasad still didn't move. His cheek stung, and he silently raised a hand to it.

"You're my mother?" Katsu said from the living room.

Vidya turned to look at her. "Katsu?" she whispered. "My little Katsu?"

She staggered to a chair and sat down with her hands over her face. The carryall fell to the floor beside her. As if in a trance, Prasad sat as well. A fruit fish floated past the pale red oval of the room's tiny window and the soft hum of water filters trickled in from Katsu's bedroom aquariums. Katsu knelt at Vidya's feet. Vidya uncovered her face, and Prasad was struck at the resemblance between the two of them.

"Mother?" Katsu said.

Vidya cautiously reached out a trembling hand to touch Katsu's face. "My baby Katsu. No longer a baby."

Katsu's face was impassive, unreadable as always. Prasad

opened his mouth to speak and found he had to force the words out.

"Vidya, what happened to you? Where did you go?"

Vidya looked up at him, anger still hard in her eyes. "I should ask the same. You disappeared. I looked everywhere for you, but I couldn't find you, even after seven days. Why didn't you come back? You left me to raise—"

"It was you who disappeared," Prasad interrupted. "I came back after I found Katsu, but the apartment was empty."

Vidya's face had gone an unhealthy ashen color. "You came back after I left? How did you find Katsu? Have you been here all this time? How did you get here?"

"That is a story."

"Then tell it!" Vidya commanded.

Prasad licked dry lips and shot Katsu a glance. It occurred to him that Katsu had never asked to know how the two of them had come here. He would tell the story for mother and daughter both.

"You remember when we found Katsu's cradle empty," Prasad began. "I was frantic—I couldn't sit and wait for the guard to try to find her, so I went out."

"This I know," Vidya said impatiently. "Tell me what I do not know."

"I am trying," Prasad said, a bit annoyed. "You must have patience. You remember also I was working as a garbage collector. Many people owed me favors for looking the other way while they dumped . . . things into my truck. I called in every one I had until someone gave me an address."

"Why did you not come to get me?" Vidya demanded.

"I was too angry to think of it," Prasad admitted. "I went to the place—a warehouse—and heard Katsu crying inside it. I did not think. I smashed through one of the doors like one of our kine would have done. Five men were there with Katsu."

Katsu, still kneeling at Vidya's feet, did not react.

"I fought them like a rabid dog, but they beat me senseless. I woke here, in this base."

"They did not kill you?" Vidya said.

"Obviously not," Prasad replied. "The men figured out

I was Katsu's father and they thought I might be valuable to their buyer as well, so they brought me here with her. Dr. Say told me—have you met her yet?"

Vidya shook her head. "I met the man named Max Garinn and I met the man with pale hair and a deep voice."

"Dr. Kri," Prasad supplied. "He and Dr. Say are in charge of the base and the project. At any rate, when I woke, Dr. Say told me I had been unconscious for ten days. Katsu was fine."

"And who were the men who kidnapped Katsu?" Vidya's hand had trailed down to Katsu's hair again. Katsu sat like a statue.

"Black market slavers," Prasad said. "Kri told me he and Say had originally arranged to buy Katsu because they were told she was an orphan and because they needed Silent. The slavers brought me along, too, hoping to get more money. Kri said I was almost dead."

"So you were rescued by people who buy infants on the black market," Vidya spat.

This reunion wasn't going as Prasad had imagined it. He could hear the anger in Vidya's voice, see it in her rigid posture. "It wasn't like that," he replied uneasily. "They saved my life."

"Your life," Vidya pointed out, "wouldn't have been in jeopardy if they hadn't wanted to buy Katsu in the first place. These people hired thugs to kidnap our daughter, and you're living with them!"

Prasad shook his head. "I'm not explaining it well. The slavers approached Kri and Say first. When they heard the slavers had a baby for . . . sale, they agreed to buy."

"And that makes it better?" Vidya said.

"You've changed, Vidya," Prasad said softly. "You've hardened."

"And your brain has softened. You work for people who stole our child."

Anger stiffened Prasad's jaw. "It was that or live in squalor and let the Unity take Katsu on her tenth birthday. Now our daughter is seventeen years old, and she is still with her father."

Vidya looked like she wanted to reply, then made her

mouth a hard line. Katsu still hadn't moved. Prasad's throat thickened.

"I missed you," he said hoarsely. "I didn't know if you were living or dead. Every day I watched Katsu grow to look like you and I wondered. Now you are here and we are fighting. Please. What happened?"

Vidya slumped back in her chair. The anger slipped from her face and her chin trembled.

"When you didn't come back, I became afraid whoever took you and Katsu would next come for me. So I ran," Vidya said. She reached down and gently stroked a lock of Katsu's hair.

"Where did you go?" Prasad asked.

Vidya barked a short, harsh laugh. "To what I thought would be a safe place. It took me seventeen years to realize it was not. You have a son, my husband."

"I have two," Prasad said, confused. "We had to give—"

Vidya cut him off with a gesture. "I was pregnant when you left. I have a daughter named Katsu, and you have a son named Sejal."

"I do? A son? Where is he?" Prasad found he was on his feet, heart thudding. "What does he look like? Didn't you bring him?"

"He is no longer on Rust," Vidya replied.

"But he is Silent," Katsu put in.

Both Prasad and Vidya turned toward her. "What?" Prasad said.

"How did you know that?" Vidya asked at the same time.

"He reaches people through the Dream," Katsu said calmly. "He touches them and changes them. And he walks the Dream."

"How do you know this?" Vidya repeated as Prasad sank back into his chair.

"I have seen him in the Dream," Katsu said. "But he does not know me."

"Your daughter is one of the few Silent who can enter the Dream without drugs," Prasad said proudly. "She is also an expert on Rustic marine biology."

"I see," Vidya said. She passed a hand over her face.

"This is not how I envisioned meeting you again, my husband."

"Nor I, my wife." Impulsively, Prasad leaned forward and took her cool hand in his. He squeezed twice. Vidya's jaw firmed, then trembled.

"I am so angry at you," she choked. "But I have also missed you. You and Katsu both."

"How did you find us?" Prasad asked, still holding her hand.

Vidya took a deep breath. Her back straightened and Prasad released her. "That is a long story as well." She told what had happened after Katsu and Prasad's disappearance, how she discovered she was pregnant with Sejal, and how she changed her name. Guilt and regret at not having been at his wife's side washed over Prasad. How hard it must have been for her, while he, her husband, had lived in luxury with the daughter she thought dead.

"I did not wish to have another Silent child," Vidya said. "I found a genegineer—Max Garinn. He said he could use a retrovirus to make Sejal non-Silent. And it seemed he did. Sejal was tested twice for Silence, once at birth and once at age two. Both tests came back negative. But I have since learned that he is indeed Silent, as Katsu says."

She continued with the story, and Prasad learned how Vidya had built the neighborhood. He blinked as she related in a dispassionate voice how she had spoken to the Children of Irfan and learned of Sejal's activities in the market. An irrational bit of anger flashed within him. What kind of mother would allow such a thing?

And, whispered a conflicting voice, what kind of father would abandon his son to do it?

"I sent Sejal to the monastery," Vidya finished. Katsu remained impassive at her feet. "I stayed behind because I had questions. I have many contacts now as well, and I used them to track down Max Garinn, though it took many days. When I told him who I was, he brought me here. Dr. Kri was extremely excited to see me."

Prasad remembered how Kri and Say had talked about Katsu's mitochondrial DNA and how they wanted to study her and her eggs. He could easily understand the sensation Vidya's arrival would generate.

"When I asked why he was excited," Vidya continued, "he mentioned you, and I refused to answer any more questions until I saw you."

Prasad grimaced. "Max Garinn was recruited for the lab only six years ago and he never mentioned you. A pity he didn't; this reunion might have taken place years ago."

Katsu shifted somewhat, but didn't leave her position at Vidya's feet. Vidya had once again taken to stroking her hair. "What exactly is the lab doing, my husband?"

"My wife has not changed," Prasad observed with grave humor. "She always wishes instant information."

"And my husband has not changed," Vidya said pointedly. "He is ever slow to deliver it."

"The lab is exploring the genetics of Silence," Prasad told her. "It began with an attempt to find a way to let Silent gestate in artificial wombs so they would no longer be ripped away from their parents."

Vidya's look became skeptical. "They are trying to end the slavery of the Silent by creating people in laboratories?"

"Not quite." Prasad squirmed a bit under her steady gaze. "They were attempting to end the slavery of women who can produce Silent children. After all, some places not only enslave the Silent, but also those who can produce them. If the project is successful, that would stop."

"Have you had any success?" Vidya's voice was hard and flat.

"Some." Prasad felt reluctant to explain about the Nursery.

"My husband, you have failed to think. I have been in this place less than an hour, but already I can see the lie in that story." She gestured at the room. "This place is expensive. It must cost billions to maintain it, not to mention what the research itself must cost. Do you honestly think whoever is paying that much money is doing it for such unselfish reasons?"

"I have thought of that." Prasad scratched one raspy cheek. He had neither showered nor shaved yet this morning. "The process, if we perfect it, would almost certainly be worth mountains of money."

"And who pays for all this?"

Prasad looked straight at her. "I don't know. The doctors refuse to say. But when they offered a haven to me and Katsu, I took it. I could have gone back to Ijhan, but that would have meant giving up Katsu on her tenth birthday. I had already lost you. I did not wish to lose her as well. So I stayed and worked for them." He traced a finger over the curly pattern in the fabric of his chair. "But now, my wife, I am beginning to have doubts."

Overcoming his reluctance, he explained about the children in the Nursery and that the lab wanted to begin experimenting with Katsu's eggs. Katsu met this news with her usual composure, but Vidya went white.

"How can you stay in such a place?" she hissed.

The words came without thought or hesitation. "I can't."

Prasad paused, startled at himself. He had spoken the truth. Words banged inside his skull, demanding release.

"I can't stay," he said again. "I do not believe that those children are not sentient. I do not believe they feel no pain. They are in physical and mental distress, and I have not let myself see this. I think . . . I *know* I blinded myself to these facts because I wanted a safe place for Katsu and for me. Can you understand that?"

"A safe place," Vidya repeated softly. Her face softened. "Yes. I can understand."

A moment of quiet fell over the room. Prasad's stomach growled, and he became aware of the smell of honey bread still hanging on the air. They should eat. They could eat together as a family for the first time in seventeen years. Was Sejal, his son, eating breakfast now?

"They are in pain," Katsu spoke up.

"Who is?" Prasad asked absently.

"The children in the Nursery."

"How do you know this, my daughter?" Vidya said. Her voice was calm and soothing. A mother's voice.

"I dance with them in the Dream," Katsu replied. "Then they don't eat so much."

"Eat?" Prasad said, his mind still on breakfast. Did Katsu mean the children wanted to eat with them?

"They don't eat other people."

Prasad snapped to full attention at this. The hackles rose on his neck. "Katsu, what do you mean?"

"The children hunger for the touch of minds denied them in the womb and in the Dream," Katsu said. "They hurt and they are angry. I dance for them sometimes, and that calms them for a while, but they still hunger. And when they eat, they make many people despondent. Sometimes these people die."

And with that she fell silent.

"You must explain more, daughter." Vidya put her hand on Katsu's shoulder. "You must tell us what you mean."

But Katsu only rose and went into her room. The door shut softly behind her. Vidya watched her go with puzzled eyes.

"She is always like this," Prasad ventured. "Sometimes I think she says so little because she expects the rest of us to follow her reasoning, even when we lack the intelligence."

Vidya rose as well. "I think my husband needs to show me these other children."

"I think," Prasad said, pushing himself up from his chair, "my wife is correct."

Dr. David Kri was murmuring to a computer pad in his hand before the clear barrier in the Nursery. He was in his early middle years, blocky and short, with pale hair, red cheeks, and narrow green eyes. Beside him stood Max Garinn studying the spiky lines crossing a readout monitor and twirling his blond mustache. In the Nursery itself, several of the dark-haired children twitched and convulsed. Their mouths opened and shut, as did their brown eyes. Saliva dribbled down several chins. Vidya stared, her face pale.

"My husband," she whispered. "They look like you."

Prasad opened his mouth to deny this, then swallowed the words. The time for denial was over. Just because he had never looked up the records stating which children had received his DNA did not mean the knowledge was hidden. Vidya was forcing him to look, and now he would see.

Dr. Kri looked up from his pad. His eyes widened at Vidya. "What the hell?" he sputtered. "Prasad, what is she doing here? This is a restricted area!"

"Vidya must see everything before she decides whether or not to join the project," Prasad said calmly.

"And I will join," Vidya put in. "I find this fascinating."

Prasad stared. Vidya ignored this and turned to Max Garinn. "But first," she said, pointing at him, "you must answer my questions."

Garinn turned the monitor off. "Go ahead."

"You told me you could change my son Sejal so he would not be Silent," Vidya said flatly. "You lied. My son is Silent, a powerful Silent."

"He's the one the Unity was looking for?" Dr. Kri said, astonished. His voice was rich and mellow. "And you're his mother?"

"Yes."

Wild anticipation mixed with amazement and . . . hunger? . . . on Dr. Kri's face. Prasad could almost see the wheels turning in the man's head.

"I told you I had an experimental process," Garinn corrected Vidya, still twirling his mustache. Prasad wanted to snatch his hand away from it. "I made no promises, and I gave you money. The process obviously worked. Your son came up negative on both scans for Silent genes, so there must have been enough change made to fool the Unity. What are you complaining about? No one came to take him when he was ten years old."

"But he is still Silent," Vidya insisted, her voice cold, and deadly calm. "Did you do that on purpose? I need to know."

Garinn shook his head. "No. It was an unanticipated side effect."

He turned the readout monitor back on. Beyond him, one of the Nursery children abruptly went limp just as another went into another fit of spasmodic behavior. Vidya looked as though she wanted to say more, then apparently thought the better of it.

"You'll join us, then?" Dr. Kri's eyes gleamed and he clapped his hands once under his chin. "That's wonderful! What we could do—it boggles the mind. I mean, Prasad's DNA alone gave us this." He gestured at the twitching bodies in the Nursery, and a wave of shame swept over Prasad. "If we combine it with yours, well—we may bring this project to conclusion in only a few more years."

"I will, of course, require compensation," Vidya said

thoughtfully. She leaned against a desk. "I will have the same benefits you are giving Prasad, plus a salary twenty percent higher than his and a twelve thousand *kesh* signing bonus."

Dr. Kri smiled. "Oh dear. We aren't made of money, you know. Our . . . sponsor does well by us, but still—"

"Yes, I see," Vidya said, waving a hand. "Very well. I shall gather my things, then, and leave you to arrange my transportation back to—"

"Now, now," Dr. Kri interrupted, his rich voice taking on a silky edge. "I didn't exactly say no."

Vidya finally settled for a salary twelve percent higher than Prasad's and an eight thousand *kesh* bonus. Prasad shook his head. Why was she bargaining? They were going to leave, weren't they? He knew he couldn't stay. Now that he could see the place through Vidya's eyes, every moment spent in the Nursery made him more and more uncomfortable, more and more ashamed.

After the dickering ended, Vidya turned to Prasad. "Perhaps my husband will help me unpack?"

She took him firmly by the elbow and all but towed him away from the Nursery. The moment they had cleared the labs, Prasad turned to her.

"What was that about? Why did you say you would stay? I thought—"

"We are staying," Vidya said in a voice that brooked no argument, "until we can figure out what to do about those children."

NINETEEN

Planet Confederation's Core
Palace of Her Most August and Imperial Majesty Empress Kan maja Kalii

People who are [s]ilent are dangerous.
—Bolivar I of the Independence Confederation

Whether Bolivar meant silent *as a proper or a common noun is a matter for conjecture.*
—Scholar Perrin Wal

"War?" Ara exclaimed.

Empress Kan maja Kalii nodded. The jewels hovering about her head bobbed like confused fireflies for a moment before settling back into their normal orbits. Although it was early morning for Ara, it was night on this part of Confederation's Core, and the Empress was holding audience in a great alabaster hall with a cathedral ceiling and white marble floors. The Empress sat on a simple gray throne on a raised platform. Lamps glowed with cold light, and the windows were shut tight against darkness and spies. The only people in the room were Ara, Grandfather Melthine, and the Empress herself, though Ara and Melthine were actually possessing the bodies of a pair of Silent slaves. They currently knelt on large pillows near the base of the Empress's platform.

"Premier Yuganovi's personal Silent delivered the ultimatum moments ago," the Empress said. "The Empire of Human Unity resents the kidnapping of Sejal Dasa on the Confederation's behalf. If Sejal is not returned immediately, the Unity will declare war."

"Over Sejal?" Ara said incredulously.

"There are other factors," the Empress said. "I am also dealing with a boundary dispute and the fact that two favored slipship routes for Confederation ships brush Unity territory. A trade agreement we negotiated ten years ago needs to be reworked due to changes in the availability of the goods concerned, but the Unity refuses to discuss the idea. Another Unity spy was caught in my court and we're trying to see if we can arrange a trade for one of our operatives found in their territory, even though neither side is officially supposed to be spying on the other."

The Empress paused to rub a hand across her forehead. "Relations between the Confederation and the Unity are a keg of powder. You can probably guess how I would describe Sejal's supposed kidnapping."

Melthine cleared his throat. He currently wore the body of the muscular male slave Ara had possessed all those weeks ago when Pitr had been alive and the Empress had put Sejal's life into Ara's hands. Ara had taken the body of a heavy-breasted human woman nearing middle age. The weight of the woman's chest dragged continuously at Ara's back and shoulders.

"Have you sent the Unity an answer about Sejal, Imperial Majesty?" Melthine asked.

"I have not." The Empress crossed her ankles beneath her simple sky-blue robe. "The situation is delicate. If the Unity goes to war, we will, of course, call on the Belmare Planets and the Five Green Worlds as allies. The Confederation would appeal to the Koloreme Senate and the Micha Protectorates, but the Prism Conglomerate could go either way. If I persuade the Conglomerate to proclaim it would side with the Confederation, the Unity might back down without bloodshed and with only small financial cost to the Confederation. If war actually breaks out, the price for the Conglomerate's aid would go up. The Unity, of course, has probably already sent a delegation to the Conglomerate, and we must move quickly to match it." She sighed. "Mother Ara, what is your assessment of Sejal's position?"

Ara shot a sideways glance at Melthine. "I have no opinion at this time, Imperial Majesty. The matter requires . . . further study."

"What matter?" Melthine asked. "Is this the subject you declined to discuss in our meeting in the Dream?"

"Yes," Ara replied simply.

"You may tell him of the duty I laid upon you," the Empress put in.

Ara did. Melthine met the news with an impassive face. "I see."

"I can stall the Premier for some time, of course," the Empress said. "This sort of thing does not move quickly. Look how long it took the Unity merely to admit that young Sejal had slipped though their fingers."

She leaned forward and the jewels bobbed again. "Practicality says I should give Sejal back to prevent many lives from being lost in a stupid skirmish. I do not think it wise, however, to hand someone with Sejal's power over to the Unity. That itself might be worse than a war. This is not an easy position to be in, Grandfather and Mother."

"I can sympathize," Ara murmured, then quickly added, "Imperial Majesty."

The Empress leaned back without changing expression. "In any case, it is obvious the Unity knows of Sejal's power. They would not normally offer war over a single, untrained Silent, even in these volatile circumstances. I am still not sure, however, how they learned of his existence."

"Other Silent were sensing Sejal in the Dream before we left Rust," Ara said. "Kendi was just the first. Premiere Yuganovi probably had every Silent in the Unity searching for Sejal, and they finally tracked him down. I suspect that when Sejal possessed the six guard at our ship, it provided the final flare of activity they needed to pinpoint his location."

"That sounds reasonable," the Empress said. "However, there is also the chance that a spy was feeding the Unity information. Is it possible this was one of your crew members, Mother Ara?"

"I very much doubt it," Ara said. "Though if you have misgivings, we could question them—and me—in the Dream, since it's impossible to lie there."

"Do that," the Empress ordered. "Though Brother Pitr Haddis died, correct? I do not wish to open wounds, Mother Ara, but is it possible he was the spy?"

Ara's throat thickened with anger. Pitr a spy? Ludicrous! And now the Empress was questioning his sacrifice. The change in wording hadn't been lost on Ara, either—"a spy" had become "the spy." Witch hunt language.

"I don't think," Ara said with seething deliberateness,

"that Pitr would have ensured our escape and saved our lives at the expense of his own if he were a Unity spy."

The Empress nodded. "And what of Chin Fen?"

"He was a student at the monastery years ago," Melthine spoke up, and Ara was glad. It gave her time to regain her composure. "But he left before completing his training. He never reached the Dream. He claims he fled to the Empire of Human Unity because it put humans first and because he was young and foolish."

"Where is he now?"

"Under house arrest until I can decide what to do with him," came the reply.

"Is it possible he is the spy? That he can indeed reach the Dream and report information to the Unity?"

Ara shook her head. "Fen figured out who Sejal was long before he leaped aboard my ship. If Fen were spying for the government, he would have turned us in the moment he even suspected we were harboring the wanted Silent."

"What of your son Benjamin?" the Empress said.

Ara's mouth fell open in utter shock, as if the Empress had dumped a load of icewater on her head.

"He ran communications on board the *Post-Script*," the Empress continued relentlessly. "It would have been easy for him to alert the Unity to anything he pleased."

Ara did the unthinkable. Still kneeling, she turned her back on the Imperial Majesty. Black anger made every muscle as rigid as a brick, and Ara would have launched herself at the Empress's throat if she had been forced to look at her for one moment more. She stared fixedly at the far end of the hall, boiling with rage.

Serene must you ever remain, she told herself. *Serene. Serene.*

"Benjamin Rymar," Melthine answered quietly, "is one of your most faithful subjects, Imperial Majesty. He is devoted to the Children, even though he is not Silent. So are Harenn Mashib and Jack Jameson. I have utter confidence in them all."

Ara did not turn around. She knew she was risking time in prison for her disrespect, but she couldn't bring herself to act properly yet.

"Here is my decision, then," the Empress said. She seemed to be ignoring Ara's breach. "Two of my slaves will enter the Dream and question all Silent who were on board the *Post-Script*, including you, Mother Ara. I expect it to be a formality and I expect that the Unity learned of Sejal through its own Silent, but we must be sure. Since Chin Fen is not my subject but wishes to defect, he will answer questions under medication. We shall, for the moment, assume Benjamin, Jack, and Harenn are innocent."

Melthine said nothing. Ara continued to stare at the far wall.

"Mother Ara," the Empress said in a kinder tone, "I know this is difficult—"

Ara whirled, heedless of Imperial protocol. "You know nothing. First you order me to decide whether an innocent boy should live or die. Then you make a mockery of the Brother who gave his life for mine, and you accuse my son of high treason. Your ass is on a throne, but your head is in a toilet."

"Ara!" Melthine gasped, horrified. "Imperial Majesty, I beg you to excuse—"

"Calm, Grandfather Melthine," Empress Kan maja Kalii said gently. She turned her brown eyes on Ara. "I understand more than you know, Mother. Shall I tell you how I spent my day? This morning I ordered emergency famine relief for a suffering planet. The planet is remote, and in order to ensure relief arrives in time to do any good, foodstuffs, medical supplies and other materials must be shipped in from the closest two planets without delay. Although the Confederation subsidizes everything, it will take time for the subsidies to catch up. This means the relief effort will put a temporary drain on these planets' economies and there is a good chance it will spark economic recessions that will change hundreds of thousands of lives. It took me over two hours to analyze the factors involved and order the implementation of this plan. In those two hours, five thousand, two hundred and twenty-four of my subjects died of hunger.

"Next, I received word that a minor conflict between a Confederation planet and one of its colonies has escalated into full-scale war because my nephew, who I sent as a mediator, was kidnapped and tortured to death by agitants."

Ara suppressed a gasp at these words. Kalii continued without changing tone or inflection.

"Hundreds of people have so far died in this war. Now I must send troops to put down this uprising, meaning still more lives will be lost or irrevocably changed, many of them innocent civilians. This is how I spent my afternoon.

"This evening, I sit here discussing the fate of a single boy and a handful of Silent monks while the nephew I loved like a son lies in a bloody grave a thousand light-years away. And I must discuss these things because if I do not, the Unity will declare a war that will make my nephew's conflict a playground scuffle by comparison."

With a single swift gesture, Kalii snatched the little jewels that orbited her head into her palm and flung them away. They bounced and scattered like marbles across the white stone floor. "I am long weary of this, Mother Ara. I inherited this crown seventy-two years ago from my father, Bolivar the First, and in that time the burden has become no easier to bear. Billions of people live and die by my words, and I sleep with their ghosts every night.

"I am not asking for your pity. I am, however, asking you to understand that you are not the only one who must make difficult decisions or watch the ones you love pay for your mistakes."

Ara had not moved. Now she bowed her head low, her anger replaced by a shame that flamed her cheeks red and raw. "My deepest apologies, Imperial Majesty. I often berate my former student Brother Kendi for speaking without thinking. It seems I must learn to take my own advice."

Kan maja Kalii nodded. "You and I are much alike, Mother Adept Araceil. People of our kind see what must be done, and we do it. Only afterward do we find time for tears."

Ara flushed at the praise, even though she recognized the words as those of a leader trying to raise the morale of a subordinate. *Interesting,* she thought, *how psychology works even when the recipient is aware of it.*

"Have the ships returned, Imperial Majesty?" Melthine asked. "The ones that were sent to investigate the Silent enveloped by the disturbance in the Dream?"

The Empress shook her head. "Not yet. They have no

doubt arrived by now and are investigating, but then it will take them some time to get back."

"Once they arrive, can't the Silent on board the ships simply report back?" Ara said.

"We have been studying the disturbance, Ara, and we advised the Empress not to send Silent to those planets," Melthine put in.

"What?" Ara said, wondering, since she had already flouted Imperial protocol and gotten away with it, if she could push a little further and sit cross-legged instead of kneeling. Kendi must be rubbing off on her. "Why not?"

"Dream mechanics," Melthine said. "Space means nothing to Silent within the Dream, but it does to non-Silent minds outside of it. When we enter the Dream, remember, we build that reality from the real-world minds closest to us before we can move on to other minds. We don't know what would happen if Silent tried to reach the Dream using minds from within the disturbance. Better first to learn what happened to the Silent already there."

A tickle at the base of Ara's skull warned her that her drugs were beginning to wear off and she would have to leave soon. As before, it seemed as if the Empress could read Ara's mind.

"Your time must be running short," she said. "You have your instructions. I will expect to hear from you soon regarding these matters. Grandfather. Mother."

"Imperial Majesty," they replied together. Then Ara let go of her body.

A dark room, the same one she always encountered before possessing an Imperial Silent, popped into existence around her. The two bits of light that represented the Silent slaves they had possessed floated in front of her, and Grandfather Melthine, no longer young and muscular, stood to one side. The furry, rotund Seneschal, Imperial silver chain hanging around its neck, ushered them out and courteously bade them good-bye. Behind them, the Dream foyer slipped into nothingness and disappeared entirely, leaving them on the familiar empty plain. In the distance, ever-present and almost taken for granted now, was the red and black chaos.

Melthine had said space meant nothing in the Dream,

and this was normally true. Where Ara was depended on where she wanted to be. If Ara thought she and her garden were worlds away from, say, Gretchen's ship, so it was. If Ara thought the ship was so close that the mast was visible over the garden wall, so it would be. If two Silent had contradictory ideas of what reality looked like, for example if Gretchen felt Ara was far away and Ara was sure Gretchen was nearby, the strongest will would win.

All this meant nothing when it came to the distant darkness. No matter how hard Ara concentrated, it stubbornly loomed on the horizon, perhaps two kilometers away. She could get closer if she wanted, but not farther.

"Ara!" Melthine grabbed her arm and pointed. "Look!"

The dark chaos, pulsing with its scarlet anger, was growing. It moved like a thundercloud, engulfing the plain of the Dream. The whispers around Ara went silent for a moment, then leaped into hysterical babble.

"We should leave the Dream," Ara urged. "Before—"

The ground rumbled beneath them. Lightning arced from the spreading darkness, stabbing the ground ahead of it like the antennae of a hungry insect. The darkness swirled like a red-cracked thundercloud. Melthine stared at it.

"Go!" Ara said, giving him a small push.

A scarlet lightning bolt smashed into Melthine's chest. Thunder blasted Ara off her feet and knocked her several meters away. She landed hard and for a moment she couldn't breathe. Her ears rang and her nose was bleeding. The ground shook again. Stunned, Ara stared stupidly upward, unable to move or think. Then she remembered Melthine. Panic jigged in her mind like a frightened frog. Ara forced herself to roll over. Melthine lay in a boneless heap perhaps ten meters away. She got up and ran toward him, ignoring the pain in her ears and her head. This was the Dream. There would be no pain.

The pain remained with her as she knelt beside Melthine. His eyes were closed and his skin was clammy. He was still breathing, though the breaths came fast and shallow. A black hole had been burnt in his chest. Horrified, Ara felt for his pulse. But even as she did so, the breath hissed heavily from his lungs. He went still and vanished beneath Ara's fingertips.

"No!" she cried. "Melthine!"

But the plain was empty.

Another bolt of lightning struck the ground and thunder crashed close enough to make Ara's ears ring anew. The darkness was still expanding, rolling toward Ara like a juggernaut. Swiftly, Ara quashed her grief and gathered together her concentration. At the last moment, the words of the Empress echoed in her mind.

You and I are much alike, Mother Araceil Rymar. People of our kind see what must be done, and we do it.

Ara opened her eyes. The familiar ceiling of her own house was above her. Quickly she sat up.

"Bruna," she said frantically, "call emergency services."

Wordlessly the house computer made the connection. In hurried tones, Ara started to tell the operator what had happened, but the woman interrupted.

"Emergency services are with him now, Mother Adept," the operator's disembodied voice said through the computer speakers. "Grandfather Melthine wears a wristband monitor when he enters the Dream and we were alerted. He will be transported to the medical center."

Ara disconnected and called the medical center. Melthine hadn't arrived yet, of course, so she made herself wait an agonizing half hour. There was no point in going down there—they wouldn't let a nonrelative see him in the emergency room.

Ara called the medical center again. Melthine was alive but comatose. Only close family members would be allowed to visit. Ara disconnected and passed a hand over her eyes, not sure whether she should be relieved that Melthine was still alive or upset over what had happened.

The house around her was quiet, and now it felt eerie, as if something were waiting to jump out of the Dream straight at her. There was plenty of empty space. In addition to several guest rooms, a dining room, living room, and computer playroom, the house contained Ara's office and her Dream Temple, the latter merely Ara's fanciful term for the comfortably furnished room she liked to use when she entered the Dream.

The house was, like most Bellerophon houses, done in glass and brown wood, and it was located only a short walk from the monastery. A wraparound balcony looked out over the misty leaves and branches, and flower boxes full of colorful blooms brightened the balcony rail. A walkway connected her balcony to the main thoroughfares, and neighbors had similar houses above and below her in the talltree. Ara shamelessly enjoyed the place. After everything she went through—was still going through—as a Mother Adept, she deserved every penny of the generous stipend that had allowed her to buy the house almost ten years ago.

"Attention! Attention!" Bruna said. "Emergency-level newscasts located."

Ara stiffened. Most house computers constantly scanned the news services for stories that might be of interest to their owners. Bruna was no exception. An emergency-level cast coming right now could only be related to the Dream incident that had nearly killed Melthine.

"Bruna, put recent newscasts on screen," she ordered. "Text and video. No holograms."

One wall flashed with videos and words. Ara watched and read. So far over two hundred Silent had been on the receiving end of some sort of Dream onslaught, and the numbers were still coming in. They had been swallowed by pits, struck by lightning, ripped apart by tornados. Some had been attacked by their own Dream furnishings. Half of the two hundred were dead. The disturbance had expanded to engulf another nine planets—twenty-eight now in all. The Silent on those worlds were unreachable through the Dream.

Ara's blood chilled. These were just reports from the Independence Confederation and the worlds friendly to it. How many Silent had been attacked on worlds that didn't report such things? What was going on?

A link to a related story caught Ara's eye, and she followed it, partly to get the frightening words and pictures off her wall. She could have disconnected, but the house was empty and Ara didn't want silent rooms right now.

After a moment's reading the news story, Ara's forehead crinkled. A new study showed rates of depression on three separate worlds had risen sharply in the last six months, as were incidents of domestic violence, violent crime, and suicide. Each of the three worlds was unrelated, except for the fact that a pair of them were two of the nineteen worlds originally swallowed by the black chaos. The third world was close by. The report had been released just before the engulfment, but with the recent attacks on Silent, someone had dug it up and rereleased it.

An increase in domestic violence, violent crimes, and suicide. Related? The Dream was, according to some theorists, made of all sentient minds in the universe. Would a worldwide increase in depression have an impact on the Dream?

Or would it be the other way around?

Ara got up to pace the hardwood floors of her bedroom. There had to be a relationship. The chaos. Depression rates. Sejal. A piece of this was missing, and Ara was sure if she had it, she would know what was going on. And the longer it remained a mystery, the more difficult everything would become. The Dream was getting more and more dangerous by the minute. If this kept up, communication between planets would die, or at least be dealt a severe blow. Governments, corporations, law enforcement agencies, and millions of individuals depended on the Dream. Messages and information that had once been instantaneous would take weeks or months if they were relegated to slipspace courier.

"Bruna," she said, "access economic and market news databases. Analyze overall trends in trading over the last three months and compare with previous decade. Answer question: Are overall market values up, down, or steady? Answer question: Is inflation up, down, or steady? Answer question: Is selling of stock up, down, or steady?"

"Please specify governments or planets."

"All governments and planets in database."

"Working." Pause. "Analysis complete. Question: Are overall market values up, down or steady? Answer: Markets in all reporting governments are down. Question: Is inflation up, down, or steady? Answer: Inflation in all reporting governments is up. Question: Is selling of stock up, down, or steady? Answer: Selling of stock in all reporting governments is up."

Ara nodded grimly. She was no economist and only had a vague idea of how buying, selling, and investing worked. However, it was easy to see that the markets were already showing a strain.

Ara wandered over to a low table with a wooden incense holder on it and lit a stick. Sweet, lightly scented smoke floated about the room. At one time, governments and companies had functioned amazingly well with slow communication. On early Earth, it had taken weeks or even months for messages to cross the ocean, yet several countries had ruled colonies thousands of miles away. Modern governments and corporations, however, were another matter entirely. They had been created with and were maintained by instant communication. Rulers and executive officers were used to making hands-on decisions for branches and worlds that lay months away by slipship. All that would disappear if the Dream were disrupted. Even the small delays caused by the current situation were causing markets to dip.

The coal at the tip of the incense stick glowed red, and gray smoke continued to trickle upward like a tiny reverse waterfall. Other thoughts Ara had been putting off crowded her mind, now that she knew Melthine was safe.

Thoughts about war.

The Empress had said a war was brewing between the Unity and the Confederation, a war that would probably never happen if Ara killed Sejal. The Empress hadn't said so, but Ara knew she was thinking it. Giving Sejal back to the Unity was not a possibility—that would cause more problems than it solved. Wouldn't it be better just to kill Sejal? What if war broke out and Ben were killed? He would be dead because Ara couldn't bring herself to raise a simple knife in his defense. The thought was unbearable.

But it wasn't Sejal's fault he could do what he could do. He had done nothing wrong. And Ara had seen nothing to indicate that Sejal would abuse his power.

Ara waved the incense stick through the air. Smoke trailed after it, leaving fuzzy gray streaks in the air. Unfortunately, the universe—and the Unity—didn't care about intentions. The fact that Sejal existed was enough to start a war. Her decision came down to simple mathematics. The death of Sejal versus the death of thousands. The death of Sejal versus the death of Ben.

People of our kind see what must be done, and we do it.

A tear trickled down Ara's cheek. Deep down, she had

known there was only one answer. She had known it from the moment the Empress had spoken those dreadful words on that dreadful day.

You are but the scalpel that does the bidding of the doctor.

Slowly, as if hypnotized, Ara set the incense down and left the Dream Temple. She went to her study and lifted a small trapdoor cunningly concealed to look like part of the wooden floor. Beneath was the door to a safe. She let the lock scan her retina, fingerprints, and voice. The locks released with a firm thump. From the safe, Ara removed a snub-nosed pistol and checked the charge. Full.

Ara knew how to use the pistol. All Children received at least basic instruction in energy weapons. When fired, this one disrupted electrochemical processes in nerve cells. At lower power, it stunned. At high power, it killed. Ara set the power as high as it would go. She put the pistol into her pocket and headed out the front door.

People of our kind see what must be done, and we do it.

Ara checked her ocular implant. It was still early morning of the day after the *Post-Script* had landed and Kendi had taken Sejal down to the dormitory. If the pattern for new arrivals from poor backgrounds held true, Sejal had first gone shopping yesterday, probably with Kendi. Today, Sejal would register for classes and be given time to explore and settle in. Tomorrow would be his first day of formal instruction. Since it was still early, Sejal was doubtless in his room sleeping.

The walk to the monastery students' dormitory took half an hour. Ara knew she was walking to put off the inevitable, but she couldn't bring herself to snag a gondola or take the monorail. The time passed as if in a dream. A few early rising students saluted her as she passed them on the swaying walkways, but Ara barely noticed.

In the dormitory foyer, she asked for and received directions to Sejal's room. As she walked the hallway, Ara put her hand on the pistol in her pocket. No doubt there would be a public outcry. No doubt Ara would be ostracized, despite interference from the Empress. At the Imperial Majesty's insistence, Ara might retain her position as Mother Adept, but that wouldn't stop the whispers and pointed fingers.

At least the whisperers would be alive to point.

Ara found herself at Sejal's door. Blood pounded in her ears and her hand shook as she raised her fist to knock.

The door swung open at her touch. It hadn't been locked, or even closed all the way. Puzzled, Ara stepped into the room. No one was inside.

The built-up tension vanished so quickly, it left Ara weak and shaky. She sat down on the unmade bed. The place was still austere and spartan, with nothing to indicate the personality of the room's inhabitant. Not surprising. Sejal had come to the monastery with almost nothing, and he'd only been here for two days. Hardly enough time to accumulate more possessions than a few clothes. The bed hadn't even been made up—the linens still sat neatly folded on the mattress. Odd.

At that moment the significance of the door came to her. It hadn't been just unlocked. It had been open a crack. Hard to believe someone who had grown up in a slum would leave his door unlocked, let alone standing open. Ara fumbled for a moment, trying to remember the name of the dormitory's computer.

"Baran," she said, "where is Sejal Dasa?"

"Sejal Dasa is in his quarters."

This was obviously not the case. Ara looked around. A scarlet glitter caught her eye. On Sejal's desk in plain sight lay his ruby student's ring. The ring carried a trace which allowed the monastery computer system to track students and monks alike. Although it was common practice to remove the ring for privacy or other reasons, this didn't seem to be the case. It felt wrong.

Ara did a cursory search of Sejal's room. No clothes hung in the closet. Maybe Kendi hadn't taken him shopping yet after all, or maybe that's where Sejal was now. No, the shops wouldn't open for another hour at least, and the bed had clearly not been slept in last night. Something else occurred to Ara, and she searched the room again, this time more thoroughly. She came up empty.

Mother Adept Araceil Rymar sat heavily on Sejal's bed. His flute was nowhere in the room. Ara's hands went cold. No flute, no clothes, unmade bed, a door standing open. It all pointed to one thing.

Sejal Dasa was gone.

TWENTY

Sejal's Journal

Day 18, Month 11, Common Year 987

I'm not on Bellerophon anymore. I'm on another ship now, a nicer one than the *Post-Script.* I wasn't even at the monastery two days before—

This is stupid. My thoughts are wandering all over the place. I don't know what to think or do or anything. I'll start at the beginning and maybe it'll make more sense.

Anyway, Kendi took me shopping. I've never had new clothes before. Most of my clothes were hand-me-downs from the neighborhood. The rest came from a secondhand store. But here, Kendi took me into real stores with real salespeople, helpful ones who didn't try to brush us off.

"There are a bunch of people who want to talk to you," Kendi said as we finished up. "They want to run some tests on what you can do, and they want to do it this evening. Is that okay with you?"

I nodded, still enjoying the feel of new clothes on my body. They still smelled new, and they were mine.

We took a gondola back to the monastery. It's like riding in a giant basket on a wire, except the basket is made of metal instead of wicker. Once we got there, we dropped off my stuff and Kendi took me to another building.

Inside was a big room that reminded me of the gymnasium back at my old school, but with a polished floor and new yellow paint. A long table was set up near the far wall. Four humans and four Ched-Balaar were there, along with four other aliens. One looked like a caterpillar, one looked like a stuffed bear, one looked like a small elephant that had been hosed with red candle wax, and one looked like some kind of lizard. The humans were dressed in brown robes with gold disks around their necks.

When Kendi and I reached the table, I remembered to put my fingertips against my forehead like I was supposed to, even though I was suddenly so nervous my teeth were almost chattering. What if they sent me back to the Unity?

The oldest human in the group stepped up to the table, which was between me and him. He used a walking stick and had big purple ring on his hand. "Sejal Dasa? I'm Grandfather Adept Melthine. You can call me 'Grandfather' or 'Grandfather Adept.' "

He introduced the others, including the Ched-Balaar and the other aliens, and they all sat down. The smaller aliens had chairs on the tabletop, and the Ched-Balaar sat on the floor like giant dogs. Kendi and I took chairs on the other side of the table. I still wanted to puke.

"Well, Sejal," Grandfather Melthine began. "We want to know more about you. You have an unusual ability, and we're fascinated."

He sounded friendly enough and he had a nice face. I was still a little wary, though. The others didn't say anything.

"We'd like to see what you can do," Grandfather Melthine continued. "Why don't you start by telling us."

I hesitated.

"Go ahead, Sejal," Kendi said. "It's all right."

"I can make people do things," I said nervously.

"Like what?" Melthine asked. His voice was still gentle, not at all stern. I concentrated on him, blocking out the aliens in the room, and was able to relax a little bit.

"I can freeze people in place," I told him, "and they don't remember what happened when I let them go. I can also make people want to do something so bad, they do it."

"Can you give an example?" Melthine said.

"Well, I froze six Unity guard in place so we could get back on the *Post-Script.* And another time I made a guard want to punch his partner so bad that he couldn't help doing it."

"A powerful form of whispering," murmured one of the other humans. "But without entering the Dream."

"I don't do it directly," I added. "I have to sort of . . .

reach through another place. It might be the Dream, but I'm not sure."

Melthine's hand was on his walking stick, even though he was sitting. "How does the freezing work, Sejal? What do you do?"

I thought about it. "It's like I can . . . see what they're feeling. Well, not really see. I just sort of know. And then I reach through the weird place and make one of those feelings really strong. The feeling already has to be there. I can't make new ones."

"Whispering," the other human said again.

"How do you 'freeze' people, as you call it?" Melthine said.

"I shut their feelings down completely," I said. "I looked it up once. It's called apathy. You don't have feelings, you don't have any reason to do anything. You don't even care enough to remember what happened."

Melthine nodded. "You don't possess people then? Put your mind into someone else's body and take it for your own?"

"No."

Everyone in the room gave a little sigh, like they were relieved or something. I didn't understand it. Several of them looked at Kendi like he had done something wrong. I didn't understand that, either. Was Kendi in trouble?

"Sejal," Kendi said quietly. "Have you ever tried to possess someone completely?"

"No."

"Can you, do you think?"

I thought about it. "Probably."

The people at the table got all tense again.

"Try it with me," Kendi said.

I looked at him. "Take over your body?"

"Sure. It's nothing new, Sejal. Silent do it all the time. Do that freeze thing, but push harder. You can't hurt me. It'll be all right."

So I did. Before any of the others said anything, I touched Kendi with my mind, like I did with that first jobber back with Jesse. Then I *pushed.*

The world jumped to the right. I was sitting in a different place. I looked down at my hands. They were bigger and darker. I drew in a sharp breath. The noise sounded different in my head. I looked sideways and saw . . . myself. My eyes were shut and I was slumped sideways in my chair. I leaped up, knocking the chair over. My heart pounded, but the rhythm was wrong. I panicked.

A hand landed on my shoulder and I yelped. It was reflex—I took that mind, too. I was seeing the room from two different points of view. There were two of me, but only one, at the same time.

The other people—and aliens—in the room scrambled to their feet. The sudden movement scared me again, and then I had three, four, five, and six people. Then seven and eight and nine. My eyes looked in a dozen different directions all at once. I had two legs—no, four legs—no, a dozen. My hearts were thumping so hard they hurt. In panic, I saw my body, still slumped in the chair. I wanted to be back inside it. I wanted to be *me* again. I lunged for myself.

And then I was there. I opened my eyes and looked down at my hands. *My* hands. *My* arms. *My* body.

I looked up, shaking. The room was dead silent. Everyone was looking at me. Then a babble broke out as everyone started talking at the same time. One of the humans, a blond man, was shouting. The caterpillar waved its arms. Kendi looked stunned. I just huddled in my chair. They were angry. They were going to do something to me. I wanted to run.

Finally Grandfather Melthine quieted the room and got everyone to sit down again. He was the one who'd put a hand on my shoulder. His face was pale.

"That was . . . impressive, young Sejal," he said. He wiped his forehead with the sleeve of his robe. "I think you made history today."

I didn't say anything.

"We'll need to analyze this more closely later," Melthine added. "We thought Brother Kendi was powerful because he can split his mind into two pieces in the Dream. But you, Sejal . . . well, your abilities go rather beyond that."

I still didn't say anything.

Grandfather Melthine took a deep breath. "Well. Mother Adept Araceil Rymar also reported that you can pull other people into the Dream. Is that correct?"

I nodded.

"Tell us about it in your own words."

I did. It took some time. Kendi got me some water, and I was glad for it. I was still nervous. Everyone listened carefully, and they didn't interrupt. I got the feeling they'd heard the story before and mentally kicked myself for not realizing that Kendi and probably Mother Ara had already told it to them.

When I was done, Melthine nodded. "Is there anything else you can do?"

I hadn't told them about my empathy talent. I was going to, but then I changed my mind. I can't say why. Eventually I'd have to tell someone, probably Kendi, but then I could say I forgot about it or that it was new. So I shook my head.

One of the Ched-Balaar chattered something from where he (she?) was squatting on the floor.

"Father Adept Ched-Farask wants to know more about this ability to bring people into the Dream," Melthine told me. "Can you do it with anyone? Including non-Silent?"

"I don't know," I said truthfully.

"Have him try it with me," said a new voice. Everyone's head swung around and I twisted in my seat. Harenn was standing in the doorway. I wondered how she had known about the meeting and figured Kendi must have mentioned it to her.

"Harenn Mashib," Grandfather Melthine said. "You weren't invited here."

Like that ever stopped Harenn. She walked straight up to the table as cool as an ice trader. "I volunteer to be a test subject," she said, "to see if Sejal can take the non-Silent into the Dream."

"Harenn—" Kendi said.

"I'll try it," I said suddenly. Until that moment, I hadn't really liked Harenn. But now here she was, facing down a council of powerful people. And I knew what she was going through. I had felt her panic and her pain for a few seconds. Harenn had told me how she was hoping to use the Dream to find her husband, the guy who'd kidnapped their kid and run off. I wanted to help.

"Sejal is too early in his training to enter the Dream

unaccompanied," Melthine pointed out. "He has been forbidden to do so."

Harenn snorted behind her veil. "Do you honestly think that has stopped this boy? As good to leave an open box of sweets on a child's bed and tell him he can only have one. He has entered the Dream often, you may be certain."

Kendi turned to me. I couldn't read his eyes. "Have you entered the Dream since I told you not to go there?"

And suddenly I was pissed. Sure, the Children of Irfan had gotten me off Rust, and sure, they were giving me an education and a place to live and some great clothes. It didn't mean they owned me.

"Damn right I have," I said. "It's easy. I can get in and out like that." I snapped my fingers. "Why shouldn't I go?"

"Dammit, Sejal," Kendi sputtered, "it's dangerous. There's something in the Dream that attacks Silent. You barely know how to create a body there. What if that thing in there hurt or killed you because you didn't know what to do? What if you—"

I folded my arms, feeling stubborn. "You sound like my mom."

That shut Kendi up.

Anyway. There was more arguing and more people yelling at me, but I just sat there. Harenn talked a lot, too, and you can guess whose side she was arguing. Finally, they all decided that I should try to take Harenn into the Dream. Kendi and Grandfather Melthine would go with me.

We moved to another room with couches and more comfortable chairs. Only the human Silent and the caterpillar came with us—the others wouldn't fit. I sat on a couch with my feet up and shut my eyes, not even waiting to see what Kendi and Melthine did. If I wanted to go into the Dream, I'd go. For a minute I wasn't sure I could trance with all those people in the room and with me being so angry, but after a short while I was fine. Voices whispered just faintly around me. I breathed deep and reached for them.

I opened my eyes in the Dream.

I was in the apartment back on Rust. The place was dull and dingy compared to the monastery, and suddenly I didn't want Kendi and Melthine there. But Kendi said each

Silent creates a Dream environment. I thought for a moment, then formed a picture in my head. I wanted to see it in front of me. I *would* see it in front of me.

And so it was. I was standing on a wide beach. White sand ran left and right as far as I could see. Reddish waves washed gently at the shore and a thick forest lay beyond the beach. Sea birds coasted by on the warm wind, and the sun shone overhead.

But not far offshore was that cracked chaos. It bubbled and boiled above the water, and just like last time, it called to me. I felt an overwhelming urge to jump into the ocean and swim toward it and even took a few steps toward the water.

I felt a ripple in the Dream, as if someone had thrown a rock into a pool I was standing in. I spun around and saw Kendi and Melthine on the sand.

"Nice beach," Kendi commented.

I nodded without speaking. If he hadn't shown up, I would have jumped into the ocean.

"It's getting bigger." Grandfather Melthine pointed at the darkness. "And it makes me feel nauseated."

I felt the pain in the darkness. It also sounded sweet and wonderful, but I didn't say anything.

"Can you feel Harenn?" Kendi asked. "Can you feel her the way you felt me that one time?"

I shut my eyes and felt around with my mind. With a start I saw that there were millions, billions, even trillions of minds everywhere. Every grain of sand, each drop of water, every leaf on every tree was a mind. Kendi had told me that the Dream was . . . what was the word? A gestalt. A combination of all the minds in the universe. But I hadn't really known what he meant until that moment. Each mind went about its business, some happy, some sad, most a jumble of emotions. I could feel them skitter around me, but at the same time they weren't moving. It was really weird.

Some of them I recognized. Gretchen, Ben, Mother Ara, Trish. And Harenn. She was around, too. I remembered how I'd called for Kendi when I got scared the first time I came into the Dream. I called for Harenn and reached for her. I touched her, and I *pulled.*

Something flickered in the air beside me like a bad hologram. Harenn stood on the beach for a tiny moment. Then she vanished.

I was suddenly tired. All my energy left me, and my legs felt like rubber. I shut my eyes and let go of the Dream.

When I opened my eyes again, I was back in the couch room. Everyone was looking at me. Melthine was lying on a couch and Kendi was standing in the corner with a stick under his knee. That was really strange, but I was too tired to think much about it. Where had the stick come from, anyway? Harenn was blinking at me like she was dizzy. I still felt tired.

"Are you okay?" I asked her.

"I am . . . uncertain," Harenn said. "I feel disoriented. One moment I was in this chair, then I was . . . on a beach? Then I was in my chair again."

"I couldn't hold you there," I said. "You slipped through my fingers."

"It failed, then," Harenn said in a flat, disappointed voice.

"The fact that you were there at all is significant," the blond Adept said from his own chair. He sounded awed. "This is astounding. A non-Silent in the Dream."

I tried to stand up, but ended up falling backward onto the couch from dizziness.

"I think my student needs rest," Kendi said beside me. He must have come out of the Dream and pulled the strange stick out from under his knee. "I'll take him back to his room. We can talk more about this later."

Grandfather Melthine blinked his eyes open. He sat up in time to catch Kendi's last remark. It seemed like he was going to object, then he looked at me.

"Take him home," he said. "And we certainly will discuss this again."

Kendi brought me back to the dormitory. We didn't talk much. I think he was still a little angry at me for going into the Dream without his permission. Tough.

Not that it matters now.

Anyway. I wasn't tired anymore when we got back to my room, but I wanted to be alone, so I let Kendi think I was exhausted. He left me sitting on my bed.

"Attention! Attention!" the computer said. "A delivery is waiting at the front desk."

Probably my clothes and stuff. I was about to go downstairs and get them when someone knocked. I thought maybe Kendi had forgotten something in my room or something, but when I opened the door, an old man was standing there. He wore white, and his clothes had that expensive, silky look I recognized from some of my jobbers. He also looked familiar. White hair, blue eyes, some wrinkles, sharp nose.

The train. It was the rude old man from the train.

"Hello, Sejal," he said. "May I come in?"

Too startled to say no, I let him in and shut the door. He sat on the corner of the bed farthest from me, keeping his clothes wrapped tight around him, as if he was afraid to let them touch me.

"Who—?" I began.

"My name is Padric Sufur," he said. "I want to make you a proposition."

He was a *jobber*? "I don't do that anymore," I told him. "So you can forget it."

The man blinked, and I could hear the tiny click of his eyelids. "You don't—oh! No, no. Nothing like that." He blinked again. "I'm the head of Sufur Enterprises, and I have some information about the Children of Irfan that might interest you. About Mother Araceil Rymar, in particular."

"What information?" I asked, tensing. This guy was setting off alarms left and right and I wished I hadn't let him in. If I shouted for help, would someone come?

"Mother Araceil has orders from Empress Kalii herself," Sufur said. "Orders to kill you."

The words were so strange, I didn't know how to react. "Kill me?" I said stupidly.

"Yes." He shifted on the bed, edging away from me. "The Empress ordered Mother Araceil to watch you and decide if you are a danger to the Independence Confederation. If she—Araceil—decides you are a danger, she is to kill you."

"She wouldn't," I said hotly, but something stirred in my gut.

"Perhaps. Perhaps not. But those were the Empress's orders."

My face was hot and my hands were cold. I remembered the way Mother Ara would look at me, as if she were sizing me up. I remembered how the Unity had sent warships to try to bring me back.

"How do you know this?" I demanded. "Who the fuck are you?"

"I told you. I'm Padric Sufur. We touched on the train, so you know I'm Silent. I touched you"—did he shudder?—"to make sure you were the person I was looking for."

My fingers were twisting my sweater like snakes. I was getting mad and found myself lapsing into my Jesse personality, the one I used with jobbers. "So you're Silent. Big fucking deal. Everyone around this shithole is Silent. How the hell does that tell you that Moth— that Ara's supposed to gash me?"

"I have connections," he said simply. "Mother Araceil Rymar has made a number of reports about you to Empress Kan maja Kalii. Twice Araceil possessed a Silent slave so they could meet in person to talk about you. In person with the Empress, Sejal. What does that tell you?"

"That she's—" And then I stopped, my Jesse instincts screaming at me to shut up. People love to talk. After I gave a jobber a mind-shattering orgasm, some of them would get weepy and want to blab about this or that. I was always surprised about what they were willing to tell a complete stranger. Why did they want to blather so much? After I broke down and cried in the restaurant with Kendi, I could kind of understand it, but Kendi had saved my life. Twice. This guy was a total stranger I didn't owe anything. So I shut up.

It didn't stop my mind from racing, though. Assuming Sufur wasn't lying—and my gut said he was telling the truth—what did Mother Ara meeting with the Empress tell me?

It told me that Harenn was right. I was important, everyone wanted a part of me, and they'd rather I was dead than end up with someone else.

When I didn't say anything, Sufur went on. "If you stay here, Sejal, they'll kill you."

The room was quiet. The French doors were still closed, keeping out the sound of breezes in the tree, though I saw green leaves fluttering beyond the glass. Footsteps trotted past my door and faded. I forced myself to think clearly before I said anything.

"You said if Ara decided I was a danger to the Independence Confederation, she was supposed to do it. How do you know she's decided I'm a danger?"

"Premier Yuganovi is very upset that you slipped away." Sufur calmly smoothed his trousers, as if he had said the weather would change. "The Unity's going to declare war."

"War? Over me?"

Sufur nodded. "You're the most valuable piece of property in history. You possess the power to topple empires and destroy governments. The Unity wants you to work for them. The Empress wants you to work for the Independence Confederation. Other governments will want you as well. Empress Kalii isn't stupid. She'll see—has seen—that she'll be fighting wars she can't possibly win. Sure, after a few years of training you'll probably be able to wipe out entire civilizations, but the Empress has to deal with the Unity *now*."

"You're exaggerating," I said. "I couldn't wipe out a civilization."

"You could make one person push all the right buttons and easily do the job," Sufur countered.

"I'd never do something like that!"

"The Empress doesn't know that. Premiere Yuganovi doesn't know that. And people change, Sejal. Who knows what you'll do in six years, or even six months, given the proper conditioning?" He crossed his arms. "No, Sejal. You're too dangerous for any government to let you live long."

I started to protest. Kendi wouldn't hurt me. The Children of Irfan had saved me, gone through a lot of trouble for me, even died for me. They wouldn't kill me after all that.

But my Jesse voice was whispering other things. Would they have come for me if it weren't for my special Silence? Would they have offered to take me off-planet if I were normal? Would Kendi have saved my life if I'd been an ordinary tricker like Jesse? I knew the answer. It wasn't me they wanted. It was my power.

I was starting to tear up, which made me mad. "Okay, so I believe you. What do *you* want? And don't give me any bullshit that you want to save my life."

Sufur chuckled. "Oh no, young Sejal. Unlike the Children and the Unity, I won't lie to you or pretend I'm talking to you for anything but selfish reasons. All humans are selfish. I'm just willing to admit it."

"Okay, then. Talk."

"Come with me. I'll give you sanctuary and I'll pay you well." He sounded like a jobber again.

"And what do you want me to do?"

Sufur wet his lips as if he were nervous. "I want you to end war."

I couldn't help it. I laughed. "Just like that, huh? You want me to end war?"

"You can do it, Sejal," Sufur said seriously. "Or at least, *we* can do it."

"How?" I asked, deciding to play along.

"What would happen," he said, "if there was a war and nobody came?"

Now I was getting nervous again. Sufur was starting to sound like a jay-head who'd had too much juice. "I don't know," I stalled.

He sighed and shook his head. "It's a rhetorical question. Look, you can possess people. More than one at a time?"

I nodded, despite the earlier advice from my Jesse voice.

"What if you got into a war, possessed the soldiers on both sides, and stopped them from fighting? What if you possessed the commanders and made them give surrender orders? What if you possessed the government leaders and made them sign peace treaties?"

"It'd work at first," I said, "until I let go. Then everyone would be back to fighting again."

"Not if they knew that you'd possess them again. And again and again until they gave it up."

"I'm one person," I protested. "I couldn't possibly do all that."

"You wouldn't need to." Sufur grinned like a cat. "It would only take the threat that you *might* do it. The Unity is willing to go to war over the mere threat that you *might* do something it doesn't like, right?"

"That's what you said."

"And they're declaring war because you're, in theory, aligning yourself with the Independence Confederation."

"Right," I said, wondering exactly where this was going.

"I'm not aligned with *any* government." He thumped himself on the chest. "If you come with me, the Unity—and everyone else—won't have a reason to declare war. You'll be neutral—and in a position to stop other wars from breaking out later."

I shook my head. This was a lot of information coming at me all at once. I wandered over to the French doors, and opened them a crack. Fresh, cool air blew into the room. I poked my head outside. A small group of other students, most of them older than me, were talking a ways up the common balcony. Good. If had to yell for help or make a fast exit, someone would hear me. I felt calmer now. Sufur didn't seem to be a whack-head, but you can never tell for sure.

"Look," Sufur said from my bed, "do you know what happened to your mother and father when the Unity invaded Rust?"

I turned. "What do you know about them?"

"I've done my research," he said. "Your parents are Prasad and Vidya Vajhur, though your mother later changed her name to Dasa. They ran a small cattle farm not far from the city of Ijhan. When the Unity invaded, it dropped biological weapons that wiped out Rust's food supply. Famine spread everywhere. Your parents, like a lot of people, headed for the city, hoping to find relief. There was none. A sea of people starving to death in their own filth and sewage surrounded Ijhan, and your parents were among them. Hundreds of thousands of innocent people died thanks to the Unity's little war."

"Where did you hear this?" I demanded, though I wanted to hear more. This was the stuff Mom never talked about.

"Your parents, however," Sufur continued as if I hadn't said anything, "did not die. They knew that they carried the genes for Silence, though they weren't Silent themselves. When their position became hopeless, they signed a contract with Silent Acquisitions, Inc."

"I know that," I interrupted. "How do *you* know it?"

"I told you—I have many contacts." He took out a white silk handkerchief and passed it over his forehead. Did I make him nervous? "Later, the Unity took over your parents' contract and forced them to hand over their first two children."

"I know that, too," I interrupted. "So what?"

"War destroyed your family, Sejal. It starved them and forced your parents to give your brothers away. War allowed the Unity to conquer your homeworld and drain it dry. Because of war, you were forced to live in an impoverished slum all your life."

"More contacts?" I said.

Sufur nodded. "More contacts. You'll have to get used to it, I'm afraid. Word about you is already spreading. No matter what choices you make, your life will be under constant scrutiny." He stood up and leaned against the door frame. "Ultimately, it all comes down to this, Sejal: Araceil Rymar has been ordered to kill you. The Empress gave her the order before either of them had even met you. Even if Araceil decides to let you live—and I very much doubt that she will—do you really want to stay in a place where such orders are given so casually?"

I didn't answer because there was only one to give. Suddenly I was angry again. Earlier today things were looking good. I had new clothes, my own place to live, and people who liked me. This jay-head was taking it all away.

"Why the hell should I go with you?" I snapped. "I don't have any proof of who you are or what you'll do to me once I leave. How do I know *you* haven't been sent to kill me?"

Sufur raised his hands, and I realized I had pretty much said I was going to leave. "You have the power to make me do—or not do—anything you want. How could I hurt you? And if I were going to kill you, wouldn't I just do it instead of talking all this time?"

I thought about it for a while. I didn't want to go, but I knew I couldn't stay.

"Can Kendi come?" I said before I could stop myself.

"Do you really think he'd want to?"

I thought about it. "No," I sighed.

"Let's go then," Sufur said gently. "I have a ship."

And then my Jesse personality spoke up. Always get the money up front. "We haven't talked terms yet."

Sufur smiled. "Altruism isn't enough?"

If he was thinking I didn't know what *altruism* meant, he was wrong. "I can't eat altruism. And you don't look exactly hungry yourself."

"Fair enough." He scratched his head. "How about this, then. Just to show you I mean what I say, I'll give you a salary and no duties. You do what you want. If you don't like what's going on, you can take your money and leave, no strings attached."

I eyed him with heavy suspicion. "What's the catch?"

"There isn't one. I'm just willing to bet you'll want to hang around."

"How do you know I won't steal you blind?"

"Two reasons," he replied instantly. "The first is that people who plan to steal me blind rarely ask that question. The second is that I've studied your history. With what you can do, you could have set yourself up pretty well, even on Rust. You didn't, and I think it's because you're not the kind of person who would steal."

I didn't like the fact that he had me so well pegged. "So what's the salary?"

"Let's see." Sufur pulled a computer pad from his pocket and started punching at it. "The Unity uses *kesh.* One *kesh* converts to point two four freemarks. So that would be . . . All right. Yearly salary of two and a half million freemarks. That's about ten million *kesh.* Full medical care and your own flitcar."

Jesse froze my face before I could show my reaction. Ten million *kesh* was a truckload. Or it was back on Rust.

Never take the first offer, Jesse whispered. I managed a sneer, despite the fact that my heart was racing. "Ten million?" I scoffed. "How much do you think I'd get if I just put myself up for auction?"

"Fifteen million."

"Thirty," I said. "And I want my own house. With a

swimming pool. And all the other stuff you said. And five million extra up front as a bonus."

"Done."

Idiot, Jesse said. *He agreed too fast. That means he thinks you're a bargain.*

But I didn't care. Thirty-five million in one year, plus a house and a flitcar. I'd never see a slum from the inside again. I crossed the room and stuck out my hand. Sufur looked at it for a long moment, then slowly brought out his own hand. His handshake was quick and limp and he pulled back as soon as he could. What was with him?

I got my flute and the computer button with my journals on it while Sufur's pad wrote up a contract. We both thumbed it, and that was that. I looked around the room that hadn't even had time to become mine. As we were heading out the door, I took off the ring Kendi had given me and dropped it on my desk in plain sight. When we left, I made sure the door was open a crack to make it clear I was gone.

"Aren't we going to go out the back?" I said as we headed down the main hallway. "This leads to the front desk."

"So?" Sufur replied. "I haven't broken the law."

Oh. "In that case . . ." I stopped at the front desk and picked up my delivery. I had been right—it was my clothes and other stuff. I made a mental note to transfer money to the Children of Irfan to pay for them. Like Sufur said, I'm not a thief.

We rode the monorail back to the spaceport. Sufur made sure there was a seat between us when we sat down. Then he put a finger to his ear and muttered to the empty air. I figured he was talking to his ship.

It was weird. Here I was on the monorail again. I was going backward, retracing the route that had brought me here. I had been happy coming in. I was depressed going out. I came in with a friend. I went out with a stranger. I came in poor. I went out rich.

Anyway. Sufur's ship at the spaceport was small but luxurious. The hallways were thickly carpeted and the walls were painted with murals and frescos. It smelled new. The elevator was a floating disk that hummed up through a hole in the ceiling/deck to the bridge. There were only two chairs, and their backs were to us.

"Are we cleared to take off?" Sufur said.

One of the chairs spun partway around. My jaw dropped and almost lost the hold on my packages. Sitting in the chair was Chin Fen.

"We're all clear," he said.

The other chair, a shorter one, also spun. An alien was in it, sort of like a giant brown spider. It waved its legs and antennae.

"Translation," said a computer voice. "I've been monitoring newscasts. Nothing so far."

"Good," Sufur said. "Let's go then."

"What the hell is he doing here?" I burst out, pointing at Fen.

Fen laughed. "You think I'm going to stay?"

"Didn't Kendi say you were under house arrest or something?" I asked.

"I was," Fen said. He cracked wrinkled knuckles. "It was low-level security. The monks watching me were nice enough. They thought the job was perfunctory, and until a couple hours ago, it was. I caught them off-guard. They'll wake up in the morning and get yelled at by their supervisor, I'm sure."

I folded my arms. "You were feeding information about me to Ara and to Sufur."

"I said I had contacts," Sufur put in mildly. "Let's take off."

Fen and the spider turned back to their consoles. Sufur stepped back onto the elevator, which started to hum downward. I jumped on it beside him and grabbed his arm. He drew away, but I didn't let go.

"I thought you said there was nothing illegal going on," I snarled. "Fen's a spy."

"Not as far as the Confederation is concerned," Sufur said tightly. "Let me go, please."

His voice was hard. I let go, and he smoothed his white sleeve. The elevator disk reached the next deck down, and Sufur went into some kind of lounge. Wide round portholes looked out at the spaceport and more thick carpets covered the floor. Half a dozen adjustable bed-couches were arranged around the room. Sufur sat in one. I took another.

"What do you mean?" I pressed. "Either Fen's a spy or he isn't."

Sufur lay back on his couch and stared at the ceiling. I couldn't read his expression. "I sent Fen to the Unity as my mole about five years ago, though I'm sure he told you and Mother Araceil that he'd been there longer. He's adept at digging up information, even classified secrets. If he told Araceil half of what he told me, I'm surprised she didn't get suspicious at what a mere clerk was able to uncover."

My stomach dropped as the ship lifted. The ships visible through the portholes fell away and were replaced with blue sky.

"I'm sure the Unity would love to talk to Fen," Sufur continued. "The Confederation, on the other hand, should be grateful to him. He was paid to feed information to *me*, not the Children or the Empress. The Confederation benefitted from his work free of charge. In any case, spying on the Unity isn't a crime in the Confederation, so they can't level charges against him."

"Why the hurry then?"

Sufur shrugged. "Courts are the same everywhere. It would take months for them to come to this conclusion. I'm just cutting through the red tape."

The sky outside darkened and stars salted the blackness. A moment later, the view exploded into slipspace color for a split second before the portholes darkened to hide it. Sufur got up.

"I have things to attend to," he said. "You'll find I prefer communicating with my employees by vid or in the Dream, so that's probably how you'll hear from me next. I'll set up a bank account for you and make the other arrangements. Good day."

And he was gone.

So now I'm updating my journal on his ship. I don't even know what it's called. The computer says we'll reach our destination—whatever it is—in six days, two hours.

I think I'll spend a lot of it in the Dream.

TWENTY-ONE

Planet Rust
Middle Ocean

If we deny our basic nature, what are we left with?
—Queen Mag of the Five Green Worlds

"She is spending more and more time in the Dream," Vidya said from Katsu's bedroom door.

Prasad nodded, his eyes still on the holographic screen. "The Dream grows worse. Pitfalls and monsters everywhere. And this darkness the Silent speak of is still there. Everyone is frightened."

Vidya strode into the living room to peer over his shoulder. "The Unity news services are reporting such things? I find that hard to believe."

"This is an underground service," Prasad said. "They aren't free of propaganda—they have their own agenda—but they are more reliable."

"What is the Unity saying?"

"Very little," Prasad's fingers moved and the screen readout changed. "The reason communications are delayed, they say, is the war brewing with the Confederation. The Confederation has reneged on trade agreements, it shows imperialistic tendencies, the Empress and her people consort with vile aliens, and so on. And now the Confederation has stooped to kidnapping Unity citizens."

"Sejal," Vidya said.

"It took the Unity a while to admit it," Prasad agreed, "but many rumors were flying about how the rogue Silent slipped out under the Unity's nose. They had to say something to explain it, so they claim Sejal was kidnapped."

Vidya pulled up a chair beside him. "How much longer can we continue to stall Dr. Kri and Dr. Say, do you think? It's been days. I will not give them my eggs, and neither will I give them Katsu's."

"I don't know," Prasad replied, eyes still on the screen. "We have manufactured excuse after excuse, but soon they will realize our words are empty." He paused. "I have been thinking. My wife is correct. The laboratory is not working to end slavery among women who bear Silent children."

"That much should have been obvious to my husband from the start," Vidya couldn't help saying.

"The question is, of course, what they are actually doing," Prasad continued, ignoring Vidya's gibe. "I wonder if they are trying to use the children to destroy the Dream."

Vidya's intake of breath was sharp. "What brings my husband to this conclusion?"

"I have never seen Dr. Say touch Katsu."

"And what has that to do with it?"

"I think Dr. Say is Silent and that she is the one who communicates with our benefactor, the person who funds this facility. Dr. Say does not wish anyone to know she is Silent, but Katsu would discover it if they ever touched. She has avoided Katsu ever since she was old enough to enter the Dream, though I never noticed until I thought about it just now."

"This does not explain—"

"The children are devouring the Dream piece by piece. As they grow more numerous and more powerful, they will destroy it."

Vidya blinked. "Why would anyone, especially a Silent, wish to destroy the Dream?"

"You would have to ask Dr. Say and our benefactor."

Vidya tapped her fingers on the table. "We must stop them, in any case, and we have still not solved the problem of what to do with the children. I refuse to accept the idea that we must kill them."

"But perhaps we can immobilize them."

"But perhaps my husband can explain, then, and with more speed?" Vidya said testily.

Prasad gave her a quiet smile, one which hadn't changed in seventeen years. Vidya suppressed a grimace. They had been together for almost a week now, and Vidya still couldn't decide how she felt about him. They shared a bed, but had not made love. They hadn't even kissed. Sometimes as Vidya lay next to him in the dark, she wanted to bury her face in his shoulder and mold her body against his. Other times she wanted to shove him onto the floor and kick and beat and tear at him. Vidya wondered if Prasad felt the same ambivalence toward her. They had not discussed it. By wordless accord they had gotten into bed together that first night, but did not touch. Now it was becoming a habit, and the longer it went on, the harder it was to broach the subject.

"As always, my wife wishes speedy answers," Prasad was saying. "I will explain. The lab is equipped with cryo-chambers. Dr. Kri had them installed in case we ever had to move the children. If the children are indeed causing the disturbance in the Dream, putting them into cryo-sleep would end it. No Silent can reach the Dream from cryo-sleep."

"Ah." Vidya nodded. "A fine idea, my husband. The only flaw I see is that we have to find a way to put thirty-one children into thirty-one cryo-chambers despite what will certainly be the best efforts of everyone else in the laboratory to stop us. Then we will have to figure out what to do with the children once they are in cryo-sleep."

Prasad shut off the terminal. The holographic screen vanished. "When we walked to Ijhan, my wife, we did so one step at a time. It appears we must once again take the same approach."

"I think," said a new voice, "that it would be better to run."

Vidya and Prasad turned to see Katsu in the doorway to her bedroom. How long had she been standing there?

"What do you mean?" Vidya asked before Prasad could respond.

"The children are angrier and hungrier than I have ever seen them," Katsu said quietly. "They will expand again soon, and more Silent will die."

"The children are killing Silent?" Prasad said, dumbfounded.

Vidya crossed the room and took Katsu's hand. "My daughter, we do not understand. You must explain to us what the children are doing. Perhaps we seem slow to you, but—"

"Communication is difficult outside the Dream," Katsu interrupted. "It is full of lies and deceits and misunderstandings."

"But your father and I are not Silent," Vidya said patiently. "It is a handicap, and one we must live with."

Still standing in the doorway to her room, Katsu closed her eyes, seeming to search for the right words to attend her thoughts.

"When a Silent child is in the womb, it feels the touch of its mother's mind," she said carefully. "The children in the Nursery crave the touch they were denied. They are hungry and they are angry at what has been done to them. They reach into the Dream, eating everything they can and destroying what they cannot. The former creates the expanding blackness, the latter brings monsters into the landscape of the Dream."

"Why have they not devoured Rust?" Prasad inquired, still at the terminal. "When Silent first enter the Dream, they build their landscapes using the minds of the people physically close to them, do they not?"

"They do," Katsu said. Her eyes were still shut. "And they do use the minds of the people on Rust to enter the Dream. They do not feed here."

"And why is this, my daughter?" Vidya asked.

"Because of me," Katsu said simply. "They like my touch and the way I dance for them. If they fed off the minds on Rust, I would not be able to enter the Dream, and they do not wish this."

A chill went down Vidya's spine. "Katsu, what happens to the worlds on which the children feed?"

Katsu opened her eyes. "All species which produce Silent have a trait in common. It is empathy. It allows them—us—to know what others are feeling, even feel it ourselves. We have this trait because the Dream connects our minds and brings us together in subtle ways. When the children devour someone, however, they remove that mind from the Dream. The victims lose their empathy and they feel disconnected from everyone around them. Some people commit crimes they would not otherwise consider because they cannot feel the impact of their actions on others. Others fall into loneliness and depression because they cannot feel love from other people, and some commit suicide because they want the pain to end. The Silent are even more sensitive to the Dream, and they feel the impact the most. They cannot feel the Dream or enter it without the minds around them to provide a foothold. It is like being simultaneously struck deaf and blind with no one to provide care or comfort."

Vidya forced herself to remain calm despite the prickling that crawled down her neck and across her arms. This was the most she had heard Katsu say in one sitting, and somehow Vidya knew that showing strong emotion would only make it more difficult for her.

"How much will the children devour if they are not stopped?" she asked softly.

Katsu shook her head. "I do not know for certain. I do know that their hunger has never once been sated, and it grows stronger as they grow older."

"There are younger children in the Nursery," Prasad croaked. "They are not old enough to enter the Dream, but they will be soon."

"Yes. They will feed also," Katsu said.

Vidya's stomach twisted. "What will happen if the children devour all the minds in the universe?" she asked, surprised at the steadiness of her voice.

"The Dream will be destroyed," Katsu replied. "The Silent will all go mad, and there will not be a single shred of empathy among any race anywhere. Life itself would not end, but we would well wish it to."

Silence reigned in the room for a long moment. Then Vidya turned to Prasad.

"I believe," she said, "that we need to run."

Padric the sprint-cat reclined on his chaise longue a safe distance away from Dr. Jillias Say. She wore lab whites and sat primly on a spindly stool as thin as she was. Her straight, dark hair was coiled into a mass of braids on the back of her head. The stone floor beneath them remained solid for the moment. Voices continued to whisper around them, though there were fewer than normal. In the distance was the rumbling blackness. Padric had not conjured up any walls to block the view, in case the chaos expanded again.

"It seems," Dr. Say said with a hint of pride, "that the children in the project are indeed causing the disturbance in the Dream."

"You call it a 'disturbance'?" Padric asked archly, something he found easy to do as a sprint-cat.

Dr. Say flushed slightly. "Dr. Kri is running numbers. With a bit of Max Garinn's viral therapy to kick them forward, the next batch of children will be able to reach the Dream within six months."

"Six months?" Padric's claws kneaded the longue, leaving tiny rips in the satin. "Not fast enough. Dreamers, Inc., and the Children of Irfan, have already set task forces to find out what's going on. I can call in a few favors and try to slow them down, but I can't imagine it won't take them more than six weeks at the outside to find you. Haven't you been able to speed things up? You have Vidya Dasa now."

"We have not begun research with Vidya Dasa yet," Dr. Say said. "I think it was a mistake to let her into the lab in the first place. I'm sure she suspects that we lied about wanting to end the slavery of Silent women, and I can't imagine she hasn't told her husband. I wish we could just kick them out, but we obviously can't do that." She leveled a hard gaze at Padric from her stool. "And no, Mr. Sufur. No matter what inducements you might offer, I will not kill them. If it becomes necessary, I will put them into cryo-sleep, but I will not commit murder for you."

Padric spread his whiskers in bemusement. She wouldn't kill. What a lie. The only reason she could say such a thing in the Dream was that she truly believed it—despite the fact that several Silent had died due to the project and Dr. Say's work. This need to deny the obvious was one of the more idiotic parts of human psychology.

"I won't ask you to do that," Padric told her. "But we do need to find a way to speed this up. Can't Garinn do better?"

Relief made Dr. Say's rigid spine slump a tiny bit. "I was coming to that. Garinn says he could do it if we had Sejal."

Padric's tail switched. "Oh?"

"Garinn joined us after the Unity raided his laboratory." Dr. Say patted the severe dark braids coiled at the back of her head. "He barely escaped with his life, never mind his notes on Sejal. Sejal's genetic structure is . . . I was going to say unique, but that's true of everyone. However, Garinn's retrovirus had its greatest success when he tried it on Sejal.

He didn't have time to study why it worked, and asking Garinn to remember every gene sequence in Sejal's DNA would be ludicrous. We have his parents, of course, but the combination that makes up Sejal is one of countless billions. Given time, we could narrow it down, but that would take months, possibly years. Having Sejal would speed the process considerably."

"How considerably?" Padric asked intently.

"Garinn estimates that if he could study Sejal, he could have a retrovirus that would bring the new batch of children into the Dream in three weeks, perhaps two. And there is another possibility."

"And that would be?"

"Sejal may be still carrying Garinn's original retrovirus," Say replied. "If that's the case, the new batch could be ready in days."

A slight tremor rumbled beneath Padric's couch. He cast a quick glance at the roiling darkness, ready to marshal his concentration and leave the Dream. How ironic that the very nature of the project he was funding made the project so difficult to complete. Already Padric had lost contact with his interests on half a dozen worlds, though he had been prepared for this. A fleet of courier ships stood ready to spring into action once the collapse began. Padric didn't want to send them out yet, though. Reports had filtered back from ships that had gone through the real-world counterpart of the chaos. Several crews had mutinied. Captains and crew had committed suicide. Many others simply failed to report. One engineer had flooded her entire ship with plasma, killing herself and everyone on board. More deaths on Padric's hands.

On the other hand, how many millions would die if the project failed? It was worth it to sacrifice a few hundred people to save millions, even if one of them was Nileeja Vo.

"I have Sejal," Padric said calmly.

Her eyes widened and she stood up. "You do? When did you get him? How did you find him?"

"I have resources," Padric replied. It was gratifying to see her startlement and surprise. "Give me a few days and he'll be back on Rust."

"But how can you—"

"That's unimportant." The iron in his voice silenced her. "For now, you need to go back to your lab and keep a close eye on the Dasa family. I'll whisper if I need you."

Dr. Say nodded once and vanished. Padric pushed his thoughts out into the Dream, questing, sensing, sorting through the hushed whispers. Eventually he found Sejal's pattern. The boy was in the Dream. Good. That would make it even easier. Padric jumped off the chaise longue and sprinted away.

TWENTY-TWO

The Dream

Even the truth can lie.
—Senator Garan Crae

The falcon soared over hot, dry scrubland, her back to the red-cracked darkness. The place made her sick, made her want to fly fast and far, though she had learned she couldn't fly so far that it disappeared entirely.

Below her, the landscape changed. A ship with sails like clouds floated on undulating waves. The falcon's sharp eyes picked out Gretchen at the helm. She made a rude sign at the sky. The falcon soared onward. A great mansion stood surrounded by tranquil pines. Black curtains were drawn across all the windows. Trish's house. The falcon soared onward. She passed over a castle, a shack, a pool of water, a hissing cloud of vapor. Each one contained one or more Silent in varying shapes and species. The falcon soared onward.

Then a faint sound caught her ear, rising above the constant whispers in the Dream. The falcon banked and turned. There it was again. Flute music. She gave a *chirrup* of excitement.

The ground below was a seashore. A calm red ocean lapped gently at white sand which eventually gave way to trees. The falcon's sharp eyes easily picked out Sejal sitting in the shade.

The falcon shot back the way she had come, wings clacking against the wind. The air grew hot and dry again, and she dove down to a naked, dark-skinned figure waiting patiently in the shade of giant rock. He put up an arm and she landed gently on it.

Kendi blinked as the falcon's memories merged with his. So Sejal was back in the Dream at last. A twinge of excitement mingled with relief.

"Thank you, sister," he said.

The falcon clacked her beak and leaped back into the sky. Kendi watched her for a moment, then took off running. As he ran, he released his expectations of what the world around him should be. The ground shifted beneath his feet, changing from sandy soil to a sandy beach. Gentle waves washed over his ankles, creating little splashes of warm water. A white shirt and blue shorts grew out of nothing to cover his body, and rubber sandals appeared under his feet. Ahead he heard flute music. After a moment, Sejal himself came into view. He was still sitting in the shade of a kind of tree Kendi didn't recognize. His music was fast and light, his fingers almost a blur. Kendi slowed. When Kendi was a few paces away, Sejal glanced at him with ice-blue eyes, then turned his gaze back out to sea. Kendi sat down in the sun.

Sejal played. Kendi waited, amazed at his own patience. He wanted to grab Sejal by the shoulders, ask him where the hell he was. Yesterday, Kendi had been woken out of a sound sleep by Ara's insistent call. Sejal, she had informed him, was gone. A frantic search of the dormitory and the monastery grounds had turned up nothing. Kendi did a quick check with the desk clerks who had been on duty the previous evening, and they reported that Sejal had picked up a delivery and left with an older human. The old man's description matched that of the rude man from the monorail.

Not much later, the monks assigned to guard Chin Fen's room were found bound and drugged in his room. Fen, of course, was nowhere to be found. Further, the spaceport reported that a slipship had taken off the previous evening without proper authorization. It wasn't difficult to link the events together.

Sejal's song slowed until it matched the leisurely pace of the red ocean waves. It was a sad song, full of disappointment, broken dreams, and tragic beauty. Kendi listened, enjoying the moment. Conflict was coming, but in this moment there was beauty.

Eventually the last note faded into the lapping water. Sejal set the flute down and hugged his knees. The silence stretched between them, and Kendi had to force himself to break it.

"Where are you, Sejal?" he asked. "We've been worried."

"I'm on a ship," Sejal replied without looking at him. "We're in slipspace, though I don't know where we're going."

"Have they kidnapped you, then?" Kendi asked urgently. "Sejal, we can—"

"I'm here because I want to be," Sejal interrupted. He let go of his knees and drew musical notes absently in the white sand. "I work for Sufur."

Kendi tried not to show his tension. "Who's Sufur?"

"Some rich guy. He came and talked to me and I decided to work for him. He's paying me a shitload."

A small flock of seabirds coasted overhead with high, wild cries. Kendi brushed a bit of sand off his leg. Sejal's sun was warm, but not nearly as hot as Kendi's.

"Is that why you left?" Kendi asked. "More money?"

Sejal drew a treble clef and added a pair of flat signs. "I was kind of hoping you'd be able to come with me," he said. "But Sufur said you wouldn't want to. I figured he was right."

"Why did you go, then?"

"He told me stuff," Sejal said. "He told me about Mother Ara's meeting with the Empress and how she's supposed to kill me. So fuck you all."

The words smashed into Kendi like an icy brick. An almost physical pain wrenched him. His stomach felt like someone had poured hot lead into it.

"Sejal—" he began.

"Shut up, Kendi," Sejal snarled. He kept his gaze out to the sea, but Kendi saw moisture gathering in the corners of his eyes. "Just shut up, okay? I thought you were my friend. But you knew about it. You knew Ara was supposed to kill me and you didn't do anything. You didn't even fucking tell me."

Kendi didn't know what to say. He cleared his throat and forced some words out. "Sejal, I didn't tell you because I didn't know if I should."

"You didn't think you *should*?" Sejal's voice rose. "You didn't think you should tell me that someone was going to *kill* me?"

"I know Ara," Kendi said. "She wouldn't . . . she wouldn't . . ."

"Yeah, right." Sejal sniffed hard. "You can't finish that sentence because you aren't sure. You can't lie here. You think she would've killed me."

Kendi shifted uncomfortably on the soft sand. "I can't justify anything, Sejal," he said. "I should have told you. I messed it up. I was stupid and I'm sorry."

Sejal didn't say anything.

"What'd this Sufur guy offer you?" Kendi asked finally.

"More than you earn in a lifetime, I'll bet." Sejal wiped the treble clef away and doodled aimless swirls instead. "Thirty million freemarks a year and five million extra to start. And that's just the cash."

Kendi whistled. "The Children can't match that. But is the money all you want? You can't buy friends."

"Friends don't let other people try to kill you. Besides, this'll stop the war."

Kendi blinked. "What war?"

"Sufur told me the Unity was going to declare war if the Empress didn't send me back right away." In a dull voice, Sejal went on to recount the conversation he'd had with Padric Sufur. Kendi listened intently, his tension growing with every word. By the end of it, his stomach was a giant knot, though he forced himself to appear outwardly calm.

"Did it ever occur to you to ask what Sufur would eventually want you to do?" he said when Sejal finished.

"I don't have to do a thing," Sejal said smugly. "It's in my contract. Besides, no one can force *me* to do anything. It's why the Unity and the Children of Irfan are so hot to get their hands on me." He picked up a small pebble and threw it out into the water.

"You know what really flames, Kendi?" Sejal said quietly. "It's that you and the Children didn't come after me because I needed help. You came after me because I'm a walking power bank and you didn't want anyone else to get hold of me. You didn't care about *me*."

Kendi winced at that. "I care about you now," he said.

"That doesn't cut it." Sejal unfolded his legs. "I'm not coming back, Kendi. You can't persuade me and you sure as hell can't make me. You're not my teacher anymore. Why don't you just leave?"

"I don't want to leave," Kendi said.

"Fine. Then I will." And he vanished before Kendi could reply. The ocean, beach, trees, and seabirds disappeared with an inrush of energy that left Kendi dizzy for a moment. Remaining was the flat, empty plain and the ever-present darkness at the horizon. He heard it wailing, even at this distance.

The dizziness cleared, and emotions jumbled through Kendi's insides. He had betrayed Sejal, played the judas goat that kept cows calm until the butcher came. The idea made him sick.

Feeling rotten, Kendi trotted in a random direction and mentally rebuilt his Outback. The sun reappeared and the gray sky became a perfect blue. His clothes vanished.

And then he smacked into a hard wall. Kendi fell backward, stunned. He heard harsh laughter mixed with a cry of pain. Dazed, Kendi sat up. He was in a stone room filled with shadows. One of the shadows stood over another with a black knife in its hand. The shadow on the floor cried out and raised its hands, but the knife descended again and again and again. Kendi watched, frozen. A smaller bit of shade slithered across the floor toward Kendi with a wet, slippery noise. Heart twisting within his chest, Kendi tried to back away, but he was already pressed against the cold bars of the cell.

"Leave me alone," Kendi croaked. "You aren't real. This isn't real. I am *here* but I want to be *there*. I am *here* but I will be *there*."

The scene didn't change. The shadow with the blade laughed harshly and turned slitted yellow eyes on Kendi. At Kendi's feet, the smaller shade stopped moving. As if in a daze, Kendi reached for it, then snatched his hand back.

"No!" he cried. "This isn't real." He clenched his eyes shut and put tight fists over his ears.

Keeeendiiiiii, whispered the shadow. *Keeeeendiiiiii. I have something for you. Keeendiiiiii.*

Kendi's breathing came in short, sharp gasps. He could felt the cold shadow sliding toward him. "If it is in my best interest and in the best interest of all life everywhere—"

Keeeendiiiiii . . .

"—let me leave the Dream. Let me leave the Dream *now*!"

Something shifted. The laughing ceased as if someone had thrown a switch. Kendi opened his eyes. He was standing in the corner of his room at the monastery, rubber-tipped spear under his knee. Sweat varnished every inch of his body and had actually made a small puddle on the floor beneath him. Slowly, Kendi put the spear away, ran a damp hand through equally damp hair, and stepped into the bathroom for a shower.

Although Kendi was a full Sibling and his stipend was easily enough to let him afford a house, Kendi preferred to live in the monastery quarters set aside for newly graduated students who needed an inexpensive place to live. Kendi put aside the money he saved in rent with the hope of buying his own slipship one day. His room was furnished with a bed, desk, two comfortable chairs, a wardrobe, and a few shelves of bookdisks. A few bits of animal statuary—a kangaroo, a koala bear, and a falcon—were the only adornments in the room.

Kendi closed his eyes under the warm spray. This was solid. This was real. He didn't need to worry or think about what had happened in the Dream. Like the nightmares, it was just a shadow not worth examining.

He shut the water off, dried, and dressed. Then he started to call Ara to tell her about his conversation with Sejal, but he found himself ordering the computer to call Ben instead. The wall flashed blue and the words PLACING CALL blinked in pleasant yellow print.

This was stupid. They had all arrived on Bellerophon three days ago, and Ben hadn't tried to contact Kendi once. Why was Kendi putting himself through this? Ben refused to discuss the idea of Sejal taking him into the Dream—not that it was likely to happen now—and it was patently obvious that Ben didn't want things to work between him and Kendi. Kendi should give it up before he turned into one of those weirdos who stalked ex-lovers until they ended up in an asylum.

The phone rang twice more. Kendi was about to hang

up when the wall flashed and Ben came onto the screen. His hair was, as usual, boyishly disheveled.

"Kendi," Ben said. "Hi. What's wrong. You look upset."

"I do?" Kendi asked, startled that it showed so readily.

"You're pale."

"Yeah?" Kendi said weakly. He stretched out dark-skinned hands. "How can you tell?"

Ben laughed, and Kendi's insides flipped a little at the sound. Then he grew more serious. "Mom told me about Sejal taking off. Is that what's going on?"

"Kind of," Kendi admitted. All of a sudden he felt weak and wrung out, as if he were a shadow fading in the sunlight. "This whole thing is a mess and I don't know what to do."

"You look like shit," Ben observed. "You want to get something to eat?"

Kendi carefully kept the surprise off his face. "Uh, sure."

"Let me put this stuff away and I'll come over. Give me fifteen minutes, okay?"

Ben disconnected, leaving Kendi staring at a blank wall. He shook his head. Was this just an overture of friendship? Or did it mean something more? Kendi suddenly remembered being back in his quarters on the *Post-Script.* Kendi still thought Sejal was a relative, and Ben had just told him not to get his hopes up.

I always get my hopes up, he had said. *Sometimes it's all that keeps me going.*

Except this time the hopes wouldn't rise. Ben went back and forth so often that Kendi just couldn't find the energy. If something happened, it happened. If it didn't, it didn't.

Kendi almost laughed. He could almost hear the approval of the Real People about this line of thought. Still feeling wrung out, he placed another call, this time to Ara. He told her about meeting Sejal in the Dream.

He didn't mention the cell or the shadows.

Sejal peered into the roaring, wailing blackness. A bone-shaking throb vibrated his teeth. Angry red cracks formed a three-dimensional lattice throughout. It was still angry. It was still in pain. And it still called to him.

Inside, he caught the occasional glimpse of the girl dancing. Was she the one calling to him? What would happen if he just walked toward her? Would he be trapped? Would he die? He wanted to know, but was too afraid to find out.

The darkness was definitely bigger. The line of Silent he had seen the last time he had gotten this close to it was nowhere to be seen. After it had expanded so quickly last time, no one dared get close to it. Except Sejal.

The throbbing hum continued, like constant thunder. Sejal backed away from it, feeling oddly at a loss. Finally he turned his back and ran until he was a safe distance away. The wailing receded. He thought about calling up his beach again, then decided to give it a miss. The gray sky and ground fit his mood better than the beach. He was still worried about his mother. Was she all right? Had she been arrested? She had promised to find a way off Rust and get to Bellerophon, but what if she couldn't and got caught? Even if she did show up at the monastery, Sejal wasn't there, and Sejal hadn't given Kendi enough information to let anyone locate him.

He tried to scuff some of the hard ground with one shoe, but the flat surface wouldn't scuff. What was it made of, anyway? He wished he could ask Kendi about it, but Kendi wasn't here. Sejal grimaced. He didn't know how to feel about Kendi. On the one hand, he was angry at him for not warning him about Ara and the Empress. On the other hand, he still liked Kendi and wanted to be his student. But what kind of teacher didn't warn you that someone would try to kill you? The betrayal hurt.

Then he heard Sufur's voice among the muted whispers around him. He cocked an ear, trying to locate the direction. Sufur sounded agitated, and that made it easier to follow the sound. Sejal eased softly closer and the terrain changed. A dozen marble steps sprang up, serving as the base for a multi-pillared hall beneath a cloudy sky. Sufur's voice came from inside.

"—not going to lie to him about it," Sufur was saying. "He'll find out eventually. Besides, lying to my employees is unpleasant."

Another voice, this one softer. Sejal couldn't make out the words.

"They're safe," Sufur replied. "The lab is well-hidden.

Chin Fen ran interference to keep it from being discovered before, and nowadays the Unity isn't paying much attention to the oceans. Sejal's parents and sister should be fine until I can get another mole into the system. But Sejal will want to see them, I'm sure."

Sejal's heart skipped. Sufur had information about Mom? And his dad? And his *sister*? He charged up the steps.

"You'd better go, then," Sufur's voice continued. "We'll talk later."

Sejal burst into the hall at the top of the stairs. A tall, willowy being with shockingly white hair turned in surprise. No one else was in the room. He hadn't felt the ripples of anyone disappearing, either.

"Where's Sufur?" Sejal demanded.

"Sejal," the creature said in Sufur's voice. "I was just talking about you. I have some news."

Sejal froze in confusion. "Sufur?"

"I don't suppose," the creature sighed, "you could put a 'Mister' in front of that name. I *am* paying you a hellish amount of money, even if you don't have any duties."

"Uh, sure," Sejal said, still confused. "Mr. Sufur. But what—?"

"I don't take human form in the Dream, Sejal," Sufur explained. "Do sit down." He gestured with long fingers at a padded chair identical to the one Sufur himself was using. It was a good five meters away from Sufur's chair. Sejal sat, then almost immediately stood up again.

"You said something about my family," he said. "What's going on?"

"I've received word that they're safe," Sufur told him. "Your mother found a . . . facility I fund on Rust. Your father and sister are there as well. It turns out they've been employees of mine for quite some time."

"Employees?" Sejal said excitedly. "What do you mean? What do they do? I need to see them!"

Sufur held up his hands. "Calm, calm. They're doing research into the Dream. But as I said, they're all back on Rust. You're a wanted criminal there."

Sejal paced in both relief and agitation. "I have to see them. I can't stay here. It's my mom. And . . . and my dad and sister. All my life I've wondered what my dad is like. I've got to see him."

"The Unity," Sufur pointed out, "makes that a difficult proposition."

"No, it doesn't," Sejal said. He circled behind the chair and grabbed the back with both hands. "I can get us through any inspection. And *you* aren't wanted. They don't even know about you. Do they?"

Padric Sufur shrugged thin brown shoulders. "They might, though as far as I know I'm not wanted by the Unity for anything."

"Then let's go." Sejal dug his fingers into the upholstery. "When the customs people inspect, I can make sure they don't even notice me. If you've got a medical kit on board, we can change my face like Harenn did and I can go anywhere I want. Come on, Mr. Sufur. We have to go."

Sufur shook his head. The mop of pure white hair contrasted sharply with the nut-brown skin and enormous dark eyes. "It might be dangerous. And you're young."

"What does that matter?" Sejal almost yelled. "I have to see my family. Don't you have a family?"

"No," Sufur replied quietly.

Sejal deflated. "Oh. But I—"

"I do, however," Sufur continued, "see your point. My drugs are wearing off, and I need to leave the Dream. I'll think about this matter further."

And he vanished. The hall instantly followed suit, leaving Sejal on the empty plain again. Sejal punched his palm with his fist. He was about to let go of the Dream when a rumble shook the plain. The whispers around him instantly went silent and Sejal automatically turned his eyes to the chaos.

It was moving forward again. Red lightning lashed out like scarlet tentacles dragging a black octopus. Sejal heard Silent shouts and screams as they fled it. Some voices vanished, swallowed into it. Thunder boomed. Sejal watched, horrified and fascinated. It was less than a hundred meters away, then fifty, then twenty. It loomed over him like a juggernaut, sucking up all the light. The screams grew louder and more intense, and it wasn't just the darkness wailing. Sejal heard thousands, millions of voices crying out with every passing second. He felt the Dream disappearing wherever the darkness touched. Sejal turned and ran, but the darkness was faster. Lightning arced overhead and stabbed the ground ahead of him. Thunder smashed into Sejal and nearly knocked him down. He flung a glance over his shoulder. The darkness was gaining. He had to leave the Dream, but he couldn't concentrate.

A tingle charged the air. Sejal threw himself flat and a scarlet streak of lightning flashed through the spot where he'd been standing. Another crash of thunder boomed into him. The voices rose in agony. Sejal huddled on the flat, hard ground with his hands over his ears. He forced himself to concentrate on his body. Something cold touched his foot. There was a sharp jerk.

Sejal opened his eyes. He was safe on his bed in his room on Sufur's ship. Slowly he rolled over and sat up, trying to calm his pounding heart. There had been no sense of the darkness calling to him when it moved forward like that, only a sense of terrible hunger and angry pain. What was going on?

After a while he noticed an insistent noise. The door chime was repeating over and over.

"Come in," Sejal called.

The door slid open, revealing the spider alien. Its—his—name was Chipk. It moved its multijointed legs and waved its antennae. The computer came on line.

"Translation," it said. "We have changed course. Mr. Sufur has ordered us to head for Rust. We will arrive in two days."

Elation poured over Sejal, washing away his earlier terror. "Thanks, Chipk."

Chipk withdrew and Sejal grinned from ear to ear.

TWENTY-THREE

Planet Bellerophon
Blessed and Most Beautiful Monastery of the Children of Irfan

Let us go on committing suicide by working among our people, and let them dream life just as the lake dreams the sky.

—Miguel de Unamuno

Kendi's mouth opened and his eyes went wide. Then he screamed.

Ben dropped his fork. Similar howls went up all over the restaurant. Several people, all of them wearing the medallions and rings that marked them as Children of Irfan, fell to the ground and curled into a fetal position. Every one of them was screaming. The people who weren't howling, about half the population in the room, stared in stunned amazement.

Ben forced himself to move. He leaped to his feet, knocking his chair over, and rushed around to the other side of the table. Kendi continued to scream. Ben grabbed him by the shoulders.

"Kendi!" he shouted over the din. "Kendi, what's wrong?"

But Kendi didn't seem to hear. Ben cast about, not knowing what to do. The other unaffected restaurant patrons were similarly confused. Like Ben, some tried to help. Some sat in dumbfounded astonishment. Others bolted for the exit.

A woman scrambled to her feet and ran toward the glass doors that opened onto the restaurant balcony, her gold medallion glittering on her chest. The doors were closed, but the woman smashed straight through them. Crying and bleeding, the woman reached the edge of the balcony and leaped over the edge. Her sobbing scream faded into the mist.

Ben slapped Kendi's face and shouted his name, but

Kendi still ignored him. A young man snatched up a steak knife. He slashed at the veins on his wrists, and blood splashed over his table. A waiter wrenched the knife away from him. The screaming continued, a roar that pounded at every square inch of Ben's skin.

And then Ben felt it. A slight, subtle twist in his head. He was abruptly so alone, so achingly, horrifyingly alone. It was as if the people around him didn't exist. A lassitude dropped over him like a heavy blanket. Just standing beside Kendi's chair cost great effort. It took some time before he noticed that the screaming had stopped. The waiter dropped the bloody steak knife. The quiet was deafening, but Ben didn't care. Kendi put his head down on the table. He was sobbing like a child. So were most of the other Silent in the room. The non-Silent stood or sat around looking tired and apathetic. Scarlet blood dripped in a steady flow from the wrists of the young man. Ben shook himself. This wasn't right. He should do something.

Ben took up a napkin from his table and went over to the bleeding man. He bound the bleeding, unresisting wrists as best he could. Every motion cost him effort. It was like his clothes were made of iron. He went back to Kendi, who was still crying quietly.

"Come on," Ben said. "We have to go."

He hauled Kendi to his feet and led him out of the restaurant. The air was brisk and the mist was heavy. Soon full summer would come, bringing gentle rains and warmer temperatures. For now, however, everything was chilly and damp. Sounds filtered through the distance-distorting mist. Ben heard weeping and shouting. A single scream rang out and abruptly hushed itself. An empty gondola coasted by. The lonely feeling welled up in Ben so strongly that tears gathered in his eyes. Kendi seemed impossibly far away, even though Ben's skin was touching his.

Ben forced himself to keep moving. The monastery felt like a war zone after the bombs had stopped falling. People wept on the walkways or stared in shock. Some moved around trying to help, but it clearly took them a lot of energy to do so. Once they passed the body of a boy who had knotted a rope around his neck and jumped off a branch. The corpse swung gently at the end of the creaking rope.

Somehow, Ben managed to get them back to his house and up all the stairs to his front door. He let Kendi drop to the couch. Ben collapsed beside him, exhausted. Clutter had already piled up—clothes, disks, computer parts. The room was warm, however, and Ben tried to soak in the warmth. He felt detached, even uncaring. Bandaging the bleeding man and bringing Kendi to the house had been acts of reflex. There had been no emotion behind them. At last, Ben turned to Kendi.

"Kendi, what happened?" he asked. He had to shake Kendi's shoulder before getting a response.

"I can't feel the Dream," Kendi answered hoarsely. "I can't feel anything at all. It's horrible, Ben. I don't—"

There was a pounding at the door. Kendi fell silent. The pounding came again. Ben blinked, then found the energy to go open the door. Harenn stood on the landing, her veil drawn haphazardly across her lower face.

"You have seen everything?" she said without preamble.

Ben nodded. "Kendi's pretty bad. Some people committed suicide. I don't know what to make of it."

"When you saw the people who committed suicide," Harenn said, "it did not much bother you, did it?"

"No," Ben answered automatically, then realized what he was saying. It *hadn't* bothered him. The boy who had hanged himself couldn't have been more than ten or eleven years old. The image should be haunting Ben, even making him ill. But Ben simply couldn't feel worked up about it.

"Yes," Harenn said, echoing his thoughts. "Other people are of small interest."

"Why not? What's going on?"

"I will come in, first." She brushed past Ben and came into the house. It hadn't occurred to Ben to ask her inside. In the living room, she surveyed Kendi, who was still on the couch. "For the first time," she said, "I believe I am glad not to be Silent."

"What's going on, Harenn?" Ben asked. "Do you know?"

She shrugged. "I have an idea. The darkness that everyone speaks of in the Dream has engulfed Bellerophon."

Ben sat down heavily on his weight bench. "You're sure?"

"It would make the most sense. I have witnessed many

Silent in apathy, just as Kendi is. They have been dealt a terrible shock."

"Kendi says he can't feel the Dream," Ben said.

Harenn nodded. "Exactly. He has effectively been struck deaf and blind. The non-Silent are affected, too, because our minds make up the Dream itself, but we are not as sensitive to it. We can therefore function, though it is difficult."

"You don't seem affected at all." Ben had to force every word and his body felt as heavy as the weights stacked in the machine behind him. Kendi stared bleakly into space.

"I learned to cope with deep depression long ago," Harenn said softly.

A problem stirred in Ben's mind. He tried to focus on it, but the effort was costly. Slowly, like a bubble rising through quicksand, it came to the surface.

"What," he asked, "about Mom?"

TWENTY-FOUR

Sejal's Journal

Day 24, Month 11, Common Year 987

Getting to Rust wasn't a problem. We ran into half a dozen checkpoints, and three times we had to let Unity troops aboard the ship to inspect it. Whenever they did, Sufur spread money around, while Chipk and I stayed in my quarters. Whenever the soldiers opened my door, I just touched their minds and pushed them away. It's been getting easier and easier to do that. I just touch their emotions, make them not want to see us. And they don't.

Anyway. Once we got down to the planet, Fen checked with the authorities and found out that my face had been removed from the "watch for this guy" list. We figured that the guard on Rust either doesn't know I'm not in the Confederation anymore or it doesn't think I'd be stupid enough to come back. It'll make it easier to get around, that's for sure.

We landed at the spaceport. Fen's picture still *is* on the guard's shit list, even if the soldiers have never heard of him, so he has to stay on Sufur's ship with Chipk. Sufur phoned someone to arrange transportation, and we went out into the city.

It felt weird. I'd been gone for weeks and I hadn't ever figured on seeing Ijhan again, but here we were. The sky was the same familiar red, the buildings gray and cracking, the cars buzzing up the street and flitcars in the air. But I didn't feel like I'd come home. I felt like a visitor.

The guard was everywhere. They carried rifles instead of pistols and they wore body armor instead of uniforms. My Jesse voice kept nudging me, telling me to run and hide, but I made myself ignore him. Running would just make them wonder what I was up to, and I was completely safe with Sufur. I hoped.

Crowds of people were wandering around on the sidewalks, just like always, but it felt different. People kept their heads down and they didn't look at the guard. They didn't talk much, either. Most of the noise came from the cars and from ships screaming in overhead. It made me nervous, but Sufur just stood at the curb, cool as you want.

Anyway. A groundcar finally showed up and we got in the back. The rear windows were tinted so you couldn't see in or out, and I couldn't see who was driving because there was a barrier between the front and backseats. I had no idea where we were going. I turned to Sufur, and he seemed to know what I was going to ask.

"It's a precaution," Sufur said. "Only a few people know exactly where the lab is."

He was sitting as far away from me as he could. I was really starting to wonder about it. He didn't act that way around Chipk. And how come he doesn't look human in the Dream? Sufur's a real weirdo, and I was wondering if I should take my first year's salary and run like hell when I got the chance.

We didn't talk on the trip. After a while, the car stopped. A second later, there was a thump against the door I was sitting by.

"You can get out," Sufur said.

That was a relief. I opened the door and found a tunnel. It was made out of flexible white plastic or a polymer. Ribs held it open. The tunnel's end narrowed enough to fit right up against the car, and I couldn't see outside. The air smelled like damp rubber.

"Go on," Sufur said.

I got out and had to duck until I got to where the tunnel widened. Then the tunnel suddenly clamped shut behind me. I heard the door slam and the car buzzed away. I was suddenly scared.

Told you, my Jesse voice said smugly.

"It's all right," said someone behind me. I spun around. It was a little blond guy with a big mustache. He was playing with one end of it, twirling it tighter and tighter. Behind him the tunnel bent downward.

"So you're Sejal Dasa." The blond guy extended the hand that wasn't twirling the mustache and I shook it automatically. He wasn't Silent, but he looked excited. "I've been looking forward to seeing you. I'm Max Garinn. Mr. Sufur told me to take you down to the base, but right now I have to hurry and get this tunnel contracted before the guard notices it."

I felt a little better, but my Jesse voice wouldn't let up. I stayed wary as Garinn lead me downward. The tunnel walls bowed inward between the ribs and I touched them. They were cool and bulgy, like a balloon filled with water. I asked Garinn what that was about.

"We're heading under the ocean," Garinn said. "The submersible is just ahead."

The tunnel leveled out and ended in a round hatchway. We stepped through onto a metal floor in an airlock. Garinn cycled the door shut and pushed a button to retract the tunnel, then took me to another room with a couple of chairs in it and a porthole. He gestured at me to sit down, and I sat.

"Wonderful," he said, still twirling that damned mustache. "We'll be on our way soon, but I need to get a blood sample from you."

My Jesse voice dinged the alarm bells. "What for?"

"DNA identification." He had already taken an injection gun from his pocket. "We need it so the lab's computers will know who you are."

Jesse was yammering at me, but I couldn't think of any reason to refuse, so I let him take the sample. He almost sprinted away with it. A minute later, motors hummed and we were moving. I watched the ocean skim past the portal. It was really interesting—beds of red plants and weird fish I'd never seen before. We moved at a pretty good clip, always staying close to the bottom. I started feeling restless. Unless Sufur had lied, I was going to see Mom and meet my dad and my sister. I wondered what they'd be like.

Eventually, we got close to what looked like a big mound of rock or coral. The tunnel extended toward it like a big white worm and attached itself to something on the rock. I was confused until I figured out the rock pile was hiding the base.

Garinn led me up the tunnel, though an airlock, and into a carpeted corridor. The walls were rounded and painted bright, cheerful colors. Garinn walked beside me, one hand playing with his mustache, the other in the pocket with the injection gun.

"You probably want to see your family," he said. "I'll take you to them."

I started getting nervous again. Garinn led me through a whole bunch of corridors. We passed lots of doors and other hallways, but didn't meet anyone else. I got completely lost. Finally Garinn stopped by one of the doors and pressed the chime. My mouth was dry as sandpaper. What did my dad look like? Was Mom really okay?

The door flew open and Mom was standing there. She cried my name and hugged me. I was so glad to see her, to know she was safe. I had completely forgotten that we had had a big fight the last time we were together. A little tear leaked out of my eye, and I hoped no one would see it.

Behind her, over Mom's shoulder, I saw a man and a girl. Both of them had black hair, though the man's—Dad's?—was going silver. I stared at them, uncertain what to do. Mom was still hugging me. The man smiled a little shyly and the girl didn't react at all. She looked familiar.

Finally Mom let me go. She looked at Garinn, who was still standing there. "You can go now," she said. Then she pulled me inside and slammed the door in his face.

"There are people you need to meet, Sejal," she said. "This is your father, Prasad Vajhur."

I looked at him. The moment was here, the one I had thought about for a long time. I was meeting my dad. When I was little, I used to fantasize that he would pick me up and swing me through the air or wrestle with me on the floor, and that was the first thing that came into my head now.

"Hi," I said. I couldn't think of anything else to say.

"Sejal." Prasad—my dad—said it like he had never said my name before. He started to stick out his hand, then pulled it back with a confused look on his face. I was wondering what to do, too. Hug him? I didn't even know him. Shake his hand? Seemed a dumb thing to do with your own father.

Mom took over and saved us both. She took me by the shoulders and turned me toward the girl. "And this is your sister, Katsu," Mom said.

"Hello," Katsu said. Her voice was low, like Mom's.

"Hi," I said again.

"Let's go and sit down," Mom put in.

We went into the living. It wasn't much bigger than the one in the apartment back in Ijhan. Two windows looked into the ocean, and I saw more red kelp waving in the water. I sat next to Mom on the couch. Katsu sat on the floor and Prasad took an easy chair.

"Sejal—" Prasad said.

"Why did you leave?" I blurted out. I was suddenly pissed at him. I had lived my whole life on Rust in a damn slum, and only after I finally manage to leave does he show up.

Prasad looked pained. He explained about Katsu being kidnapped and how he came to the lab. Then Mom explained how she had found Max Garinn, the virologist who had altered my genes and screwed up my Silence.

"Max Garinn?" I said. "The guy who brought me here? He's the guy who changed me?"

Mom nodded. I felt creeped out. "He took a blood sample before we even got here," I said. "He said it was so he could tell computers to recognize me."

Mom and Prasad looked at each. Katsu stayed in her spot on the floor. She hadn't spoken yet.

"I believe we must run faster, my wife," Prasad.

"I believe my husband is once again correct," she replied.

That was weird. I've never heard Mom call anyone her husband before. Before I could think about that much more, though, Mom asked what had happened to *me* since I had gone off with Kendi. All they knew was that someone named Dr. Say had told them I was coming.

I started from the beginning and told them about the escape and Pitr's death, Bellerophon and the dinosaurs, the Empress's orders and Padric Sufur. Mom looked enraged when I told her Ara was supposed to kill me.

"Nowhere is safe!" she cried. "Not even a monastery."

Prasad got her calmed down enough for me to finish.

Then Prasad told me about the lab and the twisted children inside it. I didn't know how to react to that, so I didn't say anything.

"So our secret benefactor is Padric Sufur," Prasad said. "The question is, why did he send you here?"

"Because I told him to," I said, a little confused. "I overheard him talking to someone about you guys and I told him he had to bring me here."

Mom shook her head. "He would not take such great risks merely so you could see your family. Even with your . . . abilities, Sejal, the risk is foolish. The fact that Max Garinn took a sample of your blood so eagerly tells me there is something else that Padric Sufur wants of you."

"He wants me to end war," I said, a little proudly. Prasad was going to know how important I am. I went on to explain.

"Foolishness," Mom said when I was done.

I stared at her. "What?"

"Foolishness," Mom repeated. "And I am unable to believe Sufur doesn't know this."

"What do you mean?" I demanded. "It would work."

"Think it through, Sejal," Prasad said gently. "At any moment there must be half a dozen wars going on between systems. You are one person. You couldn't stop all of them from going to war, no matter how powerful you are. And the potentates you threatened would certainly send assassins. One of them would find you eventually. It would be impossible for a single person to end war in this manner."

I glared at both of them. "So why is he paying me all this money?"

Mom tapped her fingers on the arm of the couch. "Any number of reasons. He may wish to ensure that no one else has control of you. Or he may want to use you for more financial gain."

"He wants Sejal's genes," Katsu said.

Everyone looked at her. I had almost forgotten she was there. Katsu has black hair like mine, but her eyes are brown like Mom's.

Anyway. Prasad started to ask her what she meant, but Mom interrupted.

"The blood sample," she said. "Garinn wanted to get it

quickly because it's important to the experiment. I won't give them my eggs, but Sejal's genes may be a better substitute. He is more powerful than any Silent in history."

"What would he want with Sejal's genes?" Prasad said.

"This place is built on lies." Katsu was staring at the carpet in front of her. "When Father first arrived, Kri and Say told him they were trying to end the slavery of women who could produce Silent babies. A lie. When Mother arrived, she said she wished to aid in the research. A lie. When Sejal met Sufur, Sufur said he wanted to use Sejal as a threat to end war. A lie. Sufur let Sejal think he was doing a great favor by letting Sejal come back to Rust. A lie. Everything here is a lie."

"So what is the truth, my daughter?" Mom said quietly.

"The Dream," Katsu replied. "There are no lies in the Dream."

"You said Sufur wants Sejal's genes," Prasad said. "Do you know why?"

"Max Garinn wants Sejal's genes," Katsu corrected. "Garinn creates viruses that change people."

"The children," Mom whispered, and I assumed she meant the ones Prasad had helped create in the lab.

"Another group will enter the Dream soon," Katsu went on. "I have felt their minds pressing on its fabric. When they enter, I don't know if I can hold all of them in one place."

Then she got up, walked into another room, and shut the door.

"Is she always like that?" I asked. I felt off-balance.

"Yes," Prasad answered. He sounded tense.

"I would gamble a great deal of money," Mom said, "that Garinn intends to use Sejal's genes and create a retrovirus that will bring the next set of children into the Dream earlier than they normally would."

"But *why*?" Prasad almost shouted. "Katsu says that would destroy the Dream. Why would they want to do that?"

"I am uncertain," Mom said. "We need to learn more. We need to know if Dr. Say is Silent, as my husband suspects. We need to know if Padric Sufur truly wants to destroy the Dream, and why he would want to do it."

She paused for a moment.

"And," she said, "we need to take over this base."

Naturally, just when things were getting really interesting, a computer chime went off and Prasad said he had to get down to the lab for the day. He squeezed my shoulder on his way out and left.

I sat on the couch next to Mom, not certain about what to do or think. So that was my dad. He seemed nice, I guess. I supposed I was expecting to feel some kind of connection with him, but he just seemed like a distracted stranger.

Mom gave me another hug and I let her. Then we talked some more. Neither of us said anything about the tricking or the fight we'd had. I told her more about Bellerophon and the dinosaurs and she told me more about the lab and the Nursery. Then I told her I was tired and wanted to take a nap. She showed me to her and Prasad's room. That was weird, too, knowing that Mom was sleeping with him.

Anyway. Mom shut the door and I lay down. I didn't really want to sleep, of course. I wanted to enter the Dream.

I closed my eyes and tranced myself. Voices whispered around me. I reached for them, and found myself on my seashore in the Dream. Right away, though, I could tell things were getting worse. The place felt almost empty. The dark place rumbled and roared over my ocean, and it was huge and closer. I thought of stories Mom used to tell about giants coming up out of the ocean and smashing whole cities to pieces with their clubs.

I took a deep breath and moved myself to the border of darkness and Dream.

It was still screaming. I looked inside, trying to ignore the noise. The figure was there, dancing, and now I saw it was Katsu. That was why she had looked familiar. I cupped my hands around my mouth and shouted to her, but she didn't hear me. I kept shouting and waving my arms and eventually she turned. I couldn't see her face very well—it was too dark—but it was definitely her. She motioned at me to come and join her. I took a step back.

Then I saw it. A shadow separated itself from the black place. It was shaped like a twisted human. It took off over the plain, and wherever it touched the ground, the earth crumbled. A small tornado whirled up behind it, and I could feel it ripping at the Dream itself. I stared.

Then Katsu appeared. She ran after the shadow, even got ahead of it, not even affected by the deep canyon it made or the whirlwind. She touched it and talked to it, though I was too far away to hear what she said. Abruptly it turned and rushed back to the dark place. Katsu watched it go, then ran over to me. We looked at each other for a long time.

"I've been calling to you in the Dream," she said. "Why didn't you answer?"

"You mean go in there?" I jerked a thumb at the darkness. "Forget it!"

"They won't hurt you as long as I'm with you."

Thunder rumbled and a cold wind rushed over us for a minute. I lengthened the sleeves on my shirt and changed my shorts into pants.

"Who are they?" I asked.

"The children in the Nursery, of course."

Katsu wore a simple blue jumpsuit in the Dream. Her hair isn't as curly as mine, but it's a lot longer. We're the same height.

"What was it like growing up with Pra—with Dad?" I asked suddenly.

She smiled. "I don't know what it's like not to. Father is gentle and he tends to believe what people tell him. He wants to see people as kind, even after it's obvious they are not. But he is not stupid."

"Mom's smart, too," I said. "She can make people do what she wants, but she wants what's good for them—or what she *thinks* is good for them. You look like her."

"And you look like Father."

We grinned at each other for a moment. Then Katsu's face got serious. Another rumble of thunder crashed over us.

"I dance for the children," she said. "It calms them and keeps them in one place, but once in a while, one of them runs away like you just saw. They see themselves as monsters, and that means when they touch the minds of other Silent in the Dream, those Silent see them as monsters too, monsters made of the Dreamscape itself. They are very powerful, which is how they can force their own picture of the Dream on other Silent."

"They're related to us, aren't they?" I said.

She nodded. "They are our brothers and sisters. That's why I dance for them, and because I dance, they haven't devoured the minds on Rust. If they did, I wouldn't be able to enter the Dream. Neither of us would. But they're getting hungrier and hungrier. When the next set of our siblings enters the Dream, I will not be able to hold them back."

I swallowed hard, feeling cold. "And if Garinn brings them in early—"

"—the Dream will be destroyed before anyone else can do anything," she finished. I saw that she was tired. The strain of what she was doing must be tremendous, and she had been doing it all by herself.

I reached into my pocket and pulled out my flute. "Do you want some music?"

She smiled at me, then took my hand.

TWENTY-FIVE

Planet Bellerophon
Blessed and Most Beautiful Monastery of the Children of Irfan

Silent grief only breaks the heart.
—Philosopher Ched-Vareed

Ben and Harenn pulled Kendi along between them on swaying walkways. Ara hadn't answered her phone, though it seemed to Ben that he should be more worried than he was. Harenn uncharacteristically kept up a running monologue as they went.

"Most people think the Dream is a gestalt of all minds in the universe," she said. "It makes us feel connected to other people. But now we are no longer part of the Dream. We feel lonely and afraid and we don't care about other people except out of habit or when the feelings are exceptionally strong."

"Not now," Ben snapped. Harenn fell silent.

Ben continued dragging Kendi along the walkways. It would have been faster to leave him behind, but something told Ben this would be a mistake. Kendi walked like he was half-asleep and his arm was cold in Ben's grip. The monastery had been transformed. It no longer bustled with life, energy. People sat on balconies and stared into space. Several times he saw people hanging from branches or rails, their bodies swinging like ghosts in the fog. Four shots sizzled in the distance and a siren wailed for a long moment before dying. A Ched-Balaar lay sprawled across one of the walkways. Ben had to guide Kendi's steps over his body. As he did so, he saw its head had been crushed.

The rest of the journey was equally nightmarish. Ben didn't dare try the gondolas or the monorail, and he avoided humans and Ched-Balaar whenever he could. If Harenn was right, if no one cared about or felt empathy for anyone else, it meant people could commit—probably already had committed—unspeakable crimes against each other. Harenn walked wordlessly with him, guiding Kendi by the other arm.

Eventually they reached Ara's house. Ben hurried Kendi across the walkway connecting her porch to the main thoroughfare. It was strange. His heart was beating fast only from exertion. He wanted to know how Ara was doing, but it was as if she were someone else's mother, perhaps Kendi's or Harenn's. The front door opened for Ben's voice.

"Wait here," he said once they were inside. He went through the house, calling out. Ara was nowhere to be seen. Ben asked the computer if it knew where she was.

"Mother Adept Araceil is on the rear section of the balcony," it said.

Feeling a bit of relief, Ben trotted out the back door. But Ara wasn't there. Confused, he asked the computer to verify her whereabouts.

"Mother Adept Araceil is on the rear section of the balcony," it repeated.

And then a gleam caught Ben's eye. On the floor of the balcony lay a gold medallion and a gold ring with a blue stone. They were Ara's.

Something inside Ben broke through the apathy. His heart beat hard in his ears and blood roared through his head. It couldn't be what he thought. It couldn't be.

Without stopping to explain to Harenn or Kendi, Ben ran to the staircase that wound down around the trunk to the base of the tree. It thudded and thumped beneath his shoes. The planks were slightly slick with moisture, but Ben avoided slipping with the ease of long practice. He passed the houses set beneath Ara's without seeing them and ran all the way to the bottom. There was no trail or sidewalk down here—the staircase was primarily for use in case of fire or other emergency. Green ferns grew shin high among beds of moss, and the impossibly thick trunk soared high above him. Ben ran several meters away from the trunk and began to circle it, trying to gauge the spot below Ara's balcony. His shoes and trousers were quickly soaked by the wet ferns. After several minutes of searching, he found nothing. Maybe he'd been wrong. Maybe he'd been—

His foot came down on something that rolled slightly.

Ben jumped back and saw the dark place where the ferns had been crushed. Ara lay facedown among them. With a choked cry, Ben dropped beside his mother, feeling desperately at her neck for a heartbeat. Her slack skin was already chilly and pale. No pulse. Feverishly Ben rolled her over.

Her face was a mass of blood. Fern leaves and bits of dirt were stuck in it. When he touched her chest, he could feel the shattered ribs move grotesquely beneath his hand.

"No," he whispered. "Mom, please, no."

There was no response. Benjamin Rymar gathered his mother's body into his arms and cried among the dripping ferns.

How long he stayed there, he didn't know. Then he felt a touch on his shoulder. Ben looked up. Harenn was standing beside him.

"I am sorry," she said.

"If I had come over earlier," Ben said, hot tears running down his face, "I could have stopped her. I could have—"

"You had no reason to be here or even to call before any of this happened," Harenn interrupted. "There was no way for anyone to do anything."

Her words didn't make Ben feel any better. "We can't leave her here," he said. "Something might— the dinosaurs will—"

"I saw a gravity sled at one of the houses on the way down," Harenn said. "Wait here. I will bring it."

Ben turned his attention back to Ara's body. Water dripped from the ferns around him with tiny spattering noises. He smoothed the dark hair out of her face and wiped the blood away with his sleeve. So many times he had heard people say that it didn't feel real when they found out someone they loved had died, but this felt achingly, bone-wrenchingly real.

Harenn arrived with the sled, a small one just the size of a stretcher. They lifted Ara's small body onto it and Ben pulled it up the stairs. The sled remained parallel to the ground and stuck out oddly from the staircase, and Ben kept checking to make sure Ara's body wasn't in danger of sliding off. They brought her to the house and let the sled drift to the balcony floor at the top of the stairs. Ben fixed the sled in place while Harenn went inside to get a sheet to draw over Ara's face. Harenn's shouts brought him hurtling into the house.

He followed her yelling to the living room. When he got there, he stared in shock. Harenn stood in the center of the room, her arms wrapped around Kendi's waist. Kendi's unmoving feet were half a meter off the floor. A rope made a loop around his neck. The other end was tied around one of the high ceiling beams. An end table lay overturned to one side.

"Help me!" Harenn shouted. "Hurry! I can't hold him up!"

Ben continued to stare. After a moment, the shock faded, replaced by his earlier crushing despondency. Nothing mattered. Ben was ultimately alone whether Kendi was alive or dead. If Kendi wanted to die, let him.

"Ben!" Harenn gasped. Kendi was slipping from her grasp.

And then more images of his mother washed over him. Her gentle hands. Her crumpled body. Her laugh. His own pain. Ben's chest tightened with grief and tears he had yet to shed. He had lost his mother. He couldn't bear losing Kendi, too.

"Ben!"

Ben moved. He rushed over and wrapped his own arms around Kendi, holding him up and preventing the noose from choking him. Harenn righted the end table and climbed up beside Kendi. She produced her knife and swiftly sawed through the rope. Ben gently lowered him to the ground and, for the second time that day, felt for a pulse. Kendi's heart was still beating, though he had stopped breathing. Training took over. Ben tilted Kendi's head back, pinched his nostrils, and breathed into Kendi's mouth while Harenn got on the phone. Ben was only dimly aware of her voice in the background. His entire world had shrunk to breathing for Kendi.

Come on, he thought. *Don't do this, Kendi. Come on!*

"There is no answer at the medical center," Harenn said behind him, but Ben barely heard. Twelve breaths, check pulse again. Still strong. Another breath and another.

Come on, Kendi. Breathe for me! I lost Mom. I'm not losing you, too.

Abruptly, Kendi coughed into Ben's mouth. He drew a shuddering breath, then blinked weakly.

"Ben?" he said in a hoarse voice.

It was only then that Ben noticed he was crying again. "Kendi. God, what were you doing?"

"It hurts," Kendi said. "All life, Ben—why didn't you let me die?"

Because I love you, you idiot, Ben thought, but he couldn't make himself say the words. Instead, he said, "We need to get you to the hospital."

"I told you," Harenn said, making Ben jump. He had forgotten she was there. "The medical center is not responding. I suspect they are overloaded or understaffed. Or both."

"We can't leave him like this." Ben sat back on his haunches. "What if he tries again?"

"We need to get him away from here," Harenn said. "We need to take him someplace where he can reach the Dream again."

"The *Post-Script*," Ben said. "It's still at port, isn't it? Maybe if we move Kendi far enough away from Bellerophon, he'll snap out of it."

"Then we should go now." Harenn helped Ben haul Kendi to his feet.

"We can't just leave Mom lying there," Ben said.

Harenn looked ready to protest, then saw the expression on Ben's face. "We will take her with us and put her in a cryo-chamber on the ship," she said.

The spaceport, however, was too far away to walk. They managed to get Kendi and the gravity sled to the monorail station where, as luck would have it, the train lay like a dead snake on the track. Ben cautiously poked his head into one of the cars. About half a dozen people and one Ched-Balaar were on board. All of them were alive, but none of them reacted to Ben.

"We're taking this train to the spaceport," he announced. "If you don't want to go, get off now."

No one reacted. Ben bundled Kendi into the empty control compartment, carefully not looking at the gravity sled and its white-draped burden as Harenn guided it into the passenger area behind him. Ben wondered what had happened to the engineer.

The controls turned out to be easy to run, but the trip itself was a nightmare. The heavy lethargy kept slowing him down, making him want to quit. Once, a series of shots rang out and one of windows shattered. This gave Ben a brief spurt of adrenaline-fueled energy, but it didn't last.

Somehow, he got the train down to the spaceport. Ben hauled Kendi onto the platform while Harenn guided the gravity sled. They rushed through the spaceport as quickly as they could, ignoring the clumps of apathetic humans and Ched-Balaar.

Ben had to get Kendi to safety. He couldn't let Kendi die like he had let his mother die. The words became a mantra as he picked his way through the port with Harenn and the sled behind him. He couldn't let Kendi die. He *wouldn't* let Kendi die.

Eventually they emerged near the landing field. Ben was jumping at every noise, afraid someone with no feelings left might have gotten hold of an energy pistol or rifle. It felt like gun sights were being trained on him from every shadow. Every corner held a potential lunatic. By the time he got to the *Post-Script,* he was wringing wet with sweat.

The hatch swung obediently open at Ben's touch and they maneuvered the sled inside. Harenn went down to the engines while Ben got Kendi up to the bridge. He parked Kendi in the captain's chair while he powered up the systems. His earlier lassitude had mostly left him, swallowed up by the need to make sure Kendi was safe, that he wouldn't end up— that he would be all right.

"Peggy-Sue," Ben said, "are you on line?"

"On line," the computer replied.

He got Harenn on the intercom and they went through the preflight checks together. Each check was a small goal, one step toward the overall one. Focusing on the little problems let him ignore the big ones.

An hour later, the checks were done and Ben tried to contact the control tower to authorize takeoff. Kendi slumped in the captain's chair, sometimes quiet, sometimes crying softly. Ben only spared him enough attention to make sure he didn't do anything foolish.

To Ben's complete lack of surprise, there was no answer from the control tower despite repeated attempts to raise one. He got Harenn on the intercom again and told her to ready herself for takeoff.

The *Post-Script* rumbled heavily into the sky. Ben didn't bother with the sound dampeners. Although fully licensed, Ben wasn't as experienced as Kendi, and the power drain from the dampeners made the ship harder to handle. If the noise spooked a few dinosaurs, that was too bad.

Ben worked the controls calmly and efficiently, as if he piloted a ship with his mother's corpse in it every day. The blue sky on the screens darkened to purple and faded to black. Stars made hard points of light. He kept a sharp eye on sensors, but picked up no other ships in flight. Several circled the planet in orbit, and he kept his distance from them. The moment he had cleared Bellerophon's gravity well, he let the ship coast while he figured out where to go. It ultimately didn't matter to him, but he didn't want to bring Kendi close to any other planets that had been swallowed by the thing in the Dream.

It was now no mystery to Ben why the Silent from the engulfed planets had remained missing and why none of the investigating ships had returned. With apathy, sorrow, and even sociopathic behavior overwhelming the people, they would not care about notifying anyone else. He only hoped taking Kendi out of the affected area would help. It might not. Ben's knowledge of Dream theory was far from expert, but he did know that the Silent built their image of the Dream from the minds closest to them. A Silent who moved to another "place" in the Dream simply leapfrogged to other minds and built his or her image from them. Getting Kendi away from the minds on Bellerophon and closer to untainted ones should make him recover.

Unless Kendi's mind kept reaching back to Bellerophon. Unless Ben's understanding was less than perfect. Unless . . .

Ben put the doubts out of his head. If he turned out to be wrong, he'd try something else. He couldn't let Kendi die like he had let his mother die.

Ben consulted the charts and decided to avoid the closest planets, since they might well be suffering under the same problem as Bellerophon. Instead he chose a planet toward the center of the Independence Confederation. If something went wrong, it'd be easier to shout for help.

No, that wasn't true. The only way to shout for help was by radio or by Silent. If the planet he went to had been engulfed, Silent communication would be worthless, and radio would be too slow to do him any good. Still, there was nothing else to do. He programmed the coordinates for Nikita, the world he had chosen, and hit the panel that shoved the ship into slipspace. The view flashed psychedelically, and Ben blanked the screens.

"Where are we going?" Harenn asked over the intercom. *"We've entered slip, but I know nothing else."*

Ben told her. "We should be there in a few hours. I'll stay at the controls."

"The engines are doing fine," Harenn said. *"I will wash Mother Ara's body and place it in a cryo-chamber."*

It. His mother had already become an object instead of a person. Ben swallowed, then bent over the boards. Traveling through slipspace required constant course corrections, and Ben wasn't experienced enough yet to make them by reflex. His entire world shrank to the instruments in front of him. One correction, and another, and another. The hours passed. They would leave slipspace in three . . . two . . . one . . . now!

The communication system leaped to life. Voices wavered in and out of hearing as the computer automatically searched for the control frequency. It found it, and the bridge echoed with instructions to other ships about entering and leaving orbit. Nikita's airwaves were bustling with life, and Ben sighed with relief.

A hand landed on Ben's shoulder. He jumped and twisted in his chair. Kendi was behind him. His brown eyes were luminous, his strong face torn with emotion.

"Thanks," he said quietly.

"Mom's dead," Ben blurted out, then turned back to the boards, embarrassed without knowing why.

"I know," Kendi said. "I remember everything." He put his arms around Ben from behind. Ben leaned back for a moment. He could feel Kendi again.

They stayed like that until the proximity alarm piped up to warn Ben that they were drifting too close to another ship—a warship. Kendi released him, and Ben felt empty, though not nearly as empty as he had felt back on Bellerophon.

"Want me to take over for a while?" Kendo offered. "I'll get us into orbit and we can figure out what to do next."

Ben nodded and got up. He took his usual place at communication while Kendi ran his hands over the flight board. Ben radioed for authorization to establish orbit around Nikita and discovered that most of the planetary orbits were taken up by warships. Ben could take a spot around the second moon, and he could only have it for two days. Then he would have to reapply and he might be denied if the military needed the spot. Kendi nudged the *Script* into place.

"Now what do we do?" Ben asked.

"I want to see her," Kendi said.

The secondary bay was a gray, echoing chamber some twenty meters on a side. Stacked six high near the entrance were a dozen black boxes the size of coffins. Each bore a window, computer screen, and keypad. The cryo-units on the *Post-Script* were meant for use in an emergency, in case all life support failed and/or there weren't enough suits to go around. A cryo-unit automatically scanned its occupant and inserted IV needles that injected a sedative followed by a series of steroidal compounds that allowed the user to survive and be revived from temperatures colder than liquid nitrogen.

Only one unit had been activated. All the lights were red, indicating the unit's occupant had died. Harenn stood nearby. She turned as Ben and Kendi entered. Her eyes were red and puffy above her veil.

"I have said good-bye," she told them. "I will leave you alone with her."

Harenn withdrew. Kendi walked up to the unit, and Ben noticed they were holding hands. He didn't remember if he had taken Kendi's or if Kendi had taken his. Ara's cryo-unit was waist high, and Kendi had to bend slightly to peer through the window. Ara, her face pale and still, was visible inside. New grief sprouted like a sodden blossom in Ben's chest, and anger, too. How could she commit suicide like that and leave him to find her broken body? He knew that it hadn't been her fault, but the knowledge didn't make him feel any better.

"The Real People are supposed to see death as a joyful transition," Kendi said beside him. "I can't do it. She was like a mother to me and I was a total jerk to her and I don't know what I'm going to do without her."

The grief filled Ben and overflowed like a waterfall. He let go of Kendi's hand so he could put his arm around Kendi's shoulder. Kendi hugged him back as they both started soundlessly to cry. After a time, they stopped and just stood in front of Ara's body before turning away. Their feet took them out of the cargo bay and toward the galley.

"What happens now?" Ben asked as they walked. "We can't go back to Bellerophon."

"I don't know," Kendi admitted. "And eventually we'll run out of places to run to if that thing in the Dream keeps growing. I don't want to go through that again, Ben. It was horrible. I can completely understand why Ara . . . why she did what she did. I wanted to die, too."

"I'm glad you didn't," Ben said.

Kendi squeezed Ben's shoulder. "Thanks again."

"You need to thank Harenn, too," Ben replied as they reached the galley.

"Thank me for what?" Harenn said. She was sitting at the table with a steaming mug of fragrant coffee before her.

"Catching Kendi before he finished the job," Ben said.

"Thank you," Kendi told her gravely.

"You are welcome," Harenn replied, equally grave. She gestured at the tiny kitchen. "There is hot water if either of you want coffee or tea."

Kendi shook his head. "Right now," he said, "I need the Dream."

TWENTY-SIX

Planet Confederation's Core
Palace of Her Most August And Imperial Majesty Empress Kan maja Kalii

The dictator needs an occasional bloodbath to renew his power.

—Breen Freerunner, *Revolution!*

Her Imperial Majesty Kan maja Kalii I, Empress of the Independence Confederation, held her regal pose on the simple throne in her marble audience chamber despite the tension humming along her nerves. Courtiers filled the balcony and occupied chairs on the floor, and over a dozen Imperial guards surrounded the throne platform. The pleasantly muscled body of her favorite Silent slave was kneeling on the cushion at the base of her dais, but the look on his handsome face was far from pleasant.

"Message begins," he said. "From Sharleman Bellimari, Executive Officer of the Prism Conglomerate Board of Directors, Chief Manager of—"

"You may dispense with the titles," the Empress interrupted, forcing her voice to remain calm. "Both his and mine. Begin with the actual message."

"Yes, Imperial Majesty," said the slave without looking up. "Message continues."

The court was holding its collective breath. The Empress realized she was clutching the arms of her throne with white fingers, but she couldn't make herself relax them. So much depended on this single message.

The slave hesitated, and the Empress wanted to scream at him to get on with it.

"It is with great regret," he said, "that we inform the Independence Confederation that the Prism Conglomerate is at this time unable to allocate resources to the Confederation for its conflict with the Empire of Human Unity. We can only hope . . ."

The court buzzed. The Empress did not sway in her seat and she did not turn pale on her throne. She did, however, stop listening. The Prism Conglomerate had turned her down. That was the only important thing. Without the Conglomerate's support, the impending Unity war would be difficult, if not impossible, to win.

When the message ended, Kan maja Kalii dismissed slave and court. Alone in the echoing, empty room, she allowed herself to slump a bit. She was so tired. She couldn't remember the last time she had slept for more than four hours at a time, and her arms and legs were heavy with fatigue. What if she just walked away? What if she just left the palace, the guards, the court, the decisions, and the bloodshed behind? What if she just told everyone they were on their own, that they would have to make their own decisions and take care of themselves?

Kalii stroked the smooth arm of the Imperial throne, the one her father had used for so many decades, and allowed herself a heavy sigh. It was pure fancy, abdicating and running away. If she did it, someone would take her place, and there was no way to know if that person would be kind or cruel, humane or inhuman. Kalii had no heirs, no one she knew well enough to put on the throne in her place. Not since her nephew had been murdered.

And how many of her subjects would see their own loved ones die in the war with the Unity?

Her Imperial Majesty Kan maja Kalii I, Empress of the Independence Confederation, forced herself to sit straight on her throne and think hard about the problems of a galaxy.

TWENTY-SEVEN

The Dream

More people die from the cure than the sickness.
—Dr. M. Rid, First Bellerophon landing party

"We were right," Dr. Say said. Her smile was uncharacteristic and small. "Sejal was still carrying the retrovirus. There was plenty in the blood sample Garinn took. He used it as a template for the new one and we injected it into the next set of children last night."

Padric clacked his beak and settled brown feathers. His talons gripped the perch in the stone room he had called up. Dr. Say sat on her backless stool, hands folded neatly in her lap. Only the slight flush and tiny smile indicated her great excitement. Padric, however, refused to share in it. He would not celebrate until the project reached its culmination. The window beside Padric displayed, as always, the roiling blackness, and the usual whispering in the Dream was all but silent now.

"We estimate," Dr. Say concluded, "that the children will begin entering the Dream sometime within the hour."

"Good," he said, the word issuing oddly from his beak. "The Dream is growing worse. Fewer Silent are using it. Not even Dreamers, Inc., employees enter lightly. Most of the traffic is military. The Unity will officially declare war on the Independence Confederation in less than a day, and they're trying to drag five or six other governments into the morass."

"They won't succeed," Dr. Say said coolly. "The project will—"

Dr. Say never finished her sentence. With a yelp, she vanished from the Dream. Padric blinked in surprise, then reached cautiously out of the Dream, feeling for her mind in the real world. He couldn't find it. Padric clacked his beak, uncertain if he should be worried or not. Reaching real world minds was not one of his better talents, especially when the minds in question were human, so the fact that he couldn't find her didn't mean much. The problem was probably completely mundane. Dr. Say's drugs may have worn off unexpectedly, or someone from the lab may have awoken her so she could deal with some laboratory emergency.

After several minutes, Padric reluctantly concluded that she wasn't coming back. He would have to check with her later. No doubt she was fine, and the explanation was perfectly innocent.

Dr. Jillias Say stared at the rod Vidya was leveling at her.

"If you fail to do exactly as I tell you," Vidya said, "I will give you another jolt, a stronger one. It will stun you and it will hurt."

"What—" Dr. Say's voice squeaked and she cleared her throat. "What do you want? How did you get into my office?"

"Get up," Vidya replied. "Come with me."

Say slowly got to her feet. Vidya kept the cattle prod pointed steadily at her. They were in Say's office, a spare place with only desk, chair, computer terminal, and couch. Say had been lying "asleep" on the latter when Vidya came in. It had been simple enough to use the cattle prod to short out the lock. One look at the dermospray on the cushion beside Say was all Vidya needed. She was indeed Silent, and she had been in the Dream.

Vidya ushered Say out into the genetics lab. Stainless steel glistened, machines hummed. The walls were a spotless white tile. Adrenaline hummed through Vidya's veins and she had to work to keep her hands from shaking. Dr. Kri, Max Garinn, and all eleven slaves sat motionless on the floor against one wall. The wrists, mouths, and ankles of two of the slaves were bound with silver tape. Katsu was busy taping up a third. None of them resisted. Sejal, perched on a stool, stared at them with glassy eyes. Prasad, meanwhile, was muttering to a computer terminal in the corner.

"What did you learn?" Vidya asked him.

Prasad's mouth was tight. "We're too late. They did it last night."

A pang went through Vidya's stomach and she almost dropped the cattle prod.

"You're trying to stop the project?" Say said incredulously. "Why?"

"Your project, whatever it is, will destroy the Dream." Vidya let some of her anger slip into her voice. "Don't you know what that would *do*?"

"Of course I know." Two spots of angry color appeared on Say's pale cheeks. "Destroying the Dream is the whole point!"

Vidya's hand tightened on the prod. "We'd guessed that."

Prasad came over to join them. His face was grave. In the background, Katsu continued plying her roll of tape. "What exactly do you think destroying the Dream would accomplish?" he asked in his quiet voice.

"It would end war!" Say almost shouted.

Prasad shook his head so calmly Vidya irrationally wanted to slap him. Then she realized he was only trying to keep her talking so Katsu could finish her work.

"I do not understand," Prasad said. "Please explain."

"The Dream allows instant communication between planets and governments." Say leaned back against one of the stone worktables. Vidya kept the cattle prod pointed at her. "Empires and armies are based on instantaneous communication. Without it, they'd fall apart. Don't you see? The Dream allows interplanetary rule *and interplanetary warfare.* Without the Dream, communication would be slowed to the speed and availability of courier ships. The governments—all of them—aren't used to that. Without the Dream, admirals couldn't communicate between ships and relay orders. Heads of government couldn't communicate with satellite planets. Once the Dream is destroyed, war will end."

Vidya's temper rose again. "You are foolish to think so."

"It will end the war between the Unity and the Independence Confederation," Say shot back.

That stopped Vidya cold. "What?"

"Didn't you know?" Say said almost sweetly. "The Unity just declared war on the Confederation. Troops and ships are already moving. Allies on both sides are gearing up as well. Billions of lives are at stake. I can—the project can—save them."

"No," Prasad said firmly. "The project won't save billions. It will destroy trillions. Perhaps more."

Now it was Say's turn to look confused. "I don't understand."

"The Dream is more than a mere communication system," he told her. "It creates a shared empathy and concern for our fellow beings. Without the Dream, there can be no compassion, no love, no joy. People will prey on one another. No one will care enough to raise children, or even have them. Within a few generations, all sentient life will simply fade away. Compared to this, war is as nothing."

Say looked at him. She was still leaning against the worktable. Vidya realized her right hand, the one that held the cattle prod, was beginning to ache, and she risked switching it to her left.

"I don't believe you," Say said at last. "You're lying to try to make me change my mind. I won't. I watched my parents and my brother die in the famine. I saw my mother and sister raped to death by Unity soldiers. The project will destroy the Unity"—she spat—"for good."

Prasad's brown eyes were implacable. "It will also destroy Rust and every other civilization in the universe."

"I still say you're lying."

"You can let go now, Sejal," Katsu said, and Vidya turned her head to look. The slaves, Kri, and Garinn were well taped. Sejal blinked, then stood up and cracked his knuckles. As one, the prisoners widened their eyes and made muffled grunts and cries.

"We won't hurt you," Katsu told them. "We will release you as soon as we are finished here."

"You can't do anything," Say said. "The final phase of the project is already underway. The next set of children will enter the Dream any moment now, if they haven't already, and they will destroy it."

Vidya's temper broke. She balled up a fist and smashed Say's face. Say's head snapped back under the impact. Vidya's knuckles stung. Say grabbed the tabletop with one hand and put the other to her mouth. It came away smeared with blood.

"Bitch," she spat. "I'm glad you lost."

Vidya was about to reply when Prasad laid a hand on her arm. "My wife should remain calm. Remember, we have a plan of our own."

"You can't stop the project." Say almost laughed.

"No?" Vidya gestured at the door that led to the Nursery. "Did you, then, find a way to let the Silent enter the Dream from cryo-sleep?"

Say's pale eyes went wide. "You can't."

"You are mistaken." Vidya put out her hand. "Katsu, would you bring me the tape please? Then you and your brother can help us with the children."

Say backed up a step. A trickle of blood oozed from the corner of her mouth. "I won't let you."

"You can't stop us," Vidya said with a hint of mean gladness in her voice. "Please hold still. I *am* going to tape you up, and it would be very painful for you if I had to use the cattle prod first."

"Tessa!" Say barked. "Emergency lockdown. All files and access. Activate emergency alert system. Scramble all—"

Vidya leaped forward and thumbed the cattle prod trigger. A spark snapped and Say collapsed to the floor with a cry of pain. Kri tried to shout something, but it was muffled by the tape over his mouth.

"Acknowledged," replied the computer. "Emergency lockdown in progress. Alert system activated."

"Tessa!" Prasad ordered. "Abort emergency lockdown."

"Access denied. Insufficient security clearance."

"Shit!" Sejal said. He ran over to Say's limp form.

"The new children are entering the Dream," Katsu said. "I can feel them."

Vidya's insides twisted and she resisted the impulse to fling the cattle prod away. Stupid! She had been so stupid! It had been foolishness itself to tell Say what they were planning before immobilizing her. Now an entire universe would pay for her mistake.

"What do we do now?" she asked.

"We need to force her to release the lockdown," Prasad said. "Otherwise the computer won't activate the cryo-units."

"The children are screaming." Katsu headed for the door that led to the Nursery. "I have to go into the Dream."

Vidya knelt next to Sejal, who was checking Say's pulse. He gasped when he touched her, further proof were it needed that she was Silent.

"The woman's a fanatic," Vidya said. "We can't persuade her with words. Are there any drugs in the labs we could use?"

"No," Prasad replied. "And I wouldn't know how to use them if there were."

"Dammit!" Vidya pounded the cold tile floor with her aching fist. "One woman. This one woman stands in our way and we can't force her to do what's right."

"You can't," Sejal said beside her. "But I can."

The Dream was almost empty. Kendi stood naked at the mouth of his cave, letting the good heat of the sun bake into his bones. He knew he shouldn't stay long, but it was such a relief to feel the Dream around him. His toes dug into the sandy soil. The scrubby vegetation of the Outback stretched away beneath the azure sky. And in the distance was the dark place.

Ara was dead. The thought pierced him like a spear, ripping through heart and lungs with a white-hot edge. She couldn't be dead. She was Mother Adept Araceil Rymar do Salman Reza. His teacher. His friend. His second mother.

The Real People saw death as something natural, nothing to grieve about. But all he knew was that it hurt. He felt trapped, hemmed in by grief and sorrow.

"Keeeennndiiii."

The harsh voice sent a chill down Kendi's spine.

"Keeeennndiiii."

He was sitting on a hard stone floor. It was cold under his buttocks. The air had turned damp and it was filled with smells of garbage and human waste. Metal bars pressed against the knobs of his spine.

Kendi lifted his head. It was the Unity prison cell. Kendi's eyes went wide and he pushed himself back against the bars. This wasn't real. He was *here* but he wanted to be *there.*

The cell remained. Nine metal bunks were stacked three

high against the walls. A crude and filthy toilet stood in the corner. Cries and conversation echoed from other cells. Six other men and four women, one of whom was pregnant, were crowded into this one. A knife blade glinted in the shadows and one of the women screamed, a high, horrible sound. It was followed by a tiny, mewling noise. Blood splashed to the ground. Kendi stared at it.

"Keeeennndiiii. Loony, loony Keeeeennndiiii!"

Kendi wrapped his arms around his knees and rocked in the corner.

Sejal sat on the floor next to Say, who glared daggers at Vidya. She had managed to pull herself into a sitting position against one leg of the worktable. Her black hair had come loose from the braid coiled above her neck and her face was pale.

"Do what you want," she croaked. "I won't release the computer."

"Look at me, Dr. Say," Sejal said. "Look at me *now*."

Almost like a puppet, Say turned her head to look at Sejal. He was staring intently at her with those strange blue eyes. The grave look on his face made him look very adult and handsome, like his father. Vidya mentally shook her head. Now was not the time for such things. She wondered if Katsu had reached the Dream yet and if she were having any impact on the children in the Nursery.

"Dr. Say," Sejal said softly, "I know you don't like my mother. But you like me, don't you?"

After a long moment, Say nodded. Sejal reached out and ran the back of his finger down Say's cheek. She shuddered delicately. Vidya stared. Where had Sejal learned that gesture? The answer followed almost immediately on the question and nausea bubbled in her stomach. Behind them, Prasad shuffled his feet.

"Dr. Say. Jillias," Sejal murmured. "Do you love me?"

Say nodded again. A little color returned to her face, and she gazed at Sejal with rapt adoration. Vidya was certain she was going to throw up.

"Jillias," Sejal said. "Will you do me a little favor? Please?"

"Yes, Sejal," she murmured. "Anything for you."

"Release the computer. Would you do that? For me?"

A long pause, and then a nod. "Tessa," she said, "lift emergency lockdown."

"Acknowledged," the computer said. "Lockdown lifted. Access restored."

A great weight lifted from Vidya's shoulders. She scrambled to her feet and turned to Prasad. "We need to begin working with the children."

"That won't help," Say said dreamily from the floor. Sejal was holding her hand.

"What do you mean?" Prasad asked sharply.

"The Unity is coming," Say told them.

"What?" Vidya, Prasad, and Sejal's voices spoke as one.

"I activated the emergency alert system." Say's hand crept up to smooth Sejal's dark hair. Vidya wanted to slap her. "It calls the Unity guard in case of a life-or-death emergency, like if we spring a leak and can't get to the submersible. Better arrest than death. They'll be here within the hour, my love."

Vidya stared at her in horror and hatred. The desire to throttle the stupid woman was so strong, her ears were ringing. Before she could move, however, Prasad's gentle hand landed on her shoulder.

"If we have little time," he said, "then we must hurry."

Practicality won out. Vidya tossed the roll of tape to Sejal. "Tape her up, then come help us in the Nursery."

Sejal obeyed. Dr. Say accepted his ministrations without comment as Vidya and Prasad left the lab and went into the Nursery. When they reached the first glassed-off area, the one with the oldest children behind it, Vidya saw that every one of them was squirming and convulsing. Not one of them made a sound. Katsu sat in the room's rocking chair, her eyes shut. Prasad opened the door to the glassed-off area. The only sound was the soft beeping of medical monitors and the eerie rustle of bedclothes sliding over convulsive flesh. The sound made the hair on the back of Vidya's neck stand up.

"Where are the children that Max Garinn injected with his virus?" Vidya asked. "We should begin with them."

Prasad quickly led her down the hallway to another glassed-off Nursery. Eight beds held eight wizened figures.

Six of them were squirming against their restraints, eyes tightly shut. The other two appeared comatose.

"Each bed has a cryo-unit beneath it," Prasad said, moving into the room. "We need to slide it out and put the child inside. The computer will do the rest."

Vidya followed as Prasad reached under the first bed. A black coffin-sized unit slid out and he pressed a release. The top slid open. Vidya began disconnecting the life support units. Touching the dry skin made her flesh shudder. Grimly she ignored the sensation and helped Prasad undo the child's restraints. It was a girl, thin and wrinkled.

One little foot lashed out and caught Vidya in the stomach. Breath left her in a *whoof.* The girl fought and gnashed her teeth, but made no sound. She was surprisingly strong, and it took some effort to wrestle her into the cryo-unit. The lid slid shut. There was a whooshing sound, and the glass fogged with condensation. Prasad wiped it away. The girl lay quietly in the unit, to all appearances peacefully asleep.

Vidya realized she was sweating and her stomach hurt where the girl had kicked her. She glanced at Prasad, who looked equally disheveled.

"Only thirty-eight more, my wife," Prasad said.

Vidya nodded and they turned together toward the second child.

Sejal stuck the last piece of tape over Say's mouth. Her emotions were a tangle. When he touched her with the back of his finger, he had seen the small part of her that found him physically attractive. It hadn't been much of a stretch to touch the emotion and make it coil around her like a mutant jungle vine until she would willingly do whatever he asked. The look she gave him, one of total adoration mixed with red lust, made him feel a bit sick. The moment the gag was in place, he let go of the emotion and it snapped back to its original state. Her eyes flickered as the false love died, replaced by confusion, then anger, then rage.

"Sorry," Sejal said. "But we couldn't have you locking down the computer again."

He left her then, moving quickly toward the Nursery. Mom and Prasad would need all the help they could—

~Sejal.~

Sejal stopped cold. "Hello?"

~Sejal, it is Katsu.~ The voice was tense.

Sejal shook his head. Kendi had told him about whispering, but he had never felt someone speak inside his mind like this.

"What's wrong, Katsu?" he asked aloud.

~I need your help. The new children are entering the Dream, and they're all angry. They're going to spread out and I can't stop them. I need your help. Quickly! They're splitting apart!~

Sejal's heart lurched. He dashed past the other taped-up prisoners and into the Nursery area. Katsu's body sat in a rocking chair in the first room. In the second, Mom and Prasad were wrestling a struggling child into a cryo-unit. Sejal did some quick math and realized it would take hours to get every child into a unit if they all struggled and fought. But what if . . . ?

He stared at the children in the Nursery and reached toward them with his mind. If he blanked them out, they would stop struggling and Mom and Prasad could get them into the units more easily. More importantly, they wouldn't tear up the Dream. Sejal *reached.*

He felt nothing. No minds. The only people he could sense were his parents.

~Because their minds are in the Dream, Sejal!~ Katsu shouted. *~I need you* here. *Help me!~*

Sejal poked his head into the Nursery. "Mom! Katsu needs me in the Dream. I'm going in."

Before Vidya could respond, Sejal slid to the floor. His insides were tightly wound, and he wondered if he would be able to concentrate enough to reach the Dream. But after two deep breaths, Kendi's training took over. The outer world faded away, and Sejal reached for the Dream.

He expected his seashore, and was therefore startled to find himself standing in front of the black space. Screams, angry and hungry, crashed over him and he put his hands to his ears.

"Katsu!" he shouted over the noise. "Katsu!"

Even as he shouted her name, he realized he knew exactly where she was. He had touched her in the real world, of course, and that now allowed him to find her in the Dream. She was in the center of the black place.

Sejal hesitated, hands over his ears. When he had played the flute for Katsu, he hadn't actually entered the blackness. The angry, horrible screams worked their way into his head, and the darkness boiled. Figures moved inside it, and he felt their hunger and their sickness. Every instinct Sejal had told him to flee far and fast. But Katsu was in there and she was fine. Sejal was her brother, and they were both half-sibling to the children. What worked for her should work for him.

Sejal took a deep breath and tensed himself to leap into the darkness. Before he could do it, however, another cry filtered its way through the noise. Sejal froze. He had felt it more than he had heard it. It was a desperate cry for help, and the voice was powerfully familiar. It came from above. Sejal looked up and saw a falcon circling overhead with desperate beats of her wings.

"Kendi?" Sejal said.

"Sejal!" Katsu's voice cut through the wailing and Sejal could now see her inside the dark place. "Sejal, I need you!"

The falcon cried again, wordless and pleading and Sejal's earlier resentment toward Kendi vanished. Kendi was in danger. Kendi needed him. But so did the universe itself. Sejal stood at the boundary of darkness.

"Sejal!" Katsu shouted desperately.

The falcon cried, begging.

Tears streaming down his face, Sejal plunged into the dark place.

TWENTY-EIGHT

The Dream

The jailer is also a prisoner, and he is jealous of the prisoner's dreams.

—Nerval d. Darge, *Diary of a Social Dissident*

It was cold, and the red cracks in the Dream fabric around Sejal offered only a dim light. He could feel the minds in this place—over thirty of them—and they were hungry. He knew it wasn't a physical hunger, but a spiritual one, a desperate, horrible feeling of loneliness and separation. He could see outside the darkness to the well-lit plain beyond. The plain was safe and pain-free and filled with other minds. This was what the children longed for, reached toward. The fact that they could see, but not touch it only made the feeling worse.

The wailing was quieter in the dark place. Perhaps it was because the children's rage and pain were directed outward. Their minds flowed around Sejal, cold shadows in a black hole. Icy fingers touched his face and neck. Sejal recoiled, but the fingers didn't draw away. More touches—hands, fingers, lips, and tongues that flickered over him. Sejal forced himself to remain stock-still, like a man confronting a strange dog that might or might not decide to tear his throat out.

A few steps away, Katsu was dancing. She moved toward him, pivoting and swaying, clearly well-practiced. As she approached, the minds around Sejal calmed. He felt from them something akin to admiration, even solace. They liked her. But before she could speak, one of the minds broke away. It flashed toward the boundary of the Dream and the dark place. Snarling gleefully, two more tensed themselves to follow. The ground rumbled.

"No!" Katsu cried, and without thinking, Sejal's mind snapped out. He reached for the escapee just as he had reached for Say. Here in the Dream, however, the action took a physical manifestation. A golden thread snaked from

Sejal's outstretched hand. The other end wrapped itself around the fleeing shadow. The shadow stiffened and halted less than a finger's length from the boundary.

Katsu sighed with relief, though she continued to sway to music that only she could hear. "This is why I need you. There are so many. If I stop long enough to chase down the ones that break away, the others—"

The shadow yanked on Sejal's thread. The sudden pain drove him to his knees. Blind fury and all-consuming hunger flooded Sejal's mind. He was flashing on the shadow, feeling what it felt. The thread flickered and weakened. The shadow yanked again and Sejal gasped in pain and confusion. No one had ever been able to fight him before. He touched people as he pleased, made them do what *he* wanted.

But, a part of him realized, these weren't normal people. They were like him. Their DNA had been given to them by the same father and shaped by the same retrovirus.

Hands landed on his head, warm and friendly. Katsu. Sejal drew strength from her, braced himself, and pulled back on the thread. The gold thread thickened. Screaming in hostility, the shadow was dragged back from the boundary. Katsu left Sejal and danced toward it. The loneliness from the other shadows lessened a bit at the sight of her graceful movements. She caressed the bound shadow and it calmed.

Another one used the distraction to leap away, but Sejal had felt its tension and another thread whipped outward to catch it. It fought, clawing and snarling, until Katsu was able to calm it down like she had the first. The others swarmed about uncertainly.

"How many can you hold?" Katsu asked.

"I don't know," Sejal replied through gritted teeth. "I could take a dozen regular people without working up a sweat, but this is something else. How many are there?"

Katsu glanced into the blackness. The red cracks formed glowing, distorted ladders in every direction, and the weird light made her face take on a spectral aspect.

"Thirty-seven," she said.

Something shifted, and the darkness rippled slightly.

"Thirty-six," Katsu amended. "Father and mother must have—"

A crashing howl broke over them. Betrayal and anger and the constant overwhelming hunger smashed at Sejal as the twisted children screamed in unified fury. Five shadows rushed away. Sejal lashed out with more threads. He caught one, two, three. But the other two broke free of the darkness and raced across the plain. The ground cracked and crumbled beneath their feet. The sky darkened as they swallowed the minds that made up the Dream plain. Katsu dashed after them, quick as a fox. She caught one by the heel, and the second stopped to see what had happened. Katsu caught that one as well. Her touch, as always, brought them some kind of comfort and she was able to bring them back. They followed her, twisting clouds of darkness and gray mist. It came to Sejal that the children had no personal physical picture of themselves, which was why they remained amorphous in the Dream.

As Katsu and her two captives re-entered the dark place, there was another delicate shudder. One of the minds Sejal had bound disappeared. Prasad and his mother had put another child into cryo-sleep. Thirty-five left. The red lattices glowed with suspicion. The children knew something was wrong, but they didn't know what it was. Sejal hoped Mom and Prasad would be able to finish the job before they figured it out. The children he held in the threads were quieter, but they were whispering to the others around them, and Sejal couldn't make out their words. He glanced uneasily at Katsu, who shook her head.

"I can't quite hear them, either," she said.

The blackness shifted, and a familiar cry rang overhead. Sejal looked up sharply and saw the falcon. In desperation she had pierced the black place. Instantly, one of the children lashed out and caught her. The falcon shrieked in pain.

"No!" Sejal yelled. "Let her go!"

Another thread snapped out and wrapped around the grasping child. It released the falcon, who dove down to land at Sejal's feet. The child drew away, hissing softly. Sejal reached down to stroke the falcon's feathers. She made soft *meeping* sounds.

"Who is this?" Katsu demanded.

"It's part of . . . of a friend of mine," Sejal told her. "He's in trouble, but you needed me more so I came here instead."

Another shudder. Another child disappeared.

"Listen," Sejal said, "Kendi must be desperate if his falcon came in here to look for me. He . . . I really want to help him. Can you hold them back for just a few minutes?"

Katsu looked at him for a long time. Then she backed away and started to dance. It was a faster dance, one with a clear rhythm. Her feet struck the dark ground, and she twisted between the red slashes cut into the Dream fabric around them. The movements were lovely and hypnotic. Sejal stared, then noticed the children had calmed considerably. He also noticed the sweat appearing on Katsu's face. This dance was clearly costing her a lot of effort. He had better move quickly.

He released his captives. The threads vanished, but the children didn't seem to notice. They were watching Katsu. Sejal put the falcon on his shoulder and wove between the red lattices toward the boundary. The moment he was clear of the dark place, the falcon exploded from his shoulder and fled across the plain.

Sejal ran after her. He hadn't gone fifty meters before he saw the stone block. It was about twice Sejal's height and six or seven meters on a side with no openings. The falcon circled over it, crying in its high, shrill voice. Sejal put out a hand. The moment he touched the block's icy solidity, he felt Kendi. His empathy switched on, and Sejal was caught in a wash of terror and . . . guilt? The falcon shrieked again.

"Kendi!" Sejal shouted. "Kendi! It's Sejal."

No response. Sejal's empathy switched off. What was going on? Could one Silent imprison another? He had never heard of such a thing, but that didn't mean much. For all his power, Sejal was still new to the Dream.

A sense of urgency tightened his chest. Katsu was holding the children back all by herself, and she must be getting tired. He had to help Kendi and get back to her. He hit the block with a fist, and yelped in pain. Nursing bruised knuckles, he next concentrated on his body. It was solid now, but when he reached toward the block, it would be insubstantial. It would be insubstantial *now.*

Sejal reached. He encountered solid stone.

"Dammit!" he spat. "Kendi! Let me in!"

The block remained unmoved. Frustrated, Sejal kicked it, though not hard enough to damage his foot. No reaction. Katsu would be more tired now. Perhaps he should give up and leave. Perhaps he should—

Then he felt it. Another familiar mind, one that wasn't in the Dream but was nearby nonetheless.

"Ben," Sejal whispered.

He had always gotten the impression that Ben and Kendi were close friends, though Kendi had almost never talked about him. Ben might better know what to do. Sejal closed his eyes, feeling for Ben's mind. When he found it, he *reached.*

Ben looked down worriedly at Kendi, lying motionless on the bed in the empty cabin. Kendi was always falling into trouble. Getting arrested, being abducted into the Dream by Sejal, going suicidal on Bellerophon. Now Kendi was spending time in the Dream when it was dangerous to do so, and according to Ben's watch, he'd been in there far too long.

Ben sighed and sat on the edge of the bed. He should walk away, sever all ties completely instead of waffling back and forth. A relationship with Kendi meant spending a lot of time waiting for him, and Ben hated the very idea. But then he would look at Kendi's face and his resolve invariably failed him. Kendi was infuriating, irreverent, and impulsive. He was also funny, kind, and surprisingly romantic. He could always think of something fun to do when Ben got bogged down by work. And Ben never felt he had to be so damned competent at everything when Kendi was around.

Kendi's face was relaxed in Dream sleep. Ben brushed his fingers over the smooth dark forehead. Maybe a little worry was all right. Concentrating on Kendi was one way to keep thoughts about his mother at bay. Maybe he should try to wake Kendi up, bring him out of the—

~Ben.~

Ben's head snapped up. "Who's there?"

~Ben, it's me. Sejal.~

"Sejal?" Ben echoed stupidly. "Where are you? What's—?"

~I'm in the Dream. I'm talking to you from the Dream.~

Ben blinked. "How can you talk to me from the Dream? I'm not Silent. What is this, a joke?"

~Ben, I don't have time to screw around. I can't leave Katsu alone much longer. Kendi needs help, but I can't reach him.~

Chill fear stabbed through Ben. He glanced over at Kendi, who hadn't moved or otherwise changed.

"What do you mean he's in trouble?" Ben demanded.

~He's inside some kind of stone block and I can't get him out. The falcon is screaming bloody murder, but I don't know what to do. Can you get him out?~

"I'll try." Ben leaned over Kendi and shook him. "Kendi, wake up! Snap out of it!" No response. He slapped Kendi's cheeks and pinched his wrists. Still no response.

~That's not what I meant,~ Sejal said impatiently. *~I need you in the Dream. You've known him longer than I have. Maybe you can reach him.~*

A stab of fear. "I can't reach the Dream, Sejal. I've tried, and it doesn't work for me." But even as he said it, an inner voice began listing contradictions. Genetically, he was Silent. There was really only one thing that had kept him out of the Dream all this time.

His own reluctance.

~You're Silent,~ Sejal countered, paralleling Ben's thoughts. *~That's why I can talk to you. And if I pulled Kendi into the Dream, I can sure as hell pull you in, too. You ready?~*

"No!" Ben had to shout to hear himself over his own pounding heart. "Sejal, I can't. I can't enter the Dream. It's impossible."

~Shit, Ben.~ Sejal's voice was startled. *~What do you mean that—oh. Oh shit!~*

"What?" Ben said. "What's wrong?"

~You and Kendi. Shit! He never told me, but now I can feel it. My God. I knew you two were friends, but Kendi never said you two were in—~

"I can't do it, Sejal," Ben interrupted. "I just can't. Can

you get him out? You're supposed to be some kind of super-Silent."

~I've tried, Ben. He's locked himself up in some kind of psycho-fantasy or something. I don't know him well enough to reach through that, and he's strong enough to keep me out. He may not be able to keep you out, though. You love him.~

It was very odd hearing it from someone else. Ben swallowed.

~Ready?~ Sejal said. *~I'll bring you in. One . . . two . . .~*

"Wait!" Ben shouted. His breathing had gone short and panicky.

~Ben, I can't wait. Katsu needs me. Ready?~

Ben looked down at Kendi's motionless form. Sejal was going to take him into the Dream, the Dream that swallowed people up and took them away from you. The Dream that made people ordinary. If Ben entered the Dream, he'd be just like the rest of his family. Ben had defined himself as special, as non-Silent, for almost twenty years. If he entered the Dream, he wouldn't be himself anymore.

And the Dream had killed his mother.

The memory of finding his mother's crumpled body at the base of the talltree flashed before him. Yes, his mother was dead. And her death had given him the strength to act, to get Kendi to safety. Now Kendi needed him again, and he was shying away? New resolve filled him.

"Bring me in, Sejal," Ben said firmly. "Go!"

~You got it.~

There was a *twist*, and suddenly Ben was standing on a blank plain. A diffuse sort of light came from no discernible direction. The air was calm and still. In the distance lay a roiling black mass, and beside him stood a massive stone block. So this was the Dream. In wonder, Ben touched his own chest and arms. They felt solid, just as they did in the real world. A wild cry sounded overhead and Ben looked up. A falcon was circling above him.

"You made it."

Ben whirled around to see Sejal. His dark hair was tousled, and his pale blue eyes looked tired in his brown face. He seemed far older than sixteen.

"Kendi's in there," Sejal said, gesturing at the block. "I have to get back to Katsu." And with that, he vanished.

"Wait!" Ben shouted. "What do I do? Who's Katsu? How do I get back?"

But he was talking to empty air.

Ben licked his lips, trying to remember everything he had heard about the Dream and how it worked. Reality was supposed to shape itself around him, becoming whatever he expected it to be. Sejal said Kendi was trapped inside the stone block. Since there were no other Silent around, that could only mean that Kendi himself had, for some reason, created the thing and he wouldn't—or couldn't—come out. But why had he created it in the first place? Ben had no idea.

Best to get him out then, and ask.

Ben put a palm on the stone. Like a sudden jolt, he felt Kendi inside. It was almost the reverse of the terrible loneliness he had felt back on Bellerophon. Kendi was *there* in a way that Ben had never felt before, even if Ben couldn't see or touch him.

Kendi was also terrified right down to his bones.

Even more worried now, Ben pushed on the stone. It was thoroughly solid. Ben paused and imagined his hand going through the rock. That was the way the Dream worked—if you imagined it, it was so. But Ben's hand remained stubbornly on the surface of the block.

"Kendi!" he shouted. "Kendi, let me in!"

No response. The falcon continued to circle overhead. Kendi had mentioned his animal friend, a fragment of Kendi's own mind, but Ben didn't see how knowing this could help.

Time for more desperate measures. Ben closed his eyes and imagined a laser pistol. When he closed his hand, he would feel it, smooth and heavy, in his palm. One . . . two . . . three. Ben closed his hand.

It remained empty. Ben puffed out his cheeks. He had no experience—or, apparently, talent—at this. His mother could have probably whipped up a jackhammer or just imagined herself inside the block, and so it would be. But Ben was stuck here by himself, abandoned by Sejal, Kendi, even his mother. Not even entering the Dream had changed that about his—

No. That was the wrong way to think. Kendi was *here.* Ben could feel him. He closed his eyes and pressed his forehead to the block.

Kendi, he thought. *Tell me how to reach you. I'm all alone out here just like you're all alone in there.*

A faint whisper of movement. Had the block shifted? Ben didn't move. Instead he thought about Kendi, his jokes, his eyes, his laugh, how much Ben missed him.

Come, on Kendi. Let me in. I'm here for you now. I'll always be here for you, even in the Dream.

The rock definitely shifted.

Kendi. Let me in the way I never let you in. I'm sorry I didn't. Come on, Kendi. Dammit, Kendi, I love you. Now let me in!

The block opened. Ben stumbled forward in surprise, and his eyes popped open. Behind him, the block sealed itself shut, leaving a blank wall. Ben found himself in a dank, dimly lit corridor. Barred prison cells lined the walls, and people moaned and muttered from their depths. Ben was wearing the black-and-scarlet uniform of the Unity guard, right down to boots and holstered pistol.

And then Ben knew what was going on. It should have been so obvious. Why hadn't he seen it sooner?

Astonished and uncertain, Ben walked slowly down the corridor, peering into each cell as he went. The people inside were ill-defined, barely more than shades. Where was Kendi? He had to be here someplace.

A horrible scream chilled every drop of Ben's blood. He ran toward the sound, boots thudding on the corridor floor, until he came to the final cell. When he peered inside, his gorge came up and he had to swallow hard. A transparent man was standing over the body of an equally transparent woman. The knife in his hand dripped scarlet blood. The woman was—had been—pregnant, but her belly had been slashed open. The baby lay on the stone floor next to its mother, bleeding, dying. Ben involuntarily backed up a step.

"Keeennnddiiii," the man with the knife said. "Want me to do you next?"

Kendi huddled on the floor against the bars, his back to Ben, and Ben realized that to Kendi the entire scene was real. The Silent did not—could not—create people in the Dream. Sentient behavior was too complex for even the subconscious mind to create and control. Shades like these were two-dimensional. Kendi, trapped in his own nightmare, didn't seem to notice.

The man with the knife advanced a step. Before Ben could react, Kendi suddenly moved. With lightning speed, his hand flashed forward and dipped into the puddle of blood. He flicked it like water at the man, then smeared some on his own forehead. With a manic grin, he threw back his head and howled at the roof. The sound sent a chill down Ben's back.

Another transparent man advanced out of the shadows of the cell. He put a restraining hand on the man with the knife.

"Leave him alone," he said in a raspy voice. "He's a lunatic. You stab a guy like that, he only gets madder."

Kendi howled again as the two men retreated into the darkness of the cell. Then Kendi slumped to the floor to huddle once again against the bars.

Ben stepped closer and opened his mouth to speak. But before he could make a sound, the scene in the cell flickered like a hologram. The two corpses, one woman and one baby, vanished. In their place stood the woman, alive and pregnant, but still transparent. The man brandished his knife. The woman screamed as he brought it down in a flashing arc. Blood flowed and the woman collapsed to the cell floor.

"Keeennndiii," the knife man said. "Want me to do you next?"

Ben watched the entire scene play out again in exact, gruesome detail. At the end, Kendi gave his chilling howl and slumped back against the bars.

How many times has he replayed this? Ben thought in horror, even as his heart wrenched in sympathy and pain. How had Kendi survived this? How was he surviving it now?

Ben put a hand through the bars and grabbed Kendi's

shoulder before the scene could reset itself. Kendi let out a snarl and twisted like a cat.

"Kendi, it's all right," Ben soothed. "It's me. Ben."

Kendi blinked owlishly up at him. "Ben? All life—Ben you have to get out! They'll catch you."

He really thinks he's in the Unity prison again, Ben thought. "I've come to get *you* out. Kendi, come on. You can do it."

"Run, Ben," Kendi pleaded hoarsely, his hands grasping the bars. "Run before they—"

"Keeeennnndiiii," the knife man rasped. "Who's your friend, Keeeennnnddiiii?"

The scene hadn't reset this time. The knife man stepped over his victims, ignoring the advice of his friend. Ben's heart leaped into his mouth. If the man stabbed Kendi in the Dream, his real body would die as well.

"Kendi, come with me," Ben said urgently. "This prison isn't real. You can walk out anytime you want."

"Run, Ben," Kendi said. "Please! Don't let them get you, too."

The man loomed behind Kendi and raised the knife. Ben reacted. He yanked out the laser pistol holstered at his side, the one Kendi had unwittingly created for him, and fired into the cell. The knife man dropped his blade and fell to the floor, twitching and writhing in pain. Kendi stared with wide eyes. Blood was still smeared on his forehead.

Ben met Kendi's gaze and held out his hand. "Come with me, Kendi."

Kendi looked at Ben's hand. "I can't, Ben. I don't deserve it."

"No one deserves this, Kendi," Ben told him. "Come with me."

"I didn't do anything to stop him," Kendi whispered. "All life, I didn't do a damn *thing*."

"There wasn't anything you could do," Ben replied. "If you had, you would both have been dead instead of just her."

"And the baby," Kendi said. "I dipped my finger in the baby's blood."

"You did it to save yourself," Ben said. "To make them

think you were insane so they'd leave you alone. But that's over now, Kendi. Come with me."

But Kendi refused Ben's hand. "I can't."

"Kendi," Ben said in sudden inspiration. "I forgive you."

Kendi continued to look at him.

"I forgive you," Ben repeated.

"That's not enough," Kendi said.

"It'll do," Ben replied, "until you can forgive yourself. Come out of the cell, Kendi. Come out of the cell for me."

With a low cry, Kendi snatched Ben's hand. The bars vanished and the stone walls melted away, leaving Ben and Kendi alone on the empty plain. Kendi dropped to the ground, dragging Ben with him. Then he buried his face in Ben's shoulder. He cried for what felt like a long time, great shuddering tears of relief. Ben just held him until the storm subsided. When it finally did, Kendi pushed himself upright.

"Wait a minute," he said, sniffling. "What the hell are you doing here? How did you get in?"

Ben gave him a rakish grin. "Present from Sejal."

A shuddering boom thundered through earth and air. As one, Ben and Kendi twisted around to look at the dark place just in time to see the darkness splinter and shatter into a thousand pieces.

TWENTY-NINE

The Dream

When dinosaurs fight, it is the grass that suffers.
—Bellerophon Proverb

The children were angrier than Sejal thought possible. They howled and shrieked and swirled around Sejal and Katsu. A shadow grabbed Sejal's arm in an icy grip, and he gave a hard, instinctive shove with his mind. The child released him with a screech that almost split Sejal's skull. Another swiped at Katsu's head, but she ducked away. Sejal spun around, trying to look in all directions at once. Angry red gashes swirled through the blackness like blood in a whirlpool.

"They're angry because Father and Mother are taking them out of the Dream!" Katsu shouted at him. "My dancing does nothing now. They will devour the people on Ru—"

Another swipe. Katsu flung herself sideways just as something cold and hungry landed on Sejal's back. He yelled and clawed at his back. It felt as if someone had thrown a bucket of icy slime on him.

"Get off me!" he snarled, and thrust backward hard. A slashing pain tore at the side of his neck. Then the icy slime vanished. Sejal whirled, neck throbbing, but the child had skittered back into the darkness. Another hand grabbed at him, and another and another. The children gibbered and laughed at him, clawing at him like a dozen grabby jobbers. Pressure built up in his head and he put his hands over his ears to shut out their noise.

"Get out of here!" he screamed.

The darkness shattered like glass. Over two dozen shadows raced howling away, leaving Sejal and Katsu alone on the Dream's empty plain. Katsu stared at him, wild-eyed and panting. In the new silence he could hear her heart beating.

"What happened?" Sejal croaked.

"Look!" she replied, pointing upward.

Sejal obeyed and saw the darkness hadn't vanished after all. From horizon to horizon, the entire sky had gone black. Thunder rumbled hungrily. The sky began to descend and he resisted the urge to fling himself flat.

"They've begun," Katsu said. "They're going to devour every mind in the Dream."

"Mom will—" Sejal began.

"Not quickly enough," Katsu interrupted. "There are thirty—no, twenty-nine—of them left, and look how easily they cover the sky. They will devour Rust, and our parents will lose interest in the cryo-units."

Not far away, a thick pillar of black dropped down from the sky like a finger as big as a city. The ground shifted and bucked where it landed. Uncountable minds cried out in despair.

"They've taken a planet," Katsu said.

Another pillar dropped near the first, and the ground shifted again. More cries like an ocean wave. Tears ran down Sejal's face in sympathy.

"We have to stop them!" he cried. "All those people—"

"We aren't strong enough," Katsu said dispiritedly. "I can't force them, only persuade them. You are able to push them, but only a little."

Thunder rumbled, a demon clearing its throat. Another pillar crashed down. There was a feeling of horrible exultation in the gesture.

Sejal grabbed Katsu's arm. "We need help."

"Who? There aren't many Silent in the Dream right now, and we'd probably need—"

"—all of them?" Sejal said in an odd voice.

Katsu looked at him. "Can you do that?"

"We'll find out."

"There must be a faster way," Vidya puffed. Sweat plastered her hair and clothes to her body and her muscles felt shaky. There were still twenty-eight more children to go.

Prasad stabbed the controls and the lid on the cryo-unit slid shut over the squirming child. The viewplate fogged over. Without speaking, he moved to the next bed.

"Sedatives?" Vidya said, moving next to him and disconnecting tubes.

"I don't know where they would be," Prasad told her, "and I wouldn't know the dosage. I'd be just as likely to kill them."

Vidya swiftly removed the last tube. "Perhaps, my husband, that would be the best choice."

"No." There was iron in Prasad's voice as he slid the cryo-unit from under the bed and undid the child's retraints. "They are *my* sons and daughters. They cannot help who they are and what they are doing."

They wrestled the child into the unit. An arm cracked Vidya in the face. Pain exploded and for a moment she saw stars. She forced her hands to keep moving, however, until the cryo-unit slid shut and condensation gathered on the viewplate. Then they moved to the next bed, and the next. Vidya moved in a sort of fog, losing all track of time. Twenty-six left. Twenty-five. Twenty-four. Twenty. Her exhausted muscles were shaking so badly she fumbled at the tubes. Her aching body was covered in bruises from the hard hands and heels that struggled against her. Nineteen left. Eighteen. Now they were in the final Nursery. Sixteen left. Fifteen.

"Freeze!"

The command startled Vidya out of her trance. A stab of terror went through her chest as she spun to face the door. Prasad straightened from the child they were working on, then took a step forward, placing himself between Vidya and the four armed guard standing at the door to the glassed-in area. The door to the main laboratory stood open behind them. Vidya thought Prasad was being stupidly romantic until he gestured sharply behind his back at the cattle prod dangling from Vidya's belt. Hiding her motions behind Prasad's body, she eased it off the loop and slid it into her waistband under her shirt.

"Who are you?" Prasad demanded, though the black-and-scarlet guard uniforms made that obvious. Dr. Say's emergency alert had done its work. "What do you want?"

"You're under arrest," the lead guard snapped.

"What for?" Prasad snapped back.

In answer, the guard fired. Prasad collapsed to the floor.

* * *

Sejal closed his eyes. Katsu's hand was cold in his. All around him, pillars of darkness dropped from the sky in an avalanche of pain and misery. Fully a third of the Dream was gone. Every so often a bit of the darkness would vanish—his parents at work—but that didn't seem to decrease the children's power. In the Dream, the Silent were limited only by willpower and self-concept. The twisted children, raised apart from humanity, did not know they were supposed to have limits. Sejal had the sinking feeling that he was dealing with an infinite set, and that one child was just as powerful as a hundred of them.

"Go, Sejal," Katsu said.

Sejal stretched out his mind. The Dream fabric stretched in all directions around him. Where the pillars touched the ground were great gaping holes. Normal people felt like threads, and here and there were the bright, sharp minds of the Silent. Only a very few were actually in the Dream.

A pillar crashed to the ground.

Swiftly, Sejal sifted through the fabric around him. It felt easy, it felt *right.* Wherever he found a Silent mind, he touched it and *pulled.* A crowd of Silent from dozens of races, hundreds of species, appeared around Sejal, all bound to him by the gleaming Dream fabric. Their bodies milled and overlapped like ghosts and their thoughts crowded his mind with questions, demands, terror, fear.

~Who are you?~ ~What are you doing to me?~ ~How dare you!~ ~Help me!~ ~Leave me alone!~ ~What's happening to me?~

Their voices rose and fell around him, threatening to engulf him. Katsu squeezed his hand, and he drew serenity from her.

Serene must you ever remain, he thought.

He found more Silent, and more and more. Padric Sufur's mind abruptly joined the pack, as did Chin Fen's and Dr. Say's. And then he felt another mind, a younger one that he didn't know, but who felt a tiny bit familiar, although he couldn't pinpoint why. It was on a planet named Klimkinnar. Then he felt two more, both on a planet called Drim. All three were slaves. Their voices joined in with the rest, rising into a fever pitch.

~No!~ ~Let go of me~ ~What the hell?~ ~Sejal, you work for me!~ ~I order you to—~

Another pillar crashed to the ground. Sejal yanked the Dream fabric with a sharp jerk. The multitude fell silent, and Sejal continued gathering. He felt Ben's and Kendi's minds and ruthlessly added them to the pool.

~Sejal, what—?~ Kendi yelped, but Sejal ignored him. Silent after Silent fell into his pool. He felt swollen with them. Lights sparked around his body. He felt like he was drinking electric water until it threatened to burst out of him. Only a few minds were left, a tiny handful. He reached for them.

"Sejal, look out!" Katsu cried.

Sejal's eyes snapped open. A black pillar was dropping straight for them. Reflexively, Sejal yanked on the Silent around them, took them into himself, possessed them fully. As one mind, they all reached up with arms suddenly grown godlike in size. The pillar landed on their shoulders. It was cold as winter, heavy as snow. But Sejal had the strength of nearly every Silent in the universe behind him, and he pushed back. His shoulders rose like Atlas, pushing the pillar back to the sky. The children stormed angrily above him, but Sejal held them back. Then he reached out with one giant hand and grabbed one of the pillars that had already reached the ground. With easy strength, he lifted it back to the sky and added it to his burden. A billion minds cleared and a thousand Silent pulled themselves out of the despair of separation. Sejal added them to his strength and reached for another pillar.

His brothers and sisters fought back, pressing down with their full weight. Sejal lifted despite their power. A small part of him marveled at what he was doing, relished in the strength. He lifted another pillar clear of the Dream, and another, and another, adding more and more Silent as they were freed. Every mind added to his own made the burden easier and easier to lift. The children howled mindlessly above him, clawed at his back, tore at his face and hair. But they did no damage. Sejal lifted the final pillar and stood with the black sky on his shoulders. Katsu was small and far below.

And then Sejal noticed that no more children had left the

Dream. There were still fifteen left, had been for quite some time. Had something happened to Prasad and his mother? A bit of uncertainty wiggled through him and his knees buckled for a moment before he could firm them again.

"Katsu," he boomed. Below, Katsu flung herself to the ground, her hands over her ears. Wincing, Sejal modulated his voice to a whisper.

"Katsu," he murmured. "Leave the Dream and go see what—"

A shudder wracked his body and Sejal's grip on the Dream weakened. A jolt of pain ripped through him. His eyes popped open and he found himself staring into the face of a Unity guard.

Ben snapped awake. He was lying on the bed in Kendi's quarters aboard the *Post-Script.* Actually, he was lying on top of Kendi. He must have fallen sideways when Sejal had taken him into the Dream. Kendi shuddered once beneath him, and Ben sat up. A pounding noise thudded through the cabin. What had happened? One minute he and Kendi had been sitting together in the Dream, and the next he had been dragged into . . . what? It was like some kind of drug-induced hallucination.

The pounding noise came again. It was the door. Ben called, "Come in," and the door slid open.

"What is wrong?" Harenn strode into the room. "You would not answer the chime."

"I'm not sure," Ben said. He looked down at Kendi, who was still unconscious. Ben put a hand to Kendi's neck. His pulse was thready, and his skin was clammy. Harenn took one look and her eyes widened above her veil.

"He is going into shock." She hurried back toward the door. "Elevate his legs with the pillow and put the blanket over him. I'll get a medical kit."

Mystified, Ben did as he was ordered. Had the fight done this? But why was it affecting Kendi and not Ben? Ben was on the verge of working himself into a panic when Harenn returned. She slapped a monitor strip on Kendi's forehead and checked the readout on the medical kit's display. Her firm, decisive movements calmed Ben down.

"Is he going to be all right?" he asked.

"He is still in shock," Harenn reported. She racked an ampule into a dermospray and pressed it to Kendi's arm with a *thump*. "This should take care of it."

A few anxious moments later, Kendi's eyes opened. "What's going on?" he asked in a blurry voice.

"What do you remember?" Ben asked.

Kendi shook his head on the mattress. "It's all fuzzy. I can't focus."

"Do you remember the fight?"

"What fight?" Harenn said.

"Sort of," Kendi slurred. "Feel like 'm . . . half outside my body. Help me sit up." They did, though Kendi had to lean heavily on Ben.

"What fight?" Harenn said again. "What happened?"

Ben explained while Kendi took several deep breaths. His head apparently cleared a little, for he sat up straighter, though he left an arm around Ben's back. Without even realizing he was doing it, Ben pulled Kendi closer while he spoke, as if he were afraid Kendi would disappear. It felt good to hold him.

"So why did you leave the Dream?" Harenn asked when Ben finished. "Did your drugs wear off?"

Ben shook his head. "I didn't need any. None of us did as long as Sejal held us there."

Harenn put the dermospray away and reached up to remove the monitor slip from Kendi's forehead. "What about these children you spoke of?"

"I don't know," Ben admitted. "Sejal disappeared. I think that broke the rest of us up."

"It hurt like hell when he did that," Kendi put in. "At least, it did me."

"Can you feel the Dream?" Harenn asked.

Kendi closed his eyes. "Sort of. It's there, but not there. I'm having a hard time concentrating, though."

"The question is," Ben said, "what the hell happened to Sejal?"

Vidya's terrified mind raced through a dozen options and discarded all of them. She was standing with her hands laced over her head in the Nursery. Prasad lay at her feet. He was breathing, which meant he was merely unconscious, ot dead. The four guard had spread into the room, pistols rained on her. They had not searched her yet. They eemed to be waiting for something. The cattle prod ressed against her stomach beneath her shirt. She could robably whip it out and get off a shot, but that would ave three other guard to react.

Life support monitors beeped softly, and over that Vidya eard shouted orders and crashing sounds from the lab itelf. Vidya's nostrils were dilated with fear. There had to e a way out of this. If she didn't find a way, life as she new it would end everywhere. It was no use trying to xplain this to the guard. It would sound like the babblings f a lunatic.

A new guard appeared at the door. "We found two nore," he said. "A boy and a girl. They were in the Dream, ut we hit them with the pistols until they came out of it."

Vidya's legs went weak. The fifth guard shoved Sejal and Katsu into the glassed-in portion of the Nursery. Katsu ooked dazed and Sejal was barely conscious. As one they tumbled and went to their knees. Vidya started to rush oward them, but two guard leveled their pistols at her, and he stopped.

"Are you all right?" she asked them.

Katsu looked up. "We're fine, but the children will soon o back to devouring—"

"No talking," the guard said, and fired his pistol at the eiling. Katsu clamped her mouth shut. Sejal slumped down eside Prasad just as another guard entered the room, a harp-faced man with a whipcord build and thinning blond air. The bars on his sleeve indicated his rank.

"I'm Lieutenant Arsula," he said. "How many are on his station?"

Vidya considered remaining mute. Out of the corner of er eye, she noticed Sejal stir slightly and changed her nind. She needed to keep the Lieutenant talking until ejal recovered.

"We are nineteen," Vidya replied. Something else, some mportant oddity, nagged at her, but she couldn't place it. "That includes the twelve slaves."

Arsula whispered something over his shoulder to someone n the hallway. The oddity continued to poke at Vidya. What was it? What was wrong besides the obvious? Her teeth trie to chatter and she kept her jaw firmly clamped to preven them. Visions of a Unity prison swam through her mind, an she almost snorted. If they couldn't do something soon abou the children, prison would be the least—

It hit her. The children. That was the oddity. The chil dren no longer squirmed in their beds. The room no longe whispered with the rustle of flesh against linen. Vidya stol a glance toward the fifteen Nursery beds and a chill trickle down her spine. Every child wore a beatific smile on it wizened face.

Kendi turned the dermospray over and over in his hand "I need to go back in."

"Out of the question," Harenn said, sounding a lot lik Ara. "It might be even more dangerous now than befor Besides, you are still weak."

"I feel fine now," Kendi objected. "And we need t know what's going on."

Ben tightened his arm around Kendi's body hard enoug to make Kendi wince. He'd forgotten how strong Ben was though it was wonderful to be reminded. It had been s long since Ben had held him.

"You aren't going in there without me," Ben told hin firmly.

"We don't even know what drug dose you need," Kend said. "And you haven't had any training."

"I did all right before," Ben replied gruffly.

"But you were only working with me," Kendi said "You've never had to move around the Dream when i was dangerous."

They argued further, but Kendi ultimately won out though he promised to exit the Dream if anything looke even vaguely dangerous. He also had to concede it woul be better if he lay on the bed instead of standing proppe up in the corner.

"Besides, you didn't bring my spear," he groused, the tousled Ben's hair to show it was a joke. Ben gave a smal smile, and Kendi's heart sang. They were together again He lay back and let Harenn administer the dose. It woul be harder for him to enter the Dream without using th proper ritual pose of the Real People, but he could do it. He breathed deeply. After a long moment, the familiar colors swirled. Kendi reached for the Dream, and opened his eyes.

Everything looked wrong. Instead of being in his cave, he was far above ground. The world spun crazily before he realized he was a falcon flying high in the air, though at the moment he was actually plummeting to his death. He regained control with frantic beats of his wings and leveled out. Below, the Outback looked thin and watery, like a spirit version of the land. Above, the sky was pitch black, and it was laughing.

Why was he a falcon? This had never happened before. Though Kendi knew Silent who changed shape in the Dream, Kendi himself couldn't do it. The falcon was a manifestation of part of himself, but never the main part. What was going on?

A black tentacle shot down from the sky to earth, followed by another and another. One of them skimmed past Kendi's right wing and he banked in panic. Where the tentacles touched the ground, a black pool oozed outward. Screams of pain erupted from the earth. Suddenly Kendi was so tired of a Dream filled with pain and screams. He longed for the time when he could go there for peace and serenity.

Kendi clacked his beak in annoyance with himself. There were real problems to concentrate on now. It was obvious the thing in the Dream was swallowing minds again. Sejal's attack may have pushed it back, but Sejal had been yanked out of the Dream. Kendi cast his mind outward, and felt a few Silent, but only weakly, as tenuous as the Outback below.

Feeling frightened and alone, Kendi continued to fly until a tentacle flashed downward and slammed him into the ground.

"We have found nineteen people," Arsula told Vidya from the doorway. "One of them a woman with dark hair, is unconscious. Do you know why?"

Vidya shook her head. "That is Dr. Say, and I do not know."

"Did you signal the alert?" Arsula said.

"What alert?" Vidya replied, deciding to play stupid.

Arsula leaned casually against a wall, though his body was tightly coiled. His expression remained calm and relaxed. Vidya found herself admiring his poise.

"The guard received a recorded emergency alert that gave us the location of this base," he said. "We had to divert a ocean battleship to investigate. No one at any level of government claims to have any idea that this place existed, and we had a hell of a time finding an airlock through all that camouflage. Who's in charge here?"

Sejal's eyes were open and he looked like he was trying to speak. Vidya willed him to remain quiet.

"Dr. Say is in charge," Vidya replied. "The woman who is unconscious."

"What is this installation doing?" Arsula demanded. "Who are these . . . children? Why are all those people out there taped up? I want answers, dammit!"

Sejal turned his head very slightly, bringing the guard and their pistols into his line of sight. Vidya flung up her hands to ensure the guards were watching her instead of him. "I know very little. I am a mere slave who only does as she is told."

"Bullshit," Arsula growled. "Someone had to tape those people up and someone had to sound the alert. That someone had to be you. You can start by telling me your—"

He stopped mid-sentence. His features froze, as did the other five guards'. Sejal stared at them with glassy eyes. Vidya all but leaped across the room and snatched the pistols out of their unresisting hands. Then she slammed the outer Nursery door shut and locked it. Katsu got dizzily to her feet. Vidya shoved aside the concern she felt and turned to her son.

"Sejal," she said, "can you make these men help us put the children into the cryo-units?"

Shouts rose from outside the Nursery door and something banged against it as Sejal nodded. The five guard and Lieutenant Arsula stiffened, then moved swiftly toward the beds. Vidya checked Prasad. His breathing and heartbeat were steady.

"Hurry, Sejal," Katsu said. "The children have retaken several planets, and they will soon devour Rust."

"I'll try," Sejal said.

"I'll try," all the guard echoed, and the sound made Vidya's skin crawl. Something slammed against the door again.

"I don't know how to do this," Sejal said.

". . . to do this," echoed the guard. They and Sejal were staring at her. Vidya would have expected them to have glassy eyes and glazed faces. They didn't, but they did look odd somehow. It was their expression. Every one of them had the same facial expression, and it looked vaguely like Sejal's face.

"Hurry, Mom," Sejal said. "Come on."

". . . come on."

Vidya went to the nearest bed. The child lay motionless. Only its breathing and the sickening smile on its face said it wasn't dead. She disconnected the first lead.

The thudding at the door was becoming rhythmic. Vidya disconnected the rest of the tubes and slid the cryo-unit out from under the bed. Two of the guard lifted the child into the unit. It slid shut and hissed into activation. The door was beginning to buckle under the repeated buffeting.

Fourteen left. The guard spread out, two to a bed, and went to work. Sejal stood to one side, watching. Eleven left. The door shuddered hard and Vidya could see light leaking through from the other side. Katsu, still looking dazed, fumbled for one of the pistols Vidya had gathered from the guard and put on a table. Vidya dashed across to the door and pulled the cattle prod from her waistband. Eight left.

Vidya set the prod at its highest level and placed the business end against the door. When the next thud came, she thumbed the trigger. Electricity snapped and there were howls of pain from the other side. Vidya nodded in satisfaction. The door was a poor conductor, but the prod put out enough power to cause some damage.

The possessed guard finished another set of children. Five left. The thudding resumed on the door, and Vidya assumed they had found another, nonconductive battering arm. The prod was drained in any case. She hung it from her belt and, like Katsu, took up a pistol. On the floor, Prasad stirred and sat up. Two left.

The door smashed open. A stone-topped table—the new battering ram—wedged itself into the doorway. Vidya crouched behind one of the beds and fired blindly in the direction of the door. Katsu did the same, and the guard outside returned fire.

"Sejal!" Vidya barked. "Take cover!"

But one of the bright beams caught Sejal's shoulder. He screamed once and dropped. Every guard in the room cried out in unison and collapsed in an eerie parody of Sejal. The last two children continued smiling on the beds.

Kendi flopped and writhed on the ground. Blackness surrounded him, thick and impenetrable. His talons curled with cold. He could feel the heat being leached from him like water being sucked from a glass. How many voices were in the blackness? He couldn't tell. Twice he had tried to leave the Dream, but the pain was too great for the necessary concentration.

"Why are you doing this?" he choked.

Concepts flooded Kendi's mind. *~anger HUNGER reach expand ANGER lonely~*

Kendi tried to rise, but the energy simply wasn't there. "You're lonely?"

~lonely HUNGER ANGER lonely~

"Come join the rest of us," Kendi replied. The response seemed to puzzle the darkness. Kendi rallied. "I meant we're all lonely."

~MOTHER~

The single concept knocked Kendi flat in its despair. A small part of Kendi's mind wondered what a trained psychologist would think of it. He shivered in the biting, horrible cold.

"I miss my mother," Kendi called out. His voice sounded thin and weak. "And I miss Ara. So does Ben. I—we—know what it's like."

The darkness hovered about him as if considering the idea. The icy heaviness lifted just slightly, as if it were pulling back from the Dream. A flicker of hope flared. Perhaps—

~HUNGRY~

There was no sympathy or empathy in the voice. Kendi, lying crushed beneath its icy weight, gave himself up to the ancestors and took his final breath.

"We surrender!" Vidya shouted, and threw her pistol toward the ruined door. It clattered on the tiles. Katsu did the same. Vidya shot a glance at Sejal, who had only been slightly stunned and was already recovering.

The result of Vidya's words was predictable. The table was shoved out of the way and a dozen more guard boiled into the room, crowding the room with warm bodies and flushed faces that sweated with fear and stress. Vidya and Katsu were swiftly handcuffed and the cattle prod was torn from her belt. The polymer bands bit deeply into Vidya's wrists, but she didn't cry out. Prasad, still dazed, was yanked to his feet and cuffed as well. Vidya watched placidly as three guard converged on Sejal, who bore a small burn on one shoulder. His strange pale eyes bore into them. At once, every guard in the room went rigid.

"Quickly!" Vidya said. "The last two!"

Four guard moved to the final pair of beds. Other guards released Vidya's, Katsu's, and Prasad's handcuffs. Vidya rubbed her wrists with relief. One more child went into the cryo-unit. The pair working on the final child had disconnected him and were sliding him toward the final cryo-unit when utter despair crashed over Vidya in a sickening tidal wave. Her legs went rubbery and she slid to the floor. Every other person in the room, including Sejal, Prasad, and Katsu, did the same, but Vidya barely noticed. Nothing she did was worth anything. She was alone in the universe. Prasad had abandoned her, stealing away her daughter and leaving her to raise a son who had turned into a prostitute. The neighborhood she had worked body and soul to build and protect had failed, and the people who lived there surely snickered at her and called her names behind her back.

One of the guard started to weep hoarse, dry sobs. So did several of the others. The first one, a handsome, dark-haired man who looked barely eighteen, picked up his pistol, put it in his mouth, and fired. His head vanished in a snapping cloud of electric blood. Vidya couldn't work up the energy to care. Part of her was aware of the fact that the final child was still active in the Dream, that it was feeding on the minds of Rust. She still didn't care.

Another guard, this one not sobbing, got up and wandered aimlessly about the room. He was a short, slender man with brown hair and a flat nose. His face was devoid of any emotion, of any sense that other people had feelings. After a moment, he slid a knife from his belt, crouched over one of his sobbing compatriots, and deliberately drew the blade across the other man's throat. Crimson liquid spouted into the air. The man's sobs dissolved into gurgling noises. The flat-nosed guard stared at the glittering table with a flicker of interest before moving purposely toward Katsu. She looked up at him with dull eyes. Blood dripped from the knife. And still Vidya couldn't bring herself to care. She had only known Katsu for a few weeks. It wasn't as if Katsu were much of a daughter to her.

And then the bleak miasma lifted for a moment, as if something had hesitated or drawn back from her mind. For some reason, the image of a falcon holding back darkness popped into her head. A spurt of adrenaline shot through Vidya's arteries and cut through the fog pressing down on her mind.

Vidya got to her feet. The despairing apathy had lifted enough to let her act, but she still felt as if a weight were pressing her down. She pulled herself upright using a cryo-unit for support. The flat-nosed guard reached down and grabbed the front of Katsu's shirt. Katsu made a small sound as he raised the knife. Vidya's fumbling fingers found one of the many pistols dropped by the guard. Katsu's shirt tore as Vidya raised her heavy hand and fired.

She missed. Energy cracked through the air and made an uneven black spot on the wall. The flat-nosed guard dropped Katsu and twisted around to face Vidya. He lunged across the room. Vidya fired again, and he dropped in his tracks to lie twitching on the floor.

Vidya turned to face the final child lying on his bed next to the open cryo-unit. The smile still lay on his distorted lips. All at once the sense of uncaring smashed back into her. Vidya wondered how she could ever have seen the twisted monstrosity as a person, as a human being worth saving. It was the cause of all the problems around her, and its self-satisfied smirk only made her angrier. It was a thing, an experiment gone wrong. Vidya raised the pistol and squeezed the trigger.

Then she jerked her hand. The shot went wide. A light fixture exploded, sending down a shower of white sparks. No. This thing would not make her a murderer, no matter how angry or uncaring she became.

Vidya bolted forward and grabbed the child by shoulder and hip. She shoved him, rolling him roughly into the cryo-unit. The slid slammed shut and the viewplate fogged over.

Instantly, the weight lifted. The despair and anger she felt melted away into something she could handle. She pushed herself erect against a bed still warm from the child that had occupied it. Around her, the guard stirred. Two were dead, and the room smelled of coppery blood and pungent bowel. Prasad came slowly to his feet and Katsu stood up as well. Sejal sat down on one of the beds. A guard blinked.

"What the hell?" he asked.

And then a shuddering boom shook the lab.

THIRTY

The Dream

We came to you in a dream,
But you were not there.
—Ched-Galar, *Silent Poetry*

Kendi huddled on the flat gray ground. One of his wings was broken, and he was so cold he had stopped shivering. He lay there bleakly, waiting to die. The Dream was absolutely quiet. Not a sound disturbed the air.

And then, like the first hesitant birds calling after the storm has passed, a whisper drifted by. It was followed by another, and another. They slowly swelled into a full chorus, but it somehow was different from the one Kendi had been hearing for so many years.

Dull pain throbbed in Kendi's wing and he couldn't find the energy to raise his head. The darkness was gone, but he could still feel the life seeping slowly from him. It wouldn't take him long to die now, and he just wished it would happen quickly. He closed his eyes.

Another strange whisper. Kendi felt something nudge him. He ignored it. Another nudge. Grudgingly, Kendi opened his eyes. Astonishment widened them. People had encircled him. Men and women, all naked, all brown skins drawn smoothly over taut muscle. They had brown eyes and brown or black hair that flared outward in ropy kinks. They were all smiling.

You did well, Kendi, they said as one. The sound of their thoughts wrapped Kendi in kind warmth and a glorious sense of belonging, a feeling he barely remembered from childhood. Their presence gave him strength, and he struggled to his feet. The pain of his broken wing faded. He was whole again. These were the Real People.

"I'm glad to see you," he said, and they smiled their acknowledgment. "What's happened to the Dream?"

It has changed, they said. *The minds of most mutants are weak, even among those who are Silent.* This statement was made without rancor or judgment. It was a simple fact, one that a parent might make about a child who had much potential but many lessons to learn. *They were unable to deal with such an abrupt merging and an equally abrupt release. A great many of them will never touch the Dream again. The few who can reach it will find their abilities severely curtailed.*

"Including me?" Kendi asked.

You were trained by mutants, they said kindly. *You will have to overcome that. There is still much for you to learn, Kendi Weaver.*

The Real People were fading into transparency. Kendi felt their minds drifting away.

"Is my family still alive?" he asked frantically. "Can I find them?"

You have to look, they said. *Start by returning to Rust.* And then they were gone.

Kendi stared at the empty plain for a long time. Then he summoned his concentration.

If it is in my best interest and in the best interest of all life everywhere, let me leave this Dream.

Another *boom* rocked the Nursery. Alarms hooted, red lights flashed.

"What's going on?" Prasad yelled above the noise.

All at once it came to Vidya. "The warship on the surface," she shouted back. "It is dropping depth charges."

Sejal grabbed one of the guard. "Tell them to stop!" he yelled.

"I can't," the guard replied, eyes wide with fright. "The Lieutenant was supposed to report in every ten minutes. If he doesn't, the Captain will assume we've been killed and destroy the installation from above."

Vidya yanked on the man's arm. He was a brawny man, with close-cropped hair and fearful green eyes. His name tag read JEREN.

"Why can't *you* tell them to stop?" she cried.

"That electric shock you used shorted out both comms."

"What about your submersible?" Sejal screamed.

"They'd have hit that first thing to make sure the enemy couldn't capture and use it," Jeren snapped.

Vidya's heart raced. They were at least twenty or thirty meters below the surface. No way to swim for it, not exhausted, and injured as they were. Another explosion rocked the floor.

"Attention! Attention!" boomed the computer. "Water breach in living sector A. Emergency doors will close in five seconds. Water breach in living Sector A. Emergency doors will close in three seconds."

"The base has a submersible," Prasad shouted. "Come on! We have to get everyone aboard!"

"What about the children?" Sejal said, waving at the cryo-units.

"Leave them!" Prasad replied. "We can't transport them now."

He strode for the door, but Jeren snagged him by the arm as he went past. "You're a prisoner!"

"If you want to live," Prasad retorted, "you had better come with us." He turned to the other guard in various poses on the floor or on their knees. "That goes for all of you as well. We will not wait for you."

Without looking back, Prasad ran from the Nursery. Vidya, Sejal, Katsu, and some of the guard followed. Several others, including Lieutenant Arsula, were either unconscious or too stunned to move. Their compatriots started lifting them firefighter style. Vidya ignored them. If they could follow, fine. She refused to risk her own life rescuing people who had tried to kill her.

Out in the main lab, Prasad came to a halt and, behind him, Vidya swore. They had completely forgotten about Kri, Say, Garinn, and the slaves. The guard had not taken the time to untape them. Say had apparently regained consciousness, for she was struggling against her bonds. Kri, Garinn, and the slaves pleaded with their eyes. Vidya considered leaving them, but only briefly. All of this might be easily blamed on Kri and Say, but the slaves, at least, were innocent. Katsu was already running over to them. The alarms continued to blare.

"No time for them!" Jeren cried. Vidya's only reply was to snatch the knife from his belt and cut the first slave free. The lab rocked under another explosion, and water cascaded almost gently down one of the hallways into the main lab. Prasad and Sejal also set to work on the captives. Most of the guard, including Jeren, looked like they wanted to leave, but they didn't know how to get to the submersible.

It only took a few moments to cut the slaves free, but they were already ankle deep in warm seawater. Katsu started to work on Garinn, but Vidya stopped her.

"No time," she shouted.

"We need him to operate the submersible," Katsu shouted back without pausing in her work. "You may as well cut Kri and Say free as well."

Swearing, Vidya did so, taking a malicious glee in ripping the tape painfully off Say's face.

"If you do anything stupid, I will kill you without hesitation," Vidya warned, hauling her roughly to her feet. Say's hair was disheveled, her face pale.

"What about the experiment?" she demanded.

"They're in cryo-sleep," Vidya told her.

"We can't leave them behind!" Say cried. "We can't!"

Katsu slashed the last of Garinn's tape just as Sejal finished with Kri. They got unsteadily to their feet.

"Stay with them, then," Vidya retorted. "We are leaving."

Say looked torn as the group sloshed their way out of the lab with Prasad in the lead. After several moments, Say sprinted after them.

The water deepened as they ran, a group of over thirty. All emergency doors had automatically slammed shut, and they had to spend precious moments cranking them open manually. People stumbled beneath another explosion, and once they opened a door on a wall of water. The released torrent swept half of them off their feet before Prasad and Sejal could get the door shut again. Prasad then hurried them down a side corridor. They couldn't have traveled more than the length of a good-size house, but it seemed to take forever. Say kept looking back over her shoulder. The hallways were a nightmare of noise and light and panicked bodies, and Vidya was sure any moment the ceiling would open up. She suspected that the only reason it hadn't was because the rock used to camouflage the base provided additional protection from the depth charges.

At last they reached the submersible airlock. Garinn

shoved his way to the controls. The submersible was a series of clear polymer and plastic bubbles. One large bubble formed a center ringed by six smaller bubbles. By some miracle it appeared undamaged. The group crowded in, body pressed against body, the need for survival overriding any sense of status or propriety. The submersible wasn't designed for so many passengers and Vidya hoped the engines were up to the challenge.

Dr. Say was the last one at the airlock. To Vidya's horror, she pulled a guard pistol from the pocket of her lab coat and pointed straight at Vidya. Her eyes were wild. The guard tensed, but most of them had lost their pistols, and those who had them, couldn't get to them in the press of bodies.

"We aren't leaving without the experiment!" Say said over the alarms.

The sub shuddered. "That one was close," Garinn shouted. "They're starting to send the charges this way."

"Get off the sub," Say screeched. "You have to get off to make room for the experiment!"

"Sejal!" Vidya cried.

"I can't see her from back here!" Sejal yelled.

"Move," Say ordered, "or I'll start—"

Vidya screamed and pointed over Say's shoulder. Say turned, and Vidya's foot lashed out. Say's pistol went spinning away.

"Get inside now!" Vidya ordered. "This is your last chance, woman!"

The look on Say's face reminded Vidya of a cornered animal. She stood in the airlock for a moment longer, then turned and ran down the corridor. Vidya slammed the airlock shut. The installation's alarms were instantly muted.

"Go!" she snapped.

Garinn released the clamps and went. The submersible lurched sluggishly. Vidya stood with her back pressed against the airlock door. Already the air was humid and close. Vidya noticed several of the passengers, including the guard, were panting.

"We need to breathe slowly and evenly," she announced in a voice much calmer than she felt. "Hyperventilating will use up more oxygen than the filters can provide. Breathe with me now. In . . . out . . ."

She kept up the exercise, using the same voice she used at meetings when she had to persuade people to do what was right for the neighborhood. At her urging, they stayed focused on their breathing and had less time to think about the dangers outside. Garinn sweated over the controls in the bubble that made up the submersible's bridge. After a while, Vidya noticed that although the explosions continued, they had less force behind them.

"I think we're clear," Garinn announced at last.

A ragged cheer went up and Vidya allowed herself to slump against the wall.

Dr. Jillias Say splashed and waded back toward the Nursery through water warm and salty as blood. Power had failed in this section, and the emergency lights provided only dim illumination. The alarms had cut out as well, leaving her breathing and sloshing as the only sounds.

There had to be a way to save the experiment. There *had* to be. She could find a solution if she just looked hard enough.

And then it came to her. The experiment could save her. All she had to do was bring one or two subjects out of cryo-sleep. Once they were awake and back in the Dream, they would fill everyone with despair again, including the sailors on the battleship. Once that happened, the crew would stop firing on the base, giving her time to work out the next step. Certainly the subjects would exclude her from whatever it was they did if she was the one who took them out of the cryo-units.

An explosion knocked her off her feet. Her mouth and nose filled with brine. For a moment she was a child again, fleeing the invaders with her family. Explosions smashed the air around them, and she saw the terror on her mother's face. They fled through the ruined city, even as Say fled through leaky hallways, until they turned a corner and ran straight into a contingent of enemy soldiers. She could still hear their laughter as they raped her sister and mother, then turned to her. She was not going to let that happen anymore. If she just saved the experiment, everything would be all right. She could sleep without hearing her mother's screams or her sister's cries.

The Nursery was waist deep in water. Say rushed into it and scrabbled at the nearest unit. It was underwater. Say would have to yank the subject above the waterline the moment she opened the unit. She was fumbling at the controls when a detonation crashed through the room. Dr. Jillias Say had time to look up and scream once before the ocean burst through the ceiling and swept down to claim her.

It took them over an hour to reach land. By then, the submersible was so hot, Vidya was drenched in sweat. She was exhausted as well, and she had no idea what time it was. It felt as if weeks had passed, but it couldn't have been more than a few hours. Her entire body ached.

As it turned out, the sun had just set when they arrived at the shore. Garinn was able to extend the tunnel up to the beach, a good thing since the submersible was too heavily laden to surface. Everyone rushed to exit except Garinn and Kri. Before Vidya realized what was going on, the exit tunnel slid back underwater and a trail of bubbles indicated the submersible was moving away. She was too tired to care.

They stood on the beach. City lights gleamed farther up the shore, perhaps a kilometer away. The air was delightfully cool after the submersible's close quarters. The slaves huddled together uncertainly and the guard did the same. Vidya gathered her husband, son, and daughter to her in a giant embrace and tears trickled down her face.

A cold hand on Vidya's arm broke the moment. She turned to see Jeren.

"You're all under arrest," he said.

Sejal tensed beside her and Vidya stared coldly at Jeren. After a long moment, he released her.

"We are all free here," Vidya said. She pitched her voice to include the slaves. "No one is enslaved to anyone else. Any who wish to come with us may do so."

The four of them turned and walked away, hand in hand. After a moment, two of the slaves followed, then four, then ll twelve. Five of the guard did so as well. The rest vatched them go.

"What is my wife doing?" Prasad asked.

Vidya smiled. "Following the advice of a wise man who aid, 'Our old community was destroyed. If we wish to survive, we must build a new one.' "

And she paused in the walking long enough to kiss him.

The Rings Around Planet Gem

Somewhere the Sky touches the Earth, and the name of that place is the End.

—Anonymous

Tears of joy trickled down Padric Sufur's face. Report were already filtering in from his courier ships, the ones h had placed in strategic spots all over the galaxy for just thi moment. He had done it. The Dream was all but useles for communication. Governments everywhere were i chaos. The war between the Independence Confederatio and the Empire of Human Unity had fallen apart. General and admirals, safely ensconced on their home worlds light years from the actual battleground, had no quick way t send orders, and all military powers were based on a quic way to send orders. A few skirmishes had managed t break out, but nothing serious. War as Padric knew i had ended.

The holographic screen winked out at Padric's command He wiped tears from his cheeks, picked up his wineglass and wandered over to the wall of the clear dome. The glit tering road of ice that circled ahead of his asteroid an around Gem, the gas giant, stood out achingly clear amon the stars. He took a smooth sip of wine, letting it pla over his tongue. One very interesting report stated that he Imperial Majesty Empress Kan maja Kalii had disappeare in all the chaos. Her bodyguards had found the crown jew els that always orbited her head piled carelessly on he throne, the Imperial robes in an untidy heap on the floor Fate—or Padric—had provided her the opportunity and sh had taken it.

Padric sighed heavily. He could no longer reach th Dream, or even sense it directly, but, he mused, it was small price to pay. His fortune was safe. He had moved al his assets to a series of banks within easy reach of a slipshi long before the Despair, as everyone was now calling it

There was also the fact that his messenger fleet was in the best position to take control of a sizeable chunk of what he was sure would become the new communication network. No human ever did anything for purely altruistic reasons. Padric knew better than to try to be an exception.

All this was thanks to Sejal.

For the first time in his life, Padric raised his glass in silent toast to a fellow human being.

How Kendi decided on a wake, Ben didn't know. It didn't strike him as particularly Australian. True, Kendi liked to drop odd bits of Aboriginal culture like a sower dropping seeds, but no matter how hard Ben tried, he couldn't imagine a tribe of Aborigines standing around a piano singing "Danny Boy."

Still, he thought, sipping from an enormous beer mug, *Mom would have laughed and joined in.*

The house, once Ara's and now Ben's, though he couldn't bring himself to live there yet, was crammed to the rafters. People—human, Ched-Balaar, and other races—occupied every inch of floor space, and the crowd overflowed onto the wraparound balcony. It felt like the entire monastery was there.

At first Ben had been surprised at the turnout. During the Despair, dozens of people had died at the monastery alone, never mind the hundreds in the main city. It didn't seem to Ben that there would be many in the mood to celebrate the life of a single Mother Adept. But as Ben circulated, he realized that people were remembering not only his mother, but their own dearly departed as well. He even heard people mention Pitr and Grandfather Melthine, who had slipped from his coma into a quiet death before the Despair fully struck.

Ben accepted condolences and hugs from various monks and listened to the stories they told about his mother. He hadn't realized how many people her life had touched. Several people had clearly held her in awe, and one man told Ben that although he had never met Mother Adept Araceil in person, she had been a role model to him all his life and he regretted not having the chance to tell her.

"I feel the same way," Ben replied around an unexpected lump in his throat.

Ben's aunt, uncle, and cousins were nowhere to be seen. They had lost all ability to enter the Dream and had so far refused to leave their homes. Ben's grandmother Salman was there, however. She caught Ben's eye across the room and raised her glass. Ben returned the salute. She couldn't enter the Dream either, but it didn't seem to faze her. Now that Bellerophon had lost touch with the Independence Confederation, the planet's council was already constructing a senatorial form of government, and Salman Reza had thrown herself into the middle of it. Ben could see where Ara had gotten her determination.

Sejal, Vidya, Prasad, and Katsu were also present. After Kendi had come out of the Dream, he had insisted they immediately set course for Rust. The planet was in chaos. A hundred factions had sprung up and the planet was almost frantically carving itself into separate countries. The Unity guard had made a half-hearted attempt at keeping order, but many of its own soldiers deserted, and there was no way to send for more.

Kendi had embarked on some extensive Dream experimentation. He learned that he was one of the few Silent who could still reach the Dream, though he could no longer keep human shape there or conjure up perfectly formed landscapes. He scoured the Dream until he ran into Sejal, who was happy to see him. Sejal, apparently, could still enter the Dream at will and was thus able to tell Kendi where to find him.

Sejal and the others with him wanted off Rust—Sejal so he could study music and Vidya so she could escape various memories. Kendi was startled to learn that Vidya's husband Prasad and her daughter Katsu had turned up alive, and it took some time to get through all the stories.

Kendi also told Ben about his meeting with the Real People. Uncharacteristically, Kendi came to the conclusion that the "family" the Real People referred to was metaphorical. He and the Vajhurs shared a common experience that made them family, which was why the Real People had told him to go to Rust.

Ben set down his mug and took a chair. Partygoers were

trickling away. A pair of drunken Ched-Balaar staggered toward the walkway as if they had trouble figuring out which of their eight legs belonged to which body. Eventually, only the Vajhurs and the original crew of the *Post-Script,* were left. Gretchen and Trish had weathered the Despair, though only Trish could still reach the Dream. Gretchen had put on a brave face, but it was clear she wasn't taking it well.

The group sat around on couches, chairs, and the floor, talking comfortably. Kendi, cross-legged on the floor in front of Ben's armchair, leaned back between Ben's knees. Ben, enjoying the warmth and closeness, rubbed the back of Kendi's neck. Kendi sighed. An emerald ring gleamed on his finger, proclaiming his recent promotion to Father.

Sejal, meanwhile, got up and crossed over to Harenn. He said something to her that Ben couldn't hear. She stiffened and her eyes went wide above her veil. They both came over to Ben's chair.

"I need to talk to you, Kendi," Sejal said in low, urgent tones. "Ben, too, I guess."

"What about?" Kendi asked.

"It's private. Can we go somewhere else?"

With a shrug, Ben got up, pulled Kendi to his feet, and led the little group toward one of the guest rooms. A little ways away, Vidya and Trish were involved in an animated discussion about the job training program they were setting up for the slaves the Vajhurs had rescued from Rust, and Prasad occasionally put in his own comments. No one glanced their way.

Ben shut the guest room door. Stray glasses and snack plates indicated the room had been used during the wake. Harenn perched on the edge of the bed, and Sejal's face was serious. Kendi looked mystified, but curious.

"I'll come straight to it," Sejal said. "In all the fuss, I forgot to tell you guys about it and I only remembered just now."

"What?" Kendi asked.

"It's about your family," Sejal said.

Ben stiffened. He and Kendi were just settling in together. Kendi had quietly moved his few possessions back into Ben's little house, and Ben found it comforting beyond words to wake up next to him. He didn't want to hare off to unknown parts on another wild hunt. But a quick glance at Kendi showed only polite interest, not thirsty curiosity, on his face.

"What about them?" Kendi asked.

"And why am I here?" Harenn put in.

"When I was in the Dream and gathering everyone together," Sejal said, "I felt every Silent in the galaxy. It was weird. We were a group, but I could still feel individuals. Three minds felt familiar to me, even though I had never touched them before. Everything got really busy after that, and I sort of forgot about it."

"Felt familiar?" Kendi repeated slowly.

Sejal nodded, his pale blue eyes full of adult seriousness. "Two of the minds felt similar to yours, Kendi. I can't describe it better than that. One of them was a man, the other was a woman, and they're both slaves on a planet named Drim."

Kendi's arms crept around his body until he was hugging himself tightly. "Drim," he whispered.

Sejal nodded again. "I think you need to go there. You can probably track them through sales records, and they might know where the rest of your family is."

Harenn leaned forward and grasped Sejal's arm. "And the third one . . . was it my son?"

"Yes," Sejal told her. "He's on a planet named Klimkinnar. He's a slave, too."

Harenn put a hand to her mouth beneath her veil. She tried to say something, but all that emerged was a choking sound. Ben sat beside her on the bed, his own heart overcome with emotion.

"Are you all right?" he asked Harenn. "Do you want something to drink?"

She shook her head and stood up. Ben saw she was shaking. "I want to get ready to leave."

Kendi put a restraining hand on her shoulder. "Not until we've both had a good night's sleep. In the morning I'll get authorization to start an expedition."

Ben stared. Kendi noticed.

"What?" he said.

"Nothing," Ben replied. "We should all get some sleep."

Harenn started for the door, halted, then came back. Moving quickly, she lifted her veil and kissed Sejal on the cheek. Ben caught sight of a pretty, lined face. Sejal blushed furiously as Harenn rushed from the room.

"Do the Children still organize hunts for Silent?" Ben asked. "I mean, the Dream's been—"

"There are still Silent who can enter the Dream," Kendi said, "and the Children still need them. Now more than ever." He leveled a hard brown gaze at Ben. "Speaking of which, Benjamin Rymar, I was wondering something."

Ben looked at him innocently. "What's that?"

"Have you tried to enter the Dream since Sejal brought you there?"

Ben tried to keep a straight face, but a smile burst through. "Once or twice. I used some of Mom's connections to get my drug dosage figured out."

"And?"

"And what?"

Kendi made an exasperated sound. "Could you do it?"

Ben kissed him. Sejal made "woo-woo" noises. The embrace became more intense, however, and after a while, a faint flush crept up Sejal's face.

"I'll just . . . I mean, I can . . . oh, shit." He fled.

When they separated, Ben patted Kendi on the cheek. "Ever think you'd see an ex-prostitute blush twice in one day?"

"You bastard," Kendi said, still irked. "You've been visiting the Dream for—what? Days? Weeks? Why didn't you tell me?"

"I wanted it to be a surprise."

"Well, I'm not surprised." He kissed Ben again, though not as intensely as before. "You always did have to be different."

Ben only smiled. "So whose family do we go after first? Yours or Harenn's?"

"Harenn's," Kendi said promptly. "She goes home to an empty house every night. I don't. We should probably—" He paused. "All life! I just realized—the Real People told me to go to Rust so Sejal could tell me where to look for my family. It wasn't a metaphor after all."

"It's amazing what you find," Ben said philosophically, "once you stop looking."

"Let's go tell the others, if Harenn hasn't already. See who wants to go."

"You go ahead," Ben told him. "Just save me a space on the crew roster. Father Kendi."

Kendi flashed a bright grin and left. Ben watched him go, then wandered over to the window, opened it, and leaned outside. The air was cool and damp on his face. Leaves rustled in a very slight breeze. Far below the house, amid the foggy ferns, lay his mother's grave. Ben had had her buried at the foot of the talltree, and already it seemed as if he could feel her presence in the leaves and branches.

"Thanks, Mom," he whispered. "Thank you for everything."

He stayed at the window, staring out into the foggy night. A long moment passed. Then Benjamin Rymar firmly shut the window and turned back to his life.